THE DEVIL'S MAKING

Seán Haldane

Stone Flower Press

Printed and bound in Great Britain by
TJ International Ltd, Padstow, Cornwall.

Cover design by Bite Design, Cork.

The cover image is *Mourning Mask* by Sandy Johnson, by permission of
Justart, Port Hardy, British Columbia.

ISBN: 978-0-9919073-0-4

And since this outward I, you know,
Must stay because he cannot go,
My fellow-travellers shall be they
Who go because they cannot stay…
Across the mountains we will roam,
And each man make himself a home:
Or, if old habits ne'er forsaking,
Like clockwork of the Devil's making,
Ourselves inveterate rogues should be,
We'll have a virtuous progeny;
And on the dunghill of our vices
Raise human pineapples and spices.

From *The Delinquent Travellers*
by S T Coleridge, 1824.

It is a world by itself, with no law ruling except
force, no compunction except fear, no religion
except that of the devil.

Description of 'The Happy Land'
from *The Sliding Scale of Life*,
by James McLevy, 1861.

To Ghislaine

1

Tellurophobia. The only word (apart from *Chad Hobbes* on the fly leaf) I have written until now in the one hundred and forty days out of Portsmouth to Vancouver Island. Perhaps it's my anger at the maniac Captain which has kept me staring at the blank first page, whenever I have opened this maroon leather journal my mother gave me. His intention – announced at the first of one hundred and forty hellish dinners in his cabin – was to make the voyage without a single landfall. The *Ariadne,* 'one of her Majesty's men of war' (she is only a three masted corvette with 18 guns) would be dependent on no Blacks (by which he meant the inhabitants of South America) or Yankees (ditto of North). He wasn't going to dirty his decks with soot, he declared glowering at Mr Scott the engineer, chugging in and out of the Plate, or Callao, or San Francisco. The *Ariadne* would enter Esquimalt Harbour as it had left Portsmouth, under pristine sail.

My first fantasy of the voyage was dashed. Not even the one or two day stops for supplies which I had expected in the parts Darwin had visited with the *Beagle.* Not even a distant sight of the pampas. Or of the Galapagos, which we avoided in a wide arc. The Captain, once underway, had a rabid phobia of land. Or to be exact it was the opposite of rabies, not a fear of water, a *hydrophobia*, but an equally furious fear of earth, a *tellurophobia*. (I am proud of this coinage.)

The closest we got to land after Land's End and the Scillies was Tierra del Fuego. Even the Captain couldn't avoid this. After crossing the Equator at English midsummer, we had gone through autumn into winter in a few weeks. There was an increasing pall of cloud and drizzle then wet snow as in early August we passed through a Strait before rounding the Horn. I leaned for a whole afternoon over the starboard rail, with snowflakes catching in my beard and dripping down my neck from my sou'wester, peering at the gloomy headlands. There Darwin, in 1835 on the *Beagle*, had seen the beacon fire lit in farewell by the poor Fuegian, Jeremy Button – who had been bought for a pearl button, taken to London for five years, almost forgetting his own language, then returned by the *Beagle* to this wilderness.

Now there was not a spark to be seen. Where was Jeremy Button?

Two months later, after passing through another brief summer on the water, with the orange sun bisecting the sky as if tracing the equatorial on the first mate's sextant, we sighted land again, a wall of dark grey, blanketed in lighter grey cloud, not unlike Tierra del Fuego. 'Forty eight North,' Robbins remarked. (He has been my only friend on this voyage). 'Where Drake gave up searching for the North West passage in fifteen-whatever-it-was, turned around, then headed South again.' Robbins had joined me at the rail for a moment and muttered, 'I'd better move on, or that bloody man will have my shore leave.'

As night fell we beat in towards the coast, which divided around us into the Strait of Juan de Fuca, and as the twin bluffs of cloud-covered land on each side darkened and disappeared, the sails were run down, the anchor dropped with a rattle and splash, and lights set. The ship strained like a dog at a leash. For a while I stared out into blackness. Then as the rain battered more heavily on the foot-smoothed familiar deck, I picked my way across it and into the hatchway. A hurricane lamp swung jerkily above the steps which I descended, as I thought, with the sea legs of an old sailor.

The 140th – I'll spell it out, the ONE HUNDRED AND FORTIETH – evening at the Captain's table. He sat at the head, with 5 naval officers, 3 officers of Marines, the ship's surgeon, and myself, cramped together down the sides. I was the only landsman, and the only one with a beard, since the navy required its officers and men to be clean shaven. I was on sufferance, an unwelcome guest. Not that the Captain was friendly with his officers either. I had given up wondering how such a man could exist, breed children as he evidently had on his poor wife in Norfolk, and go to sea and live close-quartered with his officers for months, yet keep all conversation to brief discussions of the weather, supplies, and ship's management – from which, of course, I was excluded.

This had suited me, or so I told myself on my long deck walks, or my days out of the rain looking at this blank journal or reading Darwin again, at the small table in the cabin I've shared with Robbins who was seldom there until dog-tired at night. Sometimes I could keep him awake for a while, the candle sputtering between our narrow grey-blanketed bunks, and ask him about the navy, his life at home in England, his undeclared love for the inevitable local maiden – 'a dear girl.' But nothing about the future. Robbins himself had never left home waters. He had no more clue than I about the New World, although he had found time to read a few chapters of my *Four Years on Vancouver Island* by Mayne. I had not had the courage to quizz the Captain about the place, although he had already spent a year at Esquimalt, where he was now returning with a hold full of arms and ammunition and a fresh Company of Marines.

Normally the Captain would wash down his salt beef with half a bottle of claret, then sip one glass of Port with his indescribable Stilton cheese on indestructible biscuit. But this evening he was into a second bottle of claret in no time, and the officers who had religiously followed him for 139 evenings in drinking half a bottle of claret each and one glass of Port, now sent the cabin boys for a second bottle each. I had been economizing and would have to settle my bill before leaving the ship the next day, but I finished my own bottle which had lasted me four dinners, and recklessly sent for another. Was this the Captain's way of celebrating the end of the voyage? But he was choleric as ever, fixing me with eyes like cold blue taws – as we used to call marbles at school:

'Not every immigrant arrives in British Columbia on one of her Majesty's Ships of War.'

'I dare say. I'm sorry I couldn't have made myself useful in some way.'

'Useful? At what?'

'I'm not sure.' I looked at the officers across the table for support. Robbins's face was as stony as those of the others, none of whom had ever spoken a word to me beyond 'Pass the mustard.'

'Nothing for you to do', the Captain went on. 'A Man of War doesn't usually take passengers. Unless a political bigwig. You're not that, are you? It might have looked better if you'd been hired on as something or other. But as what? You read that scoundrel Darwin, but you're not a naturalist. And this is not a survey ship. I'm damned if I'm going to let the *Ariadne* become the *Beagle!*' (This was a reference to his terror, as Robbins had described it, that his ship would be used in survey work around Vancouver Island). 'You studied Divinity at Oxford, I was told, but you're not a parson. Anyway, I'm the parson here. I conduct the services. I read the funerals. You're not a surgeon, Mr Giles here is that. So what are you?'

'No idea.' I took a large sip of my claret and studied the lumps of mashed potato on my plate.

'You're a young man with pull!' Glaring around at the stony faces. 'His uncle is Captain Hobbes, of the *Adverse*. It's his father who's the parson. Another parson's son for the Colonies!'

The others, sat tightly around the table, guffawed obediently.

'My uncle assured me I'd be a welcome guest on this ship. He insisted, in fact. I was quite ready to take passage on one of the Hudson's Bay Company's ships or another merchantman.'

'For £60 in steerage with a pack of scum, or £90 first class with shopkeepers and pen-pushing clerks.'

The Captain set down his knife and fork with a clash. The cabin boys scurried to take away the plates. They brought in dishes of pudding – prunes in lukewarm custard – at the same time setting the battered curved wall of the huge Stilton in front of the Captain, and bringing biscuits, new plates, glasses, and the crystal decanter of Port, although everyone still went on with their claret.

Later, after we had gobbled up our pudding, the Captain started up again. 'Why didn't you join the navy then?'

'I first wanted to go into the church, like my father. Then I changed my mind.'

'Another young man who believes we're descended from the apes! I know it all! The broken-hearted mother, the outraged father! The bitter arguments around the vicarage table! The crisis of faith! Am I correct?'

'More or less. Not quite as simple, if you'll forgive me.' I took a glug from my second glass of Port, come around from Mr Giles. 'Yes, of course. You're right. The family quarrels and so forth. But what happened was simply that I changed from reading Divinity to reading Jurisprudence – a new subject at Oxford, since only 1850. You might say that from studying the divine law I had changed to studying natural law.'

There was a sudden snort from Robbins, who covered it up with a cough, glancing at the Captain who said sharply,

'Yes, Mr Robbins?'

'Well, I mean, really, Hobbes, you do sound niminy-piminy.'

'I'm sorry.'

'Ah! You're a barrister.' The Captain again.

'No. I took my degree, but I had run out of money. More was not forthcoming from my family. I can't afford at the moment to go to an Inn of Court, although perhaps I shall when I return to England. The other option of course is to become articled to a solicitor. But I want to see the world, and I thought I might try British Columbia.'

'What? Try what?'

'There are at least a dozen solicitors in the Colony. I've written ahead. And I have a letter of introduction to …'

'To the Governor!' (Exultantly). 'To the Honourable Sir James Seymour! Do you know what, Gentlemen? Every young reprobate, every remittance man, every played out seedling of a good family who comes to this Eldorado, first goes to the Governor in his "castle" – a glorified shack, if you please – with a *letter of introduction*! And do you know what the first Governor, Sir James Douglas, used to do?' The Captain took a gulp of Port. Then he reached for the curved silver knife whose ivory handle stuck out of the Stilton, hacked a blue-yellow piece off the inside of the crumbling brown wall, speared it, and held it up for effect. 'He would open the letter, glance at it, then lead the young suppliant over to a *chest of drawers*. Gentlemen, I am not talking about a tiny *escritoire*. I mean damn nearly a wardrobe. Starting at the top he would open, solemnly, one drawer after another. Each drawer was stuffed with letters. In the bottom and final drawer, which was also stuffed – with letters of introduction, Gentlemen – he would put the new one. Then it was "Goodbye Sir. Very good of you to call. Goodbye now!"'

Uproarious laughter from all.

'I don't have a letter of introduction to Governor Seymour.'

'You don't? What? An immigrant without a letter of introduction to the Governor? It's unheard of.' The joke had been milked enough, so he became serious again. 'Dear boy, the Colony of British Columbia has at present no more than twelve thousand inhabitants, seven in Victoria and perhaps five on the mainland, although including a couple of thousand yellow faced Chinese – "Celestials" as they are called – and surrounded by at least fifty thousand Indians. The Gold Rush has been and gone. They are, as they would put it in their Yankee way, "flat broke". If it weren't for our base at Esquimalt, with the *Zealous* and its five hundred men, plus the company of Marines we are replacing, and the other company on San Juan Island, they would not have much to make a living by. They say Victoria is the Garden of Eden!' His audience raised its collective head at this change of tone. 'The Garden of Eden! But it's the Devil's own job to make a living there!' His laughter turned to a kind of choking. 'For whom, then, is your *letter of introduction?*'

'Mr Justice Begbie. From my tutor at Oxford. Though I believe Mr Begbie went to Cambridge.'

'Oxford. Cambridge. Landlocked, both of 'em. In the middle of marshes. Stagnant. No wind. Vile places…'

At this point the thread of the Captain's conversation became abruptly unravelled, and he wandered into myriad digressions about the landscapes of the English and other coasts. Eventually he lurched off to bed. The officers looked at each other sheepishly, and began to exchange fuddled talk about the procedures for landing in the morning, as if to prove they were still sober.

With a buzzing in my head, I got up and said Goodnight. I climbed the companionway intending to take a brief stroll on deck. When I opened the hatch door, all I could see in the shaft of golden light was rain pelting down slantwise. I shivered, closed the hatch, paid a visit to the 'head', then went to my cabin and to bed. I couldn't sleep. The wallowing of the ship at anchor was foreign after the rolling and pitching of the open sea. Images of four months on the *Ariadne* crowded my mind: the Marines in their monotonous drills on deck, the sailors with their own precise drill on sails and ropes. I wondered if they too were boozing it up on the last night of the voyage, in the bowels of the ship where they lived and I had never been. I resent my own innocence. The ship is like school with its boys and masters, and Oxford with its undergraduates and tutors. All my education has been intellectual. The crashing disillusion with Christianity. The mental gloom of a life in which the candle of faith has been snuffed, between the finger of Darwinian science and the thumb of my dislike of the deans and bishops, who were to have been my mentors. I've thrown it all over.

I've been sitting up late, writing in this diary at last, my eyes beginning to hurt in the light of the oil lamp, dimmed so that Robbins can sleep. It's all in the past tense now.

Often in that hard narrow bunk I have found myself imagining women – about which I know almost nothing. Women I had never met but who figured in the more salacious legal cases I had studied – murdered by their husbands for unfaithfulness. The whores of Oxford lingering in the shadow of St Ebbe's church, bait for divinity students. The servant girls at home, easy prey for a spoilt boy with a sovereign in his hand and the moral ascendancy of being a gentleman, well-spoken and well-groomed – but also deadly, since they could get pregnant and make claims. My dear older brother Henry was found with a maid in the summer house after dark: she was dismissed, not pregnant thank God, but with a parting gift of money. Dear weeping Mother, and indignant Father. They knew, however, that the Chad who had repudiated God would not become immoral with women. That was for Henry who went to church regularly and without a thought, and joined the army in a modest regiment our father could afford. I've shucked off my beliefs, but I've never taken my my clothes off in front of anyone. The night before Henry went off to his regiment we went for a drink in the village tavern, the Trout – it's by a stream. We both drank too much cider and when I went out to relieve myself in the moonlight I saw Sally, one of the barmaids, coming back in. She took my arm and drew me towards a hedge in the dark. 'Do you want a feel?' she said, and she pulled up her dress and apron and took my hand and stuck it between her legs, into her drawers. As I felt her my whole body buzzed with the sort of shock you get from an electricity machine, only less sharp, a sort of tingling. She kissed me on the lips and stuck her tongue into my mouth, writing down below against my fingers, then pulled back slightly and said 'Won't you do me then?' She unbuttoned my trousers with one deft movement and pulled out my member, huge like a donkey's, and pulled it into the wet of her, leaning back into the hedge. Just as my body had flooded with tingling my brain now flooded with a thousand reasons for pulling away from her – which I did with a jerk backwards. I ran away into a nearby field in the dark and my seed spilled onto the grass.

'Natural law' instead of God's. Yes, I sounded niminy-piminy at the Captain's table, too fussy in my definitions, although I feel hurt by Robbins having said so. I hope the Colony will cure me. I'm here to find myself.

I'm deciding, now, to write a full story of my experience of this New World I am entering tomorrow. I want to record my observations – as Darwin would – like a 'scientist', in the sense defined by that Cambridge philosopher Whewell: without philosophy and introspection. But these last few paragraphs are already introspections. I have drawn a line down the side of my text to mark them out. They can be discarded from the objective story. But who am I writing the story for? For Darwin, or people like him who I imagine will be *interested? To bring it out as a book? Mayne's account of Vancouver Island is humdrum. Surely I can do better than that. But I am no author, and already I am providing observations of life on the Ariadne, even an account of the Captain's table talk, which could never be published. I feel as if I am writing for an unseen friend – an unknown friend whom I have yet to meet.*

2

I was up on deck soon after dawn, in my oilskins, sipping a hot tea laced with rum. It was still raining. The sailors hauled up mainsail, mizzen, staysail, jib… Ridiculous how much sail they had to raise in order to get the *Ariadne* moving in the feeble wind. It was as if all the forces of nature were drawn downward with the rain. The *Ariadne* had covered the voyage, as the Captain had intended, with her funnel racked down and her propeller up. She would enter under sail.

We began a long tack to port where the hills of Vancouver Island were revealed grey against the lighter grey sky. To starboard, in Washington Territory, higher mountains were lost in cloud. We picked up some speed but wallowed in a swell which was still that of the Pacific. I peered towards the shore and could discern high firs on rocky slopes fringed by lines of foam, then ahead a surprisingly English lighthouse, painted white and red, perched on a rock at the end of a sandbar. The mainsail was coming down, the sailors scurrying to the sound of whistles. We entered the calm water of a wide natural harbour surrounded by low fir-clad hills. The rain pelted down. I could see three large ships at anchor, as if in a glimpse of Portsmouth Harbour, but the scene was desolate and unreal. I strained to see houses, farms, even fields, but there was nothing except sea, rocks, and slopes of dark firs through the rain. Whistles piped and the anchor went down, the remaining sails were being lowered, and the *Ariadne* stopped dead, without momentum. Now I saw a cluster of buildings in a large clearing among the firs. Wooden warehouses with a black painted monogram, HBC – Hudson's Bay Company, I knew that from the blankets. Already a few lighters were heading out to the *Ariadne*, but my attention was distracted by the sudden boom of a cannon from one of the anchored men of war, a gigantic ironclad over twice as long as the *Ariadne*, obviously the *Zealous*. Flags were being run up in some complicated naval ritual. The Captain was strutting on the poop like a bantam cock, a plump Nelson with a telescope he raised from time to time to look at the other ships. Then a sailor touched me on the elbow and informed me that my trunks were being brought up on deck, and would I please prepare to disembark? Wounded by this sudden haste after 140 days, I went to my cabin and packed my valise. Robbins turned up briefly and wished me Good Luck.

I paid a brief visit to the stores to settle my provisions bill. Then I watched my trunks being carried by sailors who clambered like apes down the rope ladder to one of the lighters. I paused at the top of the ladder for a final wave, but no one was looking.

There were two lighter-men, their faces almost invisible under their oilskins as they rowed me across a stretch of grey rain-splattered water on which huge whip-like strands of brown seaweed floated, up to twenty feet long and as thick as an arm. There was a salty stink in the air.

'I guess you're the only passenger,' one man bellowed in an American accent. 'What's your name?'

'Chad Hobbes.' I liked the man's freshness. After all, I was now in the Colonies, not in a drawing room.

'Admiralty? Colonial Office?'

'Oh no. I'm a lawyer.'

The man laughed. 'There ain't no work for lawyers in Victoria these days. No property movin' no more.' He rowed on mechanically, and without even turning their heads for a look the men steered the boat expertly to one side of the HBC quay where there was a low floating dock. 'Throw out that painter, would you,' the first man ordered.

I found the painter and threw it to a strange figure who had come running down the dock, a squat Indian wrapped in a rusty red blanket over breeches and bare feet, long-haired, brown or dirty skinned, and beardless. He caught the rope and wrapped it around a bollard.

'That'll be four dols,' said the first lighterman, pulling in his oar and pausing as if to communicate that nothing would be unloaded before money changed hands. The price, a pound, was outrageous, but I reached for my purse with its few American dollars obtained in London, and paid up. I clambered onto the floating dock. The Indian's filthy hand was stretched out for a tip. I gave him a shilling. My purse contained my worldly fortune, in the form of a few shillings, sovereigns and silver dollars, and a draft on the Bank of British Columbia for £55.

The Indian neither thanked me nor met my eyes, but jumped into the boat and set about manhandling one of my trunks. With as much dignity as I could manage in the pouring rain, I walked ahead up the dock then stepped briskly off into the mud of the New World – a world which lurched as my sea legs tensed and braced and nearly threw me into a puddle.

The life story of Jeroboam, 21 years old, driver of the cart in which I lurched along a muddy swathe through gloomy firs, in the rain, to Victoria. Childhood on a pig farm in North Carolina, living in an attic, with flitches of ham hanging to dry from the rafters, along the top of the pig pens behind the great house his forefathers had built for the Masters. The house was burned down in the Civil War and Jeroboam was freed. He went to California intending to find gold and get rich, but the white men there treated him worse than even the Masters had. So he came North. There are over two hundred Negroes here, mostly on an island called Salt Spring. They have a militia regiment of their own, raised with British approval to defend against possible American incursions. Jeroboam is married to the daughter of an Italian vegetable merchant who doesn't like the colour of Jeroboam's skin but can't do anything about it since the daughter does like it. Jeroboam laughs a lot. The funny thing is (I suppose it's a pecking order) he looks down on the 'Injuns.'

Coming into Victoria there is a sort of mirror town across the harbour called the Songhees village – a distorting mirror. Victoria itself, seen across the bay, is charming, with a regular grid of streets of wooden and brick houses and a long wooden wharf backed with a stone and brick terrace – in contrast to the irregular shore-line on either side, with its outcroppings of granite tufted with small oak trees. The Songhees village, which we drove through, is a mess of large, but low buildings of planks blackened by smoke and age, interspersed with smaller dwellings made of odds and ends – naval tents, packing cases, logs and poles. Smoke rose from the dwellings out of holes in the roofs, and from open fires. Blanketed figures moved here and there. Some of the planks are painted in a rusty red with huge designs, geometrical versions of faces and eyes, smeared with dirt and grime. The cart lurched sideways as Jeroboam steered around what I thought, with a start of horror, was a corpse lying in the mud.

'Drunken bastard. See the beach down there?' Jeroboam pointed with his whip at a stretch of mud between the plank houses and the water. 'A coupla years back, the Songhees chief – Chief Freezy we call him – cut the head off of one of his wives, right on the beach, facing across the harbour. Supposed to be because she'd been doing jig-a-jig with a white man. But usually they don't care what their squaws do, so long as they bring back money. He musta wanted to impress people.'

Victoria itself is a sort of human zoo, containing respectable-looking ladies in hooped dresses and capes, and some men as well dressed as in London, though all must pick their way along a filthy boardwalk against a backdrop of wooden buildings, mostly taverns. Other men in slouch hats and ragged clothes are sprawled asleep against walls in the drizzle. There are also some quite ferocious Indians with painted faces, wearing a mixture of white man's clothing and their own, a conical hat made of basketry and a bark-woven cape, or dirty blankets in garish colours. The men's faces are light brown, Mongolian-looking, beardless but with thin drooping moustaches, as in an engraving of Genghis Khan. I saw one woman in a petticoat with bare feet and a blanket around her shoulders, her breasts exposed completely. Her nipples were pink.

When we came to the hotel Jeroboam had recommended (I had asked for the second best), the Argyle, there were several Indian men squatting on a wooden veranda. They stared at me. One of them made a remark in his language, guttural sounds and clicks of the tongue. Then he straightened his head and shoulders, drew down his mouth, contracted his nostrils so that they developed a pinched expression, raised his eyebrows slightly, and for an instant, to my horror, I was looking at a perfect reflection of myself! The face of a haughty Englishman! After only a second or two the Indian's face reverted to its former brutish impassivity. The others burst out laughing, one of them literally rolling on the boards of the veranda.

The Argyle is a square house of yellow painted wood. Inside there is a lobby of surprising but dilapidated elegance, like a huge drawing room, with a fireplace of logs burning vigorously, armchairs, sofas, back-to-back settees, tables with waxed fruit under glass, panelled walls hung with paintings of the 'Monarch of the Glen' variety – stags or eagles standing on crags. A page boy in a shabby uniform jacket with brass buttons, but not wearing a cap, appeared promptly and took my coat and oilskin cape, holding them away from him. 'I'll dry 'em in the kitchen', he announced. Then a dramatic middle aged woman in a pink crinoline and lace mob-cap decorated with girlish ribbons appeared, and made me welcome, in an Irish accent on which genteel vowels had been superimposed. A Mrs Larose, whose poor dear husband was recently deceased. He had been a French 'homme d'affaires' in her words (pronouncing the 'h' of homme and the 's' of affaires). She swiftly negotiated a stiff price: 16 dollars, or £4 a week without meals. 'Such awful, terrible weather it is. You'll be so tired. How is Home?' she gushed as she herself undertook to show me my room, up a narrow staircase. It is just as in England, with a brass bedstead, wash-stand, wine-coloured carpet of indifferent floral design but at least clean. The walls, papered in the inevitable motif of incessantly repeated flowers, are slightly crooked as if the building were comfortably old, although nowhere in Victoria could have been built more than 15 years ago. The window looks out onto Broad Street and a row of wooden shacks which proclaim themselves to be the offices of an insurance broker and a real-estate agent, alternating with taverns.

Although I was dying to settle in, wash my hands and face, and find the water closet to relieve myself after that bumpy journey on the cart, Mrs Larose lingered in the doorway and after a few more polite questions about 'home' – meaning England where I wondered if she had ever been – began to tell me (Yes!) her life story. At least the more recent part. The purchase of the hotel. The late Mr Larose's final decline and dementia from a venereal disease...Yes, she told me that! 'Of course once I knew, I could never sleep with him,' she said, 'it became a marreeyage de conveeniaunce.' She is a great Francophile. Even Mr Larose's disease came with him from *France*, certainly *not* – and here she lowered her voice as if speaking of the dead, although she had sounded quite cheerful, even excited, speaking of the really dead Mr Larose – from a filthy Indian. He had *nothing – rien!* – to do with *them*. And the venereal disease – with French politeness, I found myself supposing – had refrained from attacking her although of course she had 'been with' her husband for many years while he must have had it – *dormant* (pronounced in the French way) of course – without knowing about it. 'I'm so sorry you're not a doctor, Mr Hobbes', she burbled, 'We *so* much need good doctors in this Colony. They are mere *horse* doctors, as I hope you are not misfortunate enough to find out. They don't understand the agonies of mature women!'

Of course I ended up apologising for not being a doctor. I was bewildered, as usual, with women. I hoped she wasn't flirting with me.

But no, there was no sidling towards me, she remained respectably in the doorway. She was simply a raving chatterbox, like a landlady at home (Oh God, I shall get the habit of calling England 'home') but with a total lack of inhibition. Eventually I made motions towards the wash-stand and she left.

My first meal in Victoria: breakfast at Ringo's restaurant – recommended to me by Jeroboam as he set me down at the Argyle. Ham and eggs, muffins with butter and jam, two glasses of coffee. All for 35 cents. Ringo is a carbon copy, as it were, of Jeroboam, and although he did not exactly tell me his life story, he let me know proudly that he had been one of the first Negroes in Victoria, before the Civil War, as a runaway slave. I sat on, browsing through the last few editions of the *British Colonist*. Victoria is in political ferment. There are indignant editorials about the horrifying prospect of annexation to the U.S.A., and the salvation promised by confederation with Canada. An election is coming up in which a Confederation Party led by someone called Amor de Cosmos is battling with a status quo party which, according to the *Colonist,* claims to maintain British interests but in fact harbours the secret agenda of annexation to the United States. Yet there are only 3,000 voters in the election. In their hands the fate of a land half as large as Europe!

The rest of the local factional conflicts are of the parish pump variety. The Governor used the prison chain gang to set out a croquet lawn at his residence, Carey Castle. The Anglican Bishop, a dandy known as Beau Brummel, is threatened by schism from his evangelistic Dean.

Ringo gave me directions to the only man I knew who might be in Victoria, Frederick Blundell, a friend of friends at Oxford, at Brasenose College. I had heard before leaving home that he was 'in trade' here, which I assumed meant banking or something such. But Ringo said, 'You'll find Fred at the ironmonger's on Store Street.'

The clouds had dissolved, and I stepped out into a surprisingly warm sun. The sky is a paler and brighter blue than in England. The wooden buildings were steaming as the rain dried. I made my way downhill to Wharf Street, now bustling with wagons and with men unloading a ship for the Hudson's Bay Company, then across a rickety bridge over a ravine whose sides were strewn with rubbish, offal, and pieces of broken wood, to Store Street. The ironmonger's had a brick front but wooden sides. Inside, tubs, kettles, buckets and watering cans were hanging from the ceiling on wires. I had to duck around them. Counters on each side were laden with boxes of nails and coils of wire. The walls were hung with shovels, picks, and more bunches of kettles and buckets. A small boy behind one counter was dealing with the shop's only customers, two men arguing quietly about nails. Behind the opposite counter Frederick was lounging on a high stool, reading a book. He looked at me blankly for a moment then broke into a smile and leapt up. 'Chad Hobbes! Old chap, it's you, isn't it?' As if long lost brothers!

Another life story. Poor Frederick, with a poor degree and always a bit dim, seems to have sunk rather than swum out here. Spent his money in the Cariboo, looking for gold. Now saving his meagre earnings in the hope of starting a private school some time in the future. From what he said of the recent fall in the local economy, this seems as unlikely a dream as finding gold. Like my own hopes of working in the law! As Frederick put it, rattling on, 'No go, old chap, I should think. Even if you'd become a barrister before leaving England there wouldn't be much work here. When people are caught red-handed in crimes they don't bother with a legal defense. There are five or six barristers who flourished on all the litigation during the Gold Rush, when everyone was suing everyone else over land frauds and money, but they seem poor as church mice now. There are a number of solicitors too, but there isn't the legal work, in conveyancing and so on, since there are so few sales. You might try Carey Castle but they're an awful crowd – sycophants and hangers-on, minor gentry from home, puffed up with importance and snobbery. And you should try the Legislature. Perhaps they need a clerk or something. Sorry, old chap, but that's the sort of possible level. Go over there and, yes, see old Matthew Begbie, the terror of the Cariboo, the dear old Indian-lover. He's an absolute gentleman, although born in South Africa or somewhere. He doesn't hear cases in Victoria. In fact there's a feud on about that. The judge here is a rather foolish chap called Needham, and although Begbie is Chief Justice he is stuck over on the mainland at New Westminster. But he comes over every couple of weeks on the steamer and sits in legislative councils. Can I sell you a pair of Wellington boots, old chap? Not strictly speaking iron, but we do "carry them", as they say. You'll need them for the Legislature. To get there. The bridge has finally rotted through and been condemned, so you'll have to walk around James Bay in the mud. Watch out for the signs that say "No bottom". They mean it. I'll draw you a map. Look, I have some splendid Wellingtons here.'

So my old acquaintance Frederick Blundell of Brasenose sold me a pair of rubber Wellingtons for the sum of three dollars.

Government Street, Victoria's main thoroughfare, comes to an end at a long wooden bridge to the Legislature buildings, known as the 'bird-cages', across a wide bay of the Inner Harbour. The bridge is closed off and is visibly rotten, with slats fallen into the water. It's necessary either to take a 'ferry' – one of the rowboats moored nearby, whose owners charge a dollar a trip – or to skirt the bay by a road which is merely a slough of mud and puddles. I took the road. There were only a few shanties here and there, with chickens or ducks running or paddling around them, stretches of long grass, and the frost-blackened remains of vegetable patches. On a rise up to my left was a wooden church – the cathedral – a humble site for the world-shaking doctrinal schisms which apparently threaten. Several horses and carts passed, with passengers in elegant coats, presumably coming from the Legislature. I was kept busy scrambling away from the road to avoid being splashed with mud. I felt pleased not to be doing the rounds of the failed lawyers, suppliant for a job. Visiting the Legislature gave me a sense of purpose, at least until I arrived there.

The 'birdcages' are indeed a grotesque architectural feat, but not disagreeable. They are faced with pink brick and half-timbered to give an Elizabethan effect, though the timbers have been painted red. The roofs are also red, and pagoda-shaped. The main building has a little square bell tower, and is fronted with wooden steps to a door with a fan-light window. Horses were hitched to nearby posts, and the drivers of carts or buggies were standing in conversation in the sun at the edge of pleasant lush lawns. There were even flowerbeds with Michaelmas daisies, asters and chrysanthemums, only slightly frost-blackened. I followed a path which led past the carts and to the back where a wider flight of steps than in front led up to a long veranda on which some men in frock coats were standing arguing. They turned to look at me with cold curiosity. I asked whether Mr Begbie was in Victoria at present.

'You're in luck. Here's here now', one man said. He had fixed intense eyes and a silly coal-scuttle shaped beard sticking aggressively forward. His accent was not quite like the local American.

The men continued to stare at me as I went in the door which was propped open on a chock of wood. There was a large panelled vestibule lined with benches, a circular staircase, and various doors. A man dressed in a black coat with silver buttons came forward and I handed him my letter of introduction. He took it and went through one of the doors. I sat on a bench and waited, twiddling my thumbs, aware that my Wellingtons were incongruous. Eventually the porter reappeared, followed by another man, who from his fussy air appeared to be a clerk. 'Mr Hobbes? Mr Begbie will see you now.'

He escorted me into a large room whose windows looked out onto the front veranda. There was a fireplace with a wood fire, a table with documents strewn over it, and leather chairs.

'Mr Hobbes. I am Matthew Begbie. Welcome to Victoria.' His voice is English, sharp, and high-pitched for such an imposing man. He is tall, dandyish, but broad shouldered. Thinning hair, a pointed grey-brown beard, aristocratic face with wide brow. Like engravings of Walter Raleigh. An elegant courtier. Frock coat, ruffed cravat, jewelled pin. Frederick mentioned, while I was trying on the boots, that Begbie was a tough customer who travelled by horseback or foot hundreds of miles on circuit, in snow or sun, pitching his own tent in the forest, living off wild game, handing out impartial judgement in the mining camps in an attempt to make Americans into peaceful British citizens. He is known both as a hanging judge and as an Indian-lover: he has hanged quite a few Indians, but believes they have title to the land they live and hunt in. This is apparently unpopular with the Legislature.

Our conversation turned out to be momentous after its initial parryings.

'An odd letter.' He held it up delicately. 'It describes you as a very able young man, but it leaves out something. You began in Divinity and concluded in Jurisprudence. But it doesn't say why.'

'I lost my faith.' I felt as if back on the *Ariadne,* and resolved not to be pompous.

'Why?'

'You know of the debate at Oxford between Dr Huxley and Bishop Wilberforce. That was eight years ago, before I was there, but it still echoed.

My father is a very earnest sort of parson with evangelical leanings. We used to argue about Low Church versus High Church, with me favouring High Church for the sake of the argument I suppose. But at Oxford, after the Wilberforce debacle, people seemed to have retreated from argument into an emphasis on ritual.' Here I began to flounder. I remembered Charles Dickens's remark that High Churchmen were all dandies. Though a Cambridge man, as a dandy Begbie would almost certainly be High Church. 'At any rate I was so wearied by the High versus Low Church question that Darwin's *Origin of Species* took me by storm.'

'Do you think Darwin is an atheist?'

'I don't know.'

'I don't think he is. He ends *The Origin* thus: "There is grandeur in this view of life, with its several powers, having been originally breathed by the Creator into a few forms or into one…" Not the words of an atheist.'

'Indeed not.'

'I've always wondered why people think he is one then. Haven't you?'

'I believe it's because of his emphasis on Natural Law.'

'Ah, that's why you changed to studying the law.'

'Yes.'

'You've come to the right place, Mr Hobbes, to pursue an investigation of Natural Law. You'll learn things about it they don't know at Oxford or in the Inns of Court – or even at Cambridge. I believe there are three laws. Natural Law, God's Law, and the Law of the Land – which in this Colony is the Common Law of England. You may have been taught it approximates to Natural Law, but I discover every day that they are different. Have you seen Mr de Cosmos?'

'No.'

'That is he.' He gestured grandly to the window and those arguing men gesticulating outside, whose heads we could see passing now and then, the man with the coal-scuttle beard, the most vehement. 'Amor de Cosmos – Lover of the Cosmos. A Canadian whose real name is Bill Smith. But that is by the by. You cannot yet practice the law of the land here. A pity you didn't go to the bar in England. It would be good to have a barrister of your background – in the long run, that is. There's no work now. And no solicitor will take you on for articling – unless you pay him a fortune for doing nothing to teach you. It's a bad time. And I should say right away, I have no personal need of your services: I have my clerk already. Have you much money?'

'Very little.'

'If you had you might go into farming. You look as if you have the energy. Then we could eventually make a Magistrate of you. But that's a time ahead. Who knows what will happen? Our Americans here are mostly good citizens. They like British orderliness. But if the United States were permitted to annex this Colony, I should leave for England at once. However, I'm not of *that* man's party.' Another glance at the window. 'Are you interested in the theatre? I mean, have you acted?'

'I'm afraid not.'

'No matter. You must come to the Amateur Dramatic Society – and of course attend the Theatre Royal. I own it.' He smiled mysteriously. 'You won't have met a judge before who owns a theatre.'

'I don't think so.' I was beginning to fear that the meeting was becoming purely social.

'I have an idea for you.' A dramatic pause. 'But it will displease you at first. Did you notice any policemen in this town?'

'Not so far.'

'There are a dozen or so, under the direction of my friend the Stipendiary Magistrate, Augustus Pemberton. They keep the peace, and they look after the jail which is part of the courthouse on Bastion Street, and is also our lunatic asylum – an unsatisfactory combination. Now, I say to myself, why shouldn't an educated young man like you, educated in the law, become a Constable?' Another dramatic pause. 'What do you think?'

'I don't see how…'

'Of course. You're a gentleman. Police Constables aren't gentlemen. Correct? But if a gentleman cannot, at present, find other employment, why not become a Constable? After all, there are university men here in Victoria who work as assistants in shops. Others have degenerated and become drunken sots. A gentleman may fall very rapidly in a Colony. I remember one man, the Honourable So-and-So, who came out here in the Gold Rush with his man-servant whom he dismissed soon after their arrival for being impertinent. Two years later the Honourable So-and-So was reduced to the point where he had to take employment in a draper's shop. The draper was his former man-servant.'

'You mean I should become a sort of Bow Street runner? – a "Peeler"?'

'I can suggest to Augustus Pemberton that you be taken on as a Constable. I believe the pay is only £25 a month. Not much, though it goes further here in Victoria than up in the Cariboo where a good meal costs over a pound. You'll have to take your shifts with the rest of them, do your stint as jailer, supervise the chain-gang, go out and arrest the more violent drunks, keep the ladies of the night within bounds. But you might also be the ideal man to do criminal investigation. The Victoria police is modelled on that of London. And if they can have a department of Criminal Investigation in London, why don't we send for an expert from the London Metropolitan police to start one here? Oh well, I see you smile. We are minuscule compared to London. If we were to have a 'detective' it could only be part time – one of the Constables at first. You will find your colleagues a rough and ready bunch. The Superintendent and Inspectors were recruited in a hurry ten years ago, as Constables then, at the start of the Gold Rush. The only requirements for entry were good character and a height of five feet nine. Mr Pemberton was formerly a barrister in Dublin and is a very capable and resolute man. I'm sure he will be more than interested in a man of your brain and calibre. I assume you can shoot a gun.'

'Yes. I grew up in the country. I've done a fair amount of rough shooting.'

'You'll learn how to use a revolver. And yes, you will learn about Natural Law, Mr Hobbes. That is, if you're the man for the job. Are you?'

'I think so. Why not? Yes. I'll give it my best.'

'Good man.' He reached forward and shook my hand earnestly. 'I'll keep this letter, if you don't mind, and I'll discuss the matter with Augustus Pemberton very shortly. Where are you staying?'

'The Argyle.'

'I shall send you a note there.'

Which he did.

Here I am, Constable 'Obbes, at your service, Sir or Ma'am!

3

I'm in prison. Or at least the court-house which also functions as police station, lunatic asylum and jail. It's less than ten years old but already decrepit. Worn and peeling paint on doors. Brick walls edged with stone and topped with fake battlements, irregular and sagging. All windows, not only those of the jail section, with bars. At £25 a month, room and board in a lodging house would have left nothing to spare. I could always have rented (or even constructed with my own hands – it's no more difficult than building a hen-house) a one room hovel, at the edge of town or along the rocks by the dead water of the Inner Harbour. But there's a spare room in the court-house, and the jailor, Archie Seeds, needs the help. Although he never says so he also needs company. His wife ran off to California last year with a returning gold-miner who although he was 'skunked' penniless in the Cariboo was able to afford to get drunk and disorderly in Victoria, and was thrown into jail – from which he departed with Seeds's wife and savings.

Lower Bastion Street is in fact a square, like a platform, once part of the HBC fort which has been pulled down. There is a fine view out over the wharves to the Inner Harbour and the Songhees village, like a smoking dump on the other side. In the square, executions are held, although none is in the offing. In the jail are a hard core of seven prisoners (a year or two for robbery or assault) and an extra one or two a night, though more at weekends, drunk and disorderly. The hard core are mostly American, including a Negro. The one-nighters are white, black, occasionally Indian. Almost never Chinamen. The 'Celestials' police themselves. The occasional corpse is found, throat slashed, butcher's knife in hand to indicate suicide, at dawn in Cormorant Street or Fan Tan Alley. Fan Tan is a Chinese gambling game. The gambling dens are also opium dens. We leave them alone. Begbie's remark about the jail doubling as a lunatic asylum is technically true, but there are no lunatics at present. 'There are too many out there to lock up' is the joke.

I have plenty of time to write my account, at night in my room. Now I am in a prison, in what seems like a lunatic world compared to any I knew in England, perhaps I should be feeling and thinking differently. But I am not. Instead I have been sparked by Begbie's brisk remarks about Darwin's possible atheism into a return of my old agonies about belief. In England I have heard both that Darwin is an atheist and that he is not. I have seen cartoons of him in the form of an ape – although his kindly face does not lend itself so readily to this caricature as that of his ferocious looking disciple Huxley. But of course he does end the Origin with the implication that good old God must have got evolution going. Perhaps it is just a debate about the time scale: God started the clock going millions of years ago, not in 4,004 BC as that mad Irish bishop Ussher calculated by adding up the life spans in the Bible.

It was never these arguments in philosophy and theology that bothered me. Since I read the Voyage of the Beagle it has been the observations. Species unfold, just as geological formations change, over millennia. And we humans unfold too. We are unstable, changing, we adapt to circumstances – also over millennia. That is what shocked me into disbelief, the realisation that the stable world of my parents was just a tiny point in circumstances. I had an argument with my father about conscience. 'It's universal', he said. 'God has planted it in every man.' 'Does a cannibal in the Pacific eating a sailor in the form of "long pig" exhibit any conscience about this?' I argued. I could also have argued that my brother Henry showed no sign of conscience in seducing village girls. Whereas I was myself so tormented with conscience – or fear – that I couldn't give in to one. Anyway I stuck with the cannibal argument, then added what could be called the Fuegian argument, mentioning the dreaded Darwin. 'I have never met a man without a conscience!' my father thundered. 'Nor a woman, and not even a child. Show me the child who does not feel a prick of conscience when he steals an extra slice of cake!' I could have shown him Henry. Instead I returned to the charge with the Fuegians who kill strangers without compunction. I said conscience was merely instilled by a particular society, and enforced by the law. But I did not really know what I was talking about.

That is why I am here. To answer questions which cannot even be easily asked in Christian circles in England. For example, to see for myself whether so called savages are really different from us in having a different, or no, conscience. So far the evidence is on my side. Chief Freezy who chopped his wife's head off on the shore as a demonstration, hardly had a conscience. Or more exactly, he did not have a conscience like mine. But he seems to have had a reason. As Jeroboam put it, she might have been doing jig-a-jig with someone. In which case Freezy can be described as having a conscience of good and evil, by his lights. I wonder if anyone asked Freezy: why? At any rate he was not punished. The police from this jail did not arrest him. In this new world I am wrong on two counts: perhaps someone like Freezy does have a sort of conscience – and the law certainly does nothing to instill one. Furthermore, I know almost nothing about jig-a-jig.

My Superintendent, Francis Parry, is not about to let his new Constable-Detective do only guard duties while waiting for a knotty investigation to challenge his intellect. He tells me that there are 80,000 prostitutes in London, and that over 20 corpses a day float down the Thames. He challenges me to believe this. I don't want to but he is a very credible man. The quintessential English Sergeant-Major. Which he was, in the Crimean War. He talks about Inkerman, the 'soldiers' battle'. In pouring rain in the dark then for a day in fog and smoke, English and Russian infantrymen fought it out hand to hand without benefit of command. They ran out of ammunition and were reduced to bayoneting each other, clubbing each other with rifle butts, braining each other with heavy stones, and strangling each other with bare hands. Parry did all these things. He also watched the magnificent charge of the Light Brigade. He says he heard its leader, Lord Cardigan, afterwards, indignantly complaining not at the folly of the charge but at the bad behaviour of the Irish officer whose message to 'Charge for the guns' neglected to specify which guns. This man realised the error too late and tried to call Cardigan back, but got his arm and shoulder shot off and, as Cardigan said furiously in Parry's hearing, 'screamed like a woman.' Parry is not a brute, but a decent man with a faded pretty wife and grown-up sons, who build houses when there is a demand for them. He seems to have had a revelation in the Crimea that without authority and hierarchy life is a hell which leads to quick and indecent death. But he is a remarkably un-snobbish man. He is not in the least embarrassed – though in English terms my social inferior, not a gentleman etc. – to be my superior in command. Why should he be? Though he sees me frankly as a protégé of Begbie and Pemberton, I must do my apprentice work. But policing in

Victoria is not an active pursuit of trouble, with regular beats and raids. The policy is to leave well alone. Most drunken brawls sort themselves out: the sawdust on the floors of the taverns (95 of them!) is there to soak up blood as well as the usual dirt and spit.

When a complaint comes in – someone knocking at the courthouse door late at night howling that a man is getting killed – the other duty constable and I throw our capes over our blue brass-buttoned tunics and set off into the rain, truncheons in hand. (Long-barrelled pistols are available but we seldom carry them). If the brawl is not over by the time we arrive we separate the combatants and haul them off to jail in handcuffs. This is easier than I had feared. The men are usually too drunk to be effective and are often pleased to have the excuse to stop fighting. The other night I did have to call for reinforcements. A sailor went berserk after rejection by a girl and attacked the entire population, male and female, of the Olympic dance hall. The reinforcements consisted of Sergeant Parry himself. He cracked the berserker's skull with his truncheon. The man survived.

A dance hall is a relatively genteel version of a brothel. Parry says they are modelled on Almack's Rooms in London, but I hardly know London. A long room lined with tables and chairs for sitting out with an over-expensive beverage, a small orchestra at one end, and a number of over-dressed young and not-so-young ladies with whom the men dance – for a fee (not apparently the practice at Almack's). There are further fees for a visit to the next door 'hotel'. The dance halls give no trouble in themselves, and we keep away from them unless an altercation occurs, which is not often, since minor quarrels are dealt with by a 'chucker-outer'. There are two dance halls: the Olympic (25 cents a dance) and the more elegant Windsor Rooms (50 cents).

Prostitution still embarrasses me. I have never seen a naked woman, after all – outside drawings and daguerrotypes. I can only imagine what the barmaid, Susan, would *look* like 'down there.' Resistance to temptation comes naturally, as a rigidity backed up by probably too much thought. Sometimes a 'lady of fashion' will 'give me the eye'. But I remain stone-faced, indifferent, as at Oxford when I strolled past the much less attractive sluts of St Ebbes, nose in the air.

The great enterprise of the winter was a raid on 'immorality'. Because of the small-pox scare, the authorities, in the form of August Pemberton, decided to enforce the bylaw which makes it illegal for any Indian woman to reside within the city limits. The only exceptions are Indian women registered as household servants, but there are few of these. They are considered to be dirty and, yes, immoral.. There are, however, no less than two hundred Indian prostitutes informally resident in an area between Cormorant and Fisgard Streets, near Chinatown, in shacks and shanties rented to them by 'Celestial' landlords. They ply their trade with seamen and the riff-raff of town, and usually we leave them alone. But now they had to be cleared out. We knew they would trickle back over the winter months, but at least a step would have been taken in the interests of public health – a blow against smallpox and perhaps, temporarily, against the other pox which provides over half the cases at the hospital.

More on Indians: I have applied myself to learning Chinook from the 'Dictionery' (spelling is not so strong in the Colony as oral fluency which is considerable) published by Hibben, the stationer. Chinook, also known as Jargon, is a lingua franca or pidgin which was developed before the coming of the white man, among the coastal Indian tribes whose languages are mutually unintelligible. Its basic vocabulary of words from various Indian languages has been added to by French Canadians and Englishmen working for the HBC. It consists of only about 600 words. It's easy to learn since it has no grammar. I think it is a remarkable human achievement, and I wonder why no such useful common pidgin has sprung up in Europe.

My reading of Darwin makes me want to feel a kinship with the Indians. But it's hard. They seem inhuman. Thoughtful people such as Begbie and Pemberton acknowledge that the Songhees in particular have been degraded by their contact with us, and weakened by venereal disease – the 'fire sickness' which is endemic in them. The Songhees are short-legged. (The story is that this has been caused by generations of sitting in canoes, but this implies a too literal interpretation of Larmarck's theories – which cause even Darwin difficulty.) Their skulls are compressed as babies, by being bound into sleeping boards, the squashed effect being seen by them as a sign of beauty. The colonists say it makes them stupid, by crushing their brains. I doubt this. They usually look expressionless, brutish, and sullen. But this is just for us. I remember the Indian who so expertly mimicked my expression on my arrival at the Argyle. In their religious rituals they act out their history through drama, though I haven't seen this yet. Occasionally a few organise themselves enough to come into town and sell basket-work which is really of exquisite skill. If a sailor in funds tosses a Songhees a sovereign, he'll take it away, beat it flat, and mould it into a perfect gold ring, which he'll give back honourably, for a few pennies or cents.

The smallpox raid was carried out at dawn on a frosty morning by almost the full police force, eight constables and two sergeants under the direction of Superintendent Parry, along with a dozen naval police, who would gather up as much of her Majesty's Navy as would be found. I was assigned with a another constable, a middle-aged Scot, Agnew, to clear out an alley of one-room shanties, like wooden boxes on the frozen mud, with wisps of smoke coming from their stove pipes. The procedure was to bang on the door then open it. If it was locked we banged again and waited for a moment, then kicked it down. The object was not to make arrests – an easy procedure since no warrant is required – but to tell the inhabitants to clear out.

From one of the larger shanties came the sound of singing and shouting, so we decided to deal with it first. The door was opened promptly by a beardless man in trousers and a grubby vest, with tattooed arms. We pushed past him. It was foetid with bodies, liquor, urine, tobacco smoke and tar (this brought me back for a moment to the *Ariadne*). Three other men, stripped to their vests, were sitting around a table, strewn with bottles and cards, as if the night had hardly begun. It was hot, from a pot-bellied stove. There were a number of sullen-looking squaws – entirely naked.

The sailors were singing lustily, not a sea shanty (associated with work for them), but that lovely West country ballad, *The Keys of Heaven*:

Madam I'll present to you a fine silver ball
To tumble in your garden on the finest day of all,
If you'll be my joy and my only sweet dear,
And walk along with me anywhere…

They finished the verse, then stopped, looking at us dopily.

I told them they'd have to leave and addressed the women in Chinook: 'Mesika maha maha house hyack hyack…' ('You leave leave house hurry hurry…') I began to explain about the danger of sickness as best I could.

'Come on you! Clear out!' Agnew ordered the sailors, who had not moved.

'Easy, Matey', one of them said. But they stood up and turned to find their clothes. 'It's cold out there', said the one who had come to the door. 'You sure we can't stay for one more bang?' But he reached for his pea-jacket which was lying on a big brass bed-stead.

The women merely sat sullenly.

'Maha maha, hyack hyack', I repeated.

'Wake' – ('No') – one of the women said. I had not expected this.

Agnew stepped over to one of the women and pulled her by the shoulder to her feet. 'Move along you slut', he said.

'Watch out, mate', said one of the sailors. 'That's my Betsy, that is. Come along now, Betsy, do as the Peeler says.'

But the woman hung heavily on Agnew's arm, so that he had to let her drop back to her seat.

I went over to one of the other women and stood beside her. She had an intense fishy smell. 'Maha house', I said as gently as I could. In Chinook, politeness or any emotion has to be expressed not by words but by the tone of voice.

'Nesika mitlite yakwa' ('We stay here') she said stubbornly.

I appealed to the sailors. 'Why don't you give us a hand? We have orders to get these ladies out of here. Couldn't you persuade them to come quietly.'

'That's your job, Matey', one man said. 'They's nice girls. You didn't orter put'em out in the cold.'

'You want to be taken by the naval police? They're out there.'

'Bastards!' The sailors then, with good humour, began to turn the occasion into a joke. 'Come on, Betsy, get your rags on.' They led the women over to the assorted blankets and skirts which had been cast here and there. They even helped them get dressed. Then they all shuffled out into the cold.

The other shanties were easier. Usually two or three couples who went quietly. Some respectable citizens who hurried furtively away. Squaws aroused naked and shameless from filthy beds. I did not look closely. Agnew did, stepping up close and yelling to them to make it quick.

The shanties were padlocked and stayed empty for a few weeks until quietly broken open and moved into again. The only obvious victims were a couple found one morning who had apparently had no shelter to go to: a sailor and a squaw, frozen into the mud in a permanent embrace.

What do I make of this? My sleep is disturbed by that night. But I was acting so quickly all the while, that I didn't look long at those women. I would have liked to study them. The hair between their thighs seemed sparse, their breasts not big. Although short legged and squat in figure, perhaps they were young girls. There was a story I heard at Oxford – that hotbed of jokes and ribaldry about sex, though of course it was denied us: we could be sent down, banished in disgrace from the university for ever, if the least relation occurred, even walking down the street hand in hand with, a young lady. If members of the university visited St Ebbes after dark, perhaps it was not unlike Cormorant Street. There was much talk of the St Ebbes whores. But I doubt if many visited them, it was too risky. Instead the colleges were rife with sentimental relations between men, which included who knows what. Wadham College was taunted in the song 'Wadham, Wadham, Sons of Sodom', but it was probably not exceptional. Luckily I had not gone to a boarding school, but to the venerable day school for boys in our local town. Anyway the story was that the writer about painting, John Ruskin, who had his marriage scandalously annulled on the grounds of non-consummation, had been horrified to find that his bride had hair between her legs. Another story in Oxford was on a similar theme, I now realise. It was about Charles Dodgson, a lecturer in mathematics at Christ Church, and a lay preacher in the Church of England. As I came up to Oxford his Alice in Wonderland was published. It was a bit of a sport to look out for him, as he had become famous, as Lewis Carroll. Whenever I walked down from Merton Lane into the Meadows, I would pause at that grilled gate in the stone wall beside Christ Church and look at the croquet lawn, where it was supposed he had imagined that game using flamingoes as mallets. Although various Christ Church men were there, Dodgson was never to be seen. It was said he had fallen out with Alice's parents, Dean Liddell and his lovely wife Lorina. I know she was lovely, because although I never saw Dodgson on the croquet lawn, I did once see the Liddell family promenading down Broad Walk – the pompous old Dean (though he had been a doctrinal rebel in his day) with the three pretty daughters all in pink and white, and I must say the quite glorious Mrs Liddell. The story was that Dodgson had taken photographs of the girls naked, or nearly naked, and that he liked little girls more than he should. If so I realise this might be, as in the case of Ruskin, because he could not tolerate the reality of women as hairy animals like ourselves, hairy men.

Unless another story was true: that in fact he was enamoured of Mrs Liddell and merely making love to her through her daughters. Rather filthy minds there were at Oxford.

Another reason I suppose the Cormorant street raid is so vivid in my mind is that I have often heard The Keys of Heaven sung at the Trout – by some man or other making up to the barmaids. At any rate I know I am not like Ruskin or Dodgson. I liked, I trembled at, what I felt under Sally's dress. I desired the whores I rounded up on Cormorant Street.

With the New Year the weather has turned clear and frosty. I supervise seven prisoners in the 'chain-gang' (without chains, in fact) repairing the James Bay bridge. I work too, lugging beams and hammering nails. On Sunday afternoons my iron-mongering friend Frederick and I hire horses and ride over to Cadborough Bay, through stretches of enormously high firs and cedars, with melting frost dripping into the gloom from sagging branches, then through patches of more open and park-like landscape of grass, scrub, brambles, native Garry oaks, 'arbutus' (madrona), and cottonwoods whose fallen yellow leaves clog the streams. We carry shotguns in holsters by the horses' saddles, and though the horses are gun-shy, they can be tied up in a patch of woods while we circle around on foot, rough shooting for grouse which are numerous and so tame that they wait on a branch after a missed shot for the deadly second. It's easy to bag a couple of dozen which I give away to the married constables, all housebound.

Frederick has suddenly lost interest in these Sunday expeditions and become busy with something or other which he does not want to talk about.

I've written to a friend in London asking for the latest text-books in criminal detection, but it will take months for them to arrive. In the subscription library I found a book by a Scottish-Irish detective, James McLevy, called *The Sliding Scale of Life* – a title which I relish for its ironical application to myself. McLevy writes about the 'stews' of Edinburgh, known as 'The Happy Land' – 'a world by itself, with no law ruling except force, no compunction except fear, no religion except that of the devil.'

Sometimes I think Victoria, the new Garden of Eden, is in its own way the kind of Happy Land McLevy describes. Even Begbie's theatre is a bore. Several of the so-called lawyers in town have fake qualifications. The doctors and surgeons are incompetent and botch diagnosis and operations. I cannot get used to the 'snake oil salesman' type of businessman. There is an advertisement at the Mechanics' Institute for two lectures, on 'Phrenology: the Science of Character', and 'Mesmerism: the Art of Magnetic Healing'. These are to be given by one 'Dr Richard McCrory, notable San Francisco Alienist who has taken up residence in Victoria.'

What would phrenology make of the compressed skull of a Songhees Indian? Dickens is said to have dabbled in Mesmerism, and it used to attract the attention of distinguished London surgeons. In England both it and phrenology are past their zenith. But 'alienist' is new-fangled. I'd use the more old fashioned term 'Mad-doctor'.

At last I've found myself with some detective work, though of a minor nature. A fraud was perpetuated on the Bank of British Columbia by a ship chandler's clerk who forged cheques. I made various enquiries and finally traced the man to New Westminster, on the mainland, where with a young Canadian constable, Joe Harding, I went to apprehend him. He had installed himself, having shaved off his beard and disguised himself as a clergyman, in a respectable but small house with a not so young lady from the Windsor Rooms. After his capture, all four of us travelled together back to Victoria, morosely, on the paddle-steamer, dining aboard at my expense. I felt sorry for them. The lady broke into tears from time to time. The criminal was pale and looked as if he had suddenly aged ten years: he'll get at least three in jail.

4

Spring in Victoria is something like England but the wind is colder and the sun hotter. Gardens recreate an English look, with daffodils crowding the flower-beds in March, tulips in April when domestic apple trees begin to come to blossom. Now it's May. In Beacon Hill Park, where people throng for their Sunday walks, the grassy slopes are covered with native 'camas' – like bluebells. Groups of Indian women move among them rooting out the occasional plant which has white flowers and therefore poisonous bulbs. They will gather the bulbs now and eat them in Autumn when the flowers will be long gone. They come from all around Victoria – Sooke, Cowitchan, Saanich. Like the Songhees, they wear a mix of civilised and native clothing – trousers or petticoats under striped HBC blankets, conical hats made of fibre, or slouch hats or bonnets. Bands of Indians from further North have also appeared, camping in the forest in makeshift tents, to trade the artefacts they have been working on during winter, and to move from farm to farm begging (stealing, some people say) or doing odd jobs. Their presence excites fear. And they seem to have given me a real adventure to write about.

I arrived back at the court house from a routine inspection of licences at about noon to find the place in a flurry. Superintendent Parry was rushing around, first to the safe, then to the armoury, yelling to Harding that he should quickly hire two horses – 'No, three!' he called when he saw me – and send a messenger for a cart to follow us 'out the Cedar Hill road and over to Cormorant Point.'

The cause of the commotion was an Indian of a kind I had not seen before. He stood motionless to one side of the vestibule, his face impassive but his eyes flickering about as if he were frightened. His feet were solidly rooted and his stance erect but he looked dog tired. There were streaks of dried sweat and dust on his face, which was of a clear coppery hue – not pocked or blotched brown like those of most Songhees – with a drooping moustache and with a red painted wooden curved pin through the septum of his nose. He was hatless and his hair was thick but cut short in the back. He wore a blanket of reddish fibre with a huge design on it in darker red and black – eyes, zigzags, circles and squares – a pair of tan coloured deerskin leggings, and moccasins streaked with mud.

'It's a body', Parry told me, more calmly, as if aware of being observed by the Indian. 'An American.' He turned to the Indian. 'Kahta mesika kumtuks man Boston?' he said loudly. ('How you know man American?')

'Tyee wawa.' ('Chief says')

'He ran all the way', Parry said. 'All right, boys? Let's go.'

Men from the livery stable brought three horses to the square outside. We mounted and set off. The Indian followed us, padding behind. Indians don't ride. The horses were not much faster than walking while still in town. People stopped and watched as we plodded uphill along Fort Street, at first lined with stores and taverns, then gardens and paddocks, stables, shanties, and towards the top of the hill some wooden houses, including Pemberton's.

We turned left at a fork and headed North along Spring Ridge onto the Cedar Hill road. After a mile we entered woods where oaks grew among out-croppings of rock and grassy patches covered with blue camas and other small pink and yellow flowers. Below us to the right, visible through the wide gaps between the oaks, was a rolling valley with a mixture of evergreens and deciduous trees – cottonwoods, maple, alder. Cedar Plains. But most of the cedars have been cut for planks to build the houses of Victoria, and now only a few huge specimens remain whose girth has discouraged the axemen.

None of us are good horsemen, and we had to pay continual attention to our rather cranky mounts. Mine needed constant encouragement in the form of kicks to the flanks. We were making better time now, and the Indian had occasionally burst into a run. Sunlight slanted down through the sparse green oak foliage. All around was the continuous ecstatic trilling of huge red-breasted 'robins' – really a form of blackbird, singing from low branches or scurrying on the grass pulling worms out with their beaks – and harsh caws from ravens, known locally as crows, which swooped down behind us to inspect the horse-droppings.

About three miles out of town we passed on the left a group of houses with a wooded cliff behind them but freshly dug gardens in front, looking down over the road towards the Plains. Then there was a newly built church of grey painted wood in a natural rockery of boulders, with cedars and oaks and a graveyard already containing several headstones.

We began to skirt around the grandly named Mount Douglas, originally Cedar Hill, on our left. We were now in a dense forest mainly of firs whose trunks were bare for the first forty feet or so, going up straight as masts to their gently swaying tops over a hundred feet above. There was a dense undergrowth of ferns and bushes. The air was suddenly cool and clammy. The sound of the horses' hooves scraping on rocks and pounding on the earth was muffled. There was no birdsong, not even the caw of a raven. One or two small colourless birds crept silently up and down the fir trunks. The shafts of sunlight were narrow and pale, like swords plunged down through the tree tops into the undergrowth. It reminded me of Salisbury Cathedral in its Gothic perpendicular lines, but there was no sense of God.

We crossed, on ramshackle bridges of cedar trunks laid over with planks, a number of ravines with streams gurgling steeply down among rocks and ferns. The road dipped into an extension of Cedar Plains where the ground was swampy, then rose into dense forest again, gloomy and sunless with boulders and crags covered with moss. We picked carefully across a washout. Then Parry, just in front of me, reined in his horse abruptly. An Indian, more squat and heavily muscled than the first but identically dressed, was standing in the middle of the road. From behind our cavalcade the first Indian came running, panting and exhausted, his face shining with sweat, and called something up to Parry. I caught the word 'kiutan' – horse. Parry ordered us to dismount, then did so himself.

We had been in the saddle an hour and a half. I stood in the dust, swaying slightly. The two Indians were talking in their own language – the usual clicks of the tongue, swishes, and glottal stops. The messenger gestured that we were to tie up the horses, and pointed to a track through the forest. Parry reached for a moment into the large pocket of his tunic where he kept his revolver, but must have decided not to bring it out. He began tying up his horse to one of the narrower firs. Harding and I did the same.

The messenger led the way down the track, dry and dusty, with a thin carpet of fir needles, winding downhill among ferns. We had to climb over dead mossy trunks in tangles of laurel-like bushes with tiny white flowers. The track descended abruptly to a stream which ran across it on a bed of stones, with occasional boulders. The Indian stopped, looking downstream. He made no gesture, but the three of us turned our heads in the direction of his gaze.

A man was sprawled on his back over a large boulder, his boots in the stream. Above the boots his trousers of checked grey and brown were crumpled, the braces dangling in the water. From the knees up he was naked, white, and bloody. The hand nearest us was in the water. The head was pillowed on the boulder, the face looking straight up at the dark treetops, with blood around the mouth, clotted and darkening in a strong carrot red beard. The stream gurgled gently.

Parry spoke. 'I know that man. McCrory. The doctor. The alienist.' He pronounced 'alienist' as if French. He stepped along the stream bank. Harding and I followed. We formed a triangle about the dead man, perching on rocks with the water gently swirling around our boots.

The blood was drying in dark streaks, but was fresh and bright red near the wounds. The most obvious one was at the crotch. The member had been cut off at the root, leaving a bloody hole. The belly had been slashed across but shallowly, not ripped open. There was an obvious stab mark just under the ribs, and one between collarbone and neck, where the wound had been somewhat widened as if the knife had been worked back and forth. There was something wrong with the thick carroty hair. It looked like a bloody wig which had been pushed out of place. A gash followed the hairline above the forehead and the ears which were beginning to turn blue-black. The arms and shoulders had also been slashed or…

Parry said, 'Notice, boys. Those are bite marks.' He squatted down and peered at the arm nearest him. 'Almost torn out a chunk of flesh'.

I crouched down at the man's right side. There were indeed the marks of teeth, a blue-black ellipse in the pallid skin of the shoulder.

'Indian work', Parry said, standing up again. 'He's nearly scalped. The medicine men run amok and sink their teeth into living flesh. I've never heard of it done on a white man though.'

I remained crouching, looking dumbly into the water at the dead man's hand.

'Look here, Sir', I said, standing upright very quickly.

Parry tried picking his way around the dead man's feet, but he splashed in the water. 'God almighty', he said, looking down. His bulldog face, normally flushed and choleric, blanched suddenly. He had seen what I thought I had seen: the dead man's hand was clutching his severed member.

'It's the Devil's making,' Parry muttered.

'Clothes down here, Sir', said Harding from a few yards downstream.

Glad to turn away from the corpse, I followed Parry to look at where a charcoal grey frock coat was flung on a rock near the bank. A shirt, waistcoat, and an elegant dove-grey hat were on the bank nearby, and beside them a small closed basket, exquisitely woven from strips of bark, dyed or painted with red and black geometrical patterns. I turned instinctively to look at the Indian who was standing perfectly still, legs planted apart on two rocks, looking straight at me. I held up the articles one by one. Frock coat, shirt and waistcoat were covered in blood, and each had rents in the front left sides below the shoulder and at the waist. 'Just these two rents', I said. 'I presume he was stabbed, then stripped and mutilated after he fell. Look, there's dirt on the back of the coat, although when it was thrown over here it landed front down.'

'It would not have sufficed to kill him', said Parry – the veteran of Inkerman. 'Nor would any other single blow. The one beneath the ribs would miss the heart and the one at the shoulder missed the artery, otherwise there would be more blood there. It probably took all the blows to do it, and even then it would take a while, bleeding to death.'

I searched the coat pockets. There was a clean handkerchief and a wallet which contained American bills, silver dollars, and a few sovereigns, but no personal papers. There was also a large clasp knife which I opened. It was clean. I crouched down and unfastened the toggle of the basket. There was a herbal smell. Plants and roots, in neat bundles tied with bark twine. 'I dare say I can have these identified by the pharmacist', I said.

'We'll take it all into town on the cart. It should be coming up behind', Parry said. He looked around at the forest. 'There won't be any tracks or footprints. Too dry, now we're down from the mountain. But we should take a look.'

For half an hour we sifted our way up and down the stream banks, and along the track in both directions. The only thing I found of interest was some fresh wood chippings on the path, near the stream, which looked as if they had been whittled off a stick. I looked for the stick but could not find it. I called Parry. 'It looks as if someone was whittling a stick while waiting.'

'Could have been the doctor himself', Parry said. 'Or an Indian. They're always whittling and carving. This is Indian work, clear as day.' He turned to face the Indian messenger, who was now squatting on his haunches in the track, staring at the ground. 'Mesika iskum nesika mesika Tyee' ('You take us your Chief'), he ordered. 'Harding, you stay here. Hobbes, you come with me.'

The Indian jumped to his feet and led the way. I followed Parry's broad back up the path. We reached the road, the horses, and the second Indian standing beneath a tree.

'It's almost a mile', Parry remarked, untying his horse. 'I'd heard there was a band at Cormorant Point. Down from the North. Trading, they say. Most likely stealing.' He scowled at the Indian.

We mounted, and this time the messenger walked briskly ahead of us. The firs became thinner, interspersed with huge arbutus, their blood red under-bark exposed where sheets of pale skin were peeling off, growing from rocks exposed to sunlight. I saw the sea ahead, glistening between the tree trunks, and smelled wood smoke.

We came out into a clearing which faced onto the sea from a bluff, which on the left became a rocky point. Tents and awnings made from densely woven matting, red but with black designs of beaks and eyes, had been slung on ropes from trees at the edge of the clearing, their lower edges tied to bushes or weighed down by stones. Other ropes held rows of split salmon hung up from poles to dry over smoky fires burning in circular hearths made from rocks. To one side was a pile of stacked cedar boxes. Some Indians were in the open, sitting on the ground, their legs spread out in front of them, men and women working at baskets, piles of cedar strips on the ground beside them. When they saw us coming they stood up and formed a straggling line. Others came crawling out of the tents and joined them. There were about ten men and twenty women, and a few children who ran to their mothers' arms to be picked up. No one said a word. The robins around the clearing sang loudly.

We dismounted. The Indians watched as we tied our horses to a tree. Parry was taking his time. Perhaps he was surprised, as I was, at the number of Indians, the well organised look of the camp, and their completely un-European clothing. All were bareheaded in the sun, the women long-haired with braids, the men's hair cut shorter. Although one or two men were wearing only deerskin trousers and loose tunics of woven fibre, most had red fibre blankets wrapped around them like cloaks. Some of the women had bare legs. Others wore leggings like the men. The Indians' skin was more coppery than the usual. Their heads had not been distorted by binding.

Two people appeared from behind a tent on one side, a man with a woman walking slightly behind him. They advanced unhurriedly. Both were quite tall, and were dressed strikingly in blankets of cream coloured cloth, with the usual geometrical patterns but in light blue and black, with long fringes of cream coloured tassels. The man was wearing deerskin leggings, the woman a sort of kilt, also of deerskin and with a fringe of tassels and zigzag patterns of tiny shells sewn onto it. Although the man was imposing, with a long nose and penetrating black eyes, a long moustache and thick but short cut hair, I could not help staring at the woman. She was young and beautiful, with light coppery skin, high cheekbones, and a narrow nose which she looked down rather haughtily, her eyes as black as the man's and more slanted, narrowing sharply. 'Arrow eyes', I found myself thinking. Her hair was not quite black, having a reddish burnished tint. It was parted in the centre into two braids which hung just behind her shoulders. She was wearing oval ear-rings of mother-of-pearl – abalone shell. My eyes were drawn lower down, to the kilt below her blanket, and her legs, naked, slim and brown, her feet in moccasins which were decorated, like the kilt, with stitched tiny shells.

They walked along in front of the others and paused near the centre of the line, the man a step in front of the woman. He was older than she, perhaps about thirty. His air was one of alertness and intelligence. But he was somewhat frightening: his mouth was so firm it looked ruthless, his eyes, which now darted to and fro between Parry and me, almost too penetrating. I glanced back at the woman. She was looking at me steadily, with a certain softness in her eyes. I felt a sudden melting feeling around my heart, and stiffened. She instantly looked downward.

The messenger joined the other Indians and squatted down to one side. 'You'd better take notes', Parry said. I took out my notebook and pencil.

Parry, who was fluent in Chinook, although he shouted rather than spoke it, asked in a bellow, who was the Tyee here?

The obvious Tyee pointed to his chest.

Who were they? What band?

'Tsalaks'. (Not a Chinook word). 'Chack chack', he added ('Eagle'). 'Tsimshian'. (Indian people, up the coast some hundreds of miles North).

'Tsimshian! Fort Simpson!' Parry bellowed, referring to the HBC headquarters 'up island.'

'Wake' ('No').

'Mektakatla?' (The name of the mission settlement).

'Wake.'

'Kah?' Parry asked impatiently. ('Where?')

'Tsalaks.'

'Mesika nem?' ('Your name?')

'Wiladzap.' The Tyee tapped his chest again.

Parry asked who had found the body.

Again the Tyee tapped his chest.

Parry shouted that the messenger had said there was a dead Boston (American). Did the Tyee know that the dead man was a Boston?

'McCloly', the Tyee said in a good imitation of the dead man's name, given that no Indian can pronounce 'R'. Then in a low but strong voice, he explained in fluent Chinook that McCrory had visited the camp four times. Once with a yellow man, a servant. After that alone. He discussed Indian medicine. He bought herbs. He also discussed the wind. Here Parry and I must have looked puzzled, because Wiladzap paused and said 'swensk', in I presume his own language. Then he explained that this meant the breath or spirit.

Parry asked if the Tyee was also a 'mestin' – a medicine man.

'Ah-ha' ('Yes').

Who had found the body?

The Tyee, Wiladzap, pointed to himself and explained carefully. McCrory had visited them in the morning, stayed for a time, then left. After a while Wiladzap heard McCrory calling for help. He ran through the forest. Again he heard the call for help. He found the body. McCrory was not quite dead, but dying. Wiladzap could do nothing, but he splashed a little water on McCrory's face. McCrory spoke in a small voice. He spoke words to Wiladzap. Then he died. Wiladzap left him there, came back to the camp, and sent a messenger to the King George men (the English – us.)

What words? Parry demanded. What words did McCrory say?

'King George Diaub'. Again, after a pause. 'King George Diaub.'

A King George is any Englishman, as opposed to a Boston. But 'Diaub' is 'Devil'.

Parry asked, How did the Tyee hear a call for help? The dead man was found almost a mile from this camp.

'Tum tum hool hool wawa chack chack'. (Literally: 'The heart of the mouse speaks to the eagle.')

Parry either lost his temper or pretended to. He bellowed that it was not a King George who had killed the Boston McCrory, it was certainly an Indian, a 'siwash'. He reached into his pocket, pulled out his long-barreled pistol, held it up for the Indians to see, then put it back into his pocket. He explained in his jerky but accurate Chinook that the Great Queen Victoria, who had given her name to the King George city, was mother of all the King Georges and all Bostons in this land. And they would make sure to find the Indian or Indians who had done this killing.

Wiladzap shrugged his shoulders.

Parry shouted: 'Mesika opitsah?' ('You have a knife?')

Wiladzap shrugged again. He reached under his blanket into the waist of his leggings and brought out a hunting knife in a sheath. He held it forward politely, handle first. I took it. It was a Bowie knife. Everyone in America has one. I do. I gave it to Parry who took it, pushed it back into his sheath and dropped it into his pocket.

Parry now followed standard procedure for dealing with Indians, and reached into his other pocket, pulled out his change purse, and took out a sovereign. He held it up and the sun caught it with a flash. He announced that this was the face of the great Queen Victoria. Her men must know who had killed the Boston, McCrory.

The Indians were motionless and quiet. Even children, clinging to their mothers' legs or in their arms, were silent.

Another sovereign. Another, and another.

Suddenly the messenger took a step forward and pointed with his whole hand, not just a finger, at the Tyee. 'Wiladzap sick tum tum Lukswaas mamook hee hee tikegh bebe bebe doctah. Doctah dollah dollah Lukswaas potlatch.' ('Wiladzap sick at heart, Lukswaas have fun, love, kiss doctor. Doctor give Lukswaas dollars.')

'Wake!' The woman beside Wiladzap spoke out in a voice that was quite loud, but choked. Her eyes were open as if horrified.

'Wake', Wiladzap said calmly. He explained that the doctor bought herbs from Lukswaas, he searched for plants with her, but he certainly did not love or kiss her. He paid dollars to her for plants.

Wiladzap turned to the woman, Lukswaas, and spoke in their own language – I suppose there is a specific Tsimshian language. She reached under her blanket and brought out a small purse made of woven fibres, holding it out in front of her. She was wearing several ornately engraved silver bracelets on her slim coppery arm. I put my notebook in my pocket, stepped forward, and took the purse, noticing that her hand was trembling. I opened the purse and poured its contents into my left hand.

'Eight silver dollars', I announced to Parry.

'We'll arrest the Tyee', he said, 'and bring in the informer and the squaw for questioning.'

Suddenly the informer dashed across in front of us and ran towards the sea. The line of Indians broke, some men running after him. But Wiladzap called out sharply, and they stopped. Parry yanked out his revolver and pointed it at Wiladzap. 'Follow the man' he bellowed, but I was already sprinting across the clearing, while clumsily stuffing the purse and silver dollars into my pockets. I dodged around the nearest Indian, leapt over a fire, and ran to the edge of the bluff, where the Indian had now disappeared. I looked down. He was already on the beach some fifty feet below, pulling a small canoe down the sand to the water.

'Stop!' I yelled ridiculously. I dashed to pick my way down a steep path through bushes. He must have leapt down it like a goat. By the time I had reached the shingle at the back of the beach, the man was already embarked, paddling vigorously, pointing the canoe out to the sea, to the North. I ran into the water, my boots splashing, then stopped. He was thirty yards away and paddling much faster than I could ever swim. Drawn up on the shingle was a dugout canoe, not less than forty feet long, of weather-blackened cedar, with high stern and prow on which boards had been placed, painted with red and black designs. I ran around it, stumbling on rocks. On the other side was a second small canoe, with two paddles in it. I looked out at the water sparkling in the sun, and the man paddling furiously Northwards. No question of catching up. Nor did I want to leave Parry alone for long, revolver or not. Even these Indians from far away would have guns, at least shot-guns for duck-shooting, and possibly rifles. I took a final look at the paddling Indian. He would pass behind an island after another mile or so and be lost.

I climbed the path to the top of the bluff. On the other side of the smoking fires, and against the background of the wall of dark green forest, the Indians and Parry were just as I had left them. I walked across the clearing as calmly as I could and reported the situation to Parry who said, as if in a daze, 'He didn't even take the money.' He glanced down at the sovereigns still in his left hand, and dropped them into his pocket. His revolver was still trained on Wiladzap. 'Arrest him', he ordered.

I walked forward. Wiladzap was about my height. I placed my hand on his shoulder and looked him in the eye. 'I arrest you on suspicion of murder', I said, then the nearest thing I could think of in Chinook, a convoluted explanation that the Tyee would have to come to the King George men's big house and answer words.

His eyes had a strange expression, not fierce, but puzzled or sad.

'Nika mahko', he said. ('I come').

I turned to Lukswaas. She was not much more than a girl. Her eyes were fixed on me, but not with fear: she was angry. She said something sharply in her own language. Then in a slower Chinook, indignation making her voice tremble, she said that Wiladzap did not kill McCrory, no Indian killed McCrory, no Tsimshian, no eagle, no man from Tsalaks.

I told her, I hoped reassuringly, that she was to come with us and she could then say more words.

She and Wiladzap exchanged a few phrases, then Wiladazp turned to face the other Indians and spoke to them at length. I waited for him to finish, not looking at Parry. Then Wiladzap turned back to us and spoke at length in Chinook. He said he had explained to his people that a mistake had been made, and that when the King George Tyees found the man who had killed McCrory, they would bring Wiladzap back to his people. In the meantime they should stay in their camp, fish for salmon, and do no trading.

I was impressed, but Parry showed no signs of being so. Perhaps this was prudent: we would have to turn our backs on the Indians while marching Wiladzap away. 'I'm wondering whether we should hand-cuff him', Parry said quietly. 'He could get away from us in the woods. We could tie him up and let him run behind the horses, or put him on the wagon when it gets here.' Parry paused and seemed to listen for the sound of reinforcements from the woods.

'The heart of the mouse talks to the eagle', I thought. The scene of the murder, where Harding and the other Indian were left waiting with the cart, was indeed too far away for any other sound to be heard.

'Perhaps that would be provocative, Sir', I said. 'You do have your revolver trained on him. And if he's their chief they won't risk having him shot.'

'Good', said Parry, as if relieved of the decision. 'Klatawa!', he said to Wiladzap. ('Go!')

Without a backward glance Wiladzap started up the path. 'Klatawa', I said to the girl.

After twenty minutes' gradual climb through the forest we reached the place where we had left Harding. The cart was there. Several horses were tied to trees, and there were were two more constables. On the cart was a grey blanket covering the body, and beside it a pile of wet and bloodstained clothing.

Wiladzap sent the other Indian back to camp, though he seemed to protest vigorously. Wiladzap and Lukswaas were told to sit on the cart at the tail, their backs to the corpse. They had to hang on tightly as the cortege set off towards Victoria and the cart lurched along the path. Wiladzap looked thoughtful. Lukswaas was almost as sullen as the whores when I had rousted them out of their shanties near Cormorant Street – a world away from Cormorant Point.

5

As we came into Victoria, the distant blue hills between us and the Pacific were sharp against a lurid orange sunset. People on the sidewalks stopped to stare at us.

At the court house, the corpse was slid onto a wide board and carried in, itself as stiff as a board now. Wiladzap was installed in a relatively secluded cell, at the end of the row. The other prisoners yelled out that they didn't want no drunken Indian murderer with them. The jailer, Seeds, roared at them to shut up and stood observing Wiladzap, as if taking stock of a new possession.

Wiladzap squatted on the cell floor, hunched in his blanket, his back against the wall, and closed his eyes.

Lukswaas was brought to make a deposition. Augustus Pemberton had been sent for, and was waiting for us in the room which we used as an officers' dining room and for interrogations. He gestured to Lukswaas to sit down at one end of the table. Her eyes were wide open in fear and she seemed almost to have stopped breathing. I had to go round behind her to show her the chair. She just stood and looked at it. I realised she did not know what to do. 'Perhaps we should put aside our good manners and show this lady how to sit down, Sir', I said to Pemberton, who instantly understood and made a deliberate show of pulling out a chair at the other end of the table, sitting down on it, and pulling himself towards the table. I pulled out a chair for Luskwaas, and she sat down on it rather clumsily as I pushed it forward. My face was just above her hair, which smelled sweetly of cedar smoke.

Parry and I sat at each side of the table. I looked at Lukswaas again, noticing for the first time a strange ornament which had slipped out from under the blanket around her shoulders, a shiny black stone shaped like a flat paddle or fishtail, hanging from a leather thong around her neck. I got out my notebook and pencil again.

Pemberton lit up his pipe. He was conducting this examination as Stipendiary Magistrate. His face is that of a dashing Irishman past his prime: resolute yet worn. He has strong eyes and a prominent nose, but his cheeks sag a little and he is going bald. Not an unkind man, but he began to question Lukswaas in a cool detached way.

'Mesika nem?' ('Your name'.)

'Lukswaas…' There followed a series of other names, which I could not transcribe.

'Mesika Tyee klootchman?' ('You Tyee's woman')

'Ah-ha.'

Pemberton asked where the Indians were from? What were they doing at Cormorant Point?

In a quiet but strong, rather deep voice, Lukswaas explained in Chinook, more hesitant than Wiladzap's but not lost for words, that it had taken them fifteen days to come South from Tsalaks and they had been at Cormorant Point for twenty days. She replied to questions about McCrory, explaining that the 'Doctah' had come to Cormorant Point with a yellow man, then three times on his own. He talked about the 'breath of life' with Wiladzap. She said Wiladzap is Tyee but also 'mestin man'. He knows how to suck and blow the breath of life. McCrory also wanted herbs for medicine. She and Wiladzap went with McCrory into the forest to show him where plants grew. She gave McCrory dried plants. He gave her money – eight silver dollars in all.

Pemberton asked if she had fun ('hee hee') or kisses ('bebe') with McCrory.

'Wake!' She looked down her nose as haughtily, I thought, as an English lady would when asked such an impudent question.

But Pemberton pursued the point, asking if Wiladzap was jealous – 'tum tum sick'.

'Wake!' But she said Wiladzap would surely now be 'tum tum sick' – meaning literally 'sick at heart' – in the big house of the King George men.

What was the name of the Indian who had told the story that Lukswaas had been kissing with McCrory?

'Smgyiik'. (My approximate transcription).

Why would he tell such a story?

'Smgyiik tum tum sick.'

Did Smgyiik want to have fun, kiss, with Lukswaas?

'Ah-ha.' Then she added, 'Nika halo tikegh Smgyiik'. ('I not like Smgyiik').

Who killed McCrory?

Luskwaas said she did not know, but it was not a 'Siwash' – not an

Indian, 'Siwash' being the Chinook pronunciation of 'Savage'.

'Do you have any questions, Superintendent?' Pemberton asked Parry.

'Nothing to add. Of course she's lying.'

'You think so?' Pemberton stared down the table at the woman, his eyes a pale icy blue. She stared back at him, calmly now, her eyes, in absolute contrast, almost black, with the pupils indistinguishable from the iris.

Pemberton turned to me. 'Any questions for her, Hobbes?'

'Might I ask her the names and functions of the plants?'

'You mean in case they are some sort of drug or opiate?'

'That was my thought, Sir. Does she know their purposes and what McCrory wanted them for?'

I asked my questions. Lukswaas gave a list of six names in Tsimshian – difficult to transcribe. She said three of these plants helped give sleep to people who found it difficult. One plant was a cure for anger. Another two were to help in making a man strong in kissing, as she put it. McCrory had been very happy to have these.

I wished I had not asked the questions.

'That's enough, I think', Pemberton said. 'Ask the clerk to write up the deposition from your notes and get her to sign it with the usual thumb print. Make sure the clerk has an outside witness. I want this done properly. But don't send her away yet. First I'll look at the victim, then I'll interview the other prisoner.' He stood up and said 'Mahse' ('Thank you') to Luskwaas.

I went to Lukswaas and escorted her from the room. The clerk had been called and in another room she had to sit down again at a smaller table with him and with Harding.

The corpse was under its grey blanket on a table in another room. I pulled the blanket off, down to the waist, as gently as I could.

'Go ahead, Hobbes, take it off completely. We're not squeamish', Pemberton said.

I took the blanket off and dropped it without folding it on a chair near the wall.

The corpse had turned a dark smoky grey, the streaks of blood almost black. The belly was swollen. A nauseating smell wafted up. Even Parry was looking a little green.

'My goodness', Pemberton said, as if mildly surprised. He strolled around the corpse, pausing every now and then to look closely. The hand with the severed member in it – now grey and wizened, like a dried slug – was sticking out in rigor mortis.

'Might I verify something?' I asked.

'Of course.' Pemberton stood aside as I went to the corpse's head. I could not avoid looking at the eyes. They had gone misty though, and were not frightening. I gritted my teeth and reached down to touch the blood-clotted beard. It felt something like my own would feel, but one finger touched through to the flesh which was like cold wax. I tried to pull the mouth wide open but of course the muscles of the jaw were locked. I had to be satisfied with leaning down and looking into the foul half-open mouth, past the yellow teeth exposed by drawn back lips, to the blue-black tongue. I explained myself to Pemberton:

'I wondered why there had been so much blood from the mouth and in the beard. There was no sign of a wound. Nor can I see any sign now – not the slightest gash.'

'What do you mean? At any rate we'll have an autopsy.'

'Perhaps this idea is macabre', I said, 'but the blood from the mouth must have come from somewhere. Yet, as the Superintendent describes the effect of these knife blows, the lungs were not punctured so as to cause an effusion of blood through the throat. If the blow near the collarbone penetrated the lung it would have bled through the wound. I believe the man's member, now in his hand, was stuck in his mouth – pointing outwards, bleeding. He then pulled it out.'

'Good God', said Parry. 'If so, it confirms the savagery of the act.'

'It may mean', I said, 'that although the murderer left him for dead – horribly mutilated and, as it were, sacrificed – he was still alive. He pulled the thing out of his mouth at least.'

'And yelled for help', Parry said sarcastically. 'And the Tyee heard him almost a mile away.'

'He would have been too weak', Pemberton interjected.

'Of course', I said. 'But alive for a while. He might have been discovered in such a state.'

'I see what you mean', Pemberton said. 'The Superintendent has briefed me on what the Tyee said.' He paused, looking at the corpse. 'One thing you may not know, Hobbes', he said gently, 'is that it's a known practice for the Indian medicine man, in a cannibalistic frenzy, to tear out chunks of flesh with his teeth.'

'I've read about that', I said. 'But if so, then this is a singularly unsuccessful effort: the bites did not detach the flesh.'

'Touché.' Pemberton smiled. 'Enough of speculation.' He turned away from the corpse.

As the others left the room, I picked up the blanket and re-arranged it over McCrory.

Luskwaas was no longer in the large room. I hoped that at least Seeds would offer her coffee or tea and somewhere to rest. Now Harding brought in Wiladzap.

He seemed to have changed already, from being in the cell only an hour. He appeared chastened, puzzled, not at all fierce. He sat down carefully, glancing around as if to note exactly what the rest of us were doing, but the chair did not seem foreign to him. He looked at Pemberton, but his eyes seemed out of focus.

Pemberton began by asking how many Indians knew Wiladzap as their Tyee.

Wiladzap explained that he was the Tyee of the people who were with him now. At Tsalak, where they came from, another man is a greater chief, his uncle, the brother of his mother. He, Wiladzap, is two men. He is an ordinary man, a warrior. He is also a spirit dancer – a 'tanse-wind', or dance breath, a 'tamanawis' or shaman.

Do the Tsalak people trade with the HBC at Fort Simpson?

Wiladzap's reply was lengthy and difficult, Chinook not being up to complicated matters. Eventually he managed to explain that he is amassing money so that eventually he will bear a great name. This name is 'Legech'. Whoever wins the name will have to do it honour, and give many potlatches. Among Tsimshian, women win names through accumulating material goods, men through accumulating money. Until last year, Tsalak people had traded up the rivers with the Interior Tsimshian, in the mountains. For example, Wiladzap's blanket is a 'chilcat', woven with the hair of mountain goats, traded in exchange for sea otter furs. Now the HBC trades up the rivers and there is no more trade for Indians.

'I believe the Bay has recently claimed a monopoly of river trading', Pemberton remarked.

Wiladzap explained that the Tsalaks do not trade with the HBC or the missionaries. In the past they had traded further South – with the Kwagiutl and the Salish. Now they are in Victoria to trade with the King Georges. Sea otter furs, baskets, and carvings of stone and wood.

Pemberton asked Wiladzap where he had obtained his knife. Parry laid this on the table as an exhibit.

Wiladzap said the Tsalak all have knives like these, bought from coastal traders who also sell guns and axes, in exchange for furs.

Then Pemberton pursued the same line of questioning as Parry had at the camp, and received the same answers, including 'The heart of the mouse speaks to the eagle.'

Pemberton observed blandly in Chinook that the eagle attacks and devours the mouse.

Wiladzap said that he had heard McCrory's voice inside his head.

'Ask your question', Pemberton said, turning to me, 'about the mouth.'

After a pause to gather my thoughts I asked whether, when Wiladzap had found the dead man, there was a thing in his mouth.

Wiladzap's eyes glittered with more focus, though as with Lukswaas it was not possible to distinguish the pupils, as he looked at me. 'Itah kop amah', he said. ('Thing in hand.'). Then 'Kulakula'. This meant 'Bird'.

'Kulakula?'

'Tsoowuts', Wiladzap said, in his own language presumably. He pointed to his lap.

'He means the member, I suppose', Pemberton said with a half smile.

I said to Wiladzap that since there was nothing in McCrory's mouth, he must have been able to talk.

Wiladzap said that although McCrory was almost dead he had said 'King George Diaub.' Nothing else.

Asked what this meant, he shrugged his shoulders and repeated separately 'King George' and 'Diaub'.

Pemberton began to ask about the basket of herbs. Did that belong to Lukswaas?

'Ah-ha.' Wikadzap explained that Lukswaas had been collecting herbs with McCrory in the forest that morning, shortly before he had been killed, and that they had come back to the camp, then she had given him the basket to take the herbs away in, asking him to bring it back when he returned next time.

This revelation, made without any apparent sense of its possible implications, caused, I thought, a sort of shudder around the table. My own heart sank.

Lukswaas spent time alone with McCrory? Pemberton asked. And when Wiladzap said 'Ah-ha' rather mechanically, Pemberton asked quickly:

'Tyee tum tum sick?' Was the Tyee not jealous of Luskwaas being in the forest alone with the doctor?

'Wake.' Then Wiladzap added that Lukswaas was safe with McCrory. McCrory had asked whether there was a 'berdash' among the Tsalak. Wiladzap said now, vehemently, that there may be 'berdash', as the traders said, among the Interior peoples, but there were none on the Coast.

Pemberton raised his eyebrows and commented in English. 'You know what a berdash is, Gentlemen? An effeminate. A pathic. Some tribes allow them to live as women. But I think the Tyee is right: the berdash is an institution of the Prairie Indians.' He went on to ask Wiladzap in Chinook whether McCrory had wanted a berdash for kissing, having fun, and so on.

'Spose.' Not surprisingly the Chinook for 'I suppose so'. Wiladzap shrugged his shoulders again.

So Wiladzap did not think the doctor desired to make kissing with Lukswaas.

'Wake. McCloly wake yaka skookum.' This meant McCrory was 'without power'. 'Skookum' has by now even entered the English language in Victoria, to mean something is 'in good condition'. Wiladzap went on to explain, using the counter-like words of Chinook skilfully, that immediately he had met McCrory he had noticed that he was without 'skookum', and he assumed this meant McCrory was ill in some way – that he was interested in herbs not only as a doctor but for himself. Now that McCrory was dead, Wiladzap realised that the lack of power was because the power had already gone out of McCrory, because he was about to die. Wiladzap should have noticed this from the first, but of course he was interested in talking to McCrory about medicines and the breath of life. McCrory was a very clever man who knew many things. When McCrory had asked about the berdash and about medicines to give power in love ('kiss kiss') Wiladzap thought another thing, that maybe McCrory was sick in that way. In any case he had not worried about McCrory being alone with Lukswaas. He added that Lukswaas also had great 'skookum'.

As I sat considering this puzzling remark, Pemberton asked abruptly whether Smgyiik had wanted kiss kiss with Lukswaas.

'Ah-ha', Wiladzap said calmly. And because Smgyiik could not have Lukswaas he was indeed 'tum tum sick'. As well, Smgyiik was the bearer of a name of bad fortune.

'Not least its being so unpronounceable', Pemberton said wearily. 'Many Indian tribes have a complicated hierarchy of names.' He asked Wiladzap why he had chosen Smgyiik to go with the message to Victoria, about the death?

Wiladzap said that Smgyiik spoke Chinook well and was fast on his feet.

Pemberton leaned forward and fixed Wiladzap with his pale eyes. He explained with emphasis that Wiladzap would have to stay in the jail until it was clear who had killed McCrory. It seemed as if Wiladzap killed him because no one else was with McCrory and no one else knew where the dead man was. No one could hear a dying man call at such a distance. Why would a dying Boston in his last breath be capable of speaking in Chinook? The only witness to McCrory having said 'King George Diaub' was Wiladzap, an Indian, and Wiladzap could have made this up – as he had made up the idea of hearing McCrory's call for help – in order to make the King Georges look among their own number for the murderer, not among the Tsalak. And in any case, no King Georges had been seen in the forest that day, or even, so far as was known, visited the Indian camp.

At this point Wiladzap leaned forward slightly and said with as much emphasis as Pemberton that he did not tell lies.

Then he allowed himself to be led off by Harding, back to his cell.

'You think the man is innocent?' Pemberton asked me.

'I don't think he's guilty. The evidence is all circumstantial, and he seems to be making no effort to tell a story which would be less incriminating.'

'Circumstantial evidence can convict a man. Innocent until proved guilty – but in practice, as you know, it is best to prove one is *not* guilty. A task, I'm afraid, almost impossible for this Indian. On the evidence we can make a charge of murder. We shall have to, for I don't think it would be wise to let him go.'

'Yet he came with us willingly. He even fetched us.'

'The savage mind is strange. Who knows what tortuous mental processes led to him sending the other man for the police? He might have wanted to place the murder on the other man. Perhaps that's why Smgyiik ran away. These are not, among the Indians, what we might call affairs of the heart – although they talk all the time about their blessed 'tum tum'. These feelings are of an animal nature, so far from our own ways of perceiving things, that it's useless to speculate. We must go on the evidence. Circumstantial evidence can convict this man Wiladzap, and undoubtedly will.'

'Hear hear', Parry interrupted. 'I've never seen such a devilish deed, and the devil who did it will be hanged.'

'Indeed, Superintendent. You must forgive my musings to Constable Hobbes who is, after all, a legal man. We shall keep the Indian in jail and charge him within a day or so. There will no doubt be an unholy hubbub in town tomorrow. Our friend McCrory may have been a somewhat dubious character, with credentials which the other medical men in town don't find impressive, but he was an American. We can't let an Indian go unpunished for murdering an American in an English Colony.'

'To hell with him being a Yankee', Parry burst in. 'Forgive me, Sir. I mean, it's as a foully butchered man that I see him, whose murderer must pay the price – and be seen by the others to pay.'

'I agree', Pemberton said blandly. 'But the crime is not fully proved, even if we must lay a charge. Mr Hobbes here has a mandate, as it were, to occupy himself with criminal detection. He must make a very thorough investigation of this case. Remember, we don't want to be as rash as the Americans so notoriously are. You know how Sitting Bull, when he was defeated by the Americans, came for refuge into the North West territories with a few hundred braves, armed to the teeth, and was disarmed by Sergeant Dickens, son of our great novelist, with only a few men, on the promise that the Great White Mother would look after them. We want, as the Canadians say, much as we may dislike their aspirations to take over this Colony, 'peace, order and good government' – not frontier wars like the Americans in their selfish pursuit of happiness. We must be seen to have left no stone unturned and to have treated these peculiar people from further North in *British* Columbia with the dignity of British subjects. Yes they have savage minds, but we have to live with them. Look how we went wrong in Ireland, in the past, in treating the Gaelic Irish, with their own civilisation, as savages. But we have been making progress, Gentlemen, I am an Irishman who is proud to be British also, and proud to be here administering British law.'

Neither of us could say anything to this unexpected peroration. Parry turned to me and said, 'You did well today, my lad, and I trust you to use your brains – which I must say are better trained than mine – to work the case out as far as you can.'

'Thank you, Sir. I must say I thought you handled the situation at the Indian camp most courageously', I said. I meant it.

'I imagine this berdash business may be a red herring', Pemberton remarked. 'As I said, it's characteristic of the Indians of the Plains such as the Pawnees and the Sioux. The word 'berdash' was brought here, I regret to say, by HBC men and French Canadian traders, who were looking for such services. A clever implication, though, on the Tyee's part. You might check, Hobbes, if there is any evidence of McCrory having been a pathic. Search his house, follow his route out to Cormorant Point, ask the people along the Cedar Hill road whether they saw him and who may have been with him. Send an electric telegraph to Fort Simpson to find if they have any knowledge of this Wiladzap.

'I hereby appoint you Acting Sergeant. It will give you more authority. You're new in the police but you've been doing well, you're a university man, and you deserve some commendation for your cool behaviour today. You can question whomever you wish, and do what you think necessary, within reason, and with the Superintendent's permission. You may start by taking care of the young lady, Wiladzap's wife. We can't keep her here. She can find her own way home, no doubt, but she had best not walk out Fort Street alone at night. Escort her out to Spring Ridge, then let her go. Ask her more questions if you wish, but do not press her. The Superintendent will inform her that she must stay near at hand. I doubt if the Tsimshian will return North without their Tyee – although they'll have to eventually, when things come to an issue. Which reminds me, Superintendent, you must alert Esquimalt about this man Smgyiik heading North in his canoe. It's not worth their pursuing him: there are a hundred islands where he could hide and lie up for a while. But they have a ship or two up the coast, and if they call in anywhere to receive messages, they should be warned. Hobbes, when you send your telegraph to the trading posts, tell them to keep their eyes open for this Smgyiik and to arrest him if they have the capability. And see if there is anyone in Victoria who can interpret Tsimshian. Chinook is hardly a fit language for evidence in a complex case like this. I think I've heard that coastal Tsimshian is different from that in the Interior. If no one knows it, ask Fort Simpson to send somebody – but that will take weeks.'

With this flurry of commands, Pemberton took his leave.

Ten minutes later I was walking up Fort Street with Lukswaas. She had apparently been offered food and drink but had refused them. Parry had told her, in front of me, that she was free to go back to the Indian camp but no further, and that I would show her to the road back. She had said nothing. I had avoided meeting her eye. I was so unreasonably nervous, in fact, that I was not hungry, although I had not eaten since noon.

It was ten o'clock. There is no public street lighting yet in Victoria, and the streets are only dimly lit by the lamps outside private buildings. I stepped slightly ahead, keeping close to Lukswaas on the outside of the sidewalk, as with any lady. She stayed just behind my right elbow. Her walk, like all her movements, was graceful. She had not a clue about crossing roads. At each cross street I held out my arm in front of her while we paused to let the occasional cart or man on horseback past.

There were people about, although every few yards we passed the door of a tavern, out of which came the usual noises of drunken singing or shouting. We passed a couple of young men who wished us good night politely. A few other men moved aside to let us pass, because of my uniform no doubt. Most people know me at least by sight. We passed a group of Indians in HBC blankets sitting on some steps from road to sidewalk, handing around a flagon of liquor. Lukswaas turned her head slightly, as if curious. Inevitably, since we were running the gauntlet of so many taverns, there was one unpleasant incident, which would have been worse if Luskwaas had been alone: no woman, white or Indian, walked alone at night, and few will do so even by day. A group of men lounging outside a tavern were slow in moving aside to let us past. I instinctively reached out and took hold of her elbow through the rough cloth of her chilcat blanket, to guide her. 'Christ', one man said, 'There goes the English copper, off to hump a squaw.'

'Shut up, you', I said, feeling a surprising viciousness. There was a roar of laughter. The man, whoever he was, had stepped back, and there was room to get through, but the laughter continued and a voice behind us said, 'Shut up, you', in a mincing English accent. I burned with anger. I let go of Lukswaas's arm and kept going, almost marching up the street, then slowed as I realised she was having to hurry to keep up.

We proceeded up Fort Street, to the end of the board sidewalk. Ahead were a few lights from widely scattered houses. A half moon, just risen in front of us over the dark line of Spring Ridge, gave just enough light to see by as my eyes adapted to the dark. It was one of those totally clear nights which are becoming more frequent as Spring advances, and the air was becoming consequently chilly. Every single star, it seemed, was visible. I had intended to say goodbye to Lukswaas at this point. She would be safe enough, surely, almost invisible in the dark, and treading quietly. No doubt, being an Indian, she could see and hear like a wild animal in the dark – or so I thought. But why assume that? I had begun the kind of internal argument I knew well. Part of me thought – or even knew that I would walk with this young woman every yard of the way back to Cormorant Point. Another part told me not to be ridiculous. She did not need my protection, and what is more she must hate it. My first part reasoned that after all it was only about five miles. I would be back 'home' at the court house by two o'clock at the latest. The second part argued that I was already tired out, and if it became cloudy I might become lost on the way back. The first part rejoined that the night would stay clear. And so on. Finally the first part won: I did not give a damn what Lukswaas or anyone else expected, I was a gentleman and I would escort her home, and that was that.

Meanwhile we kept on walking. We passed the large prosperous houses of local worthies – bankers, speculators in real estate – and the smaller house of Pemberton, with a light in its window. He would have ridden home just ahead of us. A dog barked from behind a fence, but not for long. We walked along Spring Ridge for half an hour or so, then onto Cedar Hill road, where I had ridden among the oaks and the singing robins early that afternoon. Lukswaas showed no signs of lagging. I could not see much of her, she was merely a silent figure walking beside me, about an arm's length away. I tried to imagine what she must feel, walking with the man who arrested her husband, clapping a hand on his shoulder. Useless speculation. Why not ask her? I felt the utter impossibility of speech. Could we converse as if at a ball? Remark on the moonlight? No. I concentrated on walking, and the night, and my awareness of this graceful, strange woman walking along beside me, with her faint smell of wood-smoke and cedar, occasionally stumbling slightly, as I did, on unseen irregularities in the packed earth of the road. There were no night sounds – no nightingales, bleating lambs, owls. Would there be in England at this time of year? I never spoke of England now – it was too far.

'England', I said, out loud.

'Englan', she said, in a good imitation.

I said in Chinook that I came from England, the land of the great mother Victoria – and so on. But this was official talk. She said nothing. We kept walking. I told her how on summer nights the nightingale sings from the woods. She asked, how did it sing? I made an attempt to imitate it with whistles. Then I told her about corn crakes, making their sounds from the fields at dusk. I imitated that too. She laughed, and tried to make the same sound – a rasping croak. Then we were abruptly silent. We had embarrassed ourselves and each other. 'There is nothing to laugh about', I tried saying in Chinook. 'This is a terrible day'. When I got through this, she said with what sounded like anger, that Wiladzap was alone in the King George House and he must be very tum tum sick. Then she fell silent. We walked on. Was she crying, silently? I could not see, so perhaps I imagined this. But I began to feel almost happy. It was as if we two, one man and one woman, were walking along under the stars in a bubble of our own. I had never taken a walk in the dark with a woman – other than with my mother or a maid when I was a child. But I felt strangely at ease.

The few houses along Cedar Hill were in darkness. We passed the little church on the left. After another half hour or so we entered the thick forest, where the moonlight was muted and patchy and boulders loomed up at us from each side of the narrowing track. A few times when she stumbled I took her arm to help her along. Once she grabbed my arm. Each time we let go at once.

The dirt road became even more bumpy and irregular. This had been less noticeable on horseback. There were occasional bridges across gullies, where we trod especially carefully since there were no railings. We had to walk in single file – Indian file! – with Luskwaas now in front. I could see her hair shining from time to time in the moonlight, but otherwise she was like an undulating shadow, heading on it seemed more confidently than when we were side by side.

We turned right at the fork to Cormorant Point. As the path led through the cedar swamp I could smell the fragrance of the trees – like Lukswaas herself. In Latin they are Arbor Vitae, the tree of life: they resist decay. Eventually we passed the turn off to where the corpse had been found. I could smell the dung left by the tethered horses, and managed to avoid some I could vaguely see. After this faded I became aware of the cedar smell again, of dank smells from the forest, and of Lukswaas in front of me – wood-smoke and, as my nostrils became more finely tuned, a slight animal smell of her chilcat – goat's wool. We turned toward Cormorant Point at another fork in the path, her pace not slackening – I had to almost scramble after her – as we continued down hill. Suddenly I smelled the sea – like smelling the English Channel from the downs of Dorset, not too far from home. Then fresh wood smoke – a strong smell. I no longer had Lukswaas to myself. Moonlight broke through the thinning trees. I strained my eyes ahead for the lights of camp fires and I saw them – and felt sad. Lukswaas held out a hand to slow me down, and stopped, turning to face me. She said 'Klahowya'. Goodbye.

'Klahowya', I said.

'Thank you'. She turned and ran fast down the path to the clearing, calling out. I heard calls in reply. She disappeared. I stood there stunned. Had she really said 'Thank you'? This could not have happened. I felt a tingle down my spine. It must have been a voice in my head. A hallucination. I shook myself, like a dog out of water, as if waking from a dream. I turned and began my long walk in the dark. I found I was feeling ill – heart sick – 'tum tum sick'.

6

I only had a few hours to sleep and I kept waking in a state – of ecstasy. My first thought was Lukswaas. 'I'm in love with her', I realised each time with a shock. At least that must be what I am feeling. Even on my heart-sick way back, stumbling along the path through the forest, although the moon was now higher and shafts of its light through the trees helped me on my way, I was living our walk together backwards. Here is where she said 'Thank-you' – or did she? Here is where she took my arm. Here we talked of English nightingales and she imitated my imitation of the call of the corncrake. Finally, here we walked up Fort Street almost like a shy couple on our first outing together. A couple. But she is coupled – literally – with Wiladzap. My God! I have to stop this thinking. My task is to find evidence so that we can charge Wiladzap – or let him go. But we won't let him go. On that despairing thought, my body aching from that ten mile walk, I dropped into sleep again. And when I awoke to get up I found myself ravenous for breakfast and concentrated on the case of Wildzap – not on Lukswaas. After all I am well practiced at putting things out of my mind.

The alienist's house was a small, neat, yellow painted box behind a white fence, in a side road off Fort Street between the town and the houses of the rich. A discreet and private place. Comings and goings could be observed by no neighbour, since opposite, on the hillside, was one of Victoria's typical outcroppings of rock and twisted arbutus, impossible to build on or make a garden on. Anyone turning into the street could be taking a way through to the other streets further North. Yet few people would in fact do so. It was not a thoroughfare. During my visit, not a single person passed by, so far as I could tell. There was no sound of voices from the street, or of creaking cart wheels.

I was standing in the alienist's consulting room: a typical small square farmhouse room, with fireplace and two windows, pink curtains hooked back, and a layer of opaque muslin 'drapes'. I had informed myself that this had been the house of a homesteader who had taken to drink until his wife had forced him to return to England. McCrory had bought it, taking out a mortgage from a Jew whom I would interview later.

On the walls were framed certificates with gothic lettering and gold seals – a licentiate and doctorate in medicine from the University of Virginia, made out to Richard McCrory. Perhaps this 'Yankee' was in fact a Southerner disgusted by the Confederate loss who had come all the way North and West. There was also a large chart of the human skeleton, and another of the musculature, with all parts labelled although they were of neutral sex – *those* parts were not depicted. Rather pretentious, I thought. A doctor should not need such charts. They must be there to make an impression. Like the porcelain head on a special marble topped stand, with the contour mapping of phrenology: bumps of righteousness, hope, generosity and so on. There was a desk and table oddly bare of papers except for a few journals in two neat stacks: *The Phrenologist,* and *The Zooist* – a journal I had head of. I glanced through one. It was on Mesmerism, put out by the Edinburgh surgeon Eliotson who was well known as the inventor of the stethoscope.

A high bookshelf was crammed full. Herbalist manuals, medical texts, works of Mesmer in French and Latin (these looked in mint condition and I suspected they had never been read), a book on Mesmerism by Eliotson, more copies of *The Zooist*, Herbert Spencer's huge *Principles of Psychology* which I had looked at some years before in Oxford and found unreadable. Galton on heredity. Mill's longwinded book on the rights of women. On the lighter side there were books of travels among the Indians, Eskimo, Australian aboriginals, Maori, Annamese, Javans. A shelf of novels: Dickens, Thackeray, Washington Irving, and many romances of a female kind – odd, since the alienist had no wife – by Mrs Hemans, Aphra Benn, and others whose names were new to me but whose contents, as I rifled through a few, were approximately the same: large eyed heroines pursued by heavy-breathing, fascinating sheiks, rajahs, princes and diplomats. There were of course the inevitable, for an American – even a Southerner – Emerson and Thoreau. Emerson's turgid verse was the only poetry on the shelves. My eye took in a miscellany of religious texts of the evangelistic sort. Finally, on the bottom shelf, on their sides, there were atlases and marine charts of Vancouver Island, Washington Territory, and the British Columbia coast. I looked through these briefly for annotations or pencil marks, but there were none.

I glanced around the room again. McCrory's Chinese servant, who had let me in, dressed exotically in a blue silk robe, was standing patiently just inside the door. Like one of the Indians in his immobility, I thought, but the face was entirely different in that it had a fixed smile of obsequiousness, which by compressing the cheeks upwards hid the eyes behind narrow slits. Did the Chinese face make the social manners, or the manners the face? I wondered. The kind of thing to interest Charles Darwin. I glanced again at the bookshelves. No, there was no Darwin. No Buffon, or Lyell, or Huxley. The man may have been a doctor but there was no scientific interest except for Galton and Spencer, which any educated man might be expected to have. Perhaps for McCrory, phrenology and Mesmerism were science enough.

There was a long settee of the usual kind, black horsehair – but with exotic red and gold cushions and a red quilt embroidered with gold thread. Near it was a table with the usual paraphernalia of the doctor's office, old fashioned listening horn, stethoscope, auscultator, smelling salts. Where would the man's travelling bag be? Near the desk on the floor. I crouched down and opened it. Listening horn, smelling salts, bandages in rolls, ointments. A small wooden case of surgical instruments: scissors, scalpels, knives, curved scraping-blades.

I turned my attention to the desktop again. The blotting paper pad was spotted and blotched here and there with purple ink, but there were no reversed words such as a fictional detective would have delighted to read with a mirror. There was an elaborate tray for pens and ink, of the latest style, in ormolu and brass, with the usual equipment. The desk drawers were not locked. In the upper ones were notepads, paper, prescription pads, the catalogues of pharmacists in San Francisco. Nothing surprising. I picked up a cheque book from the Bank of British Columbia. Figures but no names on the stubs. I dropped it in my pocket. In the bottom drawer were several small sealed cardboard boxes, and one which was unsealed. I opened it, but did not recognise the articles in it. I picked one out and held it up to the light of the window. It was a rolled round disc of yellowish parchment, dusted with fine powder. I began to unroll it, then stopped. A sheath! I felt embarrassed. I had never seen one of these things before. I put it carefully back in the box, now noticing a discreet label on the side: 'One doz. A1 quality Lambskin Condoms.' The box contained seven. Condom must be a new word. Absent-mindedly I wondered at its derivation but could think of none. I came back to reality, and tapped the box, looking at the Chinaman.

'Dr McCrory was not married?'

'Naw.' The Chinaman smiled more, and bobbed up and down slightly.

'Did he have a mistress?'

'Mistress? Lee not know word 'mistress'.'

At least a thousand of the three thousand Chinese in town were called Lee. I wondered, even, whether his way of talking, with 'mistress' pronounced 'mistless', was a self-parody – the stage Chinaman. Not all 'Celestials' in Victoria were incapable of prouncing 'r'.

'Lady friend?' I asked.

'Naw.' Lee's smile did not budge. 'No lady friend.'

'Then why these?'

'Lee not know.'

I put the box back in the drawer. 'Show me his bedroom please.'

Lee bowed and led me out to the stairs, stepping aside for me, then following. There were three rooms upstairs, the first with simply a bed and a chair. 'Guest room' Lee volunteered, but when I asked him about guests he said there were never any. There was a store room, bare except for two steamer trunks. I opened them and rifled through them. More books in one. Clothes in the other: brocaded waistcoats, pantaloons with silk stripes down the sides. The man was a typical American swell. Good quality linen underwear. Silk shirts neatly folded.

In McCrory's bedroom, in a wardrobe, were more shirts, trousers, jackets and coats, and a dozen or so pairs of high quality shoes. The bed was neatly made. A dressing table had a triple looking glass – an innovation I had never seen. My face looked uncouth in profile, my beard scruffy above the unbuttoned neck of my police tunic.

There was a wash-stand with the usual accoutrements: beard-trimmer, brushes, and a hair-catcher made by female hands – the kind of thing wives or daughters gave as presents. I began going through the chest of drawers beside the bed. Underclothes. A pistol: Colt 45, heavy as a rock, loaded but with the chamber opposite the breech empty and the safety catch on. A box of cartridges. He presumably had not felt he needed this on his excursions to Cormorant Point to pick herbs with….

I closed the drawers, then went over to the window and looked out at the trees across the road. Downstairs I had glanced into the kitchen, laundry room, and the waiting room, which was normal enough, with American reviews and the usual American pirated issues of the *Quarterly* and *Blackwoods*. What sorts of patients did the alienist receive?

'Why no appointment book?' I said.

'Appointment book?'

'Book with list of patients. Where book?' Oh God, I was now talking a kind of pidgin English to Lee.

'No book.'

'How did he see patients then? How many a day?'

'Patients?'

'Look, Mr Lee, I don't want to waste my time. You'll come to the police station with me anyway, and make a deposition. If necessary we shall find an interpreter. Don't pretend you know less English than you do.' I was surprised at my own rudeness, but told myself that I was tired from my long walk the night before.

'Lee not pretend,' the man said, still smiling. 'Lee do best. Dr McCrory not keep appointment book. He see two patients, three patients a day. He know when they come. He keep all in head.' Lee tapped his temple.

'Why no appointment book?'

'Lee not know.'

'Why no letters from patients, no medical notes? Have you tidied these up?'

'Naw. Lee not tidy up. Lee leave everything exactly as is. Doctor not keep notes. Not like paper.'

'Doctor receive letters?'

'Not many letters. After reading, burn them.'

'Burn them? All?'

'Doctor not like paper. Doctor *alienist*,' Lee said carefully. '*Phrenologist*. Doctor see people privately, very privately.'

'You know the names of any patients?'

'Lee never say. *Strictly* confidential. But not know. Doctor never say names to Lee.'

'But would you recognise them? Know their faces?'

'Lee easily confused white people faces.'

I almost laughed. 'Woman? Man?' I asked.

'Some women. Some men.'

I felt hot and bothered standing in a dead man's bedroom talking to this Chinaman. I turned and left the room. Lee followed me downstairs. I went back into the consulting room for a final look. Nothing much I had not noticed. As before, Lee stood just inside the doorway.

'You liked Dr McCrory?' I hazarded.

'Like? Not like, like – no difference. Good master. Pay four dollahs a day.'

Somewhat more than my own salary. And why not?

'You went to the Indian camp with the doctor?'

'One time.'

'You walked, or took horses?'

'Walk. Nice day, not far.'

'And why did the doctor visit the Indians? Or, first, how did he know they were there?'

'Everybody know Indians at Cormorant Point. Often Indians come down. Trade. Doctor interested in medicines, herbs, plants. He look for Indian medicine man.'

'How about Chinese medicine?' I interrupted, trying to put Lee off balance. 'He was interested in that too?'

'Of course. He come with Lee to Chinatown, buy medicine. Seahorse, jellyfish, ginseng, rhinocerous horn.' Seeing me puzzled, Lee added, 'In powder, for medicine.'

'What are those medicines for?'

'Seahorse for long life, wisdom. Jellyfish for blood. Ginseng, long life, much life. Rhinocerous horn for make children.'

'Make children?'

'Congress, man-woman. Make man big, strong, last long time.'

I almost asked, 'Why last a long time?' then realized what it meant. 'Where are these medicines now?' I asked.

'In kitchen. I show you.' Lee led the way into the kitchen. I had already given it a look over – stove, table and chairs, chopping blocks and cleavers, shelves of tinned and dry food, bins of grain and potatoes. What I had thought was a very large collection of spices was a kind of medical dispensary. The bottles were labelled on the top, paper stuck onto their corks, which is perhaps why I had not noticed. Valerian, fenugreek, tiger lily – scores of names of plants.

'The plants Dr McCrory bought from the Indians. What were they for?' I asked.

'Make sleep. Make strong. One like rhinocerous horn.'

'Who did he get them from?'

'Squaw, chief's wife.'

'She took him into the forest to search for them?' I had a pained feeling, thinking of the lambskins in the desk drawer and of what I knew of Indian morals. But why did I want these Indians to be innocent?

'Not when Lee there, not first time. Maybe after. He bring back plants each time.'

'What else did he do on the first visit?'

'Talk with chief – chief called Wiladap.'

'Wiladzap,' I corrected.

'Wiladzap. He knew all about breath of life. Animal magnetism. Ch'i.'

'Ch'i?'

'Chinese word for breath of life.'

'And the Indians were friendly?'

'No. At first not want to talk much. Doctor disappointed. He say to Lee he go back again, talk more, bring more dollahs – not bring Lee. He think Indians frightened Lee's yellow face.' Lee was still smiling broadly.

'And he went always alone? No one else with him?'

'First time Lee. Then by self.'

'Where were you yesterday?'

'Here.'

'All right. You must come with me now, to make a deposition. Just one more thing: show me where you live.'

Lee shifted slightly on his feet, looking oafish. 'Too humble for see,' he said, playing stage-Chinaman again.

I lost my patience. 'Stop the play acting. Show me where you live.'

Lee led the way out of the back door from the kitchen. His quarters were in a shed, near the outhouse, in an overgrown fenced garden – once presumably the vegetable plot of the failed English colonist. Lee pushed the door open. Small, lit by one window, with only a bed, wardrobe, table and chairs. It was indeed humble, but clean and not unpleasant. There was a smell of incense. There were some burned joss sticks in an enamelled vase.

Some fine pottery on a shelf.

I looked under the bed. There was a carpet bag which I pulled out and opened. In it were some fine silks. In one of them was wrapped a knife with a curved blade about six inches long. The blade looked too narrow to have made those wounds in McCrory – more suitable for filleting, I thought callously – but I re-wrapped it in its silk and dropped it in my capacious tunic pocket. Lee was looking at me with the same smile. 'I have to take this,' I said, 'for examination.'

'Everybody have knife.'

'Of course. I have one myself. Now what about this?'

In the bottom of the bag was a tin money box, locked, quite heavy to lift out.

'Do you have the key?'

Lee reached into a fold of his blue robe, brought out a big key ring, and held it out to me, pushing one key forward.

I opened the box. In it were 20 gold sovereigns, and a quantity of silver dollars – 80 or so.

'You save your pay?'

'Yes,' Lee nodded his head vigorously. 'Send home to China, venerable father, mother.' He bowed.

'And where did the doctor keep *his* money?'

'In pockets.'

I held up the moneybox and looked at the manufacturer's address on the bottom.

'San Francisco,' I said. 'Where the doctor came from.'

'San Francisco, many Chinaman,' Lee replied, quick as a shot.

I could not help smiling. I decided to leave it at that. I went back to the house for a few copies of *The Zooist* and a book on *Medical Physiology*, which I thought might come in useful. I waited while Lee locked up shed and house, then we walked down town together.

I am left uneasy by Lee. He is a caricature Chinaman. I suppose the nickname Celestial is based on such caricatures: the smiling face telling you that all is serene. "God's in his heaven, All's right with the world" as boring old Robert Browning put it. But if Lee is a caricature who else is? Parry is a caricture Welshman – all sound and fury. I dare say Freezy is a caricature

'Injun', decapitating his squaw, for effect. Begbie and Pemberton are caricature English and Anglo-Irish, respectively. The Captain of the Ariadne! And I suppose I am the caricature Oxford man of the 1860s, all agony and doubt. But is Darwin a caricature? Is Wiladzap? Wiladzap draws me to him. He is himself, not a caricature. But the others – Parry, perhaps even Pemberton (I hope not) see him as the noble savage gone wrong, as all noble savages around here have gone wrong. They have Freezy's example.

Perhaps we all have to be caricatures. As we stand for something – the navy, our country, the law, the church – we become actors on the stage of the world. But what when we are not acting? Although I am Acting-Sergeant Hobbes when on duty – and not all the time when on duty, as I have my thoughts to myself – I am still Chad. There are times when we don't act. Perhaps Mr and Mrs Pemberton together in bed – why do I think of that? – don't act. Or Begbie when he is up in the Cariboo, living rough. Were Lukswaas and I acting last night when we were like children imitating the sounds of birds?

What was McCrory acting? The alienist. The magician. His library was just a lot of stage props. His researches in the forest for herbs were for more stage props. But was he acting when he was killed? Who killed him? A savage. So someone – Wildazap or some other Indian, gone mad in the blood-rush of acting the medicine-man – lost his senses and became a force detached from being man or even animal – and stabbed him, bit his arms, slashed his flesh, cut off his member, stuffed it into his still living mouth. Why? I was taught in Jurisprudence about mens rea, 'the mind in the thing'. In Common Law you cannot convict of murder unless you can demonstrate mens rea. If a man is insane and he doesn't know what he is doing he can only be convicted of manslaughter. Hence the necessity for Pemberton and Parry to find a reason why Wiladzap killed McCrory. McCrory was attempting to seduce his wife – therefore Wiladzap killed him. He cut off that member that had dared rise at the sight of his wife, and stuffed it into the disgusting mouth that had blabbered of seduction. And as for the extra bits, the biting of the arms, the slashing across the belly, they were just the mad rage of the savage. But the law cannot have it both ways: either Wiladzap had mens rea and ruthlessly killed McCrory, or he was a raving mad, savage witch-doctor. Not both. Yes both. The law in Victoria can have it both ways. Detective Constable Chad Hobbes is not a good enough lawyer – he is not a lawyer at all! – to argue this one. And who – McCrory or Wiladzap – was the witch-doctor?

7

The next morning I rode out Cedar Hill Road as far as Mount Douglas, stopping at each house to ask if people had seen the alienist pass on the day of the murder or previously. A few had vague recollections. The best was a woman who claimed her geese honked every time someone passed along the road, causing her to look out. She therefore remembered every passer by. She had seen the alienist on his first excursion, some weeks previously, and had been intrigued by the Chinaman's silk robe. The other times the alienist had been alone, both coming and going. He always walked briskly, but if he noticed her he would take off his hat. She realised he must be an American, by his clothes, his walk, and the fact that he carried no walking stick. I asked if she had noticed anyone else passing by, either just before or just after McCrory. She had not. Most passers by were local farmers on foot, on horseback, or driving their carts or buggies. Then there was her neighbour, Parson Coulter (whose very English wife I had just talked to), of St Mark's church, and the curate, Mr Firbanks, who lodged a few houses down. Yes, she had been visited by some Indian women. All the neighbours had. Cleaner than usual, very polite, and selling the most beautiful baskets and silver bracelets, and carved stone brooches which were 'barbarous'. But she would not open her door to them *now*. It was a scandal, allowing them to stay at Cormorant Point, less than two miles away. Her husband had got the guns down and given them a good cleaning.

I rode back into town on just such a sunny day, of flowers, ravens cawing, and robins singing, as when I had come out along the same road with Parry and Harding. The other time, at night, seemed however to have occurred in another world. I did not think of it much, although when I did I felt happy, then uneasy.

I had a funeral to attend. The alienist's body, although it had been removed to the undertaker's late on the first night, and submersed in some kind of preservative, had evidently become too disgusting to leave unburied. It had been decided – with no evidence other than that perhaps McCrory was an Irish name, and that he had red hair and beard – that he was a Catholic. At least the Catholics, who were mainly Irish-Americans, had been willing to take him on, the funeral expenses paid from his bank account.

The cemetery was no more than a field with a few slabs and stone Celtic crosses, and many wooden crosses, all close together. The coffin was a deal box, the undertaker's cheapest. But it and the buggy it was lying on were covered with a profusion of wreaths and flowers. And there was a good crowd in attendance – all men, as was the custom. But they provided no material for speculation since in effect every worthy of the town short of the Governor himself had chosen to turn up, out of respect or curiosity. Even the fussy Dr Helmcken and Dr Powell were there, in solidarity with their fallen medical brother. The pall bearers were four of my convicts from the jail, out on parole, wearing borrowed clothes, and enjoying every minute. They stood turning their heads this way and that in the fresh breeze, like horses let out into a field after too long in the stables.

The service was conducted by an Irish priest, in church Latin. The old me might have found it professionally interesting. But by now, apparently, I was a new me. I was itching to get a look at the flowers and wreaths. Eventually, after the coffin had been lowered into a mucky grave, and the crowd were picking their way out of the cemetery along the cart ruts, I had my chance. The wreaths were stacked to one side as the gravediggers began filling in the hole. Most held the cards of notables – the people at the funeral. Some were without cards. Then there were bunches of the garden flowers currently in season: mainly tulips, of all colours, long stalked primulas, and forget-me-nots. I wished it had been the custom for women to attend funerals. That would have been interesting, I sensed, remembering the boxes of lambskin sheaths. Perhaps the alienist had gone with prostitutes. But he would not have needed a sheath for that. It would have been bad value, I supposed, for the money. Or perhaps sheaths prevented venereal disease… I turned over in my mind the possibilities of tracing the origins of the bunches of flowers, but gave up the idea. They could have been delivered by messengers to the sexton's door at the church, or at the undertaker's. Furthermore, they were all similar. Domestic flowers in Victoria were profuse but not varied.

'Chad, old chap!' It was my friend Frederick, whom I had not seen for weeks but had noticed in the crowd – rubber-necking, I had assumed, in the American phrase.

We exchanged the usual banalities, and agreed to walk down the street together. Frederick seemed bursting with the need to talk. When we were out of earshot of the gravediggers he asked eagerly: 'How's the investigation coming? Any dramatic news?'

'How do you know I'm investigating?'

'Steady on. Everybody knows that. You're investigating for Pemberton. And behind Pemberton, they say, is Begbie the Indian-lover.'

'That's not so. Pemberton's his own man. And so far as I know he has heard not a word from Begbie. I certainly haven't. But of course, old boy,' I added in a friendlier tone, feeling I had been too abrupt, 'I can't tell you how the investigation is going.'

'Then maybe I can help you.' Frederick seemed delighted with himself. 'I knew the man, you see.'

'McCrory?'

'Well, I didn't really know him as a friend. I never even had a private conversation with him. But we met socially.'

'Where? I must admit I haven't been able to unearth a social life at all.'

'At Orchard Farm. With the Somervilles. But of course you don't know them. I'm afraid I owe you an apology, old chap, for keeping it quiet. Wanting to keep the field to myself, as it were.'

'What do you mean?'

'You've never heard of them? I should have thought every man around here had. They are a bunch of "eligibles" of the first class. Three girls, living on a small farm out in Saanich with widowed mother – very touching. Father was an Englishman, killed by Indians almost ten years ago. He'd tried to settle up island, among the Comox, but they did him in. So mother and the girls came down here, with a little money, and bought the farm. They have help from a mixed couple – a nigger and his wife – trying to get an orchard going. You will probably have eaten their apples and pears, without knowing it. They've planted some peaches too, and say they'll do very well here. And strawberries…'

Frederick did rattle on… I interrupted: 'And the alienist?'

'He visited them. Lots of people do. On Sundays only, mind you. That's made clear. You never know what you'd see if you turned up unannounced in the middle of the week. They *work*, you see, in the orchards. One chap I met out there, Beaumont, a Marine, teased them that during the week they must put on trousers. But that was received as bad taste. Things can't be *that* difficult. They're fairly prosperous. Well, after all, this isn't England, is it? They can't sit around all day working on samplers in stuffy rooms. Between you and me the mother *is* a bit of a pill – somewhat pretentious. I suspect she married above herself. Exaggeratedly English, though she left home as a girl. Maybe that's why they emigrated, come to think of it, if she was a servant girl or something who married Somerville who had been an army Major. One is often reminded of the rank. The girls were all born over here, down in Oregon Territory, though it wasn't American then, it was ours. I think I'm reaching a certain *entente* with Cordelia, the youngest girl, who's really charming.'

'And the other sisters are called Goneril and Regan?' I interrupted, to slow down Frederick's flow, although I was becoming resigned to hearing about the alienist in Frederick's own good time.

'You mean as in *King Lear*? Ha, ha. No. Aemilia and Letitia. Well, you see what I mean, the mother is pretentious. But they're sweet girls. Aemilia is a bit, well, different – rather too serious for me, melancholic even, but very bright. I say, I think she'd be just the ticket for you, old chap. Anyway, you'll see for yourself. The thing is, I feel more secure, as it were, in my courtship of Cordelia. I wasn't telling you about it, you see. I mean, you will have noticed that I sort of disappeared from our Sunday shooting expeditions.'

'Of course I'd noticed.'

'It was very petty of me. I met them at church one Sunday morning. St Marks on Cedar Hill Road, which is nearest to them. Frankly, I'd gone out there to see the 'eligibles' once I'd heard they went there. Not very devout of me, I'm afraid. But once I'd met them, and been invited, etcetera, I thought if I told you you'd come too, and then you might take a fancy to Cordelia. There were – are still, damn it! – already other rivals. It would have been too much to add you.'

'Who are these rivals? Was McCrory one of them?'

'I'm not sure. The part he played was sort of "friend of the family", trusted advisor, and so on. In fact he hadn't been there many more times than I. I believe he only arrived in town back in the Fall – or Autumn as I suppose you still say, but I like the word Fall don't you?'

I shook my head, trying not to smile. 'Can't you see I want to know more about McCrory?' I said. 'Please tell me more about him.'

'All right. He was a bit of a swell, very sure of himself, conceited. Most definitely a ladies' man, I'd say. The old mother – well, she's not that old, quite well preserved in fact – loved to fuss around him. He would turn the pages at the piano for the girls. He would discuss varieties of apples, the necessary climate for peaches. A know-all. Walking encyclopedia. You know the type, from Oxford, although by our standards he was awfully brash. Oh yes, another act of his was "the Southern gentleman", displaced by the war, with some implication of the family mansion being razed by the invading Yankee barbarians. But on the other hand a Southerner with a conscience: the Negro our brother, all men the same under the skin, his understanding of his Celestial servant...'

'Lee went out there too?'

'Sometimes. But he would spend the afternoon chatting with the Joneses in their quarters – quite a multicoloured group that was. They have a picaninny of their own, who is coffee-coloured, and an Indian boy who is *said* to be adopted but I somehow imagine is the result of a youthful indiscretion by Mrs Jones.'

'Really, Frederick, there is no need to be so cynical.' Some of the 'old' me was still alive.

'These things do happen. In England too, as you know very well. How many children in your father's parish were conceived out of wedlock? At least half, I'd bet.'

'Admittedly. My father once calculated it to be two out of three of the first-borns, though almost always their parents married once the woman was 'enceinte'. But that is by the by.'

'All right. McCrory. I didn't like him much, as you can gather. Perhaps jealousy, because he could make the girls laugh, and keep their interest with travel stories. I don't think he had actually travelled much but he'd read a lot, about exotic customs in far off lands, women wearing discs in their noses, and so on. Then he had one of those velvety baritone voices with which he sang Negro spirituals one moment and Down in Dixie the next.'

'Did he talk about medicine?'

'He was rather coy about his work, I thought. He said an alienist saw all kinds of patients with nervous troubles, the vapours, and "incipient dementia praecox" whatever that means to medical men – and so he couldn't talk about it. Another of his acts: the mystery man.'

'How did he meet these people, the Somervilles?'

'No idea. You'll have to ask the old girl – I mean Mrs Somerville. Well, I'll tell you of a suspicion I have. I *did* find myself wondering if Mrs S was a patient of his.'

'Why?'

'There was a certain indefinable familiarity between them. She would pet him, make sure his tea was hot, and so forth.'

'I didn't know patients petted their doctors. Or was she being motherly? What's the difference in their ages?'

'She, I'd say, is in her forties. I know Aemilia, the eldest girl, is twenty-four. Cordelia is only eighteen.'

'And McCrory?'

'You don't even know his age?'

'No.' I was annoyed. I had in fact sent a letter to the University of Virginia, and a telegraph to the San Francisco police to which I had not yet received a reply. 'I only saw him dead.'

'Must have been ghastly. At any rate I'd say he was about 35. A little young for Mrs S, if that's what you're thinking.'

'Who else attended these Sunday afternoon gatherings when McCrory was there?'

'The curate from St Mark's – Firbanks. He was sweet on Cordelia but not a great worry to me. A cold fish. Now more interested in Letitia. Similarly with Beaumont, the Marine. He's a Lieutenant with the detachment on San Juan Island – some of them come over to town on weekends. He's sort of switched to Letitia too.'

'I see. They move up the line, once they've been displaced by you.'

'The girls are all pretty, though of course I think Cordy's prettiest. Aemilia is a bit intimidating – almost a bluestocking. She's very good looking, though.'

'Who else visits?'

'Mr Quattrini. You'll know him.'

'Yes. The food wholesaler. I've met his son-in-law, Jeroboam. He must be well into middle age.'

'I forgot to mention him in the list of suitors earlier. He must be secretly delighted. He really *is* courting Mrs Somerville. There are perhaps other admirers of Mrs S. Well, she's not really that old at forty five or thereabouts, is she? Such as Nally, of the Mechanics' Institute. I've seen him there twice. A local farmer, Sutherland, turned up with his wife so he's not after Mrs S. He has a gangling son who gapes at Cordelia. Then there's John Haddock, the schoolteacher. He talks books with Aemilia. But don't worry, he's married to a little woman just as mousy as himself. They seemed pretty thick with McCrory actually. But I believe they've stopped coming to the farm. I haven't seen them since February.'

'How many of these people were acquaintances of McCrory away from this Orchard Farm?'

'No idea. Now look, Chad, the trick is this. The day after tomorrow is Sunday. You can come with me out to St Mark's. Then I'll introduce you to them. Bring a bottle of ale and a sandwich and you and I shall have a picnic lunch, then stroll over there and call on them. Of course they'll be in an atmosphere of gloom because of McCrory's demise. But that should be helpful to you. Only you mustn't interrogate them.'

'Thank you. It's a good idea. I'll be discreet but I'll ask a few questions of Mrs Somerville if I can have a word with her alone. Where is Orchard Farm?'

'About a mile from St Mark's, in the valley behind Mount Douglas.'

'Ah yes.' Two or three miles from Cormorant Point, blocked from it by the mountain. 'Indians?' I said. 'Did McCrory say anything about them?'

'Nothing whatsoever. Odd, when you think of it. From what I read in the paper, he had visited them frequently. But perhaps he was being sensitive. I mean with Major Somerville having been killed by them, and probably scalped or whatever. I believe Indians don't just kill people, they chop them up. What *did* they do to McCrory? I mean, I didn't like the chap, but all the same… What does 'horribly mutilated', as the paper put it, really mean?'

'It means someone stabbed him, slashed him, tried to bite out chunks of his flesh, chopped his member off, and stuck it in his mouth.'

'Oh, I say. Not really.'

'Really.'

'Well, I'm glad you have him in jail.'

'I don't think we do,' I said hopefully.

8

'Christians awake! Salute the Happy Morn!'

It was, after all, not long after Easter. The hymn brought me back to the stone church in Wiltshire: the stained glass window I would look at of St George with a lance, his foot on the neck of the Dragon, scaly as a fish; the pew ends of oak with their carvings of lions, bunches of grapes, and the leafy face of Jack-in-the-Green; the church's six bells, each with a name – Great Tom, Jeremy, Little Isaac and the others, acquired over five centuries; my father in a state of innocent elation like mine now as I sang the hymn. I had given up the church, yet no music could stir me like church music. I had not gone to church in Victoria, not even at Christmas, which I had spent in the jail relieving Seeds who had made an increasingly merry tour of various friends, perhaps to forget the wife in San Francisco. Now I was in something more like a barn than a church, named after Mark, the youngest of the Apostles, with a smell of newly planed wood and fresh paint, six gothic windows on each side and a large triple one behind the altar, all of plain white glass. Yet Parson Coulter's robes of Ascension white were the same as my father's, and the white of the altar cloth no different from home. Coulter's sermon had been a typical English one, about charitable obligations, and delivered, like the usual prayers for the Queen, in an English voice. Although the alienist's demise was the talk of Victoria and had occurred less than two miles from this church, the parson was too much of a gentleman to give a sermon on anything to do with the sixth commandment or the revenge of the Lord against the Moabites. There was even the typical English diversion of young men and women on display, although not so many young women. There were not more than seventy people at the service, and most of them were married couples and their small, restless children, with few old people, and about a dozen young men staring at the main attraction of the service: the 'eligible' Somervilles.

The experienced Frederick had chosen an angle from which the girls and the mother could be seen in a row, from the side and slightly behind. Directly across the aisle was the delicious sight of hair curling just below the bonnet above a pink cheek, mouth opened delicately to sing, eyes under long lashes cast down modestly at the hymn book. Aemilia, the eldest, was the nearest to me, then came Letitia, Cordelia (Frederick whispered to me that this was she), and the mother. They were not exactly like peas in a pod, but the resemblance was striking. All three girls had the fine turned-up nose and chocolate-box pretty look which the mother, although stouter and with a plumper face, still possessed. I could not see much of their eyes, which might have provided more distinction between them. Aemilia, however, stood out – and literally, I noticed, stood at a slight distance from the others, even more than that required by her crinoline. She was taller, her face was thinner and less conventionally pretty, and what I could see of her hair was a chestnut brown not unlike my own, whereas her sisters and mothers were more fair. They were dressed elegantly but not, by the looks of it, too expensively. Not having had sisters, I knew little of such things.

Frederick spent the service in a state of elastic erectness, chest puffed out, eyes sparkling, voice resonant in the hymns. I found myself mimicking this involuntarily. It was a sort of mating display, in case the ladies caught sight of us out of the corner of an eye. Another person on his best behaviour was the young curate, Mr Firbanks, who was clean-shaven and had blond hair which had been incredibly smoothed, so that he looked like a porcelain angel. He read the Collects unctuously in a light and melodious tenor voice. I wondered idly why curates always seemed to be tenors, then became baritones when they matured into parsons. As if, to use the idiom of my school, their balls had dropped a notch further. I stared through the bare glass windows at a dove grey sky. The weather had turned cool and showery.

The last hymn was

There is a happy land,
Far, far away
Where saints in glory stand
Bright, bright as day…

Some contrast to McLevy's Happy Land where 'there is no religion save that of the devil'! I no longer believed in the words, but the hymn with its naïvely cheerful tune reminded me of childhood – in fact I could almost hear it in children's voices as I contentedly roared out with the others,

Come to that happy land,
Come, come away,
Why will ye doubting stand,

Why still delay?
Oh, we shall happy be,
When from sin and sorrow free,
Lord we shall live with Thee,
Blest, blest for aye.

The service ended. Frederick and I stayed in place so that Frederick could smile, and myself nod politely, at the ladies on their way out. Then as the two of us filed out of our pew we ran into a broad shouldered young man, with stiff-looking black hair and a somewhat swaggering walk. 'Hello, old chap,' he said quietly to Frederick, with a wide smile which was also stiff, almost a rictus. This was the more conspicuous for the fact that he was clean-shaven. His voice was thin and dry as if squeezed out. His eyes which, given his bearing, might have been expected to be penetrating, were of the sensitive brown kind, and moved between Frederick and me with a quick but wavering movement. The three of us paused to let others past, and Frederick made a quiet introduction: 'Hobbes. Beaumont.' Then to Beaumont: 'Hobbes was up at Oxford with me. He's acting Sergeant in the police.' And to me: 'Beaumont is a Lieutenant in the Marines.' We shook hands. Beaumont's hand was large, warm and dry. He seemed a friendly sort of chap, though odd.

We came out of church where a gently rising slope had been cleared and gravelled to provide spaces for horses and carts, although it was surrounded by wild and mossy crags under a dense cover of firs interspersed with cottonwood and oaks. Below the church was the graveyard, with a tiny yew which must have been brought from England – it was surely not native. I took in the scene before facing up to the introductions to the widow Somerville and the three 'eligibles' who had been standing outside in earnest conversation with the curate. With the forward touch of the colonies, the ladies readily held out their velvet gloved hands to be briefly clasped.

To my surprise Mrs Somerville was ready for the charge. 'Mr Hobbes! I know who you are – the constable working on the case of our poor dear Dr McCrory! So *conscientious* of the authorities to leave no stone unturned before condemning an Indian. After all, even the lowest of savages is entitled to the best of British justice. You dreadful man, Frederick. The next thing, you'll be bringing Mr Hobbes to our house for an *interrogation.*

Seriously, Mr Hobbes, you must come with Frederick to Orchard Farm this afternoon – you are *most* welcome to join our little circle – but you must promise not to question us all about our movements on the fatal day! *Poor* Dr McCrory. He was always such an *informative* man. A delight. Truly.'

All this was delivered in the imagined style of the English 'grande dame,' but in an unmistakably colonial manner. Without doubt her tactics were good. I was quite disarmed but tried to regain lost ground.

'Of course,' I said, 'I came across Frederick at the funeral – a sad occasion. But I was most offended not to have seen him for some months. We used to spend Sunday afternoons together. It was only after the deepest interrogation, I assure you, that he revealed where he had been all this time.' I smiled gallantly around at the ladies. As I had expected, I caught nothing but bland sociability in the faces of the two youngest sisters, but there was a certain 'hauteur' in that of Aemilia.

'Chad is an old friend of mine from Oxford,' Frederick put in.

'How nice!' Mrs Somerville said. 'You *will* come to see us.'

'Of course.' I was not sure how wise it was, after all, for Frederick to have played the Oxford card. The colonies, even this one, were filled with third rate Oxonians whose status as a 'university man' was the most they would ever claim. A man of action like Beaumont was well ahead in the game. The colonies needed soldiers and Marines, not Oxford men.

Beaumont was greeting the girls. They called him by his Christian name, which was George. 'King George Diaub,' I found myself thinking. The word 'George' was not much of a connection, though Beaumont like any military man, or policeman for that matter, was a 'King George' par excellence. I observed him closely. In spite of his almost mechanical stiffness he was definitely socially 'ept' (as opposed to in-). He even had a cavalry-officer lisp: 'Wather looks like wain, doncher think?' Was this natural for a Lieutenant in the Marines? They were a long way down in the social scale from the cavalry, although since the charge of the Light Brigade the cavalry were recognized as also light in brain-power. Marines were more versatile, but Beaumont hardly seemed a brain: the affable fixed smile ruled that out.

The Somervilles set off for Orchard Farm in as much style as their equipage – what was known, American style, as a two horse buggy – allowed. Their Negro farm-worker, grizzled and older than I had expected, who must have been hanging around outside, cracked his whip above the horses with panache. Beaumont, who had a satchel containing what he described as 'an American seedcake for the ladies,' plus his own sandwich, tagged on as Frederick and I followed the grandly known Cedar Hill Cross Road, really a track, through a defile between crags and firs. It was cold on this sunless day. We chatted mainly about Beaumont's rather glamorous and idle existence as part of Her Majesty's occupying force on San Juan Island.

This island, less than ten miles away across Haro Strait, is the subject of a boundary dispute between Britain and the United States. It was, like the Victoria region, occupied by both British and American settlers under the protection of the HBC. But when the boundary between Washington Territory and British Columbia was established, in 1849, the wording of the treaty was ambivalent about whether Haro Strait, or Rosario Strait on the other side of San Juan, was the boundary. In 1859 an American on San Juan shot a pig belonging to the HBC, some American army hotheads occupied part of the island, and on the pig it seemed as if a global war depended. After all the Americans once sent an expeditionary force against Morocco in the so-called 'War of Jenkins' Ear' – Jenkins being the American Ambassador whose ear had been lopped off by a Moroccan. The Americans have ambitions to extend their domain, in Manifest Destiny, all the way up to Alaska. And if they can go to war over an ear, no doubt they can do so over a pig.

But for ten years there has been a stalemate, in which a force of Marines at English Camp protects the interests of the third of the few hundred people on the island who are British, and a force at American Camp protects the rest. The Americans have been more than tied up in their Civil War, so the Pig War has remained quiescent. Now the question of the boundary has been referred for arbitration to the President of Switzerland, a neutral, who is taking his time. In the meantime the Marines at English Camp twiddle their thumbs in their quarters which have recently been rebuilt at great expense, and organize seasonal parties with their American counterparts.

'Dashed agreeable place, weally,' said Beaumont, demonstrating that his cavalry lisp only applied to the r's at the beginning of words, although I won't continue to transliterate it here. 'Not a lot to do though.' He said he came as often as he could to Victoria. It was a hard two hour row or sail across the Strait to Telegraph Cove, but every two weeks or so, weather permitting, he could get three or four Marines – he was, after all, second in command at the camp – to take him over in one of the small boats. They would tramp the four miles into Victoria and spend the day, and perhaps a night there. Or on a Sunday, when Beaumont came to visit Orchard Farm, the lads would lounge around at Telegraph Cove or nearby at Cadborough Bay, with a bottle or two of grog, and make friends with the people who came out from town to the beaches for picnics. Beaumont would walk to St Marks, then on to the farm.

The road broke out of the forest into more open country. Ahead of us was a wide valley, in which patches of trees alternated with fields and homesteads, and to the right the blunt cone of Mount Douglas, its lower slopes solid with fir, its top bare and rocky with patches of scrub.

I was trying to find an avenue of conversational approach to the subject of McCrory when Beaumont, as Mrs Somerville had done before him, brought up the subject himself: 'I heard Mrs Somerville say you're hot on the trail of the murderer of our friend the doctor.'

'Not really.' I had decided that my strategy for the day would be to play down my role as detective. 'They've already charged a man, an Indian. I'm just tying up loose ends. Very little is known about this chap McCrory. He was a bit of a mystery man.'

'Really? I always thought he was quite forthcoming – talkative, full of anecdotes. Vulgar, of course. But life and soul of the party, what?'

'You mean at the Somervilles'? Or elsewhere too?'

'Elsewhere?' Beaumont's wavering brown eyes looked almost wounded – incongruous above the tight smile and jaw. 'I'd never know a man of that sort elsewhere. I mean, I've never met him at Government House.'

This I felt, and was perhaps meant to feel, was a snub. I had never been near Government House, meaning 'Carey Castle,' a rather vulgar (to use Beaumont's term) wooden house in which Governor Seymour held court surrounded by the sort of sycophantic and rootless English who I imagined might be found in any outpost of the Empire, from Peshawar to Botany Bay.

'Now, Orchard Farm is different,' Beaumont continued. 'Very amusing. Of course the mother is a bit much, but a dear old fig, really. Lovely gels.

Quite unusual by any standards. I dare say with a bit of coaching they'd quite star at any hunt ball at home.'

'I say, Beaumont,' Frederick interrupted, hasty as always. 'Don't be patronizing. They can certainly hold their own here, which is what counts. And more than that. Cordelia is lovely too. I'm sure you don't find girls like that in your part of the world. You can't tell me the Yorkshire moors are *much* more civilised than this.'

We sat down on some rocks overlooking the valley, and pitched into our picnic lunch, Frederick and I passing our bottles of ale to Beaumont for an occasional swig. Frederick and Beaumont bantered about the respective merits of the North Riding of Yorkshire, and Kent – both 8,000 miles away.

9

The house at Orchard Farm is like the alienist's, a small two storied box, only with a wide roofed veranda or 'porch' around three sides, and extensive outbuildings, including a cottage presumably lived in by the farm help, the Joneses. Beside the house and along the road is a paddock, with a zig zag 'snake fence' of cedar poles, their ends laid over each other alternately at each joint. Behind and on each side of the house, surrounded by more snake fences on a gentle slope, is the orchard. There are at least a hundred trees, many of them now in blossom. Their scent on this dull day when perhaps the atmosphere held it down like a blanket, reached out along the road as if to greet the three of us.

We let ourselves in the front gate, closing it behind us, as a collie dog bounded cheerfully around us. At the hitching post were the Somervilles' buggy and another, more stylish one, whose two horses munched in their nosebags. The Negro, Mr Jones, appeared and began to unhitch the Somervilles' horse to lead it to stable. With him were the so-called picaninny, only a few years old, and the Indian boy, obviously a half breed white, about ten years old. Since there was no resemblance whatsoever between him and Mr Jones, the speculation about Mrs Jones was understandable.

We thumped up the steps onto the porch, and the door was opened by an angular-looking woman in a maid's costume, Mrs Jones. She was only about thirty years old but looked rather severe, I thought, to have lapsed into having congress with an Indian.

She showed us along the hall, a mere few paces, and into the drawing room, which consisted of two small square rooms connected by a wide proscenium type arch, with plaster curlicued columns. There was actually a fireplace – the more usual Victoria farmhouse would have had a potbellied stove – of brick and tile in which, for form's sake, although it would not have been chilly indoors without it, a wood fire was burning. Form was clearly important for the Somervilles, not that I thought less of them for that. Life in the Colony was not economically easy, except for government officials and some property speculators, like Mr Quattrini, who had arrived before us and rose to greet us. He was a burly red cheeked man with a thick black beard, squeezed into his Sunday best – a black suit like that of an undertaker, and a pearly grey tie on which shone an unnecessarily large diamond pin. His manner was forthright. He obviously knew better than to put on airs, as he probably would have if he had been English and therefore ashamed of money. But airs were not absent in the manners of the Somervilles, especially Mrs S, whose presence was overwhelming in a bosomy maroon coloured crinoline dress trimmed in lace. The younger girls had a simpering tendency. Aemilia, tall and elegant in a lilac coloured crinoline which complemented her eyes, which were soft grey like the sky outside, was not simpering but stand-offish.

The room was furnished in the fashionable way. Almost every inch of the walls (themselves covered with a thick-looking floral wallpaper) was covered with something. There were paintings of the Landseer 'Monarch of the Glen' type (reminding me of the Hotel Argyle) or of the sentimental type: an 'Abyssinian girl' bare-footed, casting large black eyes heavenward as if in prayer while a muffled horseman galloped into a distant landscape of mountains and minarets; some 'gypsy' children, also barefoot, selling clothes pegs outside an English Inn, their faces pretty and seraphic with unlikely innocence. The remaining areas of wall were bedecked with whatever ornament could be accommodated to its flatness: a riding crop with a woven leather handle, a sabre with a silver guard, a cavalryman's pennant – these presumably the father's – and crochet work and embroidery in frames. On the mantelpiece were the usual clock and engraved silver trays and candlesticks. The fireplace was surrounded with enough equipment in the way of brass handled tongs, pokers, scrapers and bellows to maintain three such fires at once.

The back half, as it were, of the drawing room doubled as a dining room (unthinkable in England) and had open shelves packed with china dishes and plates turned outward on display (very English, but unthinkable in more practical houses in the Colony where the shelves would have been enclosed in cupboards, so as to obviate the need for constant dusting). The front half was cluttered not only with armchairs and two settees, but with leather ottomans on which the Somerville girls perched. In view of the floor space occupied by furniture and crinolines, there was very little of the somewhat worn wine-red Axminster carpet visible, and no way of walking around. I found myself stuck on a not very comfortable hard backed chair near the door while an urgent cluster formed around the main feature of the room, an 'upright grand' piano against the wall beside the fireplace. Letitia had been playing when we came in, and now she resumed, with Beaumont turning the pages, his fixed agreeable smile and mechanical movements making him look like a huge well-dressed puppet. Cordelia abandoned her ottoman and stood fluttering with Frederick, as close together as manners and crinoline would permit, behind Letitia's other shoulder.

Letitia was playing, inevitably, one of Mendelssohn's 'Songs Without Words' – *Faith*, which I knew was one of the easiest – with competence but not much verve. They were, I thought, rather insipid girls, but they were pretty and it was a pleasure to let the eye feast on them. Quattrini and Mrs Somerville were conversing quietly. Aemilia, who might have been expected to take up the social slack by making me feel at home, had instead taken up a sampler and was stitching the usual hearts and flowers in it while listening, with a sad look, to the music. Frederick had said to me that she was melancholy, and a blue-stocking, and it was clear why she did not exert the same obvious tug on young men as her younger sisters, or even as her mother must have done in her day. Aemilia did not really look melancholy but she was obviously very serious, which was not fashionable, and considered to be intimidating. Irritated, because Frederick had predicted this, I found myself drawn to her. Her face was paler than that of her sisters, with a few freckles on her cheeks and nose, which would of course be considered a blemish, but she did not seem to have made any attempt to cover them up with powder or cream. Her skin was in fact of a milky smoothness. Her grey eyes were clear and, I imagined, wise. Her hair, out of its Sunday bonnet, was gloriously rich in colour although rather thin in texture. The turned up nose was pretty as her sisters'. Her mouth, less of a rosebud than theirs, might have been more generous but now looked severe. She must have seen I was studying her, but paid me no attention.

I felt embarrassed. Frederick's impulsive plan was clearly not a tactful one. It was only a few days since McCrory, usually present at these Sunday gatherings, had been butchered in a way of which some detail might have come to these delicate female ears. Since he had not been a family relation, one would hardly expect the Somervilles to go into mourning, and of course they had not. But they must be shocked and saddened. Perhaps a concealment of this exaggerated the mother's gushiness, Aemilia's hauteur, and the younger girls' fluffiness. Whatever they felt, they could hardly show it with a newcomer, known to be investigating the murder, sitting like a death's head in the room. They must certainly wonder why I was there and what I would do. I felt like slinking out and away.

Letitia had moved onto *Hope*, which she was finding more difficult, and she stopped as the new guest arrived, Mr Firbanks, the curate. His waxy-looking cheeks blushed as he came in. There were the usual greetings, a rather cursory introduction to me by Mrs Somerville, then at once urgings from the younger girls that he should sing. He was obviously delighted to oblige. At church it had been clear that he liked the sound of his own voice. There was much fuss over a new book of songs in Italian, bound in blue leather, which had been a present that very day from Mr Quattrini. He, at least, would not be heartbroken at the alienist's demise. Naturally the book contained *Caro Mio Ben*, a great favourite at musical gatherings and soirees. Aemilia was called on to play the accompaniment, since she was apparently the best at sight-reading. After much ritual encouragement, Firbanks sang. His voice was indeed lightly agreeable, and he launched the higher notes with a slight bobbing motion of his body, his mouth open roundly like that of a cherub. Aemilia's accompaniment was impeccable, almost nonchalant. It would have been vulgar to clap, of course, although Quattrini did smack his hands together once, then held them clasped as the others uttered quiet bravos and murmurs of pleasure. Firbanks grew quite flushed. It was becoming hot in the room, the air scented with a lemony scent all the Somervilles wore.

Then Mrs Jones brought in the 'tea' on a trolley, with flowered dishes on doilies, various pastries, and Beaumont's American seed-cake. This must mean all the afternoon guests had arrived. Perhaps the others Frederick had mentioned were keeping away, so as to leave the Somervilles with their grief at the loss of a friend, and only the inner circle of family friends would be here now. I was not quite used to 'tea.' It was very much a citified fashion in England, and not an institution at Oxford. Where I came from it was still the custom in mid-afternoon to drink a glass of sweet wine, usually Madeira, with a slice of cake. Here there was much passing around of cups and saucers. The Somerville girls and mother all crooked their little fingers as they drank. 'Oh dear!' I could almost hear my own mother say… Yet I was disposed to admire these women for putting on such a good show.

Firbanks immediately brought up the subject of the alienist, in a rather complacent tone. 'So dreadful to think of us all sitting here, in our usual happy gathering under the wing of Mrs Somerville, while our old friend Dr McCrory lies smitten down in the prime of life. It shows' – he held up a dainty forefinger – 'how frail is this civilisation, which just such a simple gathering as this may express, in a world in which savagery and barbarism stalk the land.'

'Indeed,' said Mrs Somerville, 'it has been very painful for I and the girls. It will take us a long time to get over it. A terrible blow! And in *this* family!' Here she seemed to lose her composure, and her eyes rolled upward. 'I need not say how such a deed *echoes* the loss of my dear Harry, brutally murdered by the Comox whom we had thought were our friends! No. It's almost too painful that Mr McCrory should meet such a fate. I only hope' – and here she looked directly at me, then at Beaumont – 'that the authorities of this Colony will learn from an incident like this the necessity of absolute control and ruthlessness with the native population. That poor dear Dr McCrory should be the one to pay with his life to remind us how precious our English-speaking civilisation is in this wilderness! It's too sad. A man who cared only for his work, who had detached himself from the civil conflict in his own country, who lived entirely for the light of learning and the relief of infirmity! And so interested, always, in the customs and behaviours of savages. "We can learn from them", I remember him saying in this very room. "Our ancestors themselves were savages. They are as we were. Indeed they know things about the universal life force that we have forgotten!". But he didn't know – poor, naïve Dr McCrory – that if the Indians retain an ancient knowledge, they have also retained a brutality that we spurn and reject! Do we not, Gentlemen?'

'Hear, hear,' said Beaumont, obviously moved by this peroration. 'But of course that's why we're here. Order cannot be maintained without force. I'm afraid the good Doctor was too trusting, in his American way. I venture to say an Englishman would have had more sense than to go among the Indians almost as an equal, asking them what they knew of healing and herbs.'

'Yes, he was brash!' Mrs Somerville interjected. 'Fatally brash. We found it so charming! Though we used to tease him about it, didn't we, girls? He was willing to make friends with anyone. Yet a gentleman, I assure you, as so many Virginians are. What dear Harry and I used to call a *natural* gentleman, not schooled to it perhaps, a little rough and ready, but with a measure of inborn refinement.' Here she gave a soft smile at Mr Quattrini, as if to intimate that he fell into the same category, then addressed the curate. 'Wouldn't you agree, Mr Firbanks?'

'Oh yes,' Firbanks simpered. 'Indeed. He was not of our church so I did not know him apart from here. But a most impressive man.'

'A good chap,' Frederick echoed.

I tried to assess all this. The only obvious thing was that everybody, no matter what their real, sub-latent position was in regard to the alienist, was thoroughly enjoying making their public admiration known. Even the girls – except Aemilia – added their bit. 'Dear Dr McCrory,' sighed Cordelia. And, 'Do you remember his anecdotes about Washington?' said Letitia, apparently more of an intellect. 'He could bring American history so alive!'

Quattrini said nothing, too honest, I hoped, to add his voice to the chorus.

'Frederick's friend Mr Hobbes, here, is a police Sergeant,' Mrs Somerville announced suddenly. But there was no horrified gasp of surprise. Everyone in the room knew it, except perhaps the curate. 'And I believe, from gossip about town, that he is engaged in "detective work" about poor Dr McCrory's death.'

All faces turned to look at me. 'Just tying up loose ends,' I said. 'And you know, an Indian will probably be charged with the crime. It's not as if we're looking to find out who did it.' A white lie, I hoped. 'We don't know very much about Dr McCrory. He was new in town, and something of a mystery man – a practitioner of new medical methods which clearly required more than the usual confidentiality, for one thing. Of course we have to put together a dossier if nothing else, to aid the case against the Indian.' Now the white lie was turning black. 'After all there has to be a trial. It may be that the Indian will have a defense lawyer who will attack any weaknesses in the Crown's case.' I had in fact heard the day before that Victoria's least competent barrister, Mr Mulligan, was willing to take on Wiladzap's case, 'for the public good,' given the fact there was no money in it. 'So we are particularly interested in hearing from any acquaintance of Dr McCrory's whatever information can illumine the man for us, and perhaps explain why he visited the Indians that day – just how he may have laid himself open to this crime. My task is to collect what information I can. You may have surmised that it's partly why I am here.' I managed a laugh. 'I must admit that when Frederick told me he had known Dr McCrory I plied him with questions, and he told me he had made the gentleman's acquaintance at this farm. But then I had another bone to pick with Frederick. In the darkest days of winter he and I would go riding to Oak Bay every Sunday, rough shooting for grouse. Then he disappeared! Not one squeak out of him until the other day, when he avowed he had been spending Sunday afternoon at this delightful Orchard Farm. Well of course I had to come when he intimated I might meet you all by attending Matins at St Mark's. And here I am.'

My speech seemed to ease some tension. It was at least good form, and allowed the proprieties to be observed.

'And most welcome, Mr Hobbes,' said Mrs Somerville. 'I'm only sorry you meet us in such a distressing time. Yet, life must go on!' she said brightly. The tension was eased still further. Beaumont's seed-cake, the tea, and the pastries were duly praised, and conversation wandered from the weather, to the beauty of the apple blossom, the plans for further embellishment of St Mark's, and the idea of a picnic up Mount Douglas when the weather improved. The barbarous savages in their camp on the other side of the mountain, and the loquacious Dr McCrory now reduced to eternal silence, were for the moment forgotten.

Aemilia was the least talkative, except for quiet answers to eager questions from Frederick about the order in which different varieties of apple blossomed in the orchard. She seemed to be the one who knew about the subject. Her accent was the most properly English. Perhaps, as the eldest, she had been more influenced by her English father. The mother's accent had undertones of the improper, although English. The younger girls sounded half American, a pleasant compromise.

As the tea things were being cleared away by the silent Mrs Jones, Aemilia went to the piano and began playing from the Songbook. Although the songs were in Italian they were not all by Italian composers. She was playing the thrumming accompaniment to Gluck's *O del mio dolce ardor*, but did not seem to like it, made a face, and began on Handel's *Lascia ch'io pianga*. The book was sure to be full of Handel – after Mendelssohn the rage of our epoch. I felt happy. I loved Handel, loved music, and would probably know most of the songs, since my mother and I used to play and sing through the long winter evenings at the vicarage, and I had sung in choirs all through boyhood and early manhood.

The conversation became hushed as Aemilia began to sing the words, which she pronounced quite adequately, in contrast to the curate in *Caro Mio Ben*. 'Lascia ch'io pianga, mia cruda sorte': 'Let me weep my cruel fate.' She might not understand it all, but she must have understood the words were about grief, and with a powerful instinct for the music she was uttering each syllable in a detached, almost staccato way, as if choked with feeling – which she was surely too controlled to be. I was moved. Quietly I rose and went over to her left side and stood ready to turn the page. This required a long reach since her dress on the floor kept me at a distance, and I leaned across her, close to her head and into the aura of lemon scent. I managed to turn the page noiselessly, and stood still, observing her fine long-fingered hands, and her bosom, encased in the lilac dress and an over-layer of transparent muslin and lace. I liked her creamy skin. I turned the next page. She sang to the end, quietly, as if partly for herself alone.

'Bravo,' Beaumont murmured from the other side of the room.

'Lovely, dear,' sighed Mrs Somerville. 'Do let us have another. Handel's *Largo* is there, surely.'

'Of course, Mamma.' Aemilia dutifully sought out the inevitable Largo, under its true title, *Ombra mai fu*. She began playing it, not singing, but playing louder, allowing the piece's gloomy strength to come through. But at the end of the first section, she stopped. 'Do you sing, Mr Hobbes?' she said. 'What we need is a baritone or bass for this. Or' – without waiting for my answer – 'Mr Quattrini?'

'I don't sing,' said Quattrini. But he got up and came over to the piano on Aemilia's right side, gazing down happily at the book which was causing such pleasure.

'What does this mean?' Aemilia asked him. 'Something about a dear vegetable? Not fitted to the tone of the *Largo*, surely.'

This caused a laugh, because of Quattrini's known association with the vegetable business. He took it in a good part. 'The vegetable in question is a tree,' he said. Then in an attempt at humour: 'as if you were singing to one of your apple trees.'

Aemilia smiled. '*I* can't sing it. Mr Hobbes, I think it devolves on you to give it a try.'

'I shall,' I said. Aemilia began the piece again and I gave it my best. By the time we reached the end I was almost ecstatic. Like my mother – again! – she seemed to know how to match the piano to my voice, unusually capable of listening carefully as she accompanied.

Again there was a chorus of Bravos. At least the tea party was in full swing. Aemilia flipped through the pages and stopped at Paisiello's *Nel cor piu non mi sento*. 'Another for baritone,' she said. 'One moment.' She tried the first bars of the rather difficult accompaniment, and succeeded. ' All right?'

It was a short, playful song with which I had no difficulty. But the words – which since I had done some reading in Italian and knew Latin, I understood – were embarrassing. 'Mi pizzichi, mi stuzzichi, mi pungichi, mi mastichi' must mean something like, 'You pinch me, you poke me, you prod me, you chew me.'

This song was so popular that I had to sing it again, but before starting Aemilia asked me, in her teasing way, 'Do *you* know what all this means? The words sound so dramatic.'

'It's a song about the torments of love,' I said, with a glance over Aemilia's head at Quattrini.

'Yes, yes,' said Quattrini. 'The torments of love; the words are made of suffering.' Perhaps he was embarrassed that the song was in the book he had given.

'You make suffering sound very cheerful, Mr Hobbes,' Aemilia remarked.

'That's in the song. I suppose the composer was making fun of it all.'

We did the song again, with verve. But it would not have been right for Aemilia to monopolise the piano. It was Cordelia's turn. After much rearrangement, so that Quattrini and I might be replaced by Frederick and Beamont, she played some pretty little pieces by Sullivan. A talented family indeed…

At some point in all this, the curate had taken his leave – his nose out of joint, I thought conceitedly, aware of having made a good impression and rendered my presence less baleful.

Then Beaumont looked at the ormolu clock on the mantelpiece, pulled out his fob watch to check it, and announced that he must be off. The brave lads would be waiting to row him across the Strait before it became dark.

Frederick announced that he and I would walk with Beaumont the first part of the way, but Quattrini offered us all a lift in his buggy. 'You can all squeeze in, Gentlemen'. Beaumont as far as St Mark's, Frederick and I into town. The party's ending was well timed. The alienist had had his due, but something of a cheerful atmosphere had been re-established.

'You must come again, Mr Hobbes,' said Mrs Somerville in the general melee of farewells. 'But you didn't interrogate us,' she added with an attempt at coyness. She must be relieved, I thought. But since we were face to face for a moment with no one immediately close by, I risked:

'There's just one thing I'd love to know, Mrs Somerville, since your friend was such a man of mystery. How did you happen to meet him in the first place?'

But this did not in the least faze her. 'At one of his lectures. On Mesmerism. Afterwards many of the audience remained behind in conversation. He asked if he might call, and I invited him for the following Sunday.'

How very simple it was. But I could not resist: 'It's a long way into town on a winter's evening to attend a lecture.'

This time she did seem to be put off balance for an instant. I hoped my question had not been insulting. But, 'Why that's no trouble at all,' she said. 'Whenever I go into town of an afternoon, whether with one of the girls or alone, driven by Mr Jones, and I might stay the evening, I go to the Hotel Argyle. Mrs Larose is an old acquaintance of mine. I shan't say exactly a friend because, frankly, our positions in life are rather different. But you probably understand that us older colonists were thrown together willy nilly, and English social distinctions could not always obtain. And she's a dear soul, a widow like myself. There are always empty rooms these days, I'm afraid, and I and my girls are always welcome.'

Mrs Somerville turned to say goodbye to the others. I sought out Aemilia, who held out her hand. I took it for just a moment, imagining that there was a special current of feeling between us. 'I've never so much enjoyed singing,' I said, and meant it.

10

I had received a reply from the HBC at Fort Simpson which, though remote, happens to be on the new Western Union telegraph line to Asia.

```
TSALAK RIVER ON PRINCESS ROYAL ISLAND LAT FIFTY
THIRTY STOP LOCAL TRIBES UNFRIENDLY HBC STOP
ACCORDING TSIMSHIAN INFORMANT HERE WILADZAP MEANS
LUCKY IN HUNTING INFORMAL NAME STOP REAL NAMES
CEREMONIAL STOP SEVERAL CHIEFS OF EAGLE CLANS
AT PRESENT COMPETING FOR NAME LEGEX STOP MAKING
ENQUIRIES RE COMPETENT INTERPRETER BUT UNLIKELY FIND
AS SOUTH TSIMSHIAN SKEWUNK DIALECT KNOWN TO FEW STOP
ADVISE CAUTION DANGEROUS SIGNED CAMERON HBC.
```

I had already ascertained that there was no one in the HBC in Victoria who spoke Tsimshian. I decided to visit the subscription library later in the day, to see if I could obtain further information on the Tsimshian. As it happened I was going to visit the other library, the Mechanics' Institute, but had no hope of the books there.

The Institute's director, Mr Nally, had little to say about the alienist's two public lectures. McCrory had paid £2 each time for rent of the premises. It was part of the Institute's mission to propagate knowledge, and phrenology had always proved a popular subject. Mesmerism was also of great interest. Mr Nally had enjoyed both lectures greatly, found them most enlightening. Why, the great Dr Eliotson of Edinborough, inventor of the stethoscope, had induced mesmeric trances in his patients and effected cures of certain dementias, the 'Vapours' and, in particular, women's troubles. Yes, Nally would say there were more women than men present at the lectures, but the married ones came with their husbands. Dr Powell had attended and asked some sceptical but polite questions. They had been evenings of intellectual stimulation, a credit to Victoria, if Mr Nally might say so, and he ventured to say that even though Dr McCrory had been an unorthodox practitioner, it was nothing less than a tragedy that such a fine man should be *butchered* by savages…

Before Nally began to froth at the mouth, I brought him back to earth by asking him to list for me all the people who he recalled attending the lectures. I began writing in my notebook, a formidable list which kept growing: everyone in town seemed to have attended one lecture or the other. It would have been more easy to list who had *not* attended. I stopped writing the names down. There was not much to do in Victoria in midwinter, which of course McCrory would have known. I reproached myself for a certain callousness in my attitude to the murdered man. I told myself that as an investigator I could not afford feelings of either pity or revenge. But it was going to be difficult to know the real man who had occupied that unreal corpse.

My next visit was to the bank. In England, official warrants would be necessary for some of my procedures, but the Colony was a world of its own. Although I was accountable to the Superintendent and Commissioner, I could do whatever I needed without prior authorisation. The bank manager showed me the alienist's records. His account had started from an initial cash deposit of $150. Cheques were few, and for occasional bills from clothiers and grocers. Deposits had been in cash. $100 remained in the account.

I had already discovered in the land registry, conveniently in the courthouse, that the alienist had been able to buy his house by putting down a deposit of £150. The rest of the £500 price was mortgaged to a Jewish moneylender, Rabinowicz. This was normal enough. Victoria's Jewish community, immigrants from the United States, had become prosperous enough to build the only brick house of worship in town, the Beth Emanuel synagogue. They bought and sold merchandise, travelled in the Interior selling mining supplies, and lent money at higher interest than the banks, while not insisting on letters of reference from previous places of residence – an advantage during the 'boom' years of the early '60's, now alas gone.

Rabinowicz's office was a mere shanty in a back street. Clearly no money was wasted on frills. I squeezed into a chair in a small space between Rabinowicz's desk and a wall while Rabinowicz, a little man who looked, in fact, no more Jewish than any other Victoria businessman, pored over the papers relevant to the alienist's mortgage – too long, I thought, since he would almost certainly have already revised them the moment he had heard of McCrory's death. I hoped Rabinowicz would not turn out to be as evasive as Lee. But no. Once Rabinowicz began talking he was direct.

'I shall advertise here and in San Francisco in case Dr McCrory has a successor who wishes to take the house and sell it to regain the down payment. Otherwise in three months I shall sell it myself, to pay the mortgage and expenses. There will not be much left.'

'Did he keep up his payments?'

'On the nail. First of each month. He would send the money around with his Chinese servant, Mr Lee. Cash. Never a problem.'

'Do you know why he came to you for the mortgage rather than a bank?'

'I give good terms, Sergeant. You want to buy a house and take out a mortgage, you come and see me.'

'Did he have bankers' or other references?'

'I do not require references. I make my own assessment. It's none of my business what a person's financial situation *has* been. I want to know what it *is*.'

'And what was your assessment of McCrory's situation?'

'That he was a doctor who would have patients. He mentioned he saw them on a different basis from most doctors – for regular appointments for treatment, whether at the moment they were having symptoms or not. He said the doctor should keep the patients well, not only make them better when sick. He invited me to his public lectures, and he talked to me about his methods – the use of the Mesmeric trance and vital magnetism, the diagnosis through phrenology. He even told me I had a prominent bump of benevolence, which I do not doubt. But, you'll understand, this was to encourage me to lend him the money. And he urged me that if I, or my wife or my girls had any need of either a treatment or a diagnosis, he would be happy to negotiate with regard to the fees. As one businessman to another, you might say.' Rabinowicz looked at me with his lips pushed together, an expression of amusement in his eyes. 'What more can I tell you?'

'You're giving me a good idea of the man. I never met him. Please continue.'

'I only met him a few times myself. He was energetic, very animated, an enthusiast, a sort of missionary for his methods, in that Yankee way – although I believe he was a Virginian. As a Jew I don't think like that: I make money and I'm not ashamed of it. Money is money. But for most

Americans it is something else. It has got to be not only money but *good* – a reward from God. So although they are often shrewd and even cheats, they have to *believe* in what they do, to make money. I don't *believe* in lending mortgages, I just do it. But with Dr McCrory I did wonder – to put it frankly – if he was in reality a serious doctor, or what the Yankees call a snake-oil salesman. I would not have sent my wife and daughters to him for treatment, although he was clearly an intelligent man. He did believe in his methods, but of course he had to. I did not trust him as a doctor. But I trusted him to make money. That's all I can say.'

'You're very helpful. I must ask you, though, a rather intrusive question. Do you know any patients of McCrory's?'

'No. I have no idea who they were.'

'You never visited the house when he had patients?'

'No.'

'Do you know who his friends were? Did you see him with anyone?'

'Only with Mr Lee.' Rabinowicz spread his hands, palms up, and smiled ruefully. 'But what a business it is,' he said. 'To be cut to pieces by the Indians.'

'Not cut to pieces. Stabbed and mutilated.' I got up. 'But not necessarily by Indians.'

'You think it might be somebody else?' Rabinowicz had risen to show me out, but he paused for a minute. 'You're an educated man, Sergeant, are you not?'

'I hope so.'

'So you know your history. People will say no civilised man could do such a thing – only a savage, they'll say. But ask any Jew and he will remind you that civilised men, even Christian men, or Jews themselves, are as capable of savagery as the Indians.'

On my way back to the courthouse, I visited the subscription library. There were no books whatsoever on the Tsimhian or any Indians North of Vancouver Island, though one book mentioned that the Tsimshian occupied some 200 miles of coast and coastal islands, from opposite the Northern tip of Vancouver Island almost all the way to Alaska. They were thought to be cousins of the Haida of the Queen Charlotte Islands. Both tribes were savage, prone to sudden raids on their neighbours by canoe, bringing back scores of severed heads, slaves, and goods. The Tsimshian were divided into various sub-tribes, often warring among themselves. Their language was different from that of the Kwagiutl, their Southern neighbours, but similar to that of the Interior Tsimshian who lived in the mountains up the rivers. In a booklet put out by Christian missionaries, I was reminded that the Reverend Duncan had reinstalled his mission at Mektakatla, and was building a church. The first mission had been attacked and many of its converts slaughtered so that it had to be abandoned. But Duncan was resolute that this time the medicine men, who incited the Tsimshian to dog-eating and cannibalism, and other depraved practices and Satanic orgies, would not prevail. Duncan also had the help of the HBC, with whom most Indians traded for the sake of better potlatch feasts, and which had established a monopoly.

The information was relatively useless. Mektakatla was well over a hundred miles North of Tsalaks anyway.

At the end of the afternoon I returned to the courthouse. There I read an autopsy report from Dr Powell who had examined the alienist's corpse. The report detailed the various stabs, slashes, and mutilations, and concluded as Parry had done on the spot, that no single one of them was sufficient to have caused death. The stab near the collarbone had missed arteries and only nicked the top of the lung. The stab below the ribs had penetrated the spleen. McCrory had bled to death as a result of this and the other wounds. Death might have taken twenty minutes or more.

I visited the cells. Seeds greeted me from his office which commanded a view of the row. 'Your Indian chief is having a hard time. Lucky he don't understand English. They call him a filthy savage and worse. Them bastards. He's all right. I give him to eat, though he won't take any. Won't talk neither. You know, he's not like other murderers I've had in here. They're always whiners, self-pitying, excusing themselves, blaming other people for egging them on, or the drink they've taken, or even the victim for having 'asked for it'. Wiladzap has dignity. He's probably killed plenty in his time, he's an Injun after all, but he's not fretting. I don't know as he did this one. Look for yourself.'

I walked past the cages where my chain gang were confined in pairs, playing cards or chattering. I knew I had earned their respect, insofar as they were capable of it, by working hard with them on the bridge. So when one of them called out, inevitably, 'Constable! Gee, I see you're a Sergeant now. Anyway, when you gonna settle that Injun prince? Need a hand in stringing him up?' I turned with the intention of giving them a brief sermon – what had been called at my school some 'pi-jaw' – adopting my vocabulary to its recipients although aware that my articulation was still English, which they would find prissy.

'Look here, fellows. Nobody knows the Indian did anything. He's just here on suspicion. He hasn't even been charged yet.'

'Yes he has,' Seeds interrupted from behind him. 'He was charged this afternoon, with murder, by the Comissioner.'

'Well, he hasn't been found guilty,' I said angrily. 'And until he is,' I said to the cells, 'I'd advise you to lay off.'

I walked to the end cell. Wiladzap was curled up in his bed in a grey blanket – the only place in which he was out of sight of the prisoners in the adjacent cell – but facing toward the cage door. His black eyes, slightly narrowed, were watching me.

I said, 'Nika mamook elahan nesika?' ('I do anything for you?')

Wiladzap did not answer.

'I already told him he could send out for things,' said Seeds from behind my elbow. 'If there's anything he wants special, I mean. Or maybe clothes. I offered him prison clothes but he turned up his nose at them, you might say. So long as he pays for it. Do his people have money? Anyway, my jargon ain't so good, so maybe you can explain again.'

'I'm sure his people have at least some money. Anyway, I'll guarantee his expenses for anything he needs – up to £20 or so,' I said, thinking of the remains of the money I had brought from England. I went on to explain to Wiladzap what the jailer had said, and that I could advance funds for anything Wiladzap needed.

Wiladzap said nothing for a few moments. Then he said quietly, 'Nika pittuk, tamala wawa.' ('I think, tomorrow talk.') But 'tamala' for Indians could mean tomorrow, next week, or never.

'Kloshe,' I said. ('Good.') I left Wiladzap to his thoughts, and followed Seeds back to his office apartment. I was surprised Seeds had been so understanding.

'Where have you been all day?' Seeds asked.

'On the job.'

'All hell bust loose around here. People from the newspapers, rubber-neckers. That's why the Commissioner charged him. It was getting too hot. Everybody screaming something should be done fast. He left this note for you.'

Seeds passed me a folded piece of paper, sealed with a wafer. I ripped the wafer with my thumb nail.

'Dear Hobbes: I look forward to your reports. Keep at it. You have *carte blanche*. It was necessary to place a charge, as you will have heard. But it will take several weeks at least until trial. Normally would take months, but much pressure to act. Yours truly, Augustus Pemberton.'

Nice of the old boy, I thought. It was Pemberton's way of saying that his own mind was still open.

'Then there's this news from England,' Seeds remarked.

'What news?'

'It was in the paper. By electric telegraph. The parliament in London have abolished public executions. But it don't go down well here. This Colony ain't a drawing room. What's the point of having a good hanging judge like Mr Begbie if the hanging's done sneaky, in the middle of the night or sometime when nobody can see it? I remember the last one – in '63, right outside this door. Three Injuns, Cowitchans, they was. They'd massacred three settlers on Saltspring, and the daughter of one, a fine girl though she was already married. They stripped her clothes off and cut her up something horrible, then tied a piece of a stove to her hair and threw her in the bay. We found the body. Yup, they hanged all three. They just go crazy, Injuns, from time to time. It needs an example. Why, even old Freezy knew that when he had one of his squaws' head chopped off on the beach. Anyway the Commissioner says the Legislature is goin' to debate it soon as possible, most likely to pass a law keeping executions public here. Good thing too, though not so good for the chief. But on second thoughts, who wants to be hanged sneaky-like, in the middle of the night? Myself I'd rather go out in a blaze of glory.'

'I see what you mean.'

I felt hopeless. The timing was not good. I could imagine one of the Legislature's vituperative debates, Amor de Cosmos – originally Bill Smith from Nova Scotia and the leader of a pro-Canadian sentiment – haranguing about public safety, invoking the 'Vox Populi', the voice of the people which of course spoke through him, bewailing the foul murder of a 'prominent medical man'. And everyone afraid of offending 'our American cousins, sons of a common English mother – or rather, common sons of an English mother...' I was tired. I did not give a damn for Wiladzap, the 'lucky in hunting', who had probably lopped the heads off innocent men in pirate raids. Still, I wanted to know the truth.

Yet all the while Lukswaas is in the back of my mind. I looked at Wiladzap and I wanted to help him – for her sake. At the same time I hated him for having her as his wife. He was so sure of himself when he said she would not make 'bebe bebe' with McCrory. He trusts her. Why should he? She was as open with me as if we were free to be friends. I could swear she responded to my interest in her. But she is a savage. They think differently. But how could she be so fresh with me – fresh as a girl?

Now I think of the forbidden thing. My mother. She was not quite faithful to my father. No, to be honest she was not faithful. Mr Aubrey, my father's curate, a hard-drinking, fox-hunting man with a large private income, ten years younger than my father, a frivolous man who once told me he didn't believe a word of the scriptures but it was the duty of a gentleman to promulgate them, they gave a necessary order to the minds of men. (Not women, he didn't mention them). Such a contrast to my dear old irascible father who was always ready to thunder on about God's word, and as good as gold: he would beat the bounds of his several parishes once a year as if they were so many folds and he God's sheep-dog, barking around the sheep and lambs to make sure they lived their ordained lives as he lived his. Why had my mother married him? – gay and light as she was, daughter of a baronet, from a family who had always enjoyed life, and in previous centuries had shown few signs of morality. Not for his money: he had little. I wonder if it was because she knew in herself that if she did not marry a very good man she would go to ruin. And she played the game of being the parson's wife. Until Aubrey came along. Not that there were any obvious signs between them – nothing for my father to notice. Nor Henry, absorbed in his own pursuits – hunting with Aubrey, for that matter, when he could get hold of a good mount. (We could never have afforded a hunter.) But I noticed. Well, I couldn't help it. At the age of fourteen I was out walking on the downs under the sound of the skylarks and making a private study of the various barrows and stone piles from prehistoric times: there was one long barrow I could crawl along, first between two sagging portal stones, then along a dusty tunnel between upright stones with slabs across for a roof, then where the tunnel had fallen in I could climb out through a hole to the top of the barrow, about half way along. And one day I had sat a long time in the barrow, just below the hole, my back against an upright stone, trying to recreate in my mind the druids of the stone age – while at the same time knowing that one theory about such barrows was that they were merely storage chambers or 'souterrains' for storing grain. No, I believed the other theory – based on the discoveries of charred bones in similar barrows – that they were tombs for the victims of sacrifice. And I heard laughter above me, through the hole, and the voices of my mother and of Aubrey. I sat as if frozen and listened. Eventually the voices moved away.

That evening I asked my mother what she had been doing at the barrow with Mr Aubrey. I should explain that my mother and I were close. We could talk of anything. She was what German theologians would call a Freidenker – a free thinker. She had even said to me once that when I grew up I would decide for myself whether or not I believed in Christianity, and that for herself, she had decided she did not – but that she loved my father dearly so she was prepared to believe for his sake. So I said, 'If you love my father so dearly, what were you doing laughing with Mr Aubrey on the barrow?'

She went pale. She was always pink-cheeked, so that was an event. But she looked me straight in the eye (mine and my father's and Henry's are blue but hers are brown) and she said 'I've fallen in love with Mr Aubrey, that's why. But you will have guessed that, so why should I hide it? But I do want to hide it from your father. Nothing will come of it.'

But eventually, about a year later, something did come of it. I don't know exactly what. But she was right, I can guess. Henry was staying with friends when it all blew up so I was the one who overheard, distantly echoing, their night-time arguments. In the day-time they were like ghosts: my jovial elderly father grey-faced and sad, my lighthearted mother –grey-faced and sad. I even heard her say to him – and it consoled me, somehow, for the old boy's sake – 'Even as a lover he is nothing like you, he is just a ball of fluff that wisps away in the wind. He is nothing. But I wanted some lightness. We are so serious, you and I. We sit every evening discussing the meaning of life. And I love you for it, a thousand times more than him. He is nothing. You know I stopped it even before you found out. It's over now, believe me.'

He did believe her. They reconciled. Mr Aubrey resigned his post 'for private reasons' – and took up a parish in London. Some months later he was found dead in his rectory, having drunk, it was said, three bottles of brandy in quick succession.

I suppose my mother is a powerful woman. She and my father appear close. She has even become a pious believer in the church. But sometimes I think she is happier than he is. In another context, some while ago, when he and I were discussing some piece of bad behaviour – well, I might as well write it down, the bad behaviour was an echo of my mother's, a village woman who had run off with a tranter, a man who transported goods between the local villages, then returned to her husband – my father said, using a cliché, unusually for him, 'A man can forgive but he will never forget.'

Perhaps this is why I am a prig. I don't want to live through that sort of pain. I don't want to ignore it – to forgive and forget – or whatever Henry would do. Perhaps elder sons take their own way, like him, and younger ones observe and reflect more. When I marry, I have always told myself, it will be someone whom I trust, it will be for ever. How childish, perhaps. And here I am, in love with another man's wife.

11

Mrs Larose received me in a corner of the Hotel Argyle's lobby, which when no guests were about she used as her own sitting room. 'How nice to see you again, Mr Hobbes. I was just having a glass of wine for my 'elevenses' – old fashioned of me, I know, but will you join me?' She poured me a glass of Madeira from a cut glass decanter.

It was indeed an old fashioned but respectable custom to have a glass of wine at eleven, accompanied usually by toast, which was not in evidence, besides which it was scarcely past ten. The Irish Rose was somewhat flushed, even more talkative than usual, and obviously nervous.

'What can I do for you?' she asked. 'I do hope all my permits and licenses are in order.'

'Of course. I just wanted to ask you a few questions about something else. As you may know, we still have a number of loose ends to tie up about the death of Dr McCrory…'

'I knew that was it!' Mrs Larose almost wailed. 'Oh the poor man. I shall miss him so!'

This was more than I had hoped. 'You knew him well, then?'

'Indeed I did. Or at least as well as any patient knows her doctor. He gave me a great deal of help, Mr Hobbes, and now I don't know what I shall do.'

'I'm sorry to hear it. May I ask if you have been ill?'

'Nerves, Mr Hobbes. The vapours. Melancholia. Whatever it may be called: a sense of the ineluctable complexity of life. It is difficult for a widow, in middle age – past the half century!' She paused, as if for an interruption.

'I don't believe it,' I said dutifully.

'To do the work of both a man and a woman, in managing a hotel through difficult times.'

'It must be. I admire your courage. So you became a patient of Dr McCrory's?'

'I did. I went to his lectures and I was impressed by the man. An original thinker. I made an appointment with him, and began a course of treatment.'

'Excuse me, what was the procedure for making an appointment with him?'

'I wrote him a note and sent it round by messenger. He sent a note back with an appointment.'

'And what was the form of his treatment?'

But here the talkative Mrs Larose reached a limit. 'My goodness, Mr Hobbes, you must know better than to ask such a thing. It is a matter of confidence between a lady and her physician.'

'Do excuse me. You need say nothing unless you wish.' I should leave the door open, at least. 'At any rate you found him a competent physician.'

'I did indeed. A most unusual man. Such a brilliant lecturer too.'

'You went with a friend to the lectures, I believe.'

'Mr Hobbes, you have been doing some investigation!' But this did not seem to displease her.

I paused to allow her to fill her glass again, her hand trembling slightly, and to top up my own.

'Mrs Somerville mentioned to me that she had gone with you on one occasion.'

'Ah, you know her? Bella is one of my dearest friends. She always stays here when she comes to town. Yes indeed, we went to the Mechanics' Institute together for the second lecture, on Mesmerism. I had already attended the one on phrenology, so I succeeded in interesting Bella in the other.'

'I don't know much about Mesmerism…'

'Oh, it is a most fascinating science. You see, there is an animal magnetism in all of us! A vital force. Dr McCrory thought it was something akin to electricity – the force that can be generated from a Voltic pile, I think they call it.'

'Voltaic,' I corrected automatically.

'Yes, Voltaic. And in the idea of Dr Mesmer, at least as explained by Dr McCrory, the animal magnetism, or 'Universal Fluid' – that's another name for it…'

'Really?' I was as amused as confused by this litany.

'It becomes blocked in its flow and causes illness. Physical illness, such as palpitations or numbness, but of course nervous conditions as well – melancholy, even some cases of dementia. At least it was Dr McCrory's belief that the task of the physician was not merely to cure the symptoms. No. It was to restore the flow of the vital force, allow the Universal Fluid to regain its natural movement.' She paused, as if stuck in her train of thought.

'Through animal magnetism,' I said.

'Exactly. Through animal magnetism.'

'But how did this work in practice? Was it the Doctor's method to make Mesmeric passes over the patient's body?'

I had studied the copies of Eliotson's *The Zooist* which I had taken from McCrory's office.

'Well, yes. It's the normal procedure in Mesmerism. Look. Hold out your left hand.' Mrs Larose set down her glass on the little table, and held out her own right hand, in a state of fine tremor, palm outwards and facing me.

I put down my glass and rather awkwardly held out my hand in a similar way, not sure if I should touch her.

'No, keep it there,' she said excitedly. 'Merely feel this.'

She approached my palm with her own to within an inch, then withdrew it a few inches. Then she brought it in again, and withdrew it again. She did this a few times, and by the fourth or fifth time I felt a definite tug as she withdrew her hand, as if the palm were attached by an invisible glue, and then a sensation of pressure and warmth when she approached.

'Now you feel it,' she said confidently. '*That* is the animal magnetism.'

She took up her glass again, and I did the same.

'So Dr McCrory did that?' I asked.

'Mr Hobbes, you are very persistent. Yes, at the lecture he had us, his audience, face our next neighbour and do just that little experiment. But of course the Mesmeric treatment goes much further.'

'You would go to him regularly for such treatments?'

'Once a week, in a course of ten.'

'For what fee?'

'It was negotiable. I am not very well off, Mr Hobbes, in spite of what you see.' She swept her hand to indicate the grandiose lobby. 'At times he was willing, even, to defer payment.'

'His accounting procedures were informal, I believe.'

'Indeed so. He told me specifically that he kept no written records – that the nature of his work was strictly confidential. Thus, it was possible to trust him.'

'Do tell me more about the actual procedure in treatment.'

'Mr Hobbes! Oh well, you insist. I shall tell you.' Mrs Larose emptied her glass and poured herself another, forgetting mine. For a moment I felt ashamed. I had excited her into a mood of self revelation. 'First there was a diagnostic procedure,' she said. 'That involved the usual medical things, of course – listening to the heart and lungs, looking at the tongue and eyes and into the ears – as well as a phrenological examination. It was Dr McCrory's belief that through Mesmerism it might be possible even to effect a transformation in the phrenological configuration – I believe that is the word. He had a rather complicated theory about this, involving the "surtures", or some such word, of the skull. We were none of us so hardened in life, he said, as we might think. The Universal Fluid could reinstall itself if we allowed it its way. Sometimes I believe he might prescribe a herb or medicine, to aid in the physical relaxation that would enable the vital force to flow. In my case he prescribed an infusion – a sort of tea not unlike valerian – to be taken in the morning before I came for an appointment. It made me feel a little drowsy, but in full control of my mind and senses. Then in an appointment, or a "session" as he would call it, I, the patient, myself I mean, would lie on the settee while he would sit quietly nearby. I would close my eyes and he would ask me to describe my physical sensations, whether I felt light or heavy, drowsy or alert, warm or cold, and so on. He would then ask if I had any problem in life I wanted to talk about. Sometimes I would talk a little, about my financial difficulties, my responsibilities, my dear, dear departed Mr Larose… Then after a while I would hear Dr McCrory's voice telling me to forget all the troubles of life, to let them float out of my mind, and merely to pay attention to my natural physical functions, the rise and fall of my breathing, and the beating of my heart. Oh, Mr Hobbes, do you know, lying there I could feel things that in the daily rush of existence I would suppress? I could feel the beating of my heart, the pulsing of my blood.'

Mrs Larose paused in a sort of rapture. Her eyes were looking at the ceiling and had become glazed.

'Then the doctor would do magnetic passes over my body,' she went on. 'I could feel it. He would not touch me, but I could feel the air move over my head, my chest, down over my body and my legs. After a while I could feel currents of the magnetism, the vital force!' She stopped, and lowered her eyes to look at me.

'And this was restorative,' I said encouragingly.

'My word, yes! When I left I felt I was walking on air!'

'And that was the treatment.'

'Yes. I have told you all. No, not all.' Mrs Larose's lined and powdered face suddenly blushed. 'I shall tell you, Mr Hobbes. You may find this shocking, but I assure you it was beneficial and almost miraculous.' She closed her eyes. 'I would be lying there, my eyes closed, like this,' she said in a dreamy voice. 'Then the doctor would say, or at least he did the first time: "There is a way in which you may receive a *charge*" – that was his word – "a charge of the vital force. Do not be afraid. There is a place in a man where this force resides most intensely, in a sort of Voltic'—I mean Voltaic—'pile. Reach out your hand,' he said, 'and *hold*.' I reached out my hand and he guided it very gently then he said, '*hold*.' And I held, and... You know what Mr Hobbes?' Mrs Larose's eyes sprang open, and fixed mine blazingly as she leaned forward and took my hand and squeezed it with hard but warm fingers. 'You know what? It was electric! Like the sort of shock you get from an electricity machine in a fun fair, only stronger – like a surge of the magnetic fluid which rushed up my arm and into my whole body, buzzing through me!' She let go of my hand but remained leaning forward and staring into my eyes.

'From what, Mrs Larose?' I said, my heart for some reason pounding. 'What did you 'hold'?'

'You're a man, Mr Hobbes,' she said daintily. 'As a lady I don't know all the words for these things. His – what do you call them? – his testicules? His testicules, Mr Hobbes. They were electric!'

Mrs Larose sat back in her chair and looked dreamily at me.

'But you're not saying,' I said cautiously, thinking of the lambskin sheaths, 'that Dr McCrory had congress with you?'

'Never! I assure you there was nothing *immoral* about it, nothing whatsoever.' She looked at me serenely, her face composed, Irish-looking in its oval shape and the blue of the eyes, with an expression of self-righteous purity.

'Thank you,' I said. 'I appreciate your telling me. So, to sum up, you would declare yourself satisfied with the treatment.'

'I don't know what I'm going to do without it!' Mrs Larose said in sudden anguish. 'Should I go to San Francisco, or what? I can feel my nerves coming back on me.'

'Did Dr McCrory have colleagues in San Francisco?'

'Not that he mentioned. But it will be a long time before somebody of his calibre – genius I might say – comes to this godforsaken place.' She looked around in sudden anger.

'Did you meet any other patients, or know who they were?'

'It was all confidential. I would have never met another patient, nor wanted to.'

'No one in the waiting room when you came out?'

'The appointments were at intervals. The Doctor once said that he had to concentrate his energies religiously before an appointment, in meditation, almost like a prayer to the Vital Force. No, the only person I ever saw in the waiting room was Mr Firbanks, the priest – or whatever you call him, I'm Catholic myself – from the new church out on Cedar Hill Road. But I doubt it was for an appointment. The doctor was quite surprised to see him, though he knew him. I assume it was a friendly visit.'

'No one else? How about Mrs Somerville? Was she also a patient?'

'I hope not!' Mrs Larose said vehemently, then gathered her composure. 'I mean, she would certainly have told me if she was. We're good friends and confidantes, one to the other. I know the Doctor visited on Sundays out at her Farm. He started calling there after the lecture… I dare say he liked the society.' Here Mrs Larose seemed definitely miffed.

'You mean the young ladies?'

'Oh, I don't think he was *that* kind of person. No indeed. Myself, you know how I saw him? As a priest almost. A priest of life. I only meant he might like the feeling of family, which of course I could not provide. My own children are all grown up and gone and left me.'

'I wondered if perhaps the young ladies might have been patients of the Doctor,' I said. 'I've heard the eldest one suffers from melancholia.'

'Poor Aemilia. She never got over her father's death, poor wee thing. But she'd not go to the Doctor. She's too independent, that one. Anyway,' her eyes narrowed. 'That's another good man killed by the Indians, the dirty savages. Major Somerville, God rest his soul, though I never knew him. And now they've murdered the Doctor! Tell me, Mr Hobbes.' She leaned forward, her eyes burning. 'What did the devils do to him? I've heard they cut off his…' She stopped.

'You don't need to believe everything you hear,' I said soothingly, seriously worried that the news of what had happened to the magic organ of the Doctor might unhinge Mrs Larose. 'He was stabbed to death.'

'And what are you going to do about it?' she said shrilly. 'I'll tell you, Mr Hobbes, hanging is too good for that devil. If I could get my hands on him, I'd crucify him!'

With this outburst, she seemed spent. She looked at me numbly.

I only had one more question: 'What were you doing last Wednesday afternoon?'

'You mean when he was kilt? I was here. Where else?'

'Was anyone with you?'

'I dare say the boy was, and the kitchen slut, though they're in and out. As you can see, the summer season has not yet come.'

I thanked the Irish Rose for her patience, and after begging a sample of the alienist's tea, which she gave me in a small paper bag, I took my leave.

12

MCCRORY CLEAN RECORD HERE BUT LEFT SEPTEMBER 1868
BEFORE SUIT FOR ALIENATION OF AFFECTIONS BY JOHN
REYNOLDS HUSBAND OF PATIENT ELIZABETH REYNOLDS CAME TO
TRIAL STOP SIGNED KNOWLES SAN FRANCISCO POLICE.

So McCrory had been an alienist in more ways than one... I wrote a memorandum to Inspector Wilson, the man who was in charge of police paper work, to ask him to set the long procedure in motion of sending to San Francisco for any pre-trial documents in connection with the alienation of affections case. Meanwhile the question nagged at me. Who had been the alienist's mistress? Or, more crudely, with whom did he use the lambskins? With how many women? A jealous husband might be capable, I supposed, of murder and even of mutilation. But this brought me, sadly, back to Wiladzap. It was known and freely admitted that McCrory had gone into the forest with Lukswaas. Why look further? Still – I forced myself to consider the case in the most sordid of terms – no white man would bother to use a contraceptic agent with a squaw, no more than with a prostitute. Or did they protect against syphillis, with which Indians were supposed to be riddled? I did not know. Embarrassed at my own ignorance, I made a note to consult a medical man about this. Unfortunately there was nothing about contraceptics in the *Medical Physiology* I had taken from McCrory's.

I had been sitting in a small room I used as an office. I decided I should visit Wiladzap, who had not spoken for some days. As I arrived at the cells, Seeds greeted me with, 'Here you are. He's been askin' for you. Only says one thing, though he says it in different ways: 'Hop', 'Hob', 'Hops', even 'Cop' – ha, ha.'

Wiladzap was sitting on the bed, wrapped in his chilcat, looking at the wall of his cage.

'Let's bring him into the yard,' I said. 'He'll need some fresh air. I'll talk to him there.'

'He won't come,' said Seeds. 'Least not with the others, and I ain't goin' to ast him by hisself. First exercise time he was gonna come out of the cell

– must of thought I was lettin' him lose or somp'n. Then when he saw what was up he went straight back in.'

'Does he eat?'

'Nope. Only drinks water. I dunno how he does it. Five days, it makes. He'll be dead before we get him to the rope.'

'I hope not,' I said, then realised that was not quite what I meant.

Wiladzap had clambered rather slowly off the bed. He stood facing me. 'Hops,' he said.

'Klahowya. Chahko copa nika.' ('Hello. Come with me.')

Seeds opened the cage door. This was a safe procedure since the door to the whole row had been locked behind me, and the door out to the exercise yard was directly from the cell block, just beside Wiladzap's cage.

Wiladzap stepped out unsurely, and looked around him, up the row, at the other prisoners who were whiling away their time as always playing cards. Perhaps they knew he had not been eating. He seemed to have lost his value as a source of amusement or contempt, and they ignored him. Seeds opened the door to the yard. This was a stone paved box, thirty feet or so square, within two windowless walls of the courthouse and two outside walls twelve feet high and set with spikes.

I ushered Wiladzap out in front of me. Seeds remained in the doorway, unabashedly watching and ready to listen.

Wiladzap walked into the centre of the yard, rolled his head back, and looked straight upward into the sky which, since it was noon of a clear day, was dazzling. He began rolling his eyes around as if to exercise them. His face had become thinner and paler, giving it a dusty look. He lowered his head after a while and looked at me.

'Wiladzap iskum shantie,' he said. ('Wiladzap get song.') He then uttered a short chant of words in his own language, still looking at me. He said, in Chinook again, that I must take the song to his people at the camp. They would understand it.

I asked whether the song would make any trouble.

'Wake.' ('No.')

I pulled out my notebook and pencil. Wiladzap nodded his head. Then he repeated his chant very slowly, phrase by phrase – or perhaps it was verse by verse. There were in effect four phrases, beginning something like, in my attempt at transliteration: 'Dinarhnawraw handehabewaw angurhkurhl tramawhee…' I took it down patiently.

Wiladzap moved round to look at what I had written. Then he smiled. 'Shantie,' he said, pointing a finger at it. I could not help being pleased, and thinking how strange it was that the Chinook word for song, 'shantie,' went back through the 'shanty' of English sailors, to the French 'chanter' to the Latin 'cantare.' I also smiled. Then, to my surprise, Wiladzap translated the song into Chinook, which I also wrote down. Transmitted across the simplified, almost infantile medium of Chinook, it meant something like: 'The spirit of the house of bees is punishing my body. I am stung by them but they make honey. The bear cares little for the stings of the bees when his muzzle is sticky. The bear in summer must often sleep a long way from his den.'

I asked for no further explanation, in case this would be an insult. I repeated my earlier question about the song not leading to trouble.

Wiladzap shook his head vigorously. 'Tsalak mitlite alki,' he said ('Tsalak stay a while.') Then he would say no more. He stood in the sun and began stretching his arms. He looked almost happy.

On impulse, I asked whether he would like to eat and drink.

Wiladzap said yes.

Pleased, I turned to ask Seeds to provide whatever food Wiladzap wanted.

I stood for a while watching Wiladzap doing nothing except stretching his arms and occasionally throwing his head back to look into the sky and roll his eyes. I explained to Wiladzap that it was time for him to go back to his cell, and he complied without a word. He did not look at me again, although I said goodbye.

As I left the cell block I ran into Superintendent Parry, strangely agitated.

'Look who's here,' Parry said.

Sitting in a row on the bench along the vestibule wall, with two big baskets at their feet, were three Indians. At first glance they looked ordinary, in the usual HBC blankets, of the dullest colour, which was grey, and bare legged except for moccasins. The middle one was Lukswaas, the others a man and woman whom I vaguely recognised from the camp, the man because he was unusually thick set and well muscled, and the woman because she was young, small and quite pretty. All looked at me seriously.

Parry, who was not without heart, muttered, 'Don't know whether to laugh or cry.' He probably realised, as I did, that the blankets were a disguise, for safety. 'They brought food,' he said. 'Must be dried salmon, by the smell. Mamook nanitsh!' he barked ('Make see!').

All three Indians got up. The man stood still while Lukswaas and the other woman opened the baskets, which had been smeared with dirt and dust, presumably to disguise their distinctive designs. I became absorbed in watching Lukswaas bending forward over her basket. She is so fine in her movements. Wisps of her thick hair fell forward from her braids. I noticed her earrings again, of abalone, pure mother of pearl. Everything about her fascinated me. Silly ass, I told myself, as my heart melted. Parry and I moved forward to inspect the contents of the basket: a mass of damp grass, which Lukswaas's nimble fingers folded apart as dexterously as if it had been a cloth, to reveal little bundles of green and white shoots about six inches long. I asked in Chinook what they were.

She replied softly that they came from a tall plant that grew in the water and had a brown head.

'Reeds?' I said to Parry.

'Cat tail rushes, probably. I've heard that Indians eat them.'

We turned our attention to the other basket, which was packed with sides of small salmon, smoked hard and brown and emitting a pungent but agreeable smell.

'All right,' Parry said. 'We'll send the baskets down. Seeds can dish out the food regularly. That is, if the Indian is eating.'

'He just said he was ready to,' I said, wondering at the coincidence.

'She can't see him,' Parry said, as if anticipating a question from me. 'The Commissioner and I discussed it. It would be too great a risk to permit visits, because of the 'voice of the people,' as that rabble-rouser De Cosmos is always calling it. Maybe after the Indian is sentenced.'

'That won't be for a while,' I said.

'We still can't take the risk. Halo nanitsh Wiladzap!' Parry shouted at the Indians ('No see Wiladzap!'). He added, more kindly but still in a shout, that maybe one day they could.

Without a word, in a mute accepting way, they turned to go, leaving their baskets. They had not even dared, it seemed, to make sure they would be delivered.

'Nesika iskum muckamuck Wiladzap,' I said (We take food Wiladzap).

The Indians paused to listen. 'Mahse,' Lukswaas said ('Thanks' – from the French 'Merci'). Then they left.

I thought of calling them back and giving them Wiladzap's 'Song,' but it did not seem right. I had been asked to deliver it to the whole Indian band. So I let these three go. I did not mention the song as such to Parry, but said, 'The chief gave me a message, verbally, that I should give to the Indians at Cormorant Point, about them having to stay there.'

'That's all?'

'Yes. But of course it was said in Indian language – about the bees staying in their hive. I thought I'd ride out and give it to them. At the same time there's someone I want to question out Cedar Hill Road.'

'You're on a wild goose chase, lad,' said Parry. 'Our goose is a tame one now, and we've got him in a coop.'

13

I wanted to leave the Indians time to walk back to Cormorant Point. I planned to arrive there in the late afternoon. First I would conduct two interviews.

I walked over to Quattrini's warehouse near the wharves. Quattrini imported vegetables from California during the winter, and exported them from the Saanich farms to various points South during the summer. I had to sit and wait in the front office for a while, as he was hunted down from somewhere in the warehouse or on the quay. Eventually he arrived, a very different figure from the gentleman in his Sunday best at Orchard Farm, now dressed in a checked shirt and dungarees, wearing a straw hat and smoking a cigar shaped like a long black twig.

'What can I do for you, son?' Before I could get up, Quattrini had sat down on a chair beside me, slapping me on the knee with a big hand, whose back was covered with curly black hair.

'Can we have a private talk?' I glanced at the office clerk.

'Run along, kid. Take a break.'

The clerk scurried out of the room. Quattrini had lifted his hand from my knee, but was still sitting very close, so that I was enveloped in cigar smoke. 'Smoke?' Quattrini asked, reaching into his pocket.

'No thanks. I don't want to take much of your time…'

'Take as much as you want,' Quattrini interrupted, his manner indicating that his time was very valuable indeed. 'I'm easy.'

'I'm questioning everyone who knew Dr McCrory,' I began.

'That dude? I hardly knew him. Just social-like, out at the orchard.' Quattrini's voice softened and his eyes grew moist.

'Just on Sundays?'

'Yup. Wouldn't have gone outa my way to see him any other day. But I was willin' enough to talk to him at the farm. You know, for a dear friend's sake…' Quattrini winked.

'You mean Mrs Somerville?'

'Bella. Finest woman that ever walked the earth, bar one – my wife Philomena, God bless her.'

'Passed away?' I ventured.

'Passed away,' Quattrini echoed. 'Yup. I'm a lonely man. My kids are grown up. One o' my girls married a Nigger, Jeroboam, guy who hauls freight, but the Niggers don't do too well these days, so I got him haulin' for me now. Boy, that heathen keeps *her* busy raisin' picaninnies, so I don't see much of her. Two of my boys are in Frisco learnin' the business with my brothers. Another, the kid, is helpin' around here. But I need a bit of company all right. And of course mosta the women in this town are you know what – we call 'em in Italian 'putanas'. Hell, you know Italian. Or else they're stuck up and hoity-toity. But when I first saw Bella I knew she was for me. She's been attached to that dead husband of hers for nigh on ten years. But not stuck up at all. She's a lady, of course. An English guy like you maybe knows lots of them. Not Franco Quattrini! But she's friendly. And what a looker!' Quattrini's eyes moistened again.

'And Dr McCrory?'

Quattrini scowled. 'A ladies' man. But you know what, I wonder if a guy like that really likes women. He likes himself! Me, I don't mind myself, but I don't pretend to be somethin' I ain't.' He caught my eye. 'Except on Sundays I dress up and act dignified. Why not? I can afford it. Not from this business here, though. I can tell you, if I hadn't of kept some business in Frisco I'd be broke. This place is goin' downhill so fast nothin'll save it except annexation – fast.'

'Did you know any of Dr McCrory's patients?'

'No. Why would I?'

'How do you think he ended up at Orchard Farm?'

'Well, he didn't *end* there. Some Injun got him. Probably pokin' his nose in where he wasn't wanted. They say he was doin' some squaw, and her husband got him. I don't believe it. Sure, he'd preen himself in front of a woman, like any ladies' man, but he wouldn't *do* nothin', not even a squaw.'

Quattrini seemed sure of this. Perhaps he had to believe that McCrory's presence at Orchard Farm had been harmless.

'So that's it?' he said, standing up. 'Darned if I can say any more about the guy. I know Bella went with that addle-brained friend of hers, Mrs Larose, to one of his lectures. But you can't stop women doin' these things.' He rolled his eyes. 'That's how he latched onto her and started goin' out there on Sundays. Good riddance, I say. No use wastin' any time on him.

If some Injun did it, then string him up. That's the law. But don't waste any time on McCrory.'

Time was clearly important to Quattrini. And not thinking about what he did not want to think about. I thanked him, and let myself be shown to the door. We shook hands. Then Quattrini laughed. 'I forgot to say, I thought you done well on 'mi pungichi, mi stuzzichi.' A tormented lover! Gee, I regretted for one moment bringin' that book. But they'll never take it into their pretty heads to figure out that kinda thing.'

I went to the stables near the courthouse and hired a horse, a seedy-looking roan mare. I mounted and set off up Fort Street and out of town.

I overtook the three Indians on Spring Ridge, trudging along, not turning their heads at the sound of my horse's hooves on the dusty road. I passed them, then reined in and turned around in my saddle. They stopped walking and looked at me impassively. Even Lukswaas' face was dirty and looked dull. They must be tired, having come up the hill in the heat. I called out to them in Chinook that I would be at the camp, with words to say, before the sun went low in the sky. They said nothing. My mare let out a load of droppings onto the ground. I pulled her head around and gave her a kick. She started off with a jerk and I let her break into a canter along the ridge until after a dip the road reached the Cedar Hill fork. I rode along steadily for half an hour or so at the horse's walking pace, feeling my tunic sticking to my back through my shirt.

Firbanks the curate was not at the house where he lodged. The landlady said he would be at St Mark's. I rode the few hundred yards further and hitched my horse to the rail outside the West door of the church. I opened the door. The church was empty and looked more stark than ever. But the altar, with its white and gold cloth for Ascension, the lectern, pulpit and chancel rail of polished oak, all made me homesick. I resisted an impulse to kneel down and pray. Instead I thought of my parents whom, in spite of my differences with them, I missed. I stayed for a while in the church, half hoping that Firbanks would turn up, half not. Then I went out into the sunshine again. I walked around to the North side of the church, to the graveyard, below a tumble of mossy rocks beneath fir trees.

Firbanks was lounging on the grass in the shade above one of the rocks.

He sat up when he saw me. He was smoking a pipe and had taken his jacket off: it was folded carefully beside him. The sleeves of his white shirt were rolled up and he wore no cravat. He still looked like a porcelain angel, but one more capable of falling from grace than the Sunday one. He greeted me in a languid, not very friendly voice. 'Hobbes. What are you doing here?'

'On duty,' I said. 'I want to question you.'

'Really. About what?' Firbanks looked down his nose at me. I was at a disadvantage standing below the rock looking upward. 'Have you got a warrant, or whatever you need?'

'Don't be silly,' I said, picking my way up around the rock and sprawling down beside the curate, in what I hoped was a rather brutal manner. 'Even in England I could require you to come to the police station to assist me in my inquiries. Would you like to come back with me or shall we talk here?'

'It's all right here. Sorry, I didn't mean to be rude. But your charging around the corner like that gave me a surprise. What can I do for you, old chap?' The bonhomie of this last phrase was so forced that Firbanks betrayed himself by blushing. What an odd mixture, I thought, of the crass and the sensitive.

'Where are you from in England?' I asked, stretching myself lazily, to show I had all the time in the world.

'Shrewsbury. You know it?'

'Not well.' The heart of England. Green rolling hills. Where Charles Darwin had come back to after his five year voyage on the Beagle, concluding that it was the most beautiful place in the world. 'Where Darwin grew up.'

'To Shrewsbury's eternal shame. That atheist.'

'Cambridge?' I asked, changing the subject. Unfortunately even Darwin had gone to Cambridge. I had mentally 'placed' Firbanks at Cambridge.

'Oxford.'

'Really? What college?' The usual question.

'Keble.'

I tried to keep a straight face. Keble! Founded a few years previously, a gothic monstrosity in red and yellow brick with corridors like a prison, a sort of collegiate railway station chock-a-block with evangelically inclined students of 'Divvers,' as Divinity was known.

'You?' Firbanks asked.

'Univ' – meaning University College. But I felt one of my characteristic bursts of shame at playing social games. If I had been the type to blush, I would have.

My eyes caught something moving at the bottom of the churchyard. The heads of the three Indians trudging along without a glance to either side.

'Indians,' I said. 'Have you been to see them?'

Firbanks watched the heads disappear behind the oaks. 'You mean the Tsimshian at Margaret Bay? I don't think, by the way, that those are they. They must be Saanich who've strayed off the beaten track. Yes, I did go and see the Tsimshian actually, a few weeks ago. They'd been coming along this road selling things, and everyone knew they were out at Margaret Bay, on Cormorant Point. So I walked over to see if I could do a little missionizing.'

'What?' I had not thought of something so simple as this. My question had been a shot in the dark.

'On duty,' Firbanks said smugly. 'It's my duty to try and convert the heathen, and I do.'

'You convert them, or you try?'

'Both, of course. I spend a deal of time among the Saanich on the Inlet, and among the Songhees of course.'

'You speak Chinook?'

'Goodness yes. And some Salishan.' This was the local language.

'Tsimshian?'

'Unfortunately not. Nobody speaks it, except Mr Duncan up at Mektakatla – and that's three hundred miles North of here, as you know.'

'How did these Tsimshian receive you?'

'Not very warmly. They take a dim view of Mr Duncan, somewhat to my surprise, although I know a few wretched tribes resist conversion. So as soon as I opened my mouth, they announced I was a "Mektakatla man", and I was not welcome.'

'Were they that rude? I find it hard to think they'd say you were not welcome. I doubt if there is even a way of saying it in Chinook.'

'In a manner of speaking they did. They turned their backs and went on with their business.'

'So you gave up.'

'Of course not. I began telling them in my fluent Chinook that their souls, their miserable little tum tums, would burn in Hell. Everything, even the mind, even an opinion, is a "heart" to them. So the soul is a tum

tum. With perhaps a "wind" or breath blowing through it – the "spirit" of course. Anyway I told them that their souls might go and burn up in the great "piah" of the "diaub", or devil. Hellfire is usually enough to get their attention. But for these devils it didn't work. I'm not sure why. Perhaps Mr Duncan's approach is not suitable for all of them.'

'What is his approach?' I was curious, although I disliked Firbanks' cynicism, which was of a kind Divinity students often affected among themselves.

'Plenty of hard work, cleanliness, no firewater – sorry, no 'piah chuck chuck' – no fornication, no nakedness, no eating of dogs, no eating of humans. They're cannibals, you know, in a rather specific way. At least the chiefs and medicine men are. Normally the eating of dogs, for example, is forbidden because dogs feed on corpse-flesh, which is of course forbidden too. But a really big man will eat dog or human – a slave, of course – from time to time in order to impress his enemies with his capacity to do so foul a deed. It's like their totem poles. You don't see any good ones around here. They are covered with family emblems and crests in the form of faces of animals. But the faces have expressions of terror. Nothing terrifies like terror. Like hellfire! At any rate, Duncan won't even give them the Eucharist. He's afraid it'll make them think Christians are cannibals. 'This is my body, this is my blood.' They might take it as literal encouragement.'

Firbanks would clearly have been happy to ramble on, but I interrupted. 'I've only heard of cannibalism in connection with the Nootka who met Captain Cook, and their chief Maquinna who seems to have been a monster. Maybe it's just a story they put out to impress people. Just as the Eucharist impresses us, without being literal.' In fact I felt sick at the idea Firbanks might have been telling the truth. 'So they kept their backs turned?' I changed the subject abruptly.

'Or laughed. A pretty hardened bunch, I should say. Thoroughly dangerous. People around here keep their doors locked at night, I can tell you, though they say what with the Tyee in jail the Tsimshian may not give any trouble. And with him dead they'll slink away home with their tails between their legs, or be sent home by the Navy. That's what people are waiting for.'

'And you? What do you think about McCrory's death?'

'Not in the least surprising. He should have left well alone.'

'As you did not in your missionizing,' I could not resist saying.

'You misunderstand my duty to God,' Firbanks said coldly. 'Our friend the doctor's duty was only to himself.' His face had taken on a noble cast – the prospective martyr, I thought with disgust.

'You didn't like McCrory?' I asked.

'Like him? No question of like or dislike. I didn't know the man, except at the Somervilles' little afternoon teas.'

'Hellfire,' I said softly, relishing the words. 'Piah diaub. What happens, Firbanks, to the man who lies?'

'What do you mean?' Firbanks' cheeks were burning in two patches surrounded by the usual waxy pale. His eyes, blue and rather pig-like with their very blond lashes, narrowed.

'I know you were a patient of McCrory's.'

'Nonsense. I deny it. Why would I be? What are your grounds for such an assertion?'

'A little birdie told me.' I could not help being nasty with Firbanks. Looking at him quivering finely with panic, like a white mouse, I realised that he was a reflection of something I might have been, or at least had wanted to be. A missionary among the heathen! Although Firbanks had found a comfortable berth at St Marks and was surely a mere dabbler at missionary work. There but for the grace of God go I....

'This is too much,' Firbanks blustered, sitting bolt upright as if riven to the grass.

'I only mean that a lady who had been visiting the Doctor saw you in his waiting room.'

'Damn it, who *was* that woman?' Firbanks burst out. 'There was no carriage or wagon at the door, no horse at the rail. What bad luck! And if I didn't know her, how did she know me? I wasn't wearing my dog collar.'

'Surely you know that people, especially ladies, point out of windows at passers by and say "Who goes there?" "Oh, that's the young curate out at St Mark's. Isn't he handsome?"'

'Actually, it was a social call,' Firbanks said, recovering his self control. 'I'd met the man out at Orchard Farm so I called on him on my way into town one day, to ask a few questions about his practice. I often have occasion to refer parishioners to a doctor.'

'Did you refer any to McCrory?'

'No. But I might have.'

'Let's not beat about the bush,' I said. 'I have the Doctor's medical records.'

One lie justified another, I told myself. Oddly, I felt less compunction about trapping this man through lies than about showing what I really thought of him.

'No you don't,' Firbanks shot back. 'He didn't keep any.'

'That's what *he* said. They are there, the names disguised to be sure. But they can be matched up to you no doubt. Besides, there is Mr Lee.'

'That Celestial! He knows nothing, not a word of English.'

'Wrong again. He's fluent in it.'

'Well, if you know everything, why play with me like this?'

'Because I want to hear it from your own lips. Because the records and Mr Lee's memory are ambiguous. Because I don't want to have to arrest you on grounds of suppressing evidence relevant to a crime,' (I was making this up, although I could indeed arrest anyone without a warrant and justify it later), 'And take you to Dr Helmcken for a medical examination, from which we can match you to McCrory's records.'

'All right. You will have guessed. I've got clap. That's all. Lots of people have it.'

'I imagine so. Where did you get it?'

'Among the Songhees, no doubt.'

'By doing missionary work?'

'Don't be so vile. I got it in the usual way – from fornicating with a squaw.'

'Or squaws?'

'Or squaws. Look, I'm not perfect, Hobbes. Nor are you.'

'How do you know you got it from a squaw? Perhaps you brought it with you from St. Ebbes.'

'Very funny. Anyway, who cares where I got it?'

'There are no signs on your face yet,' I said. 'I thought it spread. Didn't the Jacobean Dean of St Paul's, Dr Donne, write a treatise on "Why doth the pox so undermine the nose?"'

This was too much. Firbanks scrambled to his feet. 'I don't have *syph*,' he said indignantly. 'I have clap – gonhorrea. It's less severe, although it can be the devil to get rid off. And just you wait until clap or something like it gets you. You'll burn in hell too one day.'

'Hellfire! Don't you realise what an evil religion Christianity is? It condemns swathes of people to eternal fire if they don't do what they are told. Have you ever read Ensor's *Janus on Sion?* Christian morality enforces itself through threats of eternal vengeance – chanting that "God is Love" all the while.'

'How dare you talk to me like that?' Firbanks exploded, but his voice sounded thin and nasal. 'If you ever turn up in my church again I'll put you out the door!'

I had overdone it. Ensor's old warhorse of a book had been on one side of the pincers – Darwin being on the other – which had snipped off my Christian faith. 'Did McCrory help you?' I asked, still sprawling on the ground.

'I think so.' Firbanks became calmer, his voice urgent. 'You won't believe this, but the immediate symptoms went away. Of course they do from time to time. But there's something in this animal magnetism business. There really is a kind of force. One feels it in the treatments.'

'You mean you were allowed to touch McCrory's organs of generation?'

'What? Are you mad? Of course not. What kind of a mind do you have? You are more evil than anything in Christianity.'

'Just 'magnetic passes' then?'

'And an infusion of herbs, which I'll take until I run out.'

'None of the usual medical treatments – mercury or what not?'

'Mercury doesn't work in my case.'

'And are you celibate now?'

'None of your business.'

'You could pass it on.'

'There's no need for you to continue with this gratuitous prying.'

'Where were you last Wednesday afternoon?'

'Here. I come to pray and study.'

'What other patients of McCrory's do you know about?'

'None. He was discreet in his appointments.'

'How about the Somervilles?'

'Patients? That's hard to believe. They're not ill.'

'Melancholia.'

'You mean Aemilia? She's just an old maid in the making.'

'And you're paying court to Letitia. Are you sure you should?'

'Shut up!' Firbanks began to pace back and forth. 'Now, of course, you can wreck me', he said between clenched teeth, 'by telling people. But you don't know what it's like. I live in hope. You wouldn't understand that.'

'It's just the hypocrisy I don't like.' I stood up. 'Why be a priest at all if you're going to do such filthy things?'

'A priest must experience life', Firbanks said sanctimoniously, 'in all its squalor. He must share the humble dishes of the poor, walk among them, and yes if necessary, give into their entreaties. He should be unafraid of congress with them at any level. These Indian girls have lived like beasts since childhood, they can only be redeemed from brutality by the knowledge of something higher. Besides: better to marry than burn. Although I'm not married yet I can't pursue my mission for God if I'm burning up with filthy lust: I must get rid of it. How can I give the sacraments if my mind is polluted with these thoughts?'

I supposed this fell under the heading 'the greater the sin, the greater its redemption.' For a moment I thought of my father – that decent clergyman. Or was he like this? Did he have such a secret life? Was he fornicating with the young girls in his parish? No. It was not in his character. This was nothing to do with Christianity, or even hypocrisy. It was all character.

'I hope you don't spread the disease around', I muttered. Then I thought of something. 'Sheaths', I said. 'Does it help to use a sheath, to avoid contracting or passing on a disease?'

'You're naïve, Hobbes. Of course they are prophylactic in that sense. But why would anybody want to use one? I understand they're only used by some American husbands and wives so as to cheat God of his due while amassing material possessions. Contraceptics are profoundly unnatural – against the law of nature, in fact, and the law of God.'

'So you've never used one.'

'Of course not.'

'I suppose that's enough for now. I may talk to you again. Who do you think killed McCrory?'

'That Indian Tyee of course. McCrory got into his woman, that's all. The Tyee might not have minded at first, if McCrory was bringing money or trade goods. He could always drop the wife later, or demote her to number two by marrying a new one. But I assume something went wrong. McCrory must have been too open about it, offended the Indian's pride – something like that. I don't blame McCrory though. She's a peach, that girl. Ladylike almost, though underneath she'll be as foul a slut as the rest of them.'

'Shut up.'

'I see you don't know them, Hobbes – quite the outraged gentleman, eh? They're not ladies, Hobbes: they're devils. They're like the leech in *Solomon*. They'll suck the life out of you. They say that once you've been with a squaw you can never leave them alone. They're filthy, ugly as sin, and as soon ready to kill you as couple with you – but you can't give them up, Hobbes. No.' Firbanks' mouth had developed an ugly twist.

All I wanted to do was leave. I had been doing a good job, I thought, until the subject of Lukswaas came up. Now I was aware of an intolerable sensation, a gnawing pain in my heart and guts. I had been carrying out my interrogations like the clockwork policeman I wanted to be, and as long as I kept talking and listening I could keep this sensation at bay. No, my mind went back to the first time Lukswaas looked at me and my heart stirred, and to her trembling hand as she gave me the purse with its eight silver dollars. I clenched my jaws tight. What a bloody fool. Was this lust? She was another man's wife. Was this love? For a squaw!

'You whited sepulchre!' I said to Firbanks with all the contempt I could muster. But I didn't care a damn for Firbanks and his squalid little life. I turned away, scrambled down the bank, and walked around the edge of the graveyard to the West end of the church, where my horse was standing listlessly at the rail in the shafts of sunlight, which struck down at an angle between the branches of the oaks.

14

Yes, I thought of whether my anger at Firbanks harked back to my anger – or was it jealousy? – at that cursed curate, Aubrey, who had seduced my mother. Or had she seduced him? My head was spinning. No, Firbanks was not at all like Aubrey. By comparison Aubrey was a decent chap – frivolous, but not wicked. Not a fallen angel at least. Should never have been a curate in the first place. But he had a conscience. No, he probably killed himself simply because he could not have my mother. Could I kill myself? I doubt it. I like the world around me too much. I like pursuing this case. I like birdsong, flowers, even the gloomy Douglas firs, the peculiar greenish sunsets behind the serrated mountains to the West of Victoria. Could I kill someone? I could almost kill Firbanks – on impulse, he is such a despicable squirt. But I could hardly plan such a thing. What about mens rea? *The mind in the thing. Whoever killed McCrory could not be convicted unless it was shown that he had the deed in mind. Otherwise he would be committing man-slaughter. Or under the McNaughten Rules, House of Lords, 1843, he would be counted insane. No one I have met so far in this investigation could be called insane. Least of all Wiladzap. If he killed McCrory he must have known he wanted to. Who else could have wanted to?*

I rode slowly down the hill from St Mark's, following Cedar Hill Road along the edge of the so-called Plains – too rough and densely wooded to be a plain by English standards – then after half a mile or so up and along a ridge between the oaks. There were the usual brilliant flowers, the song of robins, and not a soul to be seen. It was much hotter than last week, though the sun was becoming lower so its light struck slantwise through the trees. The woods became thicker as Mount Douglas rose on the left, and I passed along the mountain's dark, sunless side. It was not so cold and clammy as when we had come to find the alienist. The air was pleasantly cool. Here and there small white lilies had sprung up among the mossy rocks and ferns. There was a smell of fir and cedar bark. Now and then from far above in the treetops came the piping of some kind of thrush, but there were no other sounds except the gentle pounding of the horse's hooves, and the trickle of the occasional stream through a culvert under the path. I passed the other path that struck off to the gully where McCrory had been found. I was keeping my mind busy – and the heart-sickness at bay – by reviewing my conversation with Firbanks, but it only made me feel leaden and disgusted. I turned down the path that led to the Indian camp.

Then I saw Lukswaas, sitting by the path on a rock backed by a clump of ferns. She was examining the sole of her foot, which she had crossed on the other knee. She looked up and I thought she smiled – or at least her face seemed to lighten.

I reined in my horse and swung off. 'Mesika klemahun?' ('You hurt?')

She pointed at her foot. I looked around for a handy branch, found one, and looped the horse's reins over it. I stood over Lukswaas. Her moccasins were placed neatly side by side on the path. She must have been carrying them: the sole of her foot was brown with dust. There was a streak of blood from a sliver of cedar bark, which had entered the skin at what looked like a deep angle. I knew, clear as day, that she wanted me to take the splinter out. She must have heard me coming for ages – the Indians had ears for such things – and sent her companions ahead, then stuck the splinter in. Or what? I felt confused. Had Firbanks' vile thinking got into my mind? She couldn't be as innocent as this! I knew I should not under any circumstances lay a finger on her. But I crouched down beside her and took her foot in my right hand, looking at the brown dusty sole, the top of the foot, coppery light brown, the little half-circles of pink at the base of each small-padded toe, her heel cupped soft and warm in my left hand – then the smooth brown skin and rounded calf of her leg, and under it the slim thigh of the other leg on which it was still crossed, then between her thighs the woven fibre of a short kilt or apron, under which…. I glanced up to the dull grey blanket wrapped tightly around her upper body in spite of the heat, and to her face. She was looking at me with shining, intense eyes. I clenched my teeth and returned to the foot. I took hold of the end of the splinter between the nails of my forefinger and thumb and plucked it out with a quick jerk. It was quite long and her whole body winced. A large drop of blood formed.

She could have taken it out herself, I thought. I felt a heart-sick longing to take hold of her legs and bury my head in her lap. Madness. I thought of Firbanks again. I dropped the foot abruptly and sprang to my feet. Lukswaas looked up at me with a questioning expression. As if she was innocent! I felt like yelling down at her: harlot, slut, adultress, filthy, seductive squaw! But she looked like none of these. I turned away mutely toward my horse. I could hardly mount and ride down to the camp leaving her behind. I glanced back at her. She was getting to her feet, bending down to put on her moccasins. Without looking at me, she set out off down the path, hobbling slightly on the injured foot. Well, of course it was not seriously injured, but it might hurt a bit for a while. The more fool her, if she had put the splinter in herself to entrap me.

Leading my horse, I caught up with her. She stood aside to let me pass. I could not. Too much the gentleman, I told myself ironically. But if I was a gentleman, what should I do? The other night I had walked her home five miles. So now I made a gesture that she should mount the horse, meaning I could lead her on it. She looked at me a moment, then up at the horse. Her eyes widened, and she shook her head.

I was invaded by a sort of enthusiasm which always came naturally to me. Why not get on a horse? I pointed at the stirrup, set my foot in it for a moment to show her, then stepped down again. 'Mesika mamook', I said. ('You do.') She smiled. Quite gracefully she swung her left foot into the stirrup, standing effortlessly on her right foot. I had shown my younger brother how to ride in England. I reached down, grasped her right ankle in both hands, and heaved her straight up. She flung her leg over the saddle. 'Good!', I said, moving forward. She was balancing perfectly, but I reached up, took her hand, and placed it on the pommel. Then I let go and moved to the horse's head. But when I looked back I found that Luskwaas had moved forward, to the very front of the saddle, and taken her feet out of the stirrups. She glanced behind her as if to see how much room there was. I felt utterly stumped. She had understood she was to sit in front of me! Trapped again.

I made my best, as I put it to myself, of the situation. I took the reins, stepped back, set my foot in the stirrup and swung myself up behind her. I settled into the back of the saddle but of course there was not much room and there I was with Lukswaas's back in its blanket pressed against my chest, her naked legs in front of's and touching mine, and her hair just below my chin. I reached around her with the reins and flicked them. The horse started lurching down the path. Lukswaas was holding the pommel, out of sight between her legs. Neither of us said a word. I could smell wood-smoke from her hair. It was coarse and black but with bronze and reddish flecks – perhaps from the sun. Her braids were tied with leather thongs. I held her to me with my upper arms, breathing in the wood-smoke and resisting an impulse to nuzzle her hair.

The forest became less dense, varied with arbutus. We were near Cormorant Point. I wished we could go on longer. I felt surprisingly comfortable with this strange woman – more like a girl. I almost counted the plodding of the horse's hooves, wanting them to go slower. I couldn't come riding into the Tsalak Camp like this. She must have had the same thought, and turned slightly as if to say something. I reined in and dismounted. She glanced behind her and with her usual grace, without setting foot in the dangling stirrup, she leaned forward on the pommel, swung her leg over the saddle, and let go, landing nimbly on the ground. She winced, though, and smiled ruefully down at her foot. Then she set off ahead, with me leading the horse behind. I found myself thinking of something I had blocked out of mind: had she really said 'Thank you' the last time I had left her at this spot? I must have been hallucinating, in my tiredness.

'Lukswaas', I said.

She stopped and turned to look at me. She pointed to her chest and repeated: 'Lukswaas.'

'Thank you', I said.

She simply looked puzzled, then smiled. 'Thank you', she repeated, pronouncing it correctly – but I knew by now she had a good ear.

She looked at me questioningly. I was stuck for words. Instead, at last I gave in to a simple impulse. I leant forward and gave her a gentle kiss on her left cheek – like a boy kissing his mother Goodnight – then stood back. To my surprise she leaned towards me and standing on tip-toe gave me an identical kiss, her lips brushing my cheek delicately. Then she smiled again and turned to walk ahead.

'Monkey see, monkey do', I thought. But why such cynicism? To Hell with Firbanks. What a lovely girl this was! We understood each other. I followed her, leading the horse, feeling for a moment light footed and light hearted.

We came out into the clearing on the bluff overlooking the sea. The camp had somehow changed, become more compact, with fewer tents.

There were no longer piles of boxes and baskets. I guessed they had been loaded in the big canoe, in case the Tsalak needed to depart quickly. I took all this in as I was attempting to compose my own mind and ignore the most disconcerting fact about the Indians: although much of the clearing was in the shadow of the forest since the sun was low behind it, the day was still warm, and most of the Indians were naked or nearly so. To be exact, although two or three of the men wore leggings, most were completely naked. This hardly disconcerted me – it was something like in the baths at my school, though their bodies were coppery and not very hairy. But the women wore only a kilt or double apron of bark fibre, and since most of them were plump, their breasts were conspicuous.

I dismounted and tied my horse to a tree. I turned to face the clearing. Lukswaas had disappeared. The Indians were abandoning their tasks and gathering to hear what I had to say. The thickset man, who had been with Lukswaas at the Court-house, now quite naked, took up a position in front.

'Nika Hobbes', I said, pointing to my heart.

'Nika Waaks', the man said with the same gesture.

Lukswaas reappeared from one of the makeshift tents of matting and canvas. She had changed her HBC blanket for her chilcat, wrapped modestly across her chest, pinned with a carved wooden brooch, with the flat shiny stone I had noticed before dangling outside it. She stood forward from the group but still back from Waaks, not as close as she had to Wiladzap.

I explained in Chinook that I had a song from Wiladzap. I took out my notebook and opened it and explained that I had made signs to keep Wiladzap's song. There was a murmur of interest from the Indians, and some seemed to be interpreting my words to others. Waaks turned to face them and with an air of ceremony spoke to them in Tsimshian, then faced me again.

I felt as nervous as when I had done long recitations, by rote, at my Dame School – Macauley's 'The Boy Stood on the Burning Deck' came to mind. I read out the song as best as I could:

'Dinarhnawraw handehabewaw angurhkurhl tramawhee...'

The Indians visibly strained to understand. When I had finished, Waaks said 'Weght'. ('Again')

I started reading. After the first phrase Waaks stopped me by holding up a finger. Then he repeated the phrase complete with the glottal stops and clicks of the tongue, which I had of necessity omitted. Then I read the second phrase and Waaks repeated it. Then the third and the fourth. Then Waaks turned to the Indians and pitching his voice in a chant recited Wiladzap's song from beginning to end. All listened attentively. Some nodded their heads. There was a murmur of conversation.

Waaks turned back to me. 'Kloshe', he said. ('Good'). Then he asked me if I would stay and eat with them. Surprised, I accepted. The gathering broke up, women going to the cooking fires, the few children running over the beaten down grass, throwing a tied bundle of bark to and fro like a ball. Waaks was joined by another man, taller and with a somewhat gloomy cast to his features. He wore a small bone ornament in his nose making him look like a South Sea Island cannibal in a picture book. 'Nika Tsamti', he said, touching his heart.

They led me over to a place where mats had been laid on the ground, in front of logs of wood. The Indians sprawled down in the mats, leaning against the logs. I felt extremely hot, so I unbuttoned my tunic to expose my blue flannel shirt. A woman came over from one of the fires carrying a long-stemmed tobacco pipe with a small bowl, and presented it to me. I took in a puff, and avoided sputtering – it tasted foul. Then I blew out the smoke in a long stream. Instinctively, I handed it to Waaks, who was on my left. He took a few puffs and gave it back to me, and I took another puff and gave the pipe to Tsamti on my right. This ritual continued for a few minutes, then the pipe began to taste even more horrible, and finally went out.

A social conversation began, rather as it might have in England. It was hot, yes it was hot. Even the nights were becoming warmer. But there were still salmon in the bay, and they were not yet swimming deep.

Then the tone changed. Waaks began a litany of complaint. They could not go to sell their goods. People were afraid of them. This was wrong. The Tsalak were peaceful people. Not like the Cowitchan (a bloodthirsty tribe whose territory was twenty miles from Victoria) or the Kwagiutl. The Tsalak had good hearts. Why was the Tyee Wiladzap in the big house of the King George men? The King Georges said that Wiladzap would have to die. Why? He did not kill the doctor. Now the Tsalak would stay in the camp. That was in Wiladzap's song. Wiladzap would be free soon. The King

George men would find who really killed the doctor. 'Hops' would find.

I let all this pass, making as few replies as possible, until Waaks's complaints were spent. Then I began my own questions, starting with what I hoped was polite curiosity, remarking on the fact that there were more women than men in the camp. Waaks, and Tsamti, who began putting in a word now and again, explained that on a trading mission women were more useful than men. They could work at baskets, and the cooking, and perhaps take work for short periods helping the whites in housework – although this was not possible now. Besides, each man needed a woman. And the women of the men needed women to work with them. Through more questions, I learned that there were two castes or classes, among these Tsimshian at least, although the lines of demarcation were not quite clear. Most of the ten men on this expedition were of the higher class, described as 'Tyees', but less than half of the twenty women. The rest of the women worked at the more menial duties. At home there were several hundred Tsalak, including some slaves who formed a still lower class. These slaves had been captured in war. None were with them on this voyage. They might try to escape. The slaves had 'no names' – meaning apparently no important names – although very exceptionally one might become known for bravery and skill, and therefore gain a name and become free. The higher classes had important names, and had to maintain and support these names. The Tsalak were divided into four clans, like all Tsimshian: eagle, raven, wolf, and some kind of fish whose name in Chinook they did not know.

Was Wiladzap an eagle? I asked. Yes, and Lukswaas, and Waaks – although the name Waaks meant 'tiny bird'. Both men laughed at this, reminding me that Wiladzap had referred to the alienist's member as a 'bird'. The name Tsamti meant 'light in the sky' – lightning? And what did the name 'Hops' mean?

I explained that Hobbes meant in English a man from the country, not from the town. This was a rather doubtful etymology of my family name, but I felt I should provide something.

Then I asked how many King Georges in all had visited the camp, since the Indians had first arrived. Waaks said that the first time the doctor, McCloly, had come, there had been a yellow man with him. Another time two farmers had come, looking for labour. Waaks did not know their names, although he attempted to describe them. They had gone away when told that their wages were too low. At any rate they had wanted men, not women, to work in the fields, and the Tsalak men would not pick around in the earth like women looking for roots. Then two men and a woman from the Cordova Bay direction had visited together and brought baskets. Tsamti had tried to sell them some silver bracelets he had made, but they made a face at them. Then there was an ugly man who wanted to buy women.

What? I asked for more details.

This man had come with another man, not so ugly, who had said nothing. The man who talked was called Sam. He said he wanted two or three girls to come to Victoria and make hee-hee and bebe-bebe with shipmen, Waaks said solemnly. Tsalak women did not go with King George men or Bostons at all, Tsamti added, with less tact in my presence.

I asked why.

Because then they would get fire sick. Then the Tsalak would get fire sick too.

I wondered if among themselves they lived in a state of promiscuity. My ears burned as I thought of Lukswaas and how forward she had been. But how could she not be? She lived day and night half naked in the company of naked men. At this very moment, Waaks, lounging against a log, was as naked as the day he was born. Tsamti wore leggings.

Who else had visited? I asked.

A 'Mektakatla man.' They described Firbanks' abortive visit rather as he had. Tsamti said Mektakatla men were dangerous because they wanted the Tsimshian to live in small houses, like white people. At Tsalaks, the houses were each as big as this clearing. Many families lived in each. Then, the Mektakatla men wanted the Tsimshian to give up their names! And take King George names! And only trade with King George men, not with each other. And… But Waaks interrupted in Tsimshian, and Tsamti fell silent.

I asked if anyone had visited the camp since the murder. No one had. Waaks said the King Georges were afraid of the Tsalak now.

I looked across the clearing at the fires where the women were bustling around. It was becoming cooler. The shadow of the trees, through which the sunset could be seen as flecks and cracks of fiery red, covered the whole clearing. Sea and sky had turned a dull silvery blue. Most of the Indians had flung on their blankets. They were a quiet people. There was only the occasional call or exclamation.

Waaks and Tsamti rose to their feet and I did the same. The small, pretty woman who had been with Lukswaas at the jail was coming towards us. 'Muckamuck,' she said, pointing to her mouth. She beckoned to me to follow her across to one of the fires, near which mats had been spread and people were sprawling or squatting. There were several flat stones on which salmon, wooden skewers of clams, and vegetables were spread. The women had been cooking up rice – brought by the sack from traders, I supposed – in big cauldrons. The area around the fire was cluttered with iron cooking vessels and pots. It reminded me of gypsy camps in England.

People began eating at random from oval wooden platters into which the cooks had spooned the rice. They would go to the flat stones and cut themselves a hunk of the salmon with their knife, and pick up a skewer of clams and some of the shoots I had seen at the jail. They ate these either separately from the rice, or mushed in, using wooden spoons which were like small ladles. Water was passed around in wooden cup-like bowls. Waaks and Tsamti had appeared again, Waaks in a chilcat, Tsamti in the more usual blanket of red bark fibres. They beckoned me to the fire. The young woman who had been Lukswaas's companion gave me a platter with a heap of rice, then cut me a generous piece of salmon, the tail end of a side, where there would be few bones, and helped me to the raw shoots and two skewers of clams. She then motioned to me to follow her to one side where Lukswaas was sitting on a mat, a platter on her bare knees, with her back against a log. The other woman spoke to me in Tsimshian, indicating the space beside Lukswaas. I could not help feeling amused at the formal manners which I felt clumsily incapable of matching, in the ambience of a very formal picnic.

Lukswaas seemed shy. Her braids were swung behind her shoulders so that her ears with their shiny discs of abalone were exposed, her chilcat was wrapped tightly around her shoulders, and the black stone ornament dangled in front. Stimulated by the earlier sight of the other women's naked breasts, I found myself imagining hers, but wrenched my concentration back to my food. I did not understand Indian manners or how I was being treated. It seemed always that the men were in command. They did the 'official' talking. Yet they shared certain tasks with the women, and Lukswaas seemed able to do what she wanted. Probably because she was Wiladzap's wife. And Wiladzap was at this moment in prison… Should she not be more upset or disturbed? I kept silent and watched Lukswaas for a moment. She cut pieces of the salmon with a knife, its blade very clean and obviously very sharp, then ate them with her spoon. I followed the same procedure with my bowie knife and the wooden spoon I had been given. The rice was soggy and plain, the salmon chewy but flavoursome, the clams exquisitely smoked, and the shoots like asparagus from an English garden.

It did not seem to be the custom to talk while eating. I did not look closely at Lukswaas. I liked this picnic but was embarrassed by it. As we finished eating, the other woman, who had stayed nearby without herself eating, went and fetched a carved wooden bowl with water for me. I drank some and gave it back to her, saying 'Mahse' in thanks. She then gave it to Lukswaas who drank.

I broke the silence by making a gesture toward the other woman and saying, 'Nem?'

Lukswaas smiled. 'Wan,' she said. On hearing her name, Wan smiled too.

Then Lukswaas asked me, in her Chinook which was adequate but more hesitating than Wiladzap's, how long Wiladzap would stay in 'plison' – a word she must have picked up at the courthouse.

I said Wiladzap would be free from prison once it was found who had killed the doctor.

Lukswaas said that Wiladzap had not done it.

I asked who did? Did a Tsalak do it?

'Wake,' she said emphatically.

Did a siwash (an Indian of any kind) do it?

'Wake.'

I asked her with difficulty, in Chinook which was not suited for anything but the description of material things, how she knew an Indian had not done it.

She frowned but began to explain slowly. She had not seen the body, she said, but she had been told about it by Waaks. She had been told the body had been bitten. An Indian would not do that unless he was a medicine man who was 'halayeet.' This was a word in her own language, which she tentatively explained as 'asleep but not asleep.' I supposed this meant 'in a trance.' Or, Lukswaas continued, unless he was a chief who wanted to impress – make fear in – his enemies. But there were no medicine men in

144

'halayeet' now. And no chief would expect to make fear in his enemies by biting or even killing the Boston doctor.

But Wiladzap was a medicine man, I interjected, as well as a chief.

Not now, Lukswaas explained. Medicine men were only medicine men at certain times, when healing a patient, or in winter at a spirit dance.

I remarked that Wiladzap had said in his questioning by Pemberton: 'I am a man and not a man.'

She nodded her head vigorously. 'Ah-ha.'

This had taken a long time to get clear. We were still sitting side by side. Wan was squatting opposite us as if waiting for orders, her bare thighs visible up to her bark fibre kilt.

I told Lukswaas as best I could that I was the man who had to find who had killed the doctor.

'Nika kumtuks,' she said. ('I know.') Then she looked at me intently. At close range her eyes were very clear, the dark brown iris distinct from the pupil. She said she could see that Hops' heart was sick. (Or his mind was disturbed – whatever of the many things meant by 'tum tum sick.') Hops would find who had killed the doctor if he stood in the same place as that man. She repeated this and elaborated, faltering in Chinook but at length. It was like when a hunter clothed himself in the skin of a bear, moved like a bear, growled and scratched like a bear. If Hops stood in the same place as that man, as if he were putting on that man's skin, he would see and feel the same things as that man. He would know why that man killed the doctor.

I took a moment to think about this. So far in my investigation I had been collecting information, in a hurry and under pressure. I must slow down and think more – get into each suspect's skin. Into his *mens rea*. I came out of my reverie and found Lukswaas was still looking at me, her face pink in reflected firelight although every feature was visible in the growing dusk.

'Mahse,' I said to thank her for her help, and found I was smiling at her. She smiled back. 'Chad,' I said, pointing at my chest, 'Nika Chad.' I am Chad. '*Chad* Hobbes.'

'Tsad,' she said seriously. Then she corrected herself, showing again that she had a good ear: 'Chad.' Then she said, 'Nem toketie,' meaning it was a nice name.

It was like putting one foot into water, then being tugged farther in. I could not face whatever feeling this aroused. I looked around, as if for help. Then I remembered my hallucination of 'Thank you' again.

'Thank you', I said, looking straight into her eyes.

'Thank you', she said back, as if repeating the words in a language lesson.

'You know those words', I said in English.

She looked at me questioningly.

'You said "Thank you" to me the other night – over there'. I gestured with my head towards the forest. 'Mahsi', I said in Chinook, a little impatiently.

'Ah-ha! Thank you! Mahsi!' She went on in Chinook to say she had heard traders, King Georges and Bostons, say 'Thank you' and she knew it was 'Mahsi'. Her coppery cheeks became slightly pink. She was blushing.

So there was my explanation.

The sun had gone down and the sky above was a royal blue, with a pink glow through the forest from the West. The fires in the clearing were flaring a brighter red. Most of the Indians had gone down to the edge of the bluff where they were sitting talking and looking out over the water at the blue hills of San Juan Island, behind which a cold-looking moon, almost full, had just risen. I leapt to my feet without looking at Lukswaas and said I must go. 'Waaks? Tsamti?' I said to Wan.

The woman got up and went to fetch them. I hoped it was the proper etiquette to say goodbye politely to the two men. I watched Wan reach the seated Indians, then women get up and come across the clearing. Suddenly I felt there was no time. Prey to another of the impulses which had seized me that day, I turned to Lukswaas who had risen to her feet beside me. I said – or heard my own voice say, choked with feeling – that I wanted to talk to her again. Could she come to the place where she had hurt her foot?

She said nothing. The two men arrived, and I held out my hand. 'Goodbye', I said in English.

First Waaks, then Tsamti shook my hand, or rather pumped it, and imitated 'Koodpie'. Then they all said 'Klahowya'.

I walked to where my horse was, and untied the reins. I mounted and rode slowly up the path into the darkening woods, not looking back. At the first gully I stopped and let the horse drink – something I should have done earlier – and patted her neck. Then I proceeded up the path. The trees were black but the path was clearly visible in reflected moonlight. I recognised the place. I rode a few hundred feet further, then dismounted and tied up the horse again. I walked back down the path, found the rock against which Lukswaas had been sitting that afternoon, and sat down on it, holding my knees in my hands and putting my forehead on them.

The forest grew blacker and the moon rose higher, appearing through the treetops. Every trunk and branch was picked out in black and silver. There were no night birds, no insects. Only occasionally there would be the scurry of a small animal.

I had often considered myself a clear thinker. At least, I thought a lot. But now I could not think. 'Damn her,' I cursed under my breath. She seemed to have taken away my mind. When I had said I wanted to talk to her again I had at that moment meant it. But what did I want to say? The truth was, I was completely tormented by a few intense memories of looking at her, touching her, and holding her. I could think of nothing else.

A long time passed. I stood up to stretch myself and looked down the path. It was too sharply defined in the moonlight for any mirages, or for any tree or bush to look like her. Either she would come or she would not. It was still warm in the woods but they were empty of even midges or mosquitoes. I stood rooted to the spot. It was of course possible, or even likely, that she would not come at all. But I knew I would wait stubbornly.

She appeared, walking silently up the path, carrying a bundle under one arm. She reached me. I opened my mouth to say something, an instinctive apology, but she held one finger to her mouth. She looked into the forest downhill from the path. Then she stepped forward over a clump of ferns and began picking her way around a rock. I followed, though not as silently. She plunged into the forest through a tangle of ferns, fallen logs, and bushes, then pushed through a clump of low bushes. I followed on her heels. As we came out of the bushes there was a bare patch of mossy ground with a large boulder behind. Lukswaas set down her bundle and bent to untie it. A mat and two bark fibre blankets. Then she unpinned her chilcat and set it on the ground. She was naked except for the stone around her neck. She took it off quickly and dropped it on her blanket. She plunged down onto the blanket she had spread, and pulled the other over her. She glanced at me, then unexpectedly she turned over on her side, curled up with her back to me.

I had been standing like an idiot, not even knowing how to take my clothes off, telling myself I should not, knowing I would. Now I did, dropping my heavy tunic and my shirt to the ground, stooping to take off my boots, then taking off my trousers and drawers. My body was white in the moonlight – like an ithyphallic statue. I knelt down, lifted the top blanket and slid in behind Lukswaas. I embraced her, rather as I had on the horse. I took her breasts in my hands, sank my face in her hair and nuzzled as I had wanted to earlier. We rocked gently together for a long while until suddenly she pressed back and down on me, a channel seemed to open, she rolled over on her front with a cry and rolling over with her I found that I had become no more than a coupling animal – one that moaned without words or mind but at the end called Lukswaas' name.

After a while I rolled back on my side to take my weight off her. She rolled back with me and we lay still close. I was in a daze. My mind wandered back to my few experiences of touching women. Sally of course, but I had recoiled from that. Kissing village girls behind hedges, feeling their bosoms through their dresses, being told to stop and dutifully stopping. Kissing, and the whole agonising question of when to kiss, whether to kiss an eligible girl before becoming engaged… Yet I had not kissed Lukswaas at all. We had not even caressed each other very much. This made me want to do it now. Despairingly I thought of that evil curate's saying that he had to 'get rid of it.' I had got rid of nothing. I had gained a new desire. I put out of my mind something else the curate had said, about squaws being impossible to resist. Lukswaas was impossible to resist at this moment. Or more truthfully, since she was doing nothing, I could not resist what I wanted to do. I pulled her toward me so that we were face to face and began touching her all over. I moved my face to hers and brushed her lips with mine – I did not feel like doing more. I caressed her hair, her back, her legs. She began doing the same to me. I had some vague idea of spreading her legs apart with my hands and plunging masterfully into her, the way I had always supposed men did with women, but my main impulse was tenderness, and instead she ended up rolling over and astride me, then crouching down so that her hair was against my nose and mouth, smelling of woodsmoke. Again I was overwhelmed and lost my mind. At last I came back to the smell of woodsmoke, her body warmly clasped to mine, the forest huge and dark around and above us.

Lukswaas wriggled apart from me. 'Nika klatawa,' she said quietly. ('I go.') She sat up and gathered her blanket, wrapping it and pinning it around her breasts. Then she put on the black stone which shone for an instant in the moonlight.

'Ikta yahka?' I asked. ('What that?')

She said it was for her to see herself in, in the light of the day.

A mirror. I knew the Indians had mirrors from the whites. If Lukswaas could have a knife and cook with iron pots and pans, she could surely have a looking glass. Her mirror-stone must be special. I reached out and took it in my hand for a moment, then gave it a kiss and let it go again. Then Lukswaas took it off and without a word reached out and put it over my head.

'Wake' – No, I said, beginning to take it off.

'Wake! Nika potlatch mesika.' ('No, I give you.')

There was only one thing I could give her back: the signet ring from my little finger, a gift from my mother. I pulled it off and held it out to her. I stifled a crazy impulse to put it on her wedding ring finger, then pressed it into the palm of her hand. She held it up and looked at it for a moment. Then she reached for one of the cords from her bundle, threaded the ring, and tied it deftly around her neck. Then she wrapped her chilcat over it to hide it. I reached for my shirt, then the rest of my clothes, and got dressed while she rolled up the blankets and tied them into a bundle again. She glanced at me, then set off through the bushes back to the path. I followed her.

At the path she turned and moved against me so that I could hold her. I kissed one of her ears and felt like crying. Then she pulled away and said, 'Kansih?' This meant both 'when' and 'can see.'

I managed to reply that we could see each other after three nights, at this place.

She turned and walked off down the path. I watched her until she disappeared, then walked along to where my horse, good old thing, was standing patiently, gigantic in the moonlight. In a daze, I mounted and set off, up the path to the road, then along it.

But as I rode I was invaded by all the doubts and horrors which had been, as if miraculously, put aside. You fool! I almost screamed to myself. She's somebody's wife! She's a slut! A squaw! I dug my heels into the horse and it bolted forward. Then where the road crossed a stream in a culvert, I reined in, dismounted, and ran down the bank to the silvery rippling water. I stripped all my clothes off, crouched in the stream, and washed myself frantically all over with the icy water. My member was streaked with some dark feminine secretion which I washed off in disgust. I picked up a handful of fine gravel, even, and rubbed myself with it. She was an Indian, promiscuous, filthy. She would have the fire-sickness!

Then I stood shivering by the edge of the stream, shaking the drops of water from my body, and came to my senses, only to lose them again in the opposite direction: I swore at myself for having seduced a married woman, for inviting her to meet me in the dark in the forest, for using the authority of my uniform and the power I had over her – and her imprisoned husband! – to intimidate her into giving herself. Then I clutched the stone mirror hanging around my neck and raised it to my lips murmuring her name.

15

It was an easy matter to trace the ugly Sam who had visited the Indian camp trying to procure women for the 'shipmen.' He was well known to the police as a 'crimp' who met sailors on leave with their pockets full of pay but limited time to spend it, and for a commission would find them liquor, entertainment, and whores.

I was told that Sam's usual haunt in the mornings was the Albatross Tavern, just off Wharf Street, a short stroll from the courthouse. The night had been cold toward morning (as I knew from being out in half of it) and there was a mist from the harbour, which had rolled in onto the lower streets of the town. It made me shiver, recalling my standing, a naked fool, in the moonlit stream. I was tired. But nothing could efface another feeling, of lightness and animal pleasure in my own movements, which I could not remember since childhood, running in the meadows in Wiltshire with the skylarks twittering above in brilliant skies.

I have sinned. I don't believe in God for an instant but I have sinned. I have done what Aubrey did – to my mother. Lukswaas is not my mother. Oh God, Chad you are going mad, No she is not your mother. But she is my mother, in that I have never felt so quietly at ease with any woman – with any one since my mother. Lukswaas and I understand each other. Without even a common language. Chinook is like having to squeeze yourself through a door. Meaning drops off as you speak it, you are left with bare bones and no flesh. But it is good enough for Lukswaas and me. Language is bare bones. We communicate not in words but in the flesh. As she has already done with Wiladzap! She appears to care for him, to want him free. But she has given herself to me. And what if he is free? Do we all roll together in one foul bed? Madness, Chad. This is like Hamlet, a soliloquy but in bad verse. 'with anyone since my mother... *We understand each* other...' 'She has given herself to *me. And what if he is* free?'

I pushed open the swing door of the tavern. It smelled sour from spilled liquor and was already dense with smoke, although it contained only a few men, lounging in chairs near the bar, smoking cigars, their tall glasses of ale and small 'chasers' of whisky in front of them on a table. Conversation stopped. I marched over to them, pulled out a free chair, and sat down. 'Which one of you is Sam?'

'Me,' one of them said laconically. He was indeed the ugliest of the group, with a scabrous complexion, nasty mouth like India-rubber gripping its cigar, and eyes like little brown beads. But he was also the best dressed, in a shiny frock coat with a yellow checked waistcoat and elaborate foulard. He puffed his cigar and waited.

'I need to ask you some questions in private. Do you want to come to the courthouse, or dismiss your friends so that we can talk here?'

'You can't dismiss me,' one man said. 'I own this place.'

'Fair enough,' I said. 'We can talk down at the other end. But leave us alone please.' I got up.

Sam got up too. 'Must be *extremely* important,' he said.

'It is.'

Sam followed me to another table near the door and sat down opposite me, still taking puffs on his cigar, but with one hand rather uncomfortably stroking the table, as if it was unnaturally empty without a glass on it.

'What were you doing at the Indian camp out on Cormorant Point?'

'Nothin'. Just rubberneckin'. Me and Bernie went out there, to take a look at the *view*.' He leered, as if imagining hundreds of bare-breasted women, Lukswaas among them. I surprised myself by leaning across the table and grabbing his sleeve quite viciously.

'Look,' I said, 'I know what you were doing. I have a deposition from the Indians and I can send you up for attempting to procure women for immoral purposes.'

'They ain't women, they're squaws…'

I jerked his arm so that the cigar flew out of his hand and rolled onto the sawdust floor where it lay smoking. 'They're women,' I said. 'Not only that, but *ladies*.'

'Awright, they're *ladies*.' Sam rolled his eyes to the ceiling. 'So what do you want? No squ… no Injun woman's word is goin' to stand against a white man's, a white *American's*, in court. So what's the fuss about? You tryin' to change the world?'

'The fuss is that a man, a *fellow American* in fact, was killed out there – as everybody knows. There's evidence that he too was procuring.' This was a risk of mine, and verged on slandering the dead. I might find it hard to justify in a court. But I was thinking of Wiladzap's remark about the 'berdash.' 'So maybe we'll think *you're* involved…'

'But the Injun did it, didn't he?'

'What was going on out there? Why did you go there? If you tell me, I won't hound you – *this* time – for crimping. Look, I'm not taking this down in writing.'

'It was nothin'. Just the squaws – the women. I've got sailors – you wouldn't believe it, Sergeant, bein' a clean livin' man yourself – who come rollin' off them ships just wantin' one thing. They tell me, 'I wanna bit of *smoked meat*.' You know what that is. Like in New Orleans they ask for *dark* meat, here they ask for *smoked*. But some of these men – from your Navy too – not that they're any better than our merchantmen, they're like animals if you ask me, they've got lotsa dols, they don't want just some poxed up tart from the shanties. So when I heard of them Northern Injuns comin' down, wantin' to trade, I went and saw them and offered them some trade, that's all.'

'What did they say?'

'They weren't havin' nothin' to do with it. I dunno exactly why. Maybe it wasn't that they were so fussy about the work. Some o' them gave me the eye. Nice tall girls they were too. But they were afraid of gettin' the clap, so they said. "Piah sick", The men weren't too keen on lettin' any o' that harem outa their sight, I guess. So after lookin' at the *view* for a while, Bernie and I rolled on back home. So what's goin' on? I done nothin'.'

'You didn't see McCrory out there?'

'Nah! First I heared he'd been out there was when I heared he'd been cut to ribbons. That made Bernie and me glad we'd had nothin' to do with 'em. We could of ended up the same way.'

'You mean you think McCrory proposed to the Indians the same thing as you tried?'

'I dunno. Was he a real doctor or a fake?'

'Supposed to have been real.'

'Then what was he doin' hangin' around easy girls?'

'You tell me.' I was trying not to reveal my ignorance of where Sam, who was now in a musing sort of humour, was tending.

'Waal, I seen him a lot at the Windsor Rooms.'

'You bring your, er, clients there?' I had thought the Windsor Rooms might be at a level above Sam's.

'Sure. I got some classy customers. With lotsa dols. Officers – Lootenants, midshipmen. Not all of 'em just want smoked meat.'

'What was McCrory doing there?'

'Hey, why should I tell you all this?'

'Because he's dead, and you and he may have been in the same line of business. What if the Indian didn't do it? What if somebody has it in for people like you? Anyway, where were you last Wednesday afternoon?'

'I was with a friend.'

'Who?'

'A lady. I don't need to say.'

'So you can't prove it? Maybe you were a partner of McCrory's and you had a falling out.' I was calculating on a certain stupidity in Sam. I was not wrong.

'Awright! I'll tell you all I seen. If it's not the Injun who killed McCrory you'd better find who it is, I don't want no one gettin' the wrong idea… Awright. The way I seen McCrory he was a sort of a high-class crimp. Like me, only with the people in town – the Nobs. Not that I seen him with his customers. No more than I'd see me, if you know what I mean, with mine. I don't follow my customers into bed with girls, I just make the arrangements. I won't say nothin' about financial arrangements, or you'll use it against me. But you won't often see me with my mark. Anyway it's dangerous. The longest time a man like me can be thrown in jail for in this town is for "enticin' sailors to desert". They can allus accuse me of that. So, you'll just see me with a girl or a liquorman, because I'm doin' my investigation – and sometimes it's a very pleasurable task, I must say,' Sam leered – 'of the services I provide. Likewise, I'd see McCrory at the Windsor Rooms now and then and I could tell he was like me. Not their customer. He was talkin' to 'em, workin' things out with 'em – arrangin'.'

'With any girls in particular?'

'No. He musta talked to 'em all.'

'Did he come in there alone?'

'Yeah. Now and then he'd see someone he knew and tip 'em a nod or a wink, or pass the time o' day. But no further than that. You know how it is.'

I did already know, from hearsay, that a place like the Windsor Rooms had its own code. Since well known men of the town might be found there, it was not acceptable for them ever to intimate even to each other, outside the place, that they had seen each other there. I had also heard that in such places only nicknames were used. Thus, in a town of 7,000 whites, the proprieties were observed. A professional man or business man could be walking down Government Street with his wife and encounter a pair of the Windsor Room ladies out shopping for clothes, and not a sign of recognition would be shown. Nor would a man whom he had met in the Rooms and nowhere else recognise him or greet him.

'Is that all?' said Sam, turning to look anxiously up the smoke-filled room to the table at the other end where his friends had been keeping up a steady level of boisterous conversation as if to make it known they were not listening.

'I'll let you go now. But if I find out you've kept anything from me about any transaction with the Indians, or McCrory keeping company with any particular person in your sight, I'll be back.'

'Awright, there was one fella I seen him with in the Windsor Rooms. I dunno who it was. Strong lookin' dark fella, well dressed. Could have been English, didn't look like an American. Too fussy-lookin'.'

'What do you mean?'

'Kinda stiff lookin'. Embarrassed like.'

'Describe him more. Tall? Short?'

'I only seen 'im sittin' down at the other side o' the room. He didn't get up to dance, leastways not when I was there. I didn't get too close to 'im.'

'Dark eyes? Light?'

'I couldn't see.'

'And you didn't know who he was?'

'Nope. Never seen 'im around town. But I don't hang out in the best circles. You won't find me at the Governor's levees or whatever you call 'em.'

'But this other man struck you as the kind of person who might be found at a levee?'

'Yeah. Looked like an official of some sort.'

'Why?'

'Just an impression. I hardly seen the fella. But since you're so worked up about me tellin' everythin', I thought I'd better not leave 'im out.'

'Anything else you've left out?'

'Nope.'

'That's enough for now then. But I may be back.' I got up, called out a polite 'Good morning' in the direction of the bar, and left. The fog was thinning and wispy, with streaks of blue shining through.

16

When Frederick had first told me about the Sunday afternoons at Orchard Farm, he had mentioned John Hadley the schoolmaster and his 'equally mousy wife' as having been 'fairly thick' with McCrory. Since the Hadleys were the only remaining association of McCrory's I knew of, I decided to interview them, late in the afternoon when Hadley would have finished teaching school. Then in the evening – a prospect which filled me with apprehension and some excitement – I would pay a visit to the Windsor Rooms.

I arrived at Hadley's at half past four. The house was a tiny one, near the wooden cathedral, not much more than a shack although neatly painted and with a kitchen garden and white picket fence. Hadley, a middle-sized man running to fat and with an air of shyness and plain looks, which indeed made him seem mousy, was sitting on the edge of the narrow plank deck which functioned as a 'porch', smoking a pipe, and sipping from a large glass of what looked like spirits. He seemed miserable, standing up to greet me in a weary, clumsy way.

'I'm Hobbes. Police. I'm investigating the murder of Dr McCrory.'

Hadley's face became tight, his eyes screwed up. 'That bounder,' he said. 'I'm glad somebody got him.'

'Really? Why?'

Hadley took his time in replying. He lifted his glass and gulped down some spirits, which made his eyes visibly water and his face grow red. He sat down with a bump on the edge of the porch. 'Because he was a bounder,' he said.

Not wanting to tower over Hadley, I sat down next to him on the edge of the porch. 'Where are you from?' I said. I had already found out that Hadley was a Cambridge man, but was better disposed towards Cambridge since my interview with my fellow Oxonian, Firbanks.

'Buckinghamshire. St John's, Cambridge. Got a poor degree. Too busy versifying. Came out here in '65 in response to advertisement. Took job at a school. Married Scotch girl I met here, daughter of HBC clerk. Separated. In process of becoming a drunk.' He took another swig of his spirits, and looked at me with an air of defiance in his eyes, which were pale and quite strong, but with a pouting expression of self-pity around the mouth.

'Where's your wife now?'

'With Daddy and Mummy. Name of Stevenson. Junction of Cook and View Streets.'

'When did you separate?'

'February.'

'Why was McCrory a bounder?'

Hadley reached down under the porch beside him and pulled out a bottle of cheap rum. He filled his glass and put the bottle back. He took a gulp and puffed at his pipe.

'It's not relevant to your investigation,' he said.

'Of course it is. Everything is. If you think he's a bounder perhaps it was you who did him in.'

'Wish I had. Not enough courage.' Hadley began to sing, in a surprisingly melodious voice:

Come all pretty maidens wherever you be,
Don't love a man before you try him,
Lest you should sing a song with me:
My husband's got no courage in him.

'The village girls used to sing that, at home. Quite poetic, don't you think? Double meaning of course. My wife said I had no "courage" in that sense, but it was McCrory who put her up to it.'

'Could you start at the beginning?'

'If you insist. Go and talk to Annie about it. Then you can make a judgement on who's right. You'll take her side. Everyone's sorry for her. I mean everyone who knows about it, since we're all keeping the separation quiet. But she went on her own.'

'Yes. But let's start with McCrory.'

'All right. Annie's family knew Mrs Somerville, and we would go out there from time to time on Sundays. We met the *witchdoctor* – as I call him – out there. Very ingratiating chap. But actually it was Mrs Somerville who suggested that Annie go to see him for medical advice. Isn't it *rotten…*' Hadley looked fiercely at me, 'the way women get together and discuss intimate matters?'

'I suppose so.'

'I dare say because Annie's mother is a total Scotch prude, she wanted to discuss things with another sort of mother.'

'Another sort?'

'I think she's immoral, Mrs Somerville. In fact, between you and me, I think she was McCrory's mistress. They were *so* close. But Annie thinks I have a dirty mind. I may have. Admittedly the Somerville girls are pure as pie. If I had only met Aemilia before Annie! Just my luck.'

'So what happened?' I said, trying to hurry things along.

'Annie went to see McCrory. He gave her mysterious "treatments," about which she would not tell me. Then he told her the real trouble was *me*, and that *I* should come for treatment.'

'Wait a minute. What had *her* trouble originally been?'

'Female troubles,' said Hadley darkly. 'Unmentionable. But why not? Our marriage was unconsummated. In spite of much effort. She had some kind of obstruction, it seemed to me. Everything – as it were – was *closed*. During the treatments it *opened*. I thought perhaps he had done surgery on her. But she swore he had not, and indeed there were no signs of such a thing, no blood or bandages. She actually said it was a result of 'magnetic passes.' Rubbish! And she had suddenly, after two years of lying with her legs closed, become as lubricious as a rat! And I became useless! Partly because I was worried sick at what he might have done to her.' Hadley stopped.

'And what was that?'

'Deflowered her, I imagined. Surgically might have been all right. But I suspected another way.'

'On what evidence?'

'None whatsoever, apart from the fact that she was now very definitely opened up.'

'And you accused her of…'

'Yes. She's a religious girl. Scotch Presbyterian. The "kirk." She took a bible and swore on it McCrory had never touched her. He had simply done magnetic passes over her body. These had provoked a crisis in which she cried and cried, and remembered all sorts of things, griefs and pains, from when she was a little girl. She refused to talk in detail about these. But the crisis cured her. And there I was, angry about it. Then McCrory, with whom she discussed me, had the gall to send me a note in which he said that *ejaculatio ante portae* could be cured, and why did I not come for treatment? I wrote him back referring to *ejaculatio ante portas* – correcting his Latin. It means 'to ejaculate in front of the gates,' and he muddled the cases. You wouldn't understand that. A Peeler doesn't have to know Latin.'

'What else did you write to him?'

'That the phenomenon in question was temporary, and that it was none of his business, and I was forbidding my wife to see him. She cried about it. I assumed that if the gates had been closed for two years, and opened in dubious circumstances, it was natural enough for me to become unnerved. Then it turned out she was pregnant! I was furious. I accused her of fornication with McCrory. She swore on the bible again. But she went to see him! Against my express command not to! She wanted to get him to see me here. Which he did. Stood in our parlour, smooth as a cursed ginger tom, and told me, in front of my wife, that I should come to him for treatment for *my* nerves! He also said that medical science had established beyond doubt that impregnation could occur without full penetration. He said my sperm at the 'introitus of the vagina' as he put it, had impregnated her. All this in front of Annie! I told him he was a bounder and should leave at once. Then you know what he did?'

'What?'

'He tore strips off me for almost an hour. He said I needed what he called a "criticism." And he gave it to me. He started with a physical description of me. The way I walked, the way I stood "buttocks tight together," the way my eyes were piercing but my chin and mouth weak and with "the expression of a dissatisfied baby." Then he went on to the way I wanted to "control" Annie and possess her. He said she was a weak woman, debilitated by her condition, but now she was suddenly stronger I could not tolerate the change. "You're like a dog with a bone," he said, "pushing it back and forth between his paws, snarling and biting it and letting it go. What would the dog do if the bone suddenly took on a life of its own and began to move? He'd run away with his tail between his legs – like yours is now." And other elaborate imagery of this sort. He said I was pompous about knowledge, about being a schoolmaster. He said my position gave me an authority which was not natural to me. No doubt I had come to "America," as he insisted on calling it here, because I could gain the authority of power as a missionary of English civilisation. He said my correcting his Latin was a sign of pedantry and fussiness. Who cared? he said, whether the case was nominative or accusative? I had understood what he meant, hadn't I? He said I should become dried up like an old stick if I did not change my ways. It wasn't enough for me to try and feel alive by drinking too much to get the blood circulating in my body, he said. I was frightened of the idea of the animal magnetism because it was not something I could control. But the only method of changing my ways would be to come to him for treatments. I "owed" it to my wife to do so.'

Hadley reached for his bottle again and filled his glass, his hands trembling. I was reminded of the Irish Rose. I wondered if on balance McCrory had increased or decreased human misery. Anyway drink, in Victoria, was an easy and cheap way out of most dilemmas.

'After a while I was stunned,' Hadley went on. 'I just stood there, growing hot and cold by turns. Then he said goodbye and went away. The strange thing was that although I felt as if the sky had fallen on me, and weak as a kitten, that was one moment when I did not feel angry with McCrory. Although some of what he said was too subjective on his part to be accurate, much of it was the painful truth. By itself, I should have survived it, and it even crossed my mind that since he had no illusions about me whatsoever, there was no need for me to put up a show in front of him. I felt free for a moment to be myself, such as I am. I might even have gone to see him for treatments. But in fact – and this is where I'm *really angry...*' Hadley stopped for breath, but his emphasis had been weak. He was indeed a mouse. 'In fact that bounder had, through his tirade, destroyed my marriage. Annie had been standing there all the while, and she could not bear me. Before McCrory's arrival I had been yelling at her to get out of the house, to go and live with her seducer or go back to her mother. But now it was she who said she would go. She said that although McCrory could not have made her pregnant because he hadn't touched her, she wished a man like him *was* the father of her child. He was in fact the *spiritual* father, she said ravingly. He was ten times the man I was, and so on. So she went back to her mother. And she's still there. Only three hundred yards – three hundred and fifty three paces, to be precise – from this door. She is five months pregnant and she still won't come back. And here I am. Hating that bounder, even though he's finished.'

'Did you see him after this "criticism"?'

'No. I've been nursing my wounds.'

I could easily believe it. Hadley seemed to be drowning not only in spirits but in self pity. 'When did you hear of McCrory's death?'

'Two days afterwards, from the newspaper. For a moment I felt an irrational sadness. But after that I felt pleased. For one thing, with him dead, Annie's affections may be free to come to me again.'

'Have you talked to her since then?'

'No. I'm just waiting.' Hadley took another gulp of rum. However, he was showing no signs of drunkenness.

I could not resist giving him some advice. 'I think you should get off the bottle and go and see her. Undoubtedly the child is yours.' Not that I wholly believed this.

'Don't tell me what to do. I can make up my own mind. What if the child *isn't* mine? It's easy for you to say so.'

I felt hopeless. I should leave advice to the McCrorys of this world. I contented myself with asking: 'Where were you on the afternoon McCrory was killed?'

'At school of course. Everybody there can tell you that.'

'Thank you for your help.'

'I'm sorry the Indian has to swing for it. But I gather McCrory had been tinkering with *his* wife. That's one thing that makes me suspicious again about Annie.'

'McCrory did *not* tinker with the Indian's wife,' I said sharply. 'So you can set your mind at rest.'

I went on my way. I did not have the heart to go and question the hapless Annie.

These interviews have made me calmer. I'm on the case again. I realise something: people open themselves to me, they talk to me. I am a good listener. Is this from my mother again? I would always listen to her and she to me. Actually the same was true for my father and me. But there is something more: with all the perpetual fuss about Henry, his conspicuous growing up, his mistakes and rowdiness, I was left free to observe and to listen. I am an observer. And a listener. But I could never talk to others the way they talk to me! Instead I talk to this diary. One day I want to talk to Lukswaas. I have already started. If only Wiladzap was dead! But here I am, working all day to keep him alive. And I want to. Perhaps the outcome of this will be that he is freed and he will go back to the North with Lukswaas and at least they'll be happy together. Perhaps I could take up the courtship of Aemilia. I have known Lukswaas naked – a question of her setting her chilcat aside. How strange it would be to work through the various layers of clothes around Aemilia. The idea excites me. But Lukswaas! What shall I do without her?

17

That evening, dressed in my most elegant clothes, I climbed the shabby staircase to the Windsor Rooms, paid my entrance fee to the massive door attendant who doubled as a 'chucker-outer,' and stood looking carefully around the dance hall. The orchestra, of piano, accordion, violin and cello, was playing a slow waltz rather listlessly. Nobody was dancing. The girls, brightly dressed in silks and velvets, their hair piled up on their heads in mountains stuck through by a single pin – so that with one tug the hair would fall in abandon – were clustered at several tables. At only one of these a group of men was sitting, three of whom I recognised as respectable citizens. I wandered over to a table at which four girls were sitting, and asked politely if I might join them.

'Why certainly,' one of them said, with as much poise as if she were in a drawing room.

I pulled a chair out and sat down. A waiter appeared at my elbow and I ordered a magnum of champagne for myself and the ladies. This would cost me almost a week's pay but I had decided it would be necessary. There was a murmur of appreciation, and a couple of the girls who already had drinks in front of them began to finish them off in anticipation.

'Celebrating a special occasion?' said the woman who had answered previously. She was well-spoken, American, pretty, but very heavily rouged. All of the women were bosomy, the upper halves of their dresses tight over what seemed to be less stiff stays than normal – I knew nothing of the mechanics of women's underclothes. For an instant I thought of Lukswaas and her freedom to be naked under a loose chilcat. The most striking contrast between her and these women at close range was in their artificiality. Waves of flowery scent wafted from them, and all were made up around the eyes, rouged, their lips coloured and set in a trained pouting expression. One was a Negress of no great beauty – her teeth were big – but with agreeable chocolate brown skin and an open, friendly face. The other two were sour-looking beneath a rigid mask of 'prettiness,' but one of them was relatively plump and maternal. All looked older than Lukswaas. What age was Lukswaas? I found myself thinking. But they were looking at me expectantly.

'No, I'm not celebrating. I'm Sergeant Hobbes, of the police. I'd like to talk to you for a little while, and since I'd appreciate your answering a few questions, I don't want to make it disagreeable.' There would have been no point in beating around the bush. At least some of the women would have recognised me.

The thinner of the two sour women let out a groan. The Negress said, 'Oh dear,' but philosophically it seemed.

'Sergeant Hobbes is all right,' the first woman chipped in. 'You girls remember Florence, who ran away to New Westminster with that forger? Sergeant Hobbes was the one who arrested them. She said he was a perfect gentleman. He paid their dinner on the steamer.'

'Oh yes,' another woman said. The atmosphere softened.

'How is Florence?' I asked politely.

'Went back to San Francisco,' said the first woman. 'Broken hearted. Anyway, I'm Sylvie.'

'I'm Jane,' said the Negress. The other two were Sara and Maria.

'My first name is Chad.'

'Unusual,' Sylvie remarked.

'It's not uncommon in England. Name of a saint.'

This caused a laugh, although I had not intended to be ironic. The champagne arrived in a silver ice bucket, and the first glasses were poured. We raised our glasses: 'Your health!'

'I've been investigating the awful death,' I said, 'of Dr McCrory, the alienist. And since I know he used to come here and talk to at least some of you ladies, I'd like to ask some questions about him.'

'I was surprised someone didn't come earlier,' Sylvie said unconcernedly, 'since this was after all one of his haunts. But then I supposed that since you'd caught the Indian who did it, there was no need for further enquiries.' She raised her head and looked across the room. 'Grace!' she called rather loudly, in a momentary lapse of good manners.

A very pretty honey-blonde woman got up from the table with the men, and came over to join us. As she sat down the waiter reappeared with another glass for her, filled it, and replenished the others, which had sunk rapidly. Good waiter, I thought. I looked around and realised I was enjoying myself. The orchestra was playing another waltz, very well. The champagne was good, the women attractive. Wouldn't it be nice to be as rich as Croesus and buy this sort of thing whenever one wanted? I smiled at myself. Looking at the women I found myself able to feel my attraction to them. I had a sense, as never before, of the naked bodies under all those elaborate clothes, and a curiosity I would like to have indulged – to look, and compare at least. I was at ease with them, and they, apparently with me.

During these few moments of reverie I had at the same time heard Sylvie explaining that Grace had probably talked to the alienist most. She had been his favourite, though the others all knew him too.

'Did he just talk, or did he also dance?' I asked.

They giggled. 'Dance' must have a double meaning.

'Just talked,' Grace said. 'He came to know the slack times when there weren't very many people, and he would come in then. He'd buy us drinks – not champagne though. I think he was a bit of a skinflint. A very charming man but, you know what it's like, we have to earn our living, and that means we need to 'dance'.' She too was well-spoken although her voice had the nasal quality of the Canadian or Eastern American.

'What did he talk about?'

'Well now, *there's* a delicate question,' Sylvie put in. They all laughed and sipped their champagne, looking at me with professionally flirtatious eyes.

'Let me guess,' I said. 'He asked about your relations with men.'

'Right,' Sylvie said. 'You know then.'

'I'd like to know what *kind* of thing,' I said, forging ahead but not sure if this direction would work. 'I have to understand as much as I can about his character and interests. If it embarrasses you to talk about it, I'm sorry. Would it be easier if I talked with each of you separately?'

'That's what *he* would do,' Jane the Negress interjected. 'Go sit at a side table and just *pump* for information.' The word 'pump' for some reason raised another laugh. Jane shrugged her shoulders and went on. 'I guess it's all in a night's work,' she said, 'but I didn't like it. After a while I wouldn't. I told him, look, if he wanted me to make him happy that was fine, but this talk I wouldn't take none of.'

I must have looked disappointed, because Sylvie said, 'It's more a question if *you'd* be embarrassed than us. I'm sure we don't mind talking now, since you obviously have to do your job.'

Mindful of the fact that this would keep five girls tied up for half an hour or so, I signalled the waiter for another magnum of champagne. The feeling at the table became more easy.

'You like being in the police?' Sylvie chatted as the waiter arrived, very promptly, with the new bottle in its own ice bucket.

'It's new to me. I don't like spending most of my time in jail.' They laughed, as they seemed to enjoy doing at the least opportunity. 'I find it interesting to investigate a case like this. I never met Dr McCrory. He seems to have been a complicated fellow.'

'A deep one,' Grace said. 'He took in everything a girl said. Nothing was ever lost to him.' There were words of agreement from the others.

'What was the line of his questioning?'

'There were two lines,' Grace said. 'Men. And women.' Everyone laughed. She went on: 'He wanted to know about men in bed with a girl. What size they were when excited, how long it took for them to spend. Were the ones who spent right away, or before even getting on, were they exceptionally nervous, or did they seem angry? Did they hold their breath? And the pumpers, as we call them, who wear a girl out – they're the worst – what kind of men were they? And did small men have big widdlers? And did many men want to gamahuche a girl – you know what that means? Everyone giggled, and I smiled as if I knew. 'And what kind of men were they? Did some men want to be whipped or spanked? What kind of men were they? What sort of men preferred me to take everything off, and what sort wanted me to stay in my frillies? Then there were the women questions. Did I think women spent as easily as men? What had a man to do to make me spend? I wasn't going to answer that one. "Spend money on me," I said, as a joke, and referring to his being a skinflint himself.'

'Did he have a sense of humour?' I asked, trying to maintain my calm in the face of all this strange and casual information.

'Not that I could see. *You* may say I liked him best,' Grace said to Sylvie. 'That's just because I gave him more time. I didn't *like* him. Nor did I want to go with him. Why, if he pumped like that in a mere conversation, what would he do in more *intimate* circumstances? He'd never stop!'

This raised another laugh, in which I joined. I had, after all, been drinking some of the champagne myself.

'Then there was a third line of questioning,' Sylvie put in, as if not to be outdone by Grace. 'He was very self-important about being a doctor, and finding ways of curing nervous illnesses. He said straight out he thought that what a lot of people needed was simply a good fuck – pardon my language. He said a lot of people were too nervous and they ended up merely frigging themselves instead. Now *this* sort of language is not ours.' Sylvie shook her head, and the others looked serious. 'We simply want to make people happy. And be happy, right girls? We're not doctors. But he seemed to think we'd have all sorts of professional tricks to help get a man stiff if he couldn't, or keep it hard if it went soft. That doesn't interest me. But he said I was hard-hearted! As if women don't give enough! If a man wants a good time he'll have it his way – and I'll give him a good time too. But if he wants to go to sleep on me or stay all night, or do anything dirty, or hurt me, or if after all he's not interested – then he can leave. If he won't I'll tug the bell cord and my chucker-outer will come and *make* him leave. That's our protection. If a man is a brute or a dirty pig or even just a fool, we don't have to be with him, even if we do like the money. We're not like the street girls, selling themselves in the back alleys to perverts and sodomites. But the doctor wouldn't understand that. I think he was disappointed. He wanted secrets, always secrets. But what's secret about making love? What is there that any woman don't know?' She looked around for agreement, and got it vociferously.

I saw this as a warning that my own line of questioning was over. But I tried another. 'This may be a delicate question, but do any of the men you go with ever wear sheaths?'

This caused a giggle, but also a few rueful expressions. 'And spoil their little pleasures, poor dears?' Sylvie said. 'No, we have other ways. Not that it wouldn't help. But the answer is no, I'm afraid.'

I took a new tack. 'Did Dr McCrory always come here alone?'

'The only other man I ever saw him with was Witherspoon,' Grace said. They were chums.'

One of the others groaned – Jane. 'That Witherspoon,' she muttered.

'Witherspoon?' I said. 'Could you describe him to me?'

'It's not a *real* name,' Sylvie said, amid more giggles. 'But it's not complicated. You know *spooning*?'

'Embracing.'

'Not exactly. From behind – like a girl going to sleep in a man's arms. And 'wither' means *it* would wither.'

This caused an uproarious laugh. Their table was certainly the liveliest in the room, although others had been filling up with new guests.

'Of course,' I said with a smile, although I did not find the pun very funny. 'And who was this Witherspoon?'

'Now, now,' Sylvie said. 'We can't tell you names, even if we know them, which usually we don't. Then where would our reputation be?'

'I see what you mean. But let me ask you, was this Witherspoon a stiff-looking, dark haired man?'

'You already know!' Grace said. 'Yes, a regular wooden soldier.'

'Tin, you mean,' said the plump sour woman.

'Don't be too hard on him,' said Jane the Negress. 'He was very trying but he meant the best.'

'I found him rather sweet,' Sylvie said. 'Wouldn't say boo to a goose.'

'Did he come here often with McCrory?' I asked.

'From time to time,' Sylvie said vaguely. The atmosphere at the table changed slightly. I realised that although it was permissible to discuss how many times a dead man had attended the Windsor room, the code required that a live one be protected.

'It's very nice of you to answer my questions,' I said. 'I'm most grateful.'

'Not at all…,' 'It's nothing…' The girls began looking around the room. After all, the two magnums of champagne had been finished. As if noticing this lack of tact, Sylvie said, 'Would you like to dance?'

'Of course.' I rose to my feet and bowed to the ladies, who waved their fingers and smiled. Sylvie took my arm and I led her out onto the floor. A few couples were dancing. Another waltz. I had of course danced before, but at arm's length compared to this. Before I knew it I was waltzing around slowly in a sensual embrace with Sylvie, my face against her piled up hair which smelt overwhelmingly of carnation scent – she must be bathed in it. 'I like waltzing,' she murmured into my ear. 'The polkas come later.'

Perhaps there was a double meaning in this, though I could imagine the Windsor Rooms late at night pulsing with polkas, filled with excited and half-drunk customers. 'Thank you for being so helpful,' I said. But as we waltzed around I could not help being seized with a desire to go with her, take off her clothes – petticoats, all those 'frillies' – and find underneath a naked… Lukswaas. This was ridiculous.

Sylvie pressed herself against me. How much more natural, at least, were these flowing velvet gowns than the hooped crinolines worn in polite society. She let out a sort of coo. I had the feeling she might even mean it.

'You want to come with me?' she murmured. Then since I said nothing for a moment, she added, 'Or another time?'

'Another time,' I said.

'I know.' She gave me a squeeze. 'You have a girlfriend don't you? A love?'

'Yes.'

'I know. When will men realise that a woman knows everything? That is if she's a real woman, not a mere slut.' Sylvie was now looking up at me as we were dancing. Her eyes, deep blue, were gentle but intelligent. 'You see, a man like McCrory is not really a man. Why? Because he wants to see the world from a woman's point of view. Ultimately to understand other *men*, you see? That's what really excited him. I do believe he might have been a pathic.'

'I don't think so,' I said. 'He had at least one woman in his life.'

'All right. I'm not saying he was a sodomist in action. I mean he was the sort of man who when he embraces a woman is feeling that he almost *is* that woman. Perhaps that makes a man a good doctor, with women patients. I *know* that sort of man – though I never went with him. You don't know that sort of man because you're not one. You *like* women.' She pressed against me, to make her point.

'I do, but I've not known many.'

'That's obvious. But still waters run deep, eh? I'm glad you've found a girlfriend. Is she married?'

'How did you guess?' I was genuinely shocked, and pushed Sylvie slightly away, to look down at her questioningly.

'Because if she wasn't, you'd be married to her, wouldn't you? – or engaged. But if she was the sort of girl you'd be engaged to, you wouldn't be sleeping with her. *Serious.*' Sylvie gave me a playful squeeze. The waltz was ending. 'If things don't work out with her, come and see me.'

'Perhaps I shall. Goodnight.'

Sylvie went back to the table, and I went to the door where the attendant chucker-outer had my bill – two weeks pay, even at the wage of acting Sergeant. Since the waiter had impressed me, I added half a sovereign as a tip.

18

Over coffee and a muffin, very early in the morning, for I had not slept well, I tried to plan a day's investigation. There was one person I must see again: Lee. I would have willingly (I told myself, while knowing this was not true) have put Lee to the rack and tortured him, or hung him up by his thumbs. Lee knew probably the name, and possibly the complaint, of every person who had come to see McCrory. Perhaps not very many people, since it was clear McCrory was not growing rich on his practice. The forty pounds or so in the cash-box which Lee had appropriated was not much reserve for a professional man, and McCrory's bank account had held only $100. But there had been a core of enthusiasts. I wished I knew them all. I was haunted by the idea that the murderer had been a patient of McCrory's whom I knew nothing about.

I meant to make a list, go down it by elimination, scientifically, then present my conclusions in a report to Augustus Pemberton. Before this, I should try Lee again. Besides, my single-minded pursuit of information was a help to me personally – like nursery rhymes to a child stranded over an abyss.

When I falter in my quest I fall into reveries about Lukswaas. I burn at the memory of her body and I feel like calling out 'Lukswaas, I love you!' But that is madness. I could as well hate her. Her talisman, the mirror stone which I now wear around my neck under my shirt, is like a millstone I cannot take off. While she has given herself to me, her husband, Wiladzap, sits crouched in his iron and brick cage surrounded by the coarse jests and smells of the chaingang – a bunch of crimps, rogues, thugs, and swindlers – and he will hang one day soon by the neck from the white man's gallows. Yes I hate Lukswaas. Firbanks would see her as a devil. But so clean, so innocent-seeming a devil… Hate and love. Catullus's two line poem, Odi et amo, *would be in English something like:*

'I hate and I love. How I do it, you may ask.
I do not know. But I feel it, and I suffer.'

The word for 'I suffer' is Excrucior. *I have had enough of this excruciating.*

I felt too restless to spend time in the court-house jail. I finished my coffee hurriedly, then went out into the street almost at a run.

I knew McCrory's house was already empty. Rabinowitz had put the furniture into storage and advertised the house for rent – more hurriedly than he had told me he would. But why not? The property would revert to him anyway.

The only place to look for Lee was his natural habitat, the area several blocks out of town towards the Upper Harbour which was so crowded with Celestials – some said 2,000, some 3,000 – that it was coming to be known as Chinatown. Every ramshackle building of wood and brick was a tenement in which a hundred or more Chinamen lived, in bachelor 'clubs'. Their families were mostly in China, where they sent most of what they earned. There were very few women, though those few were respectable, never prostitutes. Every other vice was available on demand. There were Chinese bum-boys for the more degenerate among our sailors, and of course the squaws in the Cormorant Street shanties with their Chinese landlords-cum-pimps. But a crimp like Sam would steer clear of Chinatown, for fear of ending up with a cleaver in his skull. It was rumoured that people disappeared there, to end up chopped in small pieces, eaten in stews with chopsticks. But then many things were said about the Celestials. Amor de Cosmos, the lover of the universe, who worked fanatically to link British Columbia with his native Canada, was a particularly virulent foe of the Chinese – and no one would want De Cosmos as an enemy. In spite of my irritation with Lee, I liked the Celestials. Where else could several thousand people live within six city blocks without any sign of disorder? Red and green banners hung from hovels and houses; ideograms of great beauty were painted on the filthy walls; the tenements had wooden balconies thick with plants and herbs in hanging pots or baskets or in window boxes; shop windows were hung with unmentionable chunks of meat on hooks, which were shining from being scrubbed every day; stalls contained open boxes and crates of fresh and dried fruits and vegetables, herbs, dried fish and crab; apothecaries in shops, which I imagined would have done credit to medieval England, presided over rows of bottled seahorses, slugs, molluscs, and jars of powders; hawkers sold so-called thousand year old eggs coated in a black crust, stored in barrels. It all showed a level of social organisation, of import of goods and export of money from China – although by the white man's ships – which existed as it were parallel to that of the white man's Victoria, and was no less efficient.

On the other hand, I imagined a sea of misery swelled and strained under the beaming sky of all those polite faces. Could the men, without women, really be happy? Not unless with opium, the snake in the Celestial paradise. In dens in the narrow alleys which linked the bustling streets, Chinamen apparently lay stacked like bales on warehouse shelves, smoking the deadly gum whose smell sometimes wafted among that of the spices, wood-smoke and ubiquitous Victorian horse-dung and sewage.

To find a particular Chinaman was not difficult. All one had to do was ask for him by name and one would be directed and redirected until at last the Chinaman would appear out of a door, an alley, or a knot of people. I started by asking the owner of a restaurant the whereabouts of the Mr Lee who had worked for Dr McCrory. The man offered me a bowl of clear tea and a sweet bun to eat while I waited and he disappeared into the street. The bun turned out to have a patch of meat stew in a gingery sauce in the centre. Strange combination, sugar and meat and spice. The tea was delicate and refreshing. The man re-appeared with word that Mr Lee would be coming shortly. But after a while another man appeared, gap-toothed and dirty, who asked me to come with him. I offered to pay for the bun and tea but the restaurant owner refused with a bow. I thanked him and followed the new man across the street and into the most notorious of dives, Fan Tan alley, where many a sailor has been made drunk, robbed, and stripped, to be pushed or kicked naked out onto the sidewalk of Fisguard Street and found there, usually alive, in the morning. It was said that absolutely anything could be bought or sold in Fan Tan alley. It was only a few hundred feet long, but very narrow and hemmed by brick walls with the occasional door. The man politely asked me to wait outside one of the doors, which as he opened it to go in let out the resinous opium smell. I ignored the passers by who ducked or squeezed past me in the narrow space. At length the door opened and the gap-toothed man appeared, literally leading Lee behind him by the silken cord of a black and gold robe. Lee blinked in the light – which was not dazzling since the sun never shines in Fan Tan alley – and stood swaying slightly. Even I, no expert on opium, could recognise the pin-point pupils, the hanging open mouth, of the stupor. I doubted if Lee knew me.

There we stood, Lee swaying on his feet, I perplexed and not knowing what to say, and the little gap-toothed man whose pigtail was monstrously long in proportion to his body, in between us looking up eagerly. I knew total defeat: not even the rack would make Lee tell what he knew. I thanked the gap-toothed man, and said goodbye to them both, then walked crossly back to the court-house – only two hundred yards but a world away.

I went to the small room which I slept in at night and, the camp bed folded, used during the day as a private office. I began working on my list of suspects, but no sooner had I dipped my pen into the ink-well than there was a bang at the door. It was Inspector Wilson, one of the original recruits from when Pemberton had hastily formed the Victoria police during the Gold Rush – the 'five foot nine men' as they were sometimes called, since height had been the only qualification apart from the usual 'good character.' Wilson in fact was scarcely up to the height, and stooped from spending most of his time at a desk, in charge of administration and paper-work. He had a peculiar sense of humour which I supposed was characteristic of the Scots Irish whose accent he retained strongly. Although he looked worried he was droll as usual.

'Hobbes, you'll be accompanying me down to the Inner Harbour. There's a young lady's met with an accident: she's lying two fathoms deep. The Superintendent's at Carey Castle cooling his heels for an audience with the Governor, so it devolved on me to take charge of this. Come now.'

I followed hastily, buttoning my tunic. We stepped out into the sun of the square and walked as quickly as we could with dignity, to the edge of the bastion foundation overlooking the harbour, clattered in our heavy boots down the stone steps which led to Wharf Street, crossed it, then clattered down another flight of steps onto the quay.

A hundred yards or so away, near Quattrini's warehouse, a small crowd had gathered, looking at the water. A few people were talking quietly but most were silent.

'Move aside now, move aside,' Wilson said. The crowd separated and we pushed through to the edge of the wharf.

The tide was low and the surface of the water was twenty feet or so below the wharf. Since the sun was behind us, the water was in shadow for some fifty yards out, although beyond that it was sparkling brightly. In the dark shadow it was possible to see to the bottom which was brown and muddy. Ten yards or so out lay the body of a woman, her outline dim but the shape of a billowing dress, perhaps pink, clearly visible, making her look like a huge submerged flower.

'Where's the lighter?' Wilson said impatiently. 'Och, there's it there.'

There was a ship moored at Quattrini's warehouse and around it a lighter appeared with several men in it.

'It was one of Quattrini's warehousemen that brought the message about the body', Wilson explained. 'I sent him back to get a lighter and a grapple. I've also sent for the undertaker and the doctor.'

'The poor dear', said a woman in the crowd. 'I dare say she must have destroyed herself.'

'The usual place,' someone else said darkly. The Inner Harbour attracted suicides.

The lighter was making its way to one of the many vertical wooden step-ladders built into the side of the wharf. Quattrini, bulky in a black waistcoat over a checked shirt, was sitting in the bow, his head turned to look up at us. One of two rowers amidships put down his oar and passed Quattrini a rope. The bow of the lighter disappeared below us. Without ado, Wilson went to the top of the steps and began to climb down backwards. I followed, peering into the black weed-smelling water between the tarred pilings of the wharf. I came down into the boat just in front of the stern, which a man was holding to the ladder, and stumbled to find a seat.

The lighter was large and flat-bottomed. Wilson and I sat facing the stern, where the man gave a shove to push the boat off, then turned his attention to a clamp he was tightening on the stern gunwale. This was attached to chains and curved iron bars in the bottom of the boat.

There was a splash at the bow. Quattrini, half standing up, had dropped the anchor. The boat swung slowly around. The rowers shipped their oars and Quattrini came climbing over the thwarts toward us, the boat lurching as he moved. His face had an odd expression of tension, his eyes bulging as if with pressure, the skin flushed on what was visible of his upper cheeks above his thick black beard. 'Good morning, gentlemen,' he said, but pushed rudely past us to look over the stern.

'Just a moment, Sir', Wilson said calmly. 'I think the Sergeant and I can assist the man. We should look carefully at the disposition of the corpse.'

Quattrini's eyes bulged under raised brows, but he said nothing and moved to take our seat, the boat lurching again as we moved to the stern where we kneeled and looked down into the water. It reminded me of the Aquarium in London. There were schools of silvery minnows and on the bottom several crabs, big as dishes, moving among the trash of the harbour – bottles, jars, pieces of metal, bricks and tins.

The woman was lying on one side and to her front. Her face was not visible. Her hair floated up towards us like a dark brown clump of seaweed. She was wearing a pink hooped crinoline.

'All right', said Wilson to the man with the grapple. 'Full steam ahead.'

From the winch clamped to the gunwale the man lowered the grapple very slowly, an open four-pointed claw on the end of its chain. Such grapples must be used fairly often in a warehouse like Quattrini's to retrieve crates fallen from ships. The man reached out with one hand to guide it in an almost stealthy descent onto the corpse. It came down on the hooped crinoline and a cloud of fine mud began to rise through the water. The man raised his hand clasping the chain and called to the oarsmen to swing the stern to the left. Then he let the grapple fall quite suddenly. 'Back up a little!' he called, and the boat's stern moved slowly over the body. 'Stop!' The chain was now vertical in the water. The man turned the winch handle a few times, then tugged at the chain with one hand. 'Got her! We should lighten the stern. I'll just need one man to help.'

Since Wilson moved promptly forward, I was that one man. The boat lurched and swung around the chain, which now seemed to anchor the stern. The man began to winch the chain in. I peered down. The body was coming up. The grapple had seized it around the waist from the back, and the head and legs drooped down and away. The grapple broke the surface of the water and the back appeared, the pink material of the dress soaking and streaked with mud. The man winched a little more. The stern dipped.

'She's very heavy', the man said. 'I don't understand it.' He winched a little more and the centre of the body came out and up to the gunwale, with water pouring off it. 'I guess we manhandle her in?' the man said uncertainly.

'All right.' My mouth had gone dry. Half-heartedly I reached and grabbed a fold of the woman's dress just below the waist and gave a tug. She hardly moved. The man beside me reached and seized the dress at the level of the neck, just below the water surface, the brown hair swirling around his hand and stroking against his wrist. Both of us pulled hard and the body came up, but it was impossible to haul all that weight by grasping the dress, so we had to let it down again. The winch held it. I decided that if I did not take charge nobody would – or Quattrini would, which would prolong the whole ghastly procedure. 'All right', I said, 'I'll take her by the waist, you take her under one arm, and we'll heave her in.'

'Awright.'

I leaned forward, my ribs pressing against the gunwale, and hooked my right arm around the woman's waist, feeling around the wet material of her dress, my arm plunged underwater. I stubbed my fingers on something hard and rocklike through the cloth and moved my hand further around to get a grip on it. 'All right', I said. 'Heave ho!' The cheerful cliché came out easily but I wished I could take it back. The man and I pulled hard, the stern dipped further, and I felt the woman's dress wet against my cheek. I was almost hugging her as she came out of the water. She lay over the gunwale, water pouring off her. We heaved again and rolled the body onto the seat where she lay facing upwards.

'Aaah!' A bellowing shriek from behind me. I turned my head. It was Quattrini, standing in the bow, looking towards us over the seated oarsmen. His face above his beard had gone pale and his eyes were bulging more than ever.

I looked at last at the body and felt a shiver up my spine. Her face! Then I realised what it was: an enormous purple starfish, about a foot across, centred on one cheek, its thick pointed arms studded with shiny protuberances spread out over the forehead, cheeks and chin. There was only one thing to do. I reached forward and seized one limb of the star. Its skin was rough, like coarse sandpaper, and cold. The whole starfish came off with a squelch. I threw it over the stern into the water with a splash.

The girl's face was pale blue and luckily the eyes were closed, though the lids were swollen and the cheeks were puffy. Just beside the nose where the starfish had been centred was a small patch of abraded flesh, but no blood. Her hair was dark brown from the water but might have been fair if dry. Her dress was dripping and tight over her nipples as if there were no undergarments. There was a huge bulge at her waist as if she were pregnant, but oddly shifted to one side. 'It's a rock', I said to fill the deadly silence. 'I could feel it.' Then I noticed that the pink of the dress, sticking up ridiculously because of its hoops, was streaked and darker in places from the upper legs downwards. This was not silt from the harbour bottom, but blood.

'Can we bring her back to your warehouse, Mr Quattrini?' This was Wilson's voice. 'If you don't mind receiving her as your guest for a short while till the undertaker comes.'

'Guest?' said Quattrini. 'Of course. My God, that was a shock – the sea star. I know this girl. She's one of my domestics. Kathleen Donnelly. Terrible business.' His voice was now completely firm. He began giving orders to the lightermen.

I looked at the body. It was still dripping. The grapple man was sitting slumped beside me. 'I knew her', he said quietly, 'Pretty gal she was. Jesus Christ.' He leaned his face forward into his hands.

The corpse frightened me less than I might have expected. But McCrory had not frightened me much either. A corpse was, after all, simply a corpse. She – whoever she had been – was simply not present. This was not 'she' but 'it'. At a given moment she had ceased to be and left this familiar thing she had lived with all her life – now embarked on decay. The starfish had only started the job the worms would finish. I had often contemplated in agony a universe in which as the mechanical meaning of things was discovered the spiritual meaning had vanished – as this girl had vanished although the abandoned machine of her body was here. It was a mere thing. But she had been more than a thing – no thing, not nothing. Although I had lost my faith I could believe that something had survived. 'She' was not here, but elsewhere.

Then as the lighter was rowed across the harbour, in the transient sparkle of the sun on the water, the comfort of my intuition began to fade. If she was elsewhere it was only as a ghost – either in her own right or in the mind of those who had known her. How long could a ghost survive? I had steeled myself to the fact that knowledge – or 'science' as we are beginning to call it – had abolished the immortal soul. But what if, as the emptiness of this corpse suggested, there was after all a soul, but not necessarily an immortal one? If body was nothing without soul, what was soul without body? The great John Donne in his sermons had insisted that at the day of judgement the *body* would be reconstituted into new life. A comforting dream. What if the soul was in turn mortal? This would be a worse nightmare than no soul at all: the girl's soul merely a ghost fading away as her abandoned body rotted.

By the time we had hauled the corpse up the steps to the wharf at Quattrini's warehouse the undertaker's wagon had arrived. The corpse was loaded onto it, grotesquely on one side, with that huge rock still inside the dress. Dr Powell would do an autopsy at the undertaker's. Wilson, showing no signs of wear, scurried back to his paper at the courthouse and I was left to find out what I could about the dead girl.

Quattrini was ready, with his usual energy, to go straight back to work, but I cornered and requested a brief word in private. Scowling, he agreed, and led me to a small cubicle overlooking the warehouse, expelling the clerk with a few rough exclamations as he had for our previous interview. Quattrini apparently imposed himself on the whole warehouse – now here, now there – not limiting himself to a particular office room. As before we made ourselves comfortable on the hard chairs available, though Quattrini sat a little further away this time. Twitching restlessly, he gave off an air of impatience.

'I tell you right away who the girl was', he said as I brought out my notebook. 'Kathleen Donnelly, though we called her Kathy. A lovely girl, very industrious, very devout. I've never employed irreligious girls in my house, and she was the best Irish type – meek, and she knew her place, never gave any trouble at all. She was twenty one or two years old and she's been in service for me for five years. My brother sent her up to me from San Francisco. Her older sister was in service with him. Why should she do a thing like this? A melancholy attack? The hysterics? Let me tell you, I'm far too busy a man to understand such things.'

He visibly strained upwards with impatience to get up from the chair and back to work.

'How many servants do you have?'

'Kathy and another girl, Ellen – also Irish. Good workers. But not too much to do. There's just me and my kid, Giuseppino, and we're both down here most of the time.'

'Did she have friends?

'I wouldn't know. Very religious girl. Like I say, she went to church regular, with Ellen. I'm generous with days off. I don't know what she done with her time.'

'Has she been in good health?'

'Why would I know?'

'So you've no idea why she did this – assuming she threw herself in deliberately.'

'I seen that rock in her dress. Of course she threw herself in. Good way to make sure she went down and stayed down.'

'Do you care about her?' This was from my heart, not my mind.

'Waddya mean?' Quattrini's eyes bulged out and he levelled a finger at me like a gun. 'Why you ask questions like that?'

'You talk about her in such a neutral fashion now, yet you were upset when we pulled her out.'

'Can you blame me? Christ! That damned sea star on her face.'

'Did you know it was she before we pulled her up?'

'Look, Sergeant, I don't know what you're getting at. I can talk to Mr Pemberton about this.'

'Of course you can. But I have to ask these questions. Did you know it was she?'

'I thought it might be her. The dress seemed familiar, and she wasn't home this morning. Ellen was flappin' about it at breakfast. But I just thought she'd made a mistake about her morning off and gone out early into town to shop or somethin'. Then when I heard someone say there was a stiff just off the quay in the water and I went out and seen that pink dress in the water I thought, Jeez, it might be her. Forgive my language, but yes, it was upsetting.' He took out a clean white handkerchief and mopped his brow.

'You say she was devout. What church did she go to?'

'Same as us. St Pat's.'

'You've nothing more to say about her?'

'Nothin'.' This gave Quattrini the excuse to rise to his feet.

I stood up too. 'You know the names of her nearest relations?'

'I can find out. In San Francisco, they'll be.'

'Please do. I'll come and see you later today or tomorrow.'

'What for?' He seemed to feel he had the upper hand again and had become belligerent. 'I'll do the right thing by the girl, give her a good funeral.'

'I mean, if I find out anything that might interest you. There'll be an autopsy of course.'

'You mean to see if she had a bun in the oven?'

'That sort of thing. It's usual.'

Quattrini's expression changed again – God, the man was volatile – to one of calm piety. 'I could swear there's nothing of that sort', he said. 'She was too good a girl for that.'

Back at the Court House, Parry told me to pursue the case of the drowned girl, to go to the undertaker's and get the results of the autopsy which was being done, and to explore whatever connections she had in order to ascertain whether it was 'the usual sort of case' – a pregnant girl killing herself in panic and despondency – or whether there was foul play involved, which Parry doubted. I could tell he was pleased to give me something to draw me away from the McCrory investigation, which he must see as a waste of time.

A telegram had arrived in response to a query I had sent to the University of Virginia. It was from the Registrar of the School of Medicine.

```
RE RICHARD MC CRORY DECEASED STOP BORN 1830 ALBANY
NEW YORK STOP RELIGION CONGREGATIONALIST STOP DEGREES
FROM THIS SCHOOL BONA FIDE BUT PERSONA NON GRATA DUE
IRREGULAR ASSOCIATIONS NOTABLY JOHN NOYES PREACHER
FREE LOVE COMMUNISM IN ONEIDA COMMUNITY NEW YORK STOP
MC CRORY LEFT ONEIDA OR EXPELLED RETURNED VIRGINIA
MENTAL ALIENIST WITH PRIVATE ASYLUM STOP UNSUCCESSFUL
STOP JOINED CONFEDERATE ARMY AND CASHIERED SUSPICION
SPYING STOP MOVED SAN FRANCISCO WHERE ALIENATION OF
AFFECTIONS SUIT CAUSED DISREPUTE THIS SCHOOL STOP NO
RELATIONS KNOWN HERE STOP SUGGEST TRY ALBANY STOP MC
CRORY NOT VIRGINIAN OR GENTLEMAN
```

I liked this last phrase, remembering Mrs Somerville's insistence that

McCrory was *such* a gentleman. My attention stuck on the name John Noyes. I had seen it somewhere. Yes: in McCrory's library, on the spine of a small book or pamphlet. I wrote a note to Rabinowitz who had McCrory's goods in storage, asking if he would be so kind as to search for the book and send to me urgently.

Since the undertaker would arrange the funeral, at Quattrini's expense, and was well equipped to deal with blood and body wastes, there had seemed no point in transporting the girl's corpse back and forth to the doctor's office. I caught Dr Powell as he had just finished his autopsy. He was brisk in manner and known to be competent. We talked privately in the undertaker's office.

'I'll write a report', Powell said. 'But I'll tell you my findings, insofar as they amount to anything. Cause of death was drowning: the lungs were full of water. She had been in the water six or seven hours: rigour had only partly set in. Thus, she entered the water some while before dawn. She had, as you will have observed, inserted a heavy rock into the front of her dress. She was not, by the way, wearing stays, by which I assume she got up in the middle of the night and did not bother with her "toilette". The rock is one such as are piled at the end of the quay near the warehouses where she was found.' Powell smiled. 'Forgive me. I'm doing your detective work for you.'

'That's all right. Your observations are to the point.'

'There are no signs of foul play. No bruises or cuts except for a small contusion on one cheek which puzzled me somewhat…'

'A star fish. It was on her face when we pulled her out.'

'How ghastly. That explains it. To repeat: no signs of foul play. And no signs of ill health. Nor was she "enceinte". She was in fact in the course of a "monthly", and wearing the usual towel. That was the blood you may have noticed. I should mention, though, that she was not 'virgo intacta'. Of course the membrane might have ruptured accidentally in the past, but then one might expect the opening to be less than it is. She was a 'nullipara' – that is, she had never had children. That is all I can report. She was not known to me personally. Must have been a pretty girl, but in spite of her swollen appearance now, I should say that she was quite thin. Sad business. She was wearing a locket on a chain. You may claim it from the undertaker if you wish.'

We shook hands and Dr Powell left. The undertaker appeared and I asked for the locket. It had been placed in an envelope. I asked permission to examine it in the undertaker's office, since I planned to be on the move and did not want to return to the court house. I sat down at a desk and opened the envelope.

The locket was quite large, of silver, oval with an imitation ribbon diagonally across it, also of silver, which gave a slightly vulgar effect. It was on a silver chain. Modestly expensive. I found the catch and pressed it with my fingernail. A small amount of water dripped out onto the table. The locket opened with the usual butterfly effect of two oval recesses connected by the hinge. In one was a curling lock of light brown hair, neatly tied with a silk thread. In the other was a photograph of a face of man wearing a straw boater. But since it had a protective cover of thin glass which was still misted from the damp, the face could not be properly seen. I debated whether to force the glass off, but decided to be patient and let it dry, in case the photograph was stuck to the glass by damp and might be damaged. I put the locket, spread open, carefully back into the envelope which I wrapped tightly around it, secured it with a rubber band from the undertaker's desk, and put it in my pocket.

My plan was to walk to Quattrini's, talk to the other servant, and take a look at the dead girl's effects. On the way I passed the Catholic church she had attended, a large barn-like building of clapboard. I knocked at the door of the priest's house, beside the church, made of the same clapboard. The door was opened by a boy in a cassock. I was shown into a parlour, where I waited for a few minutes below a picture of Jesus holding out a sacred heart with rays of light emanating from it, so that it looked like a bloody pin-cushion.

The priest entered. I had already seen him at McCrory's funeral, speaking church Latin. He introduced himself as Father McMahon. His accent was American or Irish. He was black haired, dark jowled, pale skinned, and smoothly plump.

'I'm enquiring about one of your parishioners, Miss Kathleen Donnelly, whose body was found in the harbour this morning.'

'Poor thing, poor thing, it's a tragedy so it is. I heard of it already.' He spread out his hands in an eloquent gesture of resignation to the will of God.

'What did you know of the young lady?'

'Self murder, if it be so – and I'm sure by the looks of it, it is – is a terrible thing, Sergeant. It cuts the poor girl off from her communion from God and consigns her to everlasting night. Alas, we cannot even lay her to rest among her own.'

I had forgotten about this particular Christian spite against suicides. I was almost tempted to remark, as John Donne had in an essay, that since Jesus Christ was God he must have planned his fate in advance and therefore was committing 'self homicide' at the crucifixion. Instead I asked, 'Did she ever come to you in trouble?'

'Now, now, Sergeant, I take it you are a Protestant.'

'An Anglican by upbringing.'

'A Protestant then, so you'll not know that the secrecy of the confession is sacred. It may never be divulged – not even under the most terrible tortures.'

'I realise that. I wasn't thinking about the confessional, but the possibility that she had asked your advice, or confided her worries to you.'

'Sure these poor girls, they come from country areas – she was from Donegal – they don't confide their worries to any but their own kind, and that in their own language, the Gaelic, which I don't happen to speak. It is a language of wantonness and crudeness – without refinement.'

'But she would have made her confession in English? Surely she spoke English.'

'To be sure. I did hear her in confessional, of course. And I absolved her in Latin – which your church does not know. Apart from that I never talked with her.'

'You don't remember, though, if she came to Mass with any particular friends, or…'

'Sergeant, at Holy Mass my eyes are not on my congregation as individuals, but as a community of poor sinners come to receive the power of redemption.'

'Thank you. I won't waste your time any further.' I turned to leave. But at the door I could not resist asking a question. 'Father,' (although this word almost stuck in my throat), 'may I ask if you are a Jansenist?'

Father McMahon seemed to swell with pride as he replied with a smile, 'That's an astute observation, Sergeant. I suppose it's my devotion to my calling which elicits it from you. Of course I would not admit to being a Jansenist pure and simple. I am simply a priest of the Holy Roman Church. But my seminary, at Maynooth in Ireland, was directed by priests of a definitely Jansenist persuasion.'

'I'm not sure,' I said, 'what Dr Powell's statement on this girl's death may be. I imagine he may say she died by her own hand, or as a result of misadventure. Perhaps, since she was a religious girl, you can give her the benefit of the doubt.'

Father McMahon's smile vanished. 'Of course it was self murder', he said sourly. They say she had a rock in her dress.'

'They'll say all sorts of things', I said. 'Who knows what happened?'

'*God* knows', he said triumphantly. 'It's not up to me to give her the benefit of the doubt. Do you think we can deceive the all seeing eye of God?'

Faced with the irrefutable, though circular, logic of this question, I gave up and merely said 'Goodbye.' I went on my way feeling a puff of intellectual vanity that I had recognised Father McMahon's Jansenism. This Irish priest was not the kind of warm and accepting man I imagined caring for his flocks on the warm shores of the Mediterranean – whose clear light I had seen in paintings was like the light in Victoria now that Spring had come.

By the time I had reached Quattrini's house, on the edge of town at Hillside, my new self was back again. I enjoyed being a 'detective.' After all my agonising about God's laws versus the cold inanimate laws of Darwinian Nature, I was content enough to enforce the laws of the world I lived in – which presented problems as ticklish as any in theology. Although Dr Powell had said there were no physical signs of foul play, a pretty young girl did not throw herself into the sea clutching a rock to her bosom unless there had been foul play of another sort than physical.

19

Quattrini's house was in fact a mansion, with a wide veranda and all sorts of wooden fretwork and design of the sort coming to be known as 'gingerbread' – rare, as yet, in Victoria, but apparently coming into fashion in San Francisco. The bell was answered by a servant in a mob cap and apron, no more than a girl, of perhaps sixteen, dark haired and pale cheeked. She opened the door only a few inches and told me there was no one at home.

'Are you Ellen? You're the one I'd like to talk to.'

She opened the door more fully and her eyes widened as she took in the fact that I was a policeman. 'Is it about poor Kathleen?', she said, pronouncing it almost as 'Catchleen', in a lilting, almost Scottish accent. She raised a pocket handkerchief, already in her hand, to her face and wiped her eyes. When she took it away it was clear she had been crying a lot. Her eyes were bloodshot.

'May I come in?' I entered the house past the girl. Standing in the hallway, I said 'I'd like to see Kathleen's room please. Can you show it to me?'

'We shared a room, Sir. I'd be too ashamed to let you see it. It's up in the top of the house, and of course it's full of our things. It wouldn't be right.'

I had become used to Victoria's free and easy lack of procedural restrictions. I could insist on seeing the room right away and barge up there and ransack it if I wished. But I agreed, it would not be right.

'Could we go and sit down then? So that I can ask you a few questions?'

'Yes, Sir'. Looking frightened, Ellen led the way back along the hall to a huge kitchen, where there was a mass of freshly washed dishes set to dry in racks near a double sink. She asked me to sit down at the table on which were carrots and celery she had been peeling and slicing.

'When did you hear of Kathleen's death?' I asked.

'Just now, at lunch time. When Pino came he told me.'

'Pino?'

'Mr Quattrini's son. He sometimes comes home for luncheon.' Ellen blushed, then raised her handkerchief to her eyes.

'Didn't you miss her in the morning? Or in the middle of the night?'

'Indeed I did. When I awoke this morning she wasn't there. I thought maybe she'd gone downstairs early. But she wasn't here either.'

'Did Mr Quattrini notice she wasn't here?'

'Him? No. He's in such a hurry to get to work in the morning he'd not notice anything.'

'And what did you think when she didn't come back later in the morning?'

'Nothing. I never know what to think about anything.' This remark sounded plaintive.

'Was anything missing from your room?'

'Not that I noticed.'

'All her clothes are there?'

'Yes. Pino said she had her pink dress on, that she was wearing yesterday. He saw her at the warehouse. He said she was all blue and puffed up. It's horrible.' Ellen wiped her eyes again, and let out a little sob, then surprisingly broke into an abrupt wailing sound – 'Ochone, Och a Chatchleen, mo vrone, mo vrone!' Or at least that is how I transcribe it. She paused and looked at me, wiping her tears. 'I've seen drownded people', she said. 'At home in Ireland. I never dreamed Katchleen would end up like that.'

'Are you from the same place in Ireland?'

'Och yes. Derrybeg – the Bloody Foreland, they call it. And aren't we cousins?'

'And is she what you'd call a good girl?' I asked, feeling I must be sounding like Father McMahon.

Ellen looked at me in indignation. 'Of course she was a good girl. None better. Guh mannee jeea air an anam.'

'What does that mean?'

'May God's blessings be on her soul.'

'How about her stays?' I was suddenly fed up with getting nowhere.

'What?' Her eyes widened. 'How do you know that? They're up in the room, on the chair.

'She wasn't wearing them. That's how I know.'

'Did you see her undressed?' She looked at me in horror.

'No. The doctor mentioned it to me. Did it strike you as odd that she should get dressed and leave her stays behind?'

Ellen now blushed hotly which, since the rest of her face was pale, gave a patchy clown-like appearance to her cheeks. She looked at the table. 'Not really', she muttered.

'How could she get dressed in the middle of the night and leave the room without you noticing?'

She continued looking at the table, saying nothing.

'You *did* notice it!'

'I was half asleep and I heard her getting up, but I didn't open my eyes. It's best not to notice things like that.'

'Why?'

There was no reply.

'Did you know any of Kathleen's secrets? After all, you were cousins.'

'If I did, I wouldn't tell them', she said vehemently.

'It seems she may have drowned herself. Do you think she did?

Ellen sighed. 'She might have done.' She began crying again.

'Why, Ellen?'

'I can't say, Sir.'

'Wouldn't she want you to?'

'No, she wouldn't. She said to me once: 'Aileen my girl, as you grow older you'll learn not to cry about your sorrows. You'll learn to take them into yourself and no one will ever know.'

'Did she say that recently?'

'Yes, Sir.'

'So she was suffering from a sorrow. And you knew what it was.'

'She never told me.'

'Ellen – or is it Aileen? – I can see that you're very upset and you don't like to let down your friend. But if you think she has been badly done by, you should let me know. When a person commits suicide, we have to understand why. I believe you when you say Kathleen told you no secrets. But I think you must have guessed some of them, and I know you're hiding something.'

'How can you know that?'

'Because when you mentioned Pino, and when I mentioned Kathleen's getting dressed without her stays, you blushed.'

'Well, about the stays I would, wouldn't I? It's not right for a gentleman to ask such things.'

'And Pino?'

'I *hate* Pino', she said, scrunching her handkerchief into a tight ball and squeezing it. 'If I let him do what he wanted I'd be in the same fix as *her!* I'd be lying dead upon the shore, so I would. Like father, like son!'

'You mean Mr Quattrini had relations with Kathleen?

'Of course! The beast. She would go down and visit him at night. I knew it, though she would say it was for a walk in the back yard. Even when it was raining. I knew it! So this morning at first I thought she must still be lying in the bed of the pig, having slept in. Then I remembered she couldn't have been.'

'You mean she was having her monthly?'

'You know that too! Well, of course. And very happy she was to have it, too. She had waited, I guess, three months for it, and then when it came she weren't half relieved. But it lasted over three weeks, by my count. I guess it was one week for each missed month.'

'How long had she been having this relation with Mr Quattrini?'

'Coming on a year. Mrs Quattrini died not long before that.'

'And it was a reluctant relation on her part?'

'She never liked him! Sometimes she'd feign sick. Many a night she'd complain, in the old bull's – pardon me Sir – in Mr Quattrini's hearing, like: "Oh dear, Ellen, I believe I have a headache tonight – will you smoke that old Dudeen in my ear?" It's custom we have, if a person has a headache or a cold, of blowing pipe-smoke hot into the ear. Mr Quattrini didn't like that, he thought it stupid, so he did. Maybe it put the old bull off his pleasures. Her heart was really with her young man.'

'Who was that?'

'She'd never tell me. Only she said he was a lovely young man, and quite the gentleman. When she had the day off – which wasn't often, let me tell you – she'd dress up like the dickens and off she'd go to see him, like as if she was going courting. But she would never tell me his name.'

'Did you ever see her locket?'

'Of course. Why, you know everything, don't you?' Ellen seemed by now quite perked up with talking. 'She kept his picture in it. But danged if she ever let *me* see it.'

'Didn't she worry about being gotten with child?'

'You didn't know her! She was gay and lively, like. Only when her monthlies were late she grew thin with worry. Then she went away for the night, with Mr Quattrini's permission, would you believe it, to stay with a friend. Not a friend I knew of! And whether it was the travelling, or what, the next day her monthly came, and I guess because it had been backed up so long it kinda wore her out and she was more miserable than before.'

I felt somewhat confused by all this, and I realised that Ellen's knowledge of female physiology was not necessarily more detailed than my own.

As if to confirm this, she went on: 'That's why I get upset when Pino… when he wants to do *that*. You know what I mean. I'm afraid I'll catch a child, and then what would I do? Do you think it's enough to sit on the pot and cough?'

'What do you mean?'

'Me mother – God bless her soul – always said that if a woman got up out of the bed after her husband had done *that*, and went and sat on the pot and gave a few hard coughs, that would take care of it. But she had seven of us, and she would have had more if her insides hadn't dropped out.'

'I doubt if the method works', I said. 'Listen to me. If you don't want this Pino to keep interfering with you, you must tell him so. And if he doesn't stop, you must seek another job. There's a shortage of maids in Victoria. You must know that. You'd have no difficulty at all finding employment.'

'But not in a good Catholic household like this!'

To this I had no answer. I stayed for while, telling Ellen that Quattrini would never dare treat her badly, knowing the police now knew the whole story, and assuring that Kathleen must not have suffered much – which I did not believe.

I wanted to confront Quattrini, to reverse in righteous accusation the positions we now held – of dominating Quattrini, inoffensive Chad Hobbes. But to do this I would need to know more. I had a hypothesis I could try on Dr Powell. But I felt more inclined to receive knowledge from the horse's mouth, as it were. I went to the Windsor Rooms, which were empty except for a janitor scrubbing the floors, and asked for Sylvie. Since I was in uniform I had no difficulty in being directed to a shabby rooming house just around the corner, the *Exelsior*. My ring was answered by a woman with a scarf over her curlers, who showed me into a seedy parlour with tattered armchairs and settees, where I waited for a few minutes. There was a smell of stale cigar smoke and the ash trays had not been emptied. There was an abundance of worn velvet in the upholstery. Perhaps in the dim lamplight of after dark, to men at least half inebriated, the parlour would convey sufficient elegance.

Sylvie entered, more than presentable in a canary yellow dress with a black shawl. She was rouged and eye-shadowed as if ready for the Windsor Rooms, although it was still afternoon. She held out her hand, palm downward, as if I might kiss it. I took it, held it for a moment, and let it go. She laughed, as if to let me know that her gesture had been deliberately facetious. 'To what do I owe the honour of a visit so soon?' she asked.

'I'm afraid I have to ask questions. Your advice, really. You were so helpful last night, and frankly I'm naïve about certain matters. I need to catch up on some facts.'

She motioned me to the settee and sat down beside me, though not too close, pouting in a deliberate way. 'It's not a *private* visit then', she said.

'I'm afraid not. I'm sorry to impose on you, but if there's any way I can repay you another time, I shall. I'm now investigating the case of a young lady who seems to have drowned herself this morning.'

'Yes, it is all over town I believe. Pulled out of the water with a starfish on her face. A servant girl, I was told. In the family way?'

'One might suppose so, but apparently not. Can you please tell me about such things from a woman's point of view? I've looked in textbooks of physiology and medicine for information, but there is none, or it avoids the point.' I was thinking of the *Medical Physiology* I had taken from McCrory's. 'What can a woman who has relations with men do to avoid becoming "in the family way", as you put it.'

'You mean what do we do as a contraceptic? Different girls have different ways. A "douche" of strong vinegar is the best. Some use a sponge – soaked in vinegar, or lemon juice, or quinine. Then some girls can sense when they are ready to "catch" – by a twinge in their back or stomach when they are half way between their monthlies – and they abstain at that time. *There's* an area where you find rubbish in the medical books and from the doctors! One girl showed me a book she had got hold of, by a doctor called Scales, supposed to be the most prominent medical man in the States, who said that the *safest* time was exactly between the monthlies! I'm sure a lot of women have been "caught" by that advice. Then, of course, if a girl feels she has caught, even before waiting for the missed monthly, she'll take quinine to bring it on – which it sometimes does. And after that there's always a hot bath and plenty of gin. Then there are ways of bearing down, to force a monthly on. And if all else fails, and a little "by-blow", as we call it, must come to light, then there's the baby farm. There are several here in town. If you care for your child, you pay for it to live, month by month. If not, you let it take its chances. Is that enough for you, Sergeant? I think I see you looking a little green. I could tell you worse things – of girls rolling down stairs and breaking bones…'

'In truth it's a subject I know little of. But I want to ask you about one more thing: abortion, by a specialist in that line.'

'That's a delicate subject, Sergeant, since it's against the law.'

'Can such an abortion be procured in Victoria?'

'Of course. But I could never tell you where. It's not a fair question.'

'Can you tell me – from hearsay perhaps – what the after effects of such an operation are?'

'Tiredness. Melancholia. An infection if it's not done properly.'

'Bleeding?'

'Like a stuck pig, as they say.'

'For some time?'

'Several weeks.'

'Thank you. I think that's what I wanted to know.'

'Was she bleeding, the drowned girl?'

'I shouldn't say, because it hasn't been made public. But your guess is a good one. I'd like to know who does such things, though – I mean abortions.'

'I can't say. But look, Sergeant Hobbes.' She moved closer and put her hand on my knee. 'I like you well enough, and I know you don't look down on us girls – I don't know why. Is it that your lady friend is one of us? But that doesn't fit. Anyway, since I know you're interested in the carrot-haired mad-doctor, and since he's dead and out of the way now, I'll tell you: he did some work in that line.'

'All roads lead to that man!' I could not help exclaiming. I fell silent. It all came together in my mind. I remembered the scraping tools among McCrory's surgical scalpels. 'With ladies from the Windsor Rooms?' I asked.

'No names, now. And certainly not I. But for one or two I know he did.'

I took Sylvie's hand and lifted it off my knee but again held it for a moment before letting it go.

'What do you and your friends think about McCrory's death?' I said.

'Well, it looks as though the Indian did it, doesn't it? But some of the girls say a man like McCrory could have been killed by anybody. He knew so many secrets. Yet I find it hard to believe he was a blackmailer. Once he started on that his whole life would have failed: it was built on his guarantee of absolute confidence. And though he would talk to us girls, he would never speak of his patients. His profession was like ours.' She smiled sweetly. 'We must also provide complete confidence. We too know many secrets. And a girl who tried blackmail would be swiftly ruined. She would lose all her friends and nobody would go near her.'

'You express it very clearly.'

'I was a school teacher once – in California. Then something happened to put me into this life. I'm not complaining. But when a girl becomes tired of it, she begins to slip down the scale. You see, to "dance" in a high class place like the Rooms, a girl must enjoy it. If she no longer does, she soon ends up on the street. But I'm putting by some savings, and I shall retire soon, and return to California. This will merely have been a gay episode in my life. And you Sergeant? You look less happy than the other night. Troubles with your "amour"?'

'I pulled the drowned girl out of the harbour.' But I knew that, in itself, was not the origin of my 'tum tum' sickness.

'Never worry, she'll be happier where she is now', Sylvie said.

I got up. 'Again I have to thank you', I said. 'If you should ever need me to speak up for you, I shall.'

'If something should go wrong with your "amour", come and see me.'

'Thank you.'

The appropriate way to take leave of Sylvie was apparently with a kiss on the rouged cheek which she was turning towards me. Again she smelled strongly of a heavy floral scent. I preferred the wood-smoke of Lukswaas's hair. But I liked Sylvie.

It is true, I don't look down on those girls. I don't mind what they do. Could I fall in love with someone like Sylvie? Perhaps. Could I sleep with her

*night after night knowing how many men had possessed her? I don't think
so. But I've never slept with any woman night after night. Is it because of my
mother? If I despised a woman for making love with more than one man I
would have to despise my own mother. Was my mother – is my mother –
a whore? Not for an instant. She had her own reasons. Sylvie has her own
reasons. I like her.*

I returned briefly to the court house where I sat down in my bedroom
and carefully opened the locket again. The glass had dried and become
transparent. Behind it the photograph had faded slightly, perhaps from the
water, but its browns and whites were clear enough to show the face of a
candid-looking young man in an Oxford boater. Frederick. This was what
I had feared, since seeing the boater through the misted glass. The lock of
hair, now dry, light brown with golden streaks, was Frederick's.

I decided to finish with the business of the drowned girl before the day
was over. I put the locket back in its envelope and in my tunic pocket. I
walked to the warehouse and asked to see Quattrini. The scene was at first
like a repetition of our other interviews. The clerk was shooed out of the
room, and Quattrini sat down overpoweringly close to me. He pulled out
his watch and looked at it. 'I hope this is important, my lad', he said affably.
'I'm a very busy man.' He was certainly his usual self. But I recalled the
anguished yell when the corpse had been pulled out of the water. I had
decided that since the autopsy report was not yet ready the only way to
shake Quattrini was through bluff.

'Your servant, Kathleen Donnelly, had had an abortion. What's more we
know she obtained it from Dr McCrory.'

Quattrini looked startled, but quickly said, 'Dio mio! Who'd have
thought it? A nice Irish church-going girl like her.'

'Please Mr Quattrini. We're talking about a criminal matter – the
murder of an unborn child. Why not be open with me? You can see, I'm not
taking this down in my notebook, and no charges have been laid – yet. If
you insist on providing no explanation, I shall make your life very difficult
by calling in your other servant, Ellen, your son Giuseppino, and yourself,
for questioning at the courthouse. I suggest you provide some explanation
– especially since the man who performed the abortion has since been the
victim of a murder which is under investigation.'

In fact I knew that if I wrote in my report about the dead Kathleen something like: 'suspected she was mentally deranged after a surgical abortion by Dr McCrory (now deceased)' – the police, even under the direction of Pemberton, a man of probity if there ever was, would almost certainly 'let sleeping dogs lie.'

But Quattrini was looking at me in a stunned way, the blustering gone out of him. 'You wouldn't do that, my lad', he said in a dry voice. 'It'd ruin me. And what would Mrs Somerville think? Bella!'

'It doesn't need to come to her ears,' I said, although making the mental reserve that if Quattrini had been involved in foul play it would be a different matter. 'But I want the whole story.'

'It's nothin' unusual, I guess. I got the girl in pod, and I arranged for it to be taken care of.'

'How did you know McCrory would do such a thing?'

'Like I said already. I knew him from the Somervilles.'

'You said before that was the *only* place you knew him.'

'Awright, awright. When Kathleen told me she was that way, I went to see McCrory at his house and I said, 'What do I do?' And he said he'd take care of it. So he did. That was a coupla weeks before he was killed.'

'What did you pay?'

'A hundred dols. Pretty steep, but what could I do?'

'What could *she* do? Did she not want you to put things straight another way?'

'By marryin' her?' Quattrini's eyes bulged and he became red again. 'A slut?'

'Did she suggest marriage?'

'Sure she did. She was crazy – scared to death. But when I told her I could arrange sumpn', she calmed down. Also I said I'd give her some money.'

'And did you?'

'Fifty dols.'

'Did you attempt to resume relations with her? Last night for instance?'

'Dio mio! You been talkin' to Ellen?'

'Yes.'

'She ain't got no business…'

'Wait a minute. If you give her any trouble over this, you'll be in even bigger trouble. Of course Ellen answered my questions. And by the way, your son Pino is attempting to force her. Do you know about that?'

'Christ!' Quattrini actually jumped up from his chair and stood in front of me, puffing up as if about to explode. 'Giuseppino! The little bastard! I'll have his skin! I'll send him back to Frisco!'

I think you should give Ellen her leave, with some money as compensation. In fact I expect you to do so.'

'Awright, awright, I will. Jesus! Giuseppino! He's only sixteen.'

'So you attempted to resume relations with Kathleen last night?'

'I asked her if she'd come to my room. But she said she was still bleedin' from the surgery, and she couldn't.'

'Was she upset?'

'Not that I could see. She was a great one for weepin' and wailin', but last night she was cold as ice.'

'And what did you say?'

'Whaddya mean? Look, Hobbes, I'm a man, you understand? I told you that before. I got needs. I ain't remarried. So what am I supposed to do? Am I a saint? That's what I said to Kathleen last night. 'Am I a saint?''

'And she said, "Yes, of course you are…" I couldn't help myself.

'Awright, awright. She said, "You ain't no saint, you're a devil." But she didn't mean it. She weren't cryin' or nothin'.'

'Where were you on Wednesday afternoon of last week'

'You mean when the doctor was killed? You don't think I'd do that? Hey, come on, Hobbes.' Quattrini, still standing, loomed over me.

I got up, taller than he. 'In this context you should call me Sergeant', I said. 'Please answer my question.'

'That's the damned thing,' Quattrini said, licking his lips. 'Usually I'd be here at the warehouse, but I wasn't. I was at home, with her – with Kathleen. I'd gone home for lunch, which I sometimes do. She was feelin' poorly, on account of her bein' on the rag after the surgery. She wasn't up to doin' housework. So I gave Ellen the day off and I stayed at home with Kathleen.'

'Doing what?' I was not inclined to accept that Quattrini had been acting out of loving-kindness.

'Hell, you don't need to know that.'

'Doing what?'

'I got her to give me a back rub, that sort of thing – hell, there's lots of things a woman can do for a man. You know that, Hobbes – I mean Sergeant.'

'So you still used the girl.'

'She didn't mind. Usually, like I say, she could be as cold as ice. I mean, she never really enjoyed it', if you know what I mean. But that afternoon she was feelin' low. She even said she wanted me to hold onto her and take care of her. Then over the followin' days she became cold again, sort of floatin' around, pale, like an angel, not talkin' to no one.'

'And now she's dead and she can't say you were really with her that afternoon.'

'Sergeant.' Quattrini seemed chastened. 'You can't pin that killin' on me. Why would I do that?'

'Perhaps he was blackmailing you. You're a rich man.'

'If I stay in Victoria much longer I won't stay rich… But McCrory, a blackmailer? Never. Like I told you once before, there was sumpn' funny about him. I figure he got close to women, not by cuddlin' with 'em, but by helpin' em out. Almost as if he *was* a woman. Hell, I never minded him doin' the surgery on Kathleen.'

'You might have been jealous?'

'With another man, sure. Getting' into her private parts? When I have a woman she's *mine*.' Quattrini had rebounded into his usual confidence. 'But a blackmailer? No. McCrory believed in whatever he did – all those weird ideas – he was almost religious about 'em. Made me think of some priests I've known.'

'Don't you see you contributed to this girl's ruin?' I said, lapsing into priggishness. I tried to correct this by being more worldly. 'Why take advantage of your servant? Why not get your needs met elsewhere? Say, in a dance hall.'

'And throw away good money on whores? *Putane*? What do you take me for?'

'So you had no quarrel with McCrory.'

'Nope. The girl went over there one day. I sent the 100 dols with her. He kept her overnight and sent her back in a buggy. No receipt, but I didn't expect that. I saw him the Sunday after, out at the Farm. We had a private word together. He said Kathleen should come and see him once a week for a while. I should give her time off on Friday mornings, and send her to him with an envelope with ten dols, and he would give her a treatment. He said she needed it for her nerves, after the operation. Now you might think it was a kinda blackmail – to get ten dols a week outa me. And I did get annoyed, like it was an extra fee I hadn't bargained for. But he said it was for her own good. And you know what? I believed him.'

'I suppose that will be all', I said. 'As you see, I haven't taken this down. I may want to ask you more questions though. Oh yes. If you have any influence with that priest of yours, Father McMahon, see if you can get him to turn a blind eye to how that girl died, and bury her in consecrated ground. He thinks God doesn't turn a blind eye on anything. But you know, Mr Quattrini, that the girl would never have killed herself, had her life not been made intolerable.'

'Don't you play God!' Quattrini flared for a moment. 'But I'll talk to the Father. He's hard man. Sergeant!' Quattrini took my arm and looked wildly into my eyes. 'Never a word of this to Bella Somerville! That woman's pure as the driven snow. If she heard one word that I was sleepin' with Kathleen, I'd be finished! Then I might as well walk off the quay into the harbour myself!'

'Of course I won't mention it to her.' I was becoming a keeper of secrets.

Quattrini believed McCrory – the Southern gentleman. Similarly he trusts me, and reveals himself to me – the English gentleman. McCrory and I apparently have it in common that we appear gentlemen. Quattrini referred to McCrory as a 'devil'. Then there is the 'King George devil.' All Englishmen are' King George'. Witherspoon. King George par excellence – George Beaumont. Another gentleman. There is something devilish about Beaumont – his rictus smile, his woodenness. But that is a caricature. What is wooden about the devil? The devil is surely like a snake. He creeps along, he is subtle, deceptive, two faced. If I were the devil how would I want to appear in Victoria? What would be my outer face? Perhaps a wooden soldier like Beaumont. Or a whited sepulchre like Firbanks. My father used to joke that the Devil if he wanted to incarnate himself as a person would surely choose to do so as a clergyman. 'I mean, why the devil would the devil want to appear as he is – evil and twisted?,' he said. 'He would appear as some smooth and jovial country vicar – like me!' It was generous of him, or perhaps cautious, not to say 'like some smooth country curate', meaning Aubrey. But he had a point. Everyone here is afraid of the Indians. They are devils. Freezy obliges, he lives up to the fears, by chopping his wife's head off on the beach facing town. Wiladzap, Lukswaas, the whole lot of them out at Cormorant Point, are devils. Of course Wiladzap butchered McCrory. That's what devils do. To hell (as it were) with mens rea, *Wiladzap doesn't need a* reason *to kill. He just kills, that's all.*

But that is not enough for me. McCrory's death may be, as Parry said, the devil's making. If so I should seek the devil in the smooth faces of my friend Frederick, of Firbanks, of George Beaumont. Quattrini? No devil he. Just a bad man. And why a man? Could a woman have killed McRory? Should I seek the smooth faced devil in Lukswaas? In one of the Somerville 'eligibles'?

This is ridiculous. If I were not myself, Chad Hobbes, I would start suspecting Chad Hobbes, the smooth faced, upright, priggish young detective constable – sorry, Acting Sergeant – another devil.

I reached the ironmongers just as it was closing. Frederick was showing the last customers to the door, and the other clerk was nowhere visible.

'Chad, old chap. On the prowl?'

'Yes. I'd like to have a word with you.'

'Of course. Just let me lock up.'

Frederick locked the door and swung the sign behind it around so that from the inside it read 'OPEN'. Since the sun, low in the sky, shone from behind the building, it was gloomy in the store, although the street outside was in a glare. Frederick pulled out two tall stools and set them beside the counter. We sat facing each other as if at a bar.

Looking carefully at Frederick's face, I brought out the envelope and opened it, setting the locket on the counter between us.

Frederick's eyes widened. 'I say, that's my locket', he said. 'Where did you find it?'

'Where do you think?'

'No idea. I lost it a few weeks ago. Thought it was stolen.'

'You wear a locket, Frederick?'

'Steady on. Of course not. I was merely going to send it home to my sister.'

'Frederick, you know perfectly well where I got this. Don't lie to me.'

'Lie to you?' Frederick's face had its usual expression of candour and innocent enthusiasm, but he had gone very pale.'

'It was worn on a very cold bosom', I said.

'What do you mean, old chap?'

'I know Kathleen was a reticent sort of girl, but she did tell some things to the other maid, Ellen, with whom she shared a room – and a language, come to that.'

'Damn it!', Frederick said rather feebly. 'We did become rather fond of each other. That's when I gave her the locket. And then this morning I heard she had drowned herself. Poor Kathy!', he said in a hollow, mournful voice.

'You're leaving out all the interesting bits,' I said cruelly, 'such as her becoming "enceinte"'.

All right, Chad old boy. But I didn't know if it was by me or that old beast Quattrini. She said it was by me – she said she could feel it was. But that was only because she wished it, I suppose. Anyway, I said there was nothing I could do about it. We had a row, actually. But I wasn't about to acknowledge the paternity of a child that might not be mine. She was, of course, in a dreadful stew. Then she came and said Quattrini had arranged for some surgery to get rid of the child. Of course he didn't know I was in the picture. That was a relief. But it gave her the "blues", as she put it – meaning she cried a lot, as she tended to do anyway. It was with McCrory, by the way, the surgery. You know that?'

'Yes. Did you talk to him about it?'

'Not beforehand. He had a word with me out at Orchard Farm the following Sunday. Quite decent about it, actually. He said he knew I had been Kathy's lover. She had told him. He said she would come to see him for a while, to deal with the after-effects of the operation. He said she would be prone to hysteria, after such an assault on the uterus – "hysteros", as you know. It would seem he was right, too. And …'

'What?'

'"I'll see if I can mend a broken heart", he said. Made me feel quite bad, actually. I forgot to mention … I broke with her before the operation. It was time. I couldn't go on with it. Anyway, McCrory knew this too, and he very kindly offered to give *me* what he called "lessons in contraceptics". For a fee, of course. Who knows, I might have taken him up on it. Then he got killed.'

'Where were you that afternoon?'

'I was here. On the job. I didn't kill McCrory, if that's what you're insinuating.'

'Did you know from the beginning of your relationship with the girl that she was Quattrini's mistress?'

'No. Only that she was easier than she should have been.'

I felt disgusted but let it pass. 'What did she tell you about Quattrini?'

'That he was a beast. That he had forced her, originally. But of course maids get into these situations.'

'Was she in love with you?'

'I dare say she was. She said she'd never known anyone like me – gentle, and all that.'

'Were you in love with her?'

'Don't be silly, Chad. I said I was fond of her, that's all.'

'Why did you meet in secret? Plenty of young men court their young ladies openly.'

'A serving maid? I wasn't going to *court* her.'

'But you're an ironmonger's clerk. As you would say yourself, "this isn't England". The same distinctions just don't quite obtain here. The Americans in this town would see you on the same level as she. She would too, as a matter of fact – "gentle" or not. Did she not find you cruel?'

'What's this got to do with police work, Chad? You're moralizing. You know perfectly well I would not take seriously a relation with a servant girl – any more than you would yourself if you stooped to it. But one has one's needs, doesn't one? Or don't you? You're such a prune.'

'So you never considered marriage with her.' Here I knew vaguely that I was pursuing a line of questioning for my own good. It was indeed not police work.

'Of course not. Not merely because she was an Irish kitchen-maid, but because she was, to put it bluntly, second hand goods. Would you marry a woman who gave herself easily to you? It's the worst thing they can do. She was spoiled already, by Quattrini.'

I paused in my questioning. My mind had wandered to Lukswaas. She had given herself to me – though perhaps under the pressure of my authority. She was spoiled – if that was what it was – by her relations with who knows how many men, not to speak of her husband Wiladzap whom she had apparently betrayed willingly. She was a 'bad' woman. Yet what she and I had done together seemed so different from what other people did. I imagined Quattrini using the girl Kathy, herself seeing him as a 'beast', and the gentle Frederick also using her, less beastly perhaps, but surely not with the sort of self-dissolving passion I felt for Lukswaas. It went further than the 'need' which both Quattrini and Frederick talked about so glibly. Real desire was more than need … or was I deceiving myself?

'When did you last see her?' I resumed wearily.

'Last night. I do feel bad about that. About three in the morning it was. She threw gravel against my window. It's on the second floor – meaning, in English terms, the first. I opened the window and there she was in the street, like a wraith. She wanted to come in and see me. But I couldn't let her. It was all right for her to visit my rooms during the day, ostensibly for 'tea'. But not at night. My landlady would have thrown me out. So I told Kathy to go home, in a sort of loud whisper. She stood looking at me. I closed the window. She must have gone away.'

'Did it not strike you,' I burst out, 'that with McCrory dead, when he had said he would see her every week, and with you deserting her, she was left in the lurch? Don't you think you could have helped her?'

'I couldn't get involved with her again. You're naïve if you think it's possible to see a girl you have been involved with that way, and not get back into it. If I'd let her in we would have gone and done it again, no question. But there's Cordelia! She's the only girl I think about now. Dear Cordy!' Frederick seemed near tears.

I could say nothing. I did not like my own moral indignation very much. I had never felt very close to Frederick, but had found him good company, and liked his ingenuousness. Now Frederick was not merely boyish but weak, not merely amusing but cynical.

I got down from my high stool, and walked out of the store, unlocking the door for myself, not saying a word to Frederick who hovered behind me like a ghost.

I wrote a brief report for the Superintendent and Pemberton. I concluded that Kathy had procured an abortion from Dr Richard McCrory (now deceased); that Dr McCrory had undertaken to give her a series of treatments for the nervous effects of the operation; that since the doctor was dead and she had become alienated from the putative father of the aborted child, she must be assumed to have fallen into a mental state, of extreme melancholia or hysteria (which Dr. McCrory had warned of) which had caused her to commit suicide. Insofar as the information I had received was pertinent to the death of Dr McCrory, I would summarize it in the report I was preparing on my preliminary investigation of the murder.

I knew that Pemberton, at least, would read between the lines of this, and if he decided to pursue charges, would know he could obtain the details from me. But I still thought Pemberton would let sleeping dogs lie. What would I do, if I were in Pemberton's place? The question kept me awake half the night.

20

Although I had slept little, I woke shortly after dawn. The memory of the day before, my thoughts while trying to go to sleep, and dreams from after that, compounded themselves into one nightmare. I felt an urge to exorcise myself of it. I told myself that in order to write my report on the McCrory case that day, I would have to ask a few more questions of Lukswaas. This thought made me feel lighter. I sprang out of bed, washed and dressed, and rushed out to hire a horse.

It was still very early, and there had been a heavy dew. The air was chilly, and I rode as fast as I could so that the jogging movement might keep me warm. The last stretch through the woods was dark and gloomy, the trees dripping onto my head and shoulders – I was in uniform but not wearing my helmet. It was still only eight o'clock, and I felt some trepidation as I approached the camp. I smelled smoke and heard voices. I came out of the trees, dismounted, and tied my horse to a tree.

The camp was much as usual, although there were less people visible. At least, since it was chilly, they were fully dressed. The tall Tsamti came to greet me, explaining that Waaks and some of the others had gone fishing. I asked if I could speak with Lukswaas. Tsamti pointed to a group of women nearby, working at something on the ground.

I walked over to them, and Lukswaas got up, wiping her hands, which were bloody, on a woven bark napkin. She looked far from being an Indian princess. She was wearing a worn-looking fibre blanket, with no silver bracelets on her blood-streaked arms, and brown leather leggings above bare, dirty feet. She was still, however, wearing her abalone earrings. I did not dare smile at her in front of the others, and she did not smile at me. Her face was extremely beautiful, as always, but it had an intense, strained look.

I told her that I needed to ask her some questions. She nodded and said that she would go and wash her hands first. She went over to one of the fires where there was a big pot of water from which she dipped with a ladle and began washing her hands and arms. I looked down at the women beside me. I recognized Wan, who glanced up at me shyly. They were gutting and plucking about a dozen waterfowl – geese, ducks and coots.

Lukswaas returned and led me over to the edge of the forest. She sat down on the ground, crossing her legs under the long tattered fringes of her blanket. I sat down opposite her, leaning on one arm. I looked into her eyes. They seemed worried.

Chinook, as always, reduced my thoughts to their most simple form. I said I wanted to see her because when I talked to her she said things which helped me. Then, since she still looked worried and I felt it would be wrong to conceal myself from her, I said I liked seeing her. I liked seeing her in the woods. But I liked talking to her also.

I realized with a shock which made me stop talking for a moment, that if I were speaking English I would reassure her by telling her I loved her. But that could not be true. Instead I changed the subject and told her brusquely that I had to ask her some questions about the dead man, McCrory. After that, we could talk of other things.

She nodded her head, her face still serious.

I began to reiterate the story of McCrory going into the forest with Lukswaas. Lukswaas had said McCrory had asked for herbs to make a man powerful in loving, herbs to make a person sleep, and herbs to give long life. Had he also asked for herbs a woman could take so as not to have a baby when she had been with a man?

'Ah-ha', Lukswaas nodded. She blushed slightly, with that natural innocence of hers which seemed to belie what I knew of her. Then she said that she had told McCrory the truth, that Tsimshian women did not take herbs for that purpose, and she knew of none.

I felt surprised by this. I went on to ask if McCrory had enquired about herbs that a woman could take, when she was carrying a child in her body (I pointed at my abdomen) so that the child would come out dead.

Lukswaas nodded. The doctor had indeed asked her about such herbs. But again she had told the truth, that Tsimshian women know of no such herbs.

Again I was surprised. I had read that quinine was used for such purposes among the South American Indians. I had imagined the Tsimshian might have an equivalent. These questions had seemed important to me, when I woke up in the morning, because of the nightmares of the previous day. Asking them was part of the purpose of, as Lukswaas herself had put it a few days before, 'getting into the skin' of McCrory. But now I felt no further ahead in my case. Out of curiosity I asked what a Tsimshian woman would do if she lay with a man and did not want to get a child.

Lukswaas replied that most women knew from the feeling in their body, (this time it was she who pointed to her abdomen), when they could get a child. And at that time they might decide to be with a man, or not, depending on whether or not they wanted a child. But of course there were sometimes mistakes.

I wanted suddenly to ask her if she had risked having a child by me. But I didn't dare. Instead I asked more generally, what happened when a woman had a child and she was not married. The word in Chinook for 'married' was 'malie', which came from the French 'Marié'. I knew nothing of marriage customs among the Tsimshian.

Lukswaas replied with her usual seriousness that among the Tsalak, at least, if a woman had a child then she would say who the father was. If the father was a chief or a rich man he would either provide for her, or marry her. Some men had two wives, she added. The child, at any rate, would be known as his, and the child's standing depended on who the father was as well as who the mother was. If the father was of low standing or a bad man, then the child would have no standing, although of course the mother would look after it. And sometimes such a child might grow up and become known for beauty or great deeds or gathering goods or money.

I asked if a woman who had had a child but was not married to the father could marry another man.

Lukswaas frowned, as if puzzled. Of course the woman could. But it depended on her standing.

Clearly, I reflected, there were social barriers among the Tsimshian as among the whites – by the sound of it as well defined as in England. But there did not seem to be a moral barrier. I thought of asking her if a Tsimshian woman could marry two men. But that would be too close to the bone ... And I had never heard of such a thing among Indians – only of men having several wives.

I asked if it was a good thing for a young girl to lie with a man if she did not want to be married to him.

'Wake'. Lukswaas shook her head vigorously, and seemed upset. She said it was best for a young woman to keep herself for the man she wanted to marry.

I was baffled by this statement, as rigid as any to be heard from an

English girl's lips. It was not fair of me to ask Lukswaas all these questions without explaining why. She would take everything I said as an oblique reference to our own love-making. But I felt, inexplicably, as if I wanted to confide in her.

I told her, slowly and carefully, the whole story of Kathy Donnelly, and my work in finding out what had happened – though I did not mention Sylvie or the Windsor Rooms, out of delicacy. Delicacy, in talking to a 'squaw' …

Lukswaas listened carefully, making no comments except to get the meaning of a word clear from time to time. When the story was finished she said in Chinook that it was a story to make a person cry. It showed that when a girl had two men at once it led to trouble.

It was my turn to look puzzled.

Lukswaas went on to say that if the woman knew which man was the father of her child, then she could go to that man and say: this is your child. Then of course he would have to provide for it, or marry her. Lukswaas said she could understand how the young man in my story would not want to marry the girl, if the child might be that of the old man. In a case like that, among the Tsalak and other Tsimshian, the two men would provide for the child. But it would be an unlucky child and an unlucky woman. Every child should know its father. But it was terrible that McCrory had cut the child out of the woman. The result was worse than an unlucky child, it was a dead child. Or were the King George men so cruel that it would be worse for the girl to have the child?

I admitted ruefully that yes, it would be worse. I felt ashamed.

It was worse still, that the girl had killed herself, Lukswaas added. Were the King George men always so cruel to their women?

I replied that since the girl had been of low standing in society she had had no power – no 'skookum' – so of course it had been worse for her. But I felt that was a lame excuse.

Lukswaas asked as abruptly as the repetitions of Chinook allowed, what I myself would have done if I were the young man?

I said, meaning it, that if I loved the girl I would marry her. But if the child was by the other man, I would feel 'tum tum sick'. Perhaps if I loved the girl very much I would want to be with her anyway. If she loved me, I added. But it would be very difficult, I said, trying to be honest. In all this

I had used 'tikegh' the nearest Chinook word to 'love', though it also meant pleasure and liking.

'Nika tikegh tikegh mesika'. (I love love you), Lukswaas said, looking intently at me.

I felt a wave of emotion run through me and said back to her: 'Nika tikegh tikegh mesika.'

But this was impossible. I felt a sudden reaction, almost a sickness. I scrambled to my feet. She did the same and looked at me questioningly. I said I was sorry, but I had to go, since I had much work to do that day. I thanked her, and said I would see her the following night. As I said this, I almost melted with the desire which I had somehow managed to put aside during our conversation. But I looked away from her eyes.

'Kloshe', she said. ('Good'). Then she asked if I was going to find who killed McCrory.

I looked back at her, and said that I hoped so. I explained that, as she had said to me before, I was trying to get into the skin of everyone who might have killed McCrory, and of McCrory himself.

Lukswaas looked concerned. I marvelled at the transparency of her expressions, which I could always read without difficulty – as it seemed she could read mine. She said that I should be careful to come back inside my own skin. This was why, she said, it was necessary for me to see her.

The simplicity of this was too much for me. I turned away.

But Lukswaas spoke again. She said that if there were several people whom I thought might have killed McCrory, then probably there were some whom I wanted to be the murderer, and others whom I did not want to be. I should be sure that those feelings did not stop me from seeing clearly. I would only see who the murderer was when my heart (or mind or soul – the 'tum tum' again) was clean.

I smiled and said I agreed. I said I felt sad to be going.

We clung to each other with our eyes for a moment. Then I went over to my horse. Lukswaas was already walking away to join the other women.

When I got back to Victoria just before noon, I was pleased to find that Rabinowicz had been prompt in his search for the book by John Humphrey Noyes: he had sent it by messenger to the courthouse, where its title, *Male continence: Self Control in Sexual Intercourse* (on the front of the book where I had not seen it: Noyes's name was on the spine) had attracted the interest of Parry and Wilson, who had each leafed through it. Parry said it was a 'damned perverted tract', and Wilson that its title should be *Self-Gelding*. But Parry, as he handed it over to me, added, 'it shows McCrory was up to mischief', which I hoped meant he was becoming tolerant of the investigation.

After a quick lunch on a cheese sandwich and a glass of ale, I retreated to my office with the book. It was not much more than a pamphlet really, although McCrory had had it bound in leather, privately published at Oneida, New York, in 1866. It was not only well thumbed, but full of McCrory's own notes, in the margin and sometimes on pieces of paper which had been gummed in like extra pages. These notes, in a larger, messier and more childish hand than that of an educated Englishman, added comments which must have come from McCrory's own experience at Oneida, beginning with such statements as 'According to Noyes ...', or 'JHN says ...' There were also enlargements of the pamphlet's points, and notes on a few new topics.

The members of the Oneida Community, under Noyes's direction, called themselves Perfectionists. Noyes, although not proclaiming himself to be God, claimed to speak for God in the same way Christ had done. The Perfectionist way to salvation was a practice called either 'male continence' or 'magnetation'. This meant that in sexual intercourse, the man would penetrate the woman and move gently in such a way that an exchange of magnetism via the genital organs would take place; however, he would restrain himself from ejaculation by stopping movement if this threatened. With experience, magnetation could be continued for hours. Its essence, in fact, was to continue until the male member shrank of its own accord, but without ejaculation having occurred, while still in the vagina. This process caused no risk to health – whereas if the man withdrew while still in a state of erection or, still worse, if he practised coitus interruptus or onanism and ejaculated outside the woman, then dire physical and spiritual consequences would ensue.

McCrory had annotated Noyes's description of magnetation with the comment: 'Possibility of eventual retrograde ejaculation or seeping into bladder? Not physiologically out of the question. Do Elders have cloudy urine?' There was no answer given to this, and I was not sure if it was deliberately irreverent, though it seemed so.

The practice of magnetation was, according to Noyes, the answer to all problems. First, it meant that women would not conceive unless they wanted to, so they would not be burdened by frequent childbirth. However the decision that a woman should conceive was not entirely hers: it was taken, or confirmed, in a Community meeting. I gathered from a note of McCrory's, perhaps added after he had cut his association with Oneida, that there was a constant problem of jealousy because the Community Elders, and in particular Noyes himself, were those selected to father the women's children. There was surely an inconsistency, I thought, in the rule of Male Continence, which was proclaimed to be infinitely superior to sexual intercourse with normal ejaculation, being broken only by the most privileged of the Community's members ...*(no pun on 'member' intended – be careful, Chad!)*

The second point about magnetation was that it enabled the communal sharing of everyone by everyone. The Perfectionist ideal was a total 'communism' (although not, it seemed of the anarchic varieties that had brought workers to the barricades in Paris in 1848), in which all properties and sexual favours were shared. The woman and man have congress in private (after approval at a community meeting), but a woman must not restrict her favours to one man. Individual attachments were the root of all evil.

The third point was that the exchange of magnetism at the physical level accompanied the union of the man's and the woman's souls. This was apparently impossible if intercourse led to climax. Climax, in fact, led to the sort of attachment ('falling in love', McCrory had scrawled in the margin) which was banned in the community.

One insert which caught my eye was headed '*Criticism*: in Community meetings, Criticism can last two or three hours. Some subjects reduced to state of nervous prostration, carried from room. But following day in state of elation and spiritual renewal. 'The storm is past, the lightning has cleft me to the root, and Lo, I am miraculously new!' as one woman said to JHN. A *technic of enormous power*, susceptible to individual application.'

On another of McCrory's inserts was a summary of the principles of 'Ascending and Descending Fellowship', from which I gathered again that the Elders must have the best bargain at Oneida. If they had intercourse with younger, less spiritually advanced Community members, there was a certain loss of magnetism! On the other hand it was only through intercourse with the Elders that the younger members, through 'Ascending Fellowship' could gain and store magnetism. In other words, a young man and woman together would be squandering their magnetism and impeding their spiritual development. McCrory had scribbled: 'JHN himself initiates all female virgins.'

I laughed out loud at this solemn American version of the medieval 'jus primae noctis' – the 'right of the first night': Noyes had the same power over his community's virgins as that of a medieval baron over the daughters of his serfs. What humbug!

Another interesting marginal comment was: 'Lambskin condoms, being made of gut, transmit the animal magnetism. Vulcanized rubber condoms, as proposed in Chicago, being vegetable matter, would obstruct it.'

All was becoming clear. After reading the pamphlet and its notes, I sat doodling for a while, thinking about it. First I could not help applying it to myself. I had just discovered the animal in myself, with Lukswaas, and at times I felt a return of the physical horror which had made me wash myself in the ice cold stream. But at times I felt that I had also discovered my soul. This made my heart pound with fear as well as desire. I had always known I would fall heavily in love some day: I had waited so long! But Lukswaas was an insane choice – not that such an event was really a choice. I could *not* be in love with her. So I tried, constantly, to extrapolate my experience with her to other circumstances. I had suddenly become intensely and openly interested in sex. I could imagine doing it with all sorts of women. Yet I had not been able to, or wanted to, with Sylvie. (Yes, I could get the clap, the firesickness, from a woman like Sylvie. But from a squaw too!) Could I do it with Aemilia? There I imagined a spiritual union as well as the physical. But not to melt into her, not to give myself, not to 'come' into her? Now I thought not of Aemilia, but inevitably of Lukswaas again. There was a melting on the woman's part too. A 'spending', in the current term. The ethos of my time is, so far as I can understand it – a difficult task, like that of a fish understanding the water it lived in – accumulative. 'Spending' is frowned upon in financial terms, and also in sexual. The proper thing to do is to *save* – both money and sexual energy. John Noyes joined a long list of cranks whom even I had heard of, who felt that the spending of male seed depletes body and mind; that abstaining from it is rather like keeping money in a bank account at a good percentage of interest. The original idea of Noyes's Community was that they could have their cake and eat it too: fornicate and 'save' (salvation!) at the same time. (Except for Noyes and other Elders allowed to impregnate the young women …) I find all this repugnant. Like 'utilitarianism', another part of the contemporary ethos. Darwin's theory of evolution is based in it: a species survives if its adaptation is *useful*. Although this is materialistic, it is also common sense. It is not useful to accumulate: there is also time to spend. And for every crank with a fear of spending, there is a sexual utilitarian (a London physician by the name of Acton came vaguely to my mind) who points out the dangers of saving …

But all this is theory. In practice, I know simply that whomever the woman I love, I would want to lose myself in her. Lukswaas has shown me, to my surprise, that a woman can also lose herself in a man. I gave myself. She gave herself. What have we found? I would rather not think.

Here I find mysef in a quandary. My 'introspections' are now occurring in my narrative. I have been assuming that the narrative would one day be read – by someone, if not in print, in manuscript by my friends or – even – my descendants. These passages with the line down the side are marked so as to be discarded, so that the narrative is not too private, too intimate. But I cannot keep the private out of the public. My introspections are becoming mingled with my 'extrospections', my insights with my 'outsights'. This whole story is not a narrative for the world. It can only be for a few. For Lukswaas, I find myself thinking – though she doesn't know a word of English. Except for 'Thank you'.

From now on I shall see if I can include my instrospections in my narrative.

I turned my mind back to the case of McCrory. The annotations in Noyes's booklet made it clear that McCrory had spent time in the Oneida Community but was, at least in retrospect, highly sceptical about it. I wondered if McCrory had left voluntarily or been ejected. Sceptical or not, he had brought some ideas and technics with him. He was, I felt, above all an opportunist, disguising self interest under a cloak of high-mindedness. Perhaps that came from his Congregational background, thought the 'old' me. McCrory would easily have been tempted by religious communism. But he was, I suspected, too much of a prima donna to stay within any community. He had, opportunistically, lived within the Oneida Community and taken away what he wanted from it. This he must have blended with Mesmerism, phrenology, medicine, French 'aliénisme', herbalism, the technics of anti-conception, a rather old fashioned humanitarianism (as opposed to utilitarianism), and a belief that he must save people – primarily women. This mental synthesis no doubt corresponded with his more base desires. For as I see it, a Perfectionist of other people is ultimately a Perfectionist of himself, and therefore a monster of vanity. McCrory's Perfectionism led to his death.

21

My report to Pemberton was brief. I set out as strongly as I could the flaws in the case against Wiladzap and summarized what I had learned from my various interviews about the professional and private life of McCrory – in such a way, I hoped, as to make a convincing case that in view of the imbroglio of secrets and (in conventional terms) vice that was McCrory's life, it was necessary to be prudent before jumping to conclusions about the Indians. 'It must be concluded', I wrote in the pompous style that an official report required, 'that whatever vices, unrestrained passions, and indifference to society's rules of conduct may be assumed to exist among the Tsimshian Indians, also exist, in an equal plenitude of facts shocking to the civilized mind, among the citizens of this Colony who were Dr McCrory's patients and associates. The blows which struck him down, in their barbarity have been assumed to have been smitten by Indians, whereas they might equally be the result of the inflamed passions of a person in whom, in a nervous condition of the kind which the doctor specialized in treating, the veneer of civilization, already cracked and crazed by nervous tensions, had suddenly shattered. Until further investigation has been established beyond doubt that the victim's demise was not the result of a passionate explosion of hatred or revenge on the part of one of his patients or associates in the demi-mode of prostitution and abortion, it would seem prudent to delay bringing the Tyee Wiladzap to trial, for fear of having him convicted and hanged as a result of evidence which, although strong, is never more than circumstantial.'

It was with such flourishes that legal reports concluded. But I knew in my heart that my argument was weak until the 'further evidence' was forthcoming.

Once written, the report could not even be presented to Pemberton right away, since he was out of town on one of several trips to remonstrate with the Chiefs of the Cowichan, twenty miles North, over their intransigence in disputes over the boundaries of their recently established reservation. There is in fact an upsurge of news concerning Indians, underlying to Victorians the fact that their garden of Eden is surrounded by a howling and barbarous wilderness. On Saltspring Island an Indian has come to trial and been convicted to hang for the murder of two white settlers. The British Columbia legislature has rushed to denounce the reformatory zeal of the mother country, and has confirmed that in the Colony executions will continue to be public. No doubt they had the Saltspring case, and Wiladzap, in mind. Public opinion, Amor de Cosmos's infernal 'vox populi' as expressed in the *British Colonist,* is also incensed by news of the shipwreck of a small Navy boat further up the coast. The sailors' bodies were found on the beaches. They had not been drowned but instead had received a welcome from the local Indians, the Clayoquot: the bodies were headless, and pieces of flesh had been stripped from the bones. No 'almost scalped', or 'almost bitten off' flesh', I can't help thinking. But the details are not fully in. The fact that the news comes piece by piece, like the instalments of a serial, keeps interest high.

All this Indian news might make a jury act quickly and harshly to condemn Wiladzap. But at the same time, it diverts attention from him. Perhaps his trial can be delayed.

I wrote out my report to Pemberton on the morning of the day I was due to meet Lukswaas at night, in the forest. The work kept my mind off her, although my body had gone into a state of excitement on its own. No matter what I had been thinking of, each time I came back to my physical sensations I found that my heart was pounding, my head light, my genitals stirring. It was as if my body was an animal living independently of my mind.

At noon I received an unexpected visit from Mr Giles, the surgeon of HMS *Ariadne*, whom I only remembered as a gaunt, silent observer of the humiliation of the under-officers by the Captain. Giles had come to the courthouse to speak to 'whoever is investigating the murder of Dr McCrory', and was quite startled to see me.

'Why Hobbes,' he said, 'I thought you would be prospecting for gold up in the Cariboo, or perhaps pushing paper at Government House. You look like a London "peeler". But, my goodness, you've become a Sergeant already.'

'Acting.' I said. 'For this investigation at least.'

'Yes. Dr McCrory. We just got back to Esquimalt yesterday and it was mentioned to me that he had been savagely murdered – by an Indian apparently, but the officer who told me said there was talk of there being other involvements and that McCrory had been a regular charlatan. So I thought I should report to you my own meeting with the man.'

'With McCrory?'

'Yes. In January. He came out to Esquimalt and wanted to meet some of the naval surgeons. 'In the interest of professional friendship', as he put it in his unreticent Yankee way. We had a few tots of grog together and a chat. He tried to make himself agreeable. But it soon turned out that what really interested him was that we might send him patients. He explained, in a very learned way, which seemed utter balderdash to me, that many physical illnesses were mental in origin. He gave me an exposition about the 'calenture' which, as you must know, is a disease which sometimes attacks sailors when they have been too long at sea, causing them to see strange visions, develop a fever which is not associated with any discernible organic condition, and to commit odd or self destructive acts, such as jumping overboard. McCrory tried to convince me that the calenture was akin to hysteria in women! I ask you! He was trying to impress me, I thought. He explained that he was a qualified "alienist" – you know, it's a French term for a doctor whose patients are "aliénés", that is alienated by mental disorders. And he proposed that I send him any officers who seemed afflicted by nervous or mental disease. Very forward of him. I told him politely that there was no question of any officer in Her Majesty's navy being treated by any doctor other than a naval surgeon. Surprisingly insensitive man. He actually pressed me to make an exception. Went on about the Hippocratic oath. What a nerve! At last I got rid of him, but not before he had subjected me to a veritable quizzing, which I answered in words of one syllable, about where the *Ariadne* had been surveying, what was her compliment of men and guns, and so on. So much so that when I saw him off down the ladder I said to myself: "That damned Yankee is a spy." Giles, who had never uttered a squeak at the Captain's table, but was now revealed as excitable and long-winded, seemed quite delighted at this supposition. 'So when I learned he was dead in mysterious circumstances, I thought I should tell the police of our conversation.'

'Very good of you,' I said as I finished scribbling a summary of Giles's account in my notebook. 'From what I know of McCrory, he was a conspiratorial type, and always had his nose in other people's secrets. But, may I ask, what would be the point of spying on the navy? What is there to discover? A corvette of the *Ariadne* type carries 200 officers and men and is armed with 20 heavy guns. Everyone knows that. I've never been on the *Zealous*, but I know she carries 500 men. Our naval presence here is meant to be in the open, isn't it?'

'Yes, so that the Yankees don't get any wrong ideas. I agree with you, it's hard to imagine what secrets a spy could find out. Our men are not even told to keep their mouths shut when they go ashore, in spite of the fact that every other person in Victoria is a Yankee. It's a puzzle. Nevertheless, I'm almost sure this man McCrory was a spy – or interested in spying, which is the same thing.'

'You could be right,' I said. 'I've made a note of it and I'll give it the utmost consideration.' To placate the surgeon and to make his trip into town worthwhile, I invited him out to Ringo's for lunch. This kept my mind off Lukswaas.

Back in the courthouse, I added a paragraph to my report, about Giles's visit. I had only mentioned in passing the telegraph from Virginia with its claim that McCrory had been 'cashiered' from the Confederate army on suspicion of spying: this could simply have meant that although McCrory's loyalties were to the South, his New York Yankee origins had been discovered. But now it took on a new dimension. Whether or not McCrory was a spy, either officially or independently, there were now two indications that he had behaved like one. I concluded: 'Although it is impossible to imagine what useful function an American spy might have in this Colony where it is the policy of the authorities to be entirely open about military and naval activities, nevertheless McCrory's curiosity about the navy and his having been accused of spying for the winning side in the American Civil War, must raise the question whether his friendship with the Marine Lieutenant, George Beaumont, was in part motivated by spying.'

This was, indeed, the nub. I was ready to seize on any fact, no matter how bizarre, that might explain McCrory's relationship with Beaumont. I sent the report to Pemberton's house, to await his return, then went to deliver an oral summary to Superintendent Parry.

Though more roughly than Pemberton might, Parry expressed a view which Pemberton would probably share: that my investigation had uncovered 'a lot of dirt' about McCrory's patients and associates, but that I was probably too young to realize that almost any respectable life revealed an equal amount of dirt under investigative scrutiny. 'There are Quattrinis in every town,' Parry said, 'and more of them in Victoria than him. I dunno how many girls in the family way have thrown themselves into the Inner Harbour in the past ten years, but it runs into dozens. Leave well alone, lad. Though I know the doctor stands exposed as a beast. No doubt he was up to all kinds of beastliness with the Indians too.'

Anyway, Parry explained, the circumstantial evidence with regard to the murder, and leaving all the other 'dirt' aside, was overpoweringly against 'the Indians.' Parry admitted easily enough that it was unclear whether Wiladzap, Lukswaas, or even the defaulting Smgyiik, had murdered McCrory. But as Parry put it succinctly: 'It's an Indian crime, and for it an Indian will hang.'

'It's almost not relevant,' Parry went on, 'whose hand drove in the knife. Or whether it was one or many hands. Or whether the Indians are covering up for one of them, which no doubt they are. Your man in the cells, Wiladzap, may even be what they call a Noble Savage – as I believe you want to think, my lad – and taking the rap for a deed done by his wife. Then so be it. Do you really want to charge the woman with murder instead? No matter if she claimed McCrory attempted to violate her – as no doubt she would, not that I'd believe it, beast though he was – and cried her pretty eyes out in court, she'd hang sure as him.'

Parry concluded by reminding me that I had other duties. Starting with my usual Sunday night guarding the jail with Seeds, I would be expected from the following week to put in half a day with the others. This would be more agreeable now I had my Sergeant's stripes, which Pemberton would no doubt make permanent. And apart from the usual drudgery of license fees and drunks, there was even some detective work to be done: many of the recent burglaries showed what the Superintendent was pleased to call, probably having heard the words from Pemberton, 'the same modus operandi' – entry through the roof hatch which most buildings had for ventilation.

Of course I should keep eyes and ears open. But the case against Wiladzap was clear and the way was free for a trial within a few weeks. 'We don't want to keep that Indian camp in existence much longer, and once a couple of 'em, and the woman Lukswaas, have testified and it's all over, we can let 'em depart for home.'

I tried to encourage myself by remembering I still had Pemberton's 'Carte blanche'. But I knew that Pemberton would be under worse pressures than I. Then, to make me even more gloomy, I met Mulligan, the Irish-American lawyer who had volunteered to undertake Wiladzap's defense. Mulligan had a reputation as a vicious shark in civil cases, who would not stop at destroying a man's name, or breaking his purse by prolonging a case through procedural manipulations. Indeed Mulligan's own reputation was so bad that he had recently lost business. Since the gold rush had ended, and with it the rush of frantic litigation over property and land deals, Mulligan would have had less work anyway. There was no money in his defending Wiladzap, but he might see it as a way to gain lost ground by posing as a selfless champion of a wretched savage who was sure to lose.

Mulligan's face was concave, with forehead and chin both ahead of a small nose and thin lipped mouth out of which cigar smoke billowed as he announced that Wiladzap would not talk to him, but that did not matter. 'He's not goin' to be saved by any new facts. They're all against him – as you know, havin' collected the evidence. Nope. But he deserves a defense all the same, and by Christ I'll give it to him. Ultimately ...' Here Mulligan stuck his thumbs into his trouser tops, as if his hands were on a pair of 'six gun' butts, and stuck his stomach forward. He was one of those Americans who could – and worse, would – talk with a cigar between the teeth. 'Ultimately, the chief is a victim as much as McCrory was. Why? Because the authorities shoulda protected him against contact with the intolerable riches of the White man. To kill for a few dollars? Or because the White man accepted the services of the chief's squaw? He shoulda been kept in a reservation, back where he came from. What are these people doin' wanderin' around like this? Settin' up camp near a responsible town? Worryin' the lives outa respectable citizens? Where is our protection against these Injuns? And' – he took the cigar out of his mouth and waved it for emphasis, squinting narrowly through the smoke – 'how come the government of this Colony, a *British* government, cannot better protect the lives of its citizens, its *American* citizens?'

'We do our best,' I said, wearing as I did a version of the Queen's uniform.

'In the States we know how to treat Injuns. They give any trouble, they *get* trouble – big trouble. In a while the lot of 'em'll be on reservations. They don't belong next to civilized people, lookin' sneakily at our women, measurin' up our children…'

'Wait a minute,' I said in the frosty English manner which this provoked. 'If you don't like Indians, why defend this man?

'Like 'em? Nobody could *like* 'em – unless your taste runs to squaws…'

'Mr Mulligan, if you talk like this in court, I'm afraid…'

'I'm talkin' to you, sonny boy,' Mulligan interrupted. 'Of course in a *British* court, I shall know how to modulate my language. I shall nevertheless…' It was true, he did know how to talk English. '… emphasize to the court that the government of this Colony would be remiss not to keep in constant consideration the rights of its American residents, especially in view of the inexorable logic of Annexation to the larger society, the United States of America, where the problems of an indigenous population are addressed – so far history informs us – in a more resolute manner.'

'Good point,' I said. 'For the prosecution. But what's your defense going to be?'

'Non legitimis in locus.'

'In loco,' I corrected, feeling as 'fussy and pedantic' as a schoolmaster, but unable not to be. 'Not legitimate in place?'

'Non legitimis in loco. It's a new defense: that since the Indian Wiladzap was only allowed by lapses in Government resolution and policy to freely move from his natural trading area on the North Coast down to here, he cannot be held fully responsible for his actions faced with civilisation – in the form of an educated American, a Southern gentleman into the bargain. Yes, Sergeant, we have mended our fences since the War between the States – rancour is a sentiment foreign to the free-flowing blood of the American heart. After all, if a dangerous dog runs wild and bites a child, do we shoot the dog or fine the owner? We do both, do we not? The British authorities in this Colony…'

'You mean, we hang Wiladzap and excoriate the government,' I said wearily.

'He'll be hanged, but the point will be made.'

'Mr Mulligan, I must tell you, having a degree in Jurisprudence myself that such a defense is simply untenable…'

'Have you been called to the Bar?' Mulligan interrupted with a flourish of his cigar.

'No.'

'Then, forgive me Sergeant, you are not a lawyer.' Mulligan turned and stalked out of the room.

'Oh Jesus Christ,' I said quietly. I resolved to have a word about Mulligan with Pemberton. No defense at all for Wiladzap would be better than that…

I went down to the cells. The prisoners were out at exercise. Wiladzap must have refused to go. Seeds was standing in the doorway to the exercise yard, taking the sun, glancing in at Wiladzap.

'Klahowya,' I said in greeting.

Wiladzap, squatting with his back against the wall, looked up at me, eyes calm.

I asked him why he had not talked to Mulligan.

Wiladzap merely said, 'Mulligan pelton. Cultus pelton.' Meaning that Mulligan was a worthless fool.

Since I had intended to warn Wiladzap against Mulligan, I felt relieved.

Then Wiladzap asked if I had found who killed McCrory. If so, Wiladzap explained, then Wiladzap could go free.

I said I did not know. My despair probably showed in my eyes.

Wiladzap, who was studying me closely, said, 'Spose mesika halo klap man mamook opitsah opitsah doctah, alki nika wind.' Literally: 'If you not find man make knife knife doctor, by and by I dead.'

'Alki nika klap,' assured Wiladzap. ('By and by I find') But now Wiladzap's eyes too were showing despair.

There was one minor piece of investigation which I had thought of before but had not had the nerve to pursue. I visited the pharmacist who had analyzed the herbs in the alienist's basket, who was also Victoria's main supplier of surgical goods – Mr Newton. I asked for a brief private talk. Newton asked his assistant to look after the store, and led me behind misted glass windows into a small room full of boxes and lined shelves of drugs, trusses and surgical corsets. Newton was a lean skeletal man, not at all welcoming. I started by asking him if he sold lambskin sheaths.

'Of course,' Newton said resignedly. 'But you didn't need to request a private interview. You might have asked for the "special supplies depot".'

'I didn't intend to buy any. I'm investigating the McCrory murder, as you know, and I believe he may have bought his supplies of sheaths here.'

Newton actually laughed, with a dry crackling sound. 'He did indeed. Now *you* tell me what he used them for.'

'All I know is that he used a lot of them,' I hazarded.

'He did indeed!' Again Newton laughed, a startling event as if a shroud suddenly moved on a corpse and shed dust. 'By the gross! I reckon he went through a dozen a week anyways. And since there wasn't a Mrs McCrory, it made a person wonder. I even joked with him that maybe he was re-selling them – only half a joke really, since doctors have been known to buy supplies from a pharmacist and sell them at a profit.'

'What do *you* think he used them for?' But I nearly bit my tongue off after these words escaped, since they would provide fuel for this pharmaceutical humorist.

'For prophylactic purposes, I assume.' Newton looked at me with a skeletal grin, as if challenging my education.

'Prophylaxis of what?' I said, rising to the bait in spite of myself. 'Conception or disease?'

'Darned if I know. Could be either.'

'You mean they're known to be a precaution not only against conception but against venereal infections.'

'They're thought to be the latter. I believe they were originally invented for that purpose, but then human ingenuity realized they could be used for unnatural purposes – by which I mean as contraceptics. Do you know the one about the man who went to the doctor and said he'd caught a venereal disease in a public water closet?'

'No.'

"Funny place to take a woman!", said the doctor. And there's another use.' Newton's voice had become stealthy.

'What?'

'Onanists. Afraid of polluting themselves!' He cracked into laughter again.

I walked, not rode, out Cedar Hill Road as the sun was setting pink behind a grey wall of cloud. As I entered the forest the dusk was becoming murky, blurring the details of the trees. I halted, somewhat tired after the four and a half miles of uphill and down, at the place where Lukswaas and I had met before. I waited, but not as I had thought I would. My brain had been crowded with speeches, remonstrations, arguments, well-considered phrases in Chinook… I must tell Lukswaas how dangerous the situation was for Wiladzap. I must say our own relation must be finished – now.

But as I waited, my body grew taut and swollen like that of a satyr: I could have thrust myself against a tree, or thrown myself onto the nearest bush, although I could think only of Lukswaas. As soon as it was completely dark she appeared, like a piece of the darkness detaching itself and moving towards me. I could not stand still as she approached, I hurried forward and in a few steps caught her and held her, smelling her woodsmoke hair, feeling the rough chilcat blanket under my hands as I stroked instinctively up and down her back. We broke apart and went into the pitch dark down from the path, and fell in the first clear space, she fumbling with her bundle to lay out the blankets, I unlacing my boots and tearing off my clothes. Then I pulled her to me although this time face to face, and we did the same thing as before, again crying out like animals. We lay for a while floating on the sea of night but still joined, then appallingly – although now should have been the moment to talk and reason, with our lust put behind us – we began to move again.

At last we slipped apart, and I rolled over on my back, putting my arm under her head as she pulled the blanket over our shoulders. We lay quietly. I gazed up into the darkness which had become a purple shifting mist with dots of evanescent light. But before I had gathered my thoughts it was Lukswaas who spoke, asking me if I had yet found the man who had killed the doctor.

'Wake', I said. ('No') I found my voice was almost a groan. As best I could, I explained sadly that I could not find that evil man, although I worked on finding him night and day. But it was difficult because the King George men had so many secrets.

Lukswaas said that the Tsimshian had many secrets too: it was difficult to hear the 'tum tum' of a man, to know what else he was besides a man. She said every man or woman was not only a man or woman, but something else: it could be a bear, a salmon, an eagle, a dolphin. Or even something changeable – a salmon one minute, a raven the next. It was almost impossible to follow a man or woman through these changes, she said. I realized as she spoke that they were 'transformations' or 'metamorphoses.' The so-called savage mind was that of the ancient Greeks at the time of Homer, before philosophy. The 'tum tum' was the equivalent of Homer's 'thymos', the point near the heart where feeling centred. And the 'wind' was the 'psyche' and the 'pneuma' or breath of divine life in the human body.

Lukswaas went on to say that the man who killed McCrory must have been entrapped in something, like a salmon in a weir of woven cedar strips, or a bear in a pit; he was a man who wanted to be free, to run wild like an animal or like an Indian. King George men were not free to run, she said to me, they were like planks or axes. They had shiny, greedy eyes, wanting always what they could not have. They did not 'potlatch' or give, they took to themselves. Yet their uprightness often made her heart happy. The Indian could be too much like a willow branch that bent in all directions. I made her heart happy, she said, because I was straight and strong, and I was also clean and deep, like a whirlpool which pulled her in. Tsalak, the place they had come from, meant a whirlpool. She recognized the whirlpool in me, and the big Coho salmon, old and wise, turning slowly at the bottom. Only I did not feel the movements of the salmon, she said. I did not yet know what it was.

It took some time for her, with my assistance, to express herself in Chinook where even the word 'whirlpool' took minutes to explain, using other words for 'water' and 'turning'. Eventually she came back to the murder of McCrory. She said that he wanted to be an animal, an Indian, but he could not be. His trap must have made him so enraged that he was ready to kill in the way an animal or an Indian – especially a medicine man Indian – could. She said the killer of McCrory must have wanted something from him, in that greedy King George way, which McCrory could not give. But McCrory probably had said he would give it. McCrory was a man who thought he could give to men and women. He was like a Mektakatla man, a missionary. But really he had no power.

This was abstract to me. I tried to bring Lukswaas and myself back to earth. I asked if McCrory had wanted to make love to Lukswaas in the forest.

Lukswaas said she was not sure. But McCrory had shown her his bird.

What?

His bird. Lukswaas felt for my member and stroked it. His bird.

McCrory had shown her that?

Yes. It had been big as if he had wanted to make love with Lukswaas. And he asked her if it was bigger than an Indian bird. She had said it was not the bird that went in her nest. He replied that it was a magic bird with power, that could make her very happy. She had picked up her herb basket and walked back to the camp. He had followed. By the time they had reached the camp he had put the bird back into his clothes.

What had Lukswaas thought of that? I asked.

No doubt McCrory thought he was an eagle, but he was really a very small bird. Her word for this was 'waaks', as in the Indian's name, which I gathered meant a bunting or wren. I almost asked what Lukswaas thought I was, but she anticipated me by touching me again and telling me I was an eagle. At this my pride and my own 'bird' swelled, then it diminished slightly as she told me that the eagle's strength was not because of its size, but its sharp eye, its straight dive, its finding the mouse.

Then she grew quiet and motionless, as if sad. At last she said that if I did not find the killer of McCrory, Wiladzap would die.

To hear this truth yet again, and from her mouth, drove me almost mad. My body grew taut, I thumped my fist on the ground, and said that there was still time, I would find the man. Then *that* man would die, and Wiladzap would be free. For the moment, I meant it.

But Lukswaas was still sad. When Wiladzap was free, she said, she and I could not be with each other like this.

My whole resolution had been to tell her that our meetings were impossible, but I was at a loss for words. I reassured her with gestures, and these became more intimate until we came together again.

There was now a dull white glow from the moon through the overcast night. We had been in the forest a long time. We got up, naked but blurred. Through all this I had worn her stone on the thong around my neck, and she my gold ring – which perhaps she would hide, I reasoned, during the day. We got dressed. Lukswaas was either no longer sad, or not wanting to be. She remarked lightly that she would like to see me under the sun, not always at night. I cast ahead in my mind for an afternoon I would not be on duty, and said I could meet her the following Monday just after noon.

We felt our way up the path which seemed to undulate like an inky snake in the blurring light, embraced fiercely – perhaps she, like me, felt both love and hate – and parted. I wended my way slowly back through the forest, the oak woods, and finally down Fort Street to Victoria.

22

On the Sunday I walked out to St Marks alone, but for form's sake I shared a pew with Frederick who seemed chastened and willing to be friends. I muttered to Frederick that I wanted to question Beaumont on the walk over to the farm, so Frederick should hang back. Luckily we had both arrived before Beaumont who, when he did appear, shared our pew, so that I was standing between the two. The scene was déja vu: the three fascinating faces of the Somerville girls under their bonnets, the unctuous voice of Firbanks reading the prayers, the 'English gentleman' type sermon from Coulter, hymns of praise stirring me in the familiar way. I suddenly recalled that the last time I had met Firbanks he had threatened to throw me out of his church. But of course he had not done so. And wasn't I as much of a hypocrite as he? If I believed that Christianity was evil, what was I doing here?

I noticed that Beaumont had no musical ear – he spoke, or whispered, rather than sang. A strange mechanical fellow. But possibly a murderer? It was only too easy, in the church, to believe that murders were committed by naked savages – out there, in the wilderness. But then it was not easy to believe that the curate was in fact a sexual degenerate. That the fussily conventional Mrs Somerville might have been the mistress of a murdered abortionist. Or that I, upright and respectable in my stiff Sunday collar, had spent the best part of two nights in the past week locked in animal embraces with an Indian woman, in the bushes in the heart of the forest only two miles from this church, under a moon which it would seem had never seen Christ.

Afterwards there was the same polite exchange of compliments and invitations outside the church. But I noticed a change in Aemilia – an excitability which had not been there before, an edge of nervousness in her greeting. Perhaps she had been numbed, the previous week, by the shock of the news about McCrory. Now she was not quite so much at ease, but certainly not melancholic. As I watched her drive away with her family in their buggy, I thought that if anything she looked cross.

Frederick Beaumont and I walked together along Cedar Hill Cross Road to our picnic place. Looking sullen, Frederick fell back. Beaumont did not seem to notice. He kept straight ahead, tapping in the dust with a walking stick, in a rhythm which was so precisely in time with his footsteps that he seemed clockwork, a tin soldier.

'I'm still working on the McCrory case,' I remarked. 'I'm wondering if you could help me. I hate to pester you with questions, but no one seems to have known the man at all, and I understand you did – to a certain extent.'

Beaumont's clockwork pace did not falter, and he spoke straight ahead, although with the usual fixed smile, as if he were looking at someone. 'What do you mean, old chap?'

'Well, I heard you knew him somewhat.'

'From whom?'

'A crimp by the name of Sam.' This of course, was not careful.

'A crimp? You can't be serious.' Still Beaumont looked ahead. 'I don't know any crimps.'

'Of course you wouldn't. But I was questioning him about McCrory and he said he'd seen you together.'

'Impossible! How would a rotten little crimp even know my name?'

'He described you.'

'And where was I seen with our friend McCrory?'

'In the Windsor Rooms.'

'Ah!' Although his mechanical step did not change, Beaumont for the first time showed some vehemence. 'One can get away with nothing,' he said. 'I should have known better.'

'What do you mean?'

'A chap can't spit in a town like Victoria without being observed and reported on. I can't visit a simple dancehall without being spotted. Just my luck!'

'What were you doing there?'

'Looking for a girl of course. Have you never done that?'

'Of course ...'

'Well, what's wong with it?'

'I had understood, from something you said last Sunday, that you didn't know McCrory apart from at Orchard Farm.'

'Did I say that? Well, one doesn't want to admit one's low connexions – though they're hardly a crime, what? Something of a joke, really, his capering around with the Somervilles like a rose in Spring. But of course none of us is what he seems. No doubt you're not either.'

'How many times did you see him in Victoria?'

'Perhaps your crimp counted them. Too boring really. When I wished to be amused, McCrory was there: he liked slumming it.'

'Why?'

'For his researches, I suppose. Interested in sex, above all, I should think – not in doing it, necessarily, but in finding out about it. Sort of medical Casanova.'

'You mean you don't think he had a sexual life? A mistress, for instance?'

'Damned if I know. I did meet him a few times at the Windsor Rooms, 'cos he suggested it. He thought I might enjoy it – suggested it as we were riding into town one Sunday evening, from the Farm.'

'Why would he think you'd enjoy it?'

''Cos I asked him, as a man who seemed to know his way around, though he had not been in Victoria very long, what there was to do there. I manage to go there rarely, since San Juan is so far. I'm too busy fighting the Pig War, you see. Silly business, damned boring, and no society on San Juan really, since they are such a rustic lot.'

'So you visited the Windsor Rooms with McCrory.' I was already tired of going round in circles. It was as if we had been talking an hour, not just a few minutes, Beaumont was so opaque.

'That's what I said, old boy.'

'And you weren't a patient of his?'

'Don't be silly. Animal magnetism? Mesmerism? Rubbish!'

'You think so?'

'Of course. He was a very *silly* man – a sort of intellectual worm with a digestive system which would reduce all facts to, well, earth.'

'But you liked him,' I said, playing for time while I considered Beaumont's unexpected image of the intellectual worm…

'One does what one can. I mean, do I like *you*? Beaumont was still looking straight ahead. 'You're a bit pi, I'd expect. Not really much fun, not the sort of chap I'd choose as a friend really. Yet here we are, strolling along cheerfully enough.' His pace did not falter.

'When did you hear about McCrory's death?'

'In the *British Colonist*. A day or two late. When it reached English Camp. I forget what date it was.'

'What were you doing the day he was killed?'

'I don't know. I'd have to think. Could have been on duty or off – we're not very busy. Was it a Wednesday or a Thursday? I forget.'

'Wednesday.'

'I went rough shooting on the island. Super grouse.'

'Do you ever come over here by boat on your own?'

'I've done it. I'm here now aren't I? But not often. We have a sort of skiff with a centre board. I've rowed and sailed her across but it's awfully hard work. Better on the way back, with the wind. Not worth it really, since it's a long walk to Victoria from Telegraph Cove, and it's not always easy to hire a horse.'

'Where do you put up when you stay the night in town?'

'Hotel Argyle. McCrory recommended it to me, actually. Frightful bore, Mrs Larose, but it's better than the more expensive one I'd stayed at before, the St George.'

'Ah yes, Mrs Larose,' I said, giving up my interrogation for now. I went on to describe my arrival in Victoria. I knew that if I continued questioning Beaumont we would arrive quickly at accusation and denial. I decided, on the spot, that I would have to go to San Juan somehow and find out more about this inscrutable machine-man. But now we were, after all, going to spend a Sunday afternoon together.

At Orchard Farm we were met by the three Somerville sisters, all fluffy and filmy in their summer dresses over crinolines, who had been waiting for us in the sun. They maintained a certain poise, like flamingos in a park, on the rough grassy patch in front of the house. But they were excited, in a breathless, girlish way, about the project of going for a walk up Mount Douglas. At least the youngest two were excited, above all Cordelia who called out gaily: 'Mamma has a headache so she's staying to talk to Mr Quattrini. He, poor man, is most upset at the death of his Irish servant girl in a fit of hysteria. Do come with us. Jones will bring us the first part of the way, then we can walk. It's such a *perfect* day.' And in her voice there was the thrill of the other perfect thing: that there were three girls and three young men. Firbanks or other admirers were nowhere to be seen. Typically going slightly beyond good taste, Cordelia mentioned this: 'Three escorts! What more could we ask?'

This frothiness was not quite shared by Aemilia, I sensed, but even she was, as at the church, less sombre than the previous week. As we waited for Mr Jones to come up with the buggy, it was natural for us all to pair off and stand talking. Frederick, come out of his sulk, with the bubbling Cordelia; Beaumont, the wooden man, with the insipid Letitia; me with Aemilia. I asked her about music. My mind and senses had been so indelibly marked by my encounters with Lukswaas that I found it unnerving to be standing close to a young woman yet not embracing her, not being aware of what she was like underneath her clothes. It was a struggle between surges of impersonal man-woman lust and a refined conversation which seized on everything ethereal – whether it was the cadence of a phrase of Handel, or the clear light on the few puffy clouds – as evidence that here were two souls talking, not two bodies.

Yet I told myself I did not actually lust after Aemilia. It was the awareness of her as a physical woman that was new. The barrier of my former innocence had broken through. At the same time I could, to my pleasure, feel Aemilia warming to me. Her grey eyes lingered more in mine than they had before, and her body, tall and slim like Lukswaas but seeming to reflect or emit more light, perhaps because of her dress, swung to and fro slightly as she leaned on her parasol, its point pressed into the rough grass of the 'lawn'.

Mr Jones appeared, driving the four-wheeled buggy pulled by two horses, with its facing seats under a canopy, his own seat raised in front. He was not exactly in livery – this was, after all a free country and the Somervilles not aristocrats. But he was wearing a dark coat, which must have been stifling in the heat, with silver buttons. It looked not unlike my police uniform coat, a fact with Frederick, no doubt in revenge, latched upon. 'We should have Mr Hobbes here recruit you into the police, Mr Jones,' he said, as patronizing as if he were a young squire at home in England, not an ironmonger's clerk stranded in a Colony. 'You and he would make a great show together.' The girls laughed merrily.

'Do you wear a *uniform*, Mr Hobbes?' Aemilia asked. We were getting settled, side by side, Beaumont on the other side of her, and Frederick ecstatically between the other two girls in the seat opposite. I could not tell, in the bustle, whether Aemilia was teasing or not.

'Oh yes. Brass buttons an' all, wiv a brand new Sergeant's stroipe, or chevron, on the sleeve.' I said this in a joke Cockney voice, imitating a London 'Peeler', then realised that such an accent would be foreign to these girls who had never been to England.

'Tell me where you come from in England, Mr Hobbes,' Aemilia said gently.

I realized she was saving me from making a fool of myself, and I melted with gratitude. I went on to talk about Wiltshire at this time of year – the miles of green corn waving in the wind, with the few forlorn oaks and ashes in clumps on the high ridges which the Romans and Saxons had used as roadways, the scattered prehistoric stones and ramparts of earth where in places burnt bones and pottery shards could be dug out, the villages of pink brick houses covered with climbing roses – no, it would be wisteria coming into bloom now, as it had on the peeling stone walls of the quad in Univ. Here there was a diversion to Oxford in the late Spring, and the medieval carols sung from Magdalen tower on May morning at dawn. Then back to the sky larks hovering in song over the windswept Wiltshire downs: they never sang for more than three minutes, I was saying. But I was interrupted by Frederick beginning to chatter about Kent. Then Beaumont in his dry voice was saying that the bleakness of the North Yorkshire moors was 'most agreeable when a man has grown up in it'. A general competitive cacophony intervened, with me talking merely to keep my end up. For a moment I had felt like an English skylark trilling a solo for Aemilia's ears, but now I was more like one of the Vancouver Island bluejays who in flocks of three or four, iridescent inky blue, black-crested, and quarrelsome, would squabble over last year's berries with raucous cries.

So we gabbled away about England, that Mecca of civilisation which all three of us men for one reason or another had left – although in that respect Beaumont had most assurance, since as the Queen's man wherever he went was a sort of England. The buggy was lurching along a dusty road, not much more than a path, between newly cleared farms in the valley bottom, with the thick firs of Mount Douglas forest behind, the mountain itself rising above the treetops, rocky and scrubby and singularly uninteresting from this distance. At length Mr Jones steered the horses up a trail through firs and cedars – like those on the other side of the mountain. As so often around Victoria, the impression was of having suddenly crossed aeons of time. This quiet, dark forest, with its trunks as straight and bare as masts, tufted branches far above, and its undergrowth of broad leaved bushes and ferns, its lack of birdsong except for very occasional, muffled twitterings, its grudging admittance of sunlight in the form of narrow shafts striking down like lightning bolts here and there, seemed primeval.

The trial came to a fork, each side of which was too narrow for the buggy, which stopped. Mr Jones would wait for us here. The men and I jumped down and handed the ladies out. As Aemilia stepped down, a few inches of bloomer showed, tied with pink ribbon at the ankle. Formerly it might have caused me to lose a night's sleep in wondrous retrospect. Now it seemed rather ridiculous. Must she not be hot? My own grey trousers were heavy and itchy.

We walked, as three couples, up one of the paths. It became steeper, and dustier. We stopped to examine the bark of a huge fir, perhaps six feet in diameter at chest height. Its deeply ridged bark was studded with layers of resin, some of which had swollen to bubbles and burst, so that trickles of it ran down the trunk, fragrant, and sticky to the touch – but leaving the fingers stained with black, as the over-eager Frederick discovered. We began walking again, almost climbing now, and gradually the path rose up along a ridge to the levels of the fir tops it was leaving behind, and was surrounded by another kind of vegetation – oaks and brambles among rocks and dry gullies.

Then the path broke out onto the shoulder of the mountain and we entered a third sort of region, where the oaks were suddenly dwarfs not much taller than a man, and there were grassy patches between rocks and boulders, carpeted with pink, yellow, and purple flowers. The resinous smell of the forest was replaced by the smell of dry grass. The sun beat down. The dwarf oaks were twisted, gnarled, and sparsely leaved. There were occasional arbutuses, blotched with green bark peeling from red, dense with thick green leaves, although last year's lay yellow on the stony ground.

'We shan't look back until we reach the top,' Aemilia announced. We kept on climbing, the dainty shoes of the girls becoming dusty, we men offering our arms from time to time but just as often having to scramble for ouselves. The girls had courage, I thought, but they obviously had made the climb before. It was an odd struggle: to climb a mountain on a fiercely hot day, and yet to preserve civility. On my own I knew I would have cursed at the dry rocks, panted and puffed. As it was, our little procession mounted the narrow path serenely, at least in appearance, even as the wind began to tug at the bonnets of the girls, and the frock coats of the men.

At the top was a cairn of stones. A cool wind blew strongly around us. We now turned to look at the view, admiring it with oohs and aahs. It was very much the fashion to admire such 'prospects'. We had come from the Southwest side, where we looked down over scrub and rocks to the top of the fir forest, then further to the fields of the valley, and rolling, forested hills all the way to the Western horizon. To the South, across forest then oak woods on steep small hills, we could see Victoria, about five miles away, nestling on its tiny mirror-like harbour, and beyond it the Straits with a fog bank starting about half way across, and above this, about twenty miles away, in Washington Territory, the bluish wall and level snowy crests of the Olympics or, as Aemilia explained to me 'Hurricane Ridge.' To the East was dense forest covering a wide peninsula indented with bays. There was Cormorant Point. I thought I could see wisps of smoke from the camp fires, hovering above the trees, although the prospect was more hazy to this side. Across Haro Strait, San Juan Island was a gentle, wooded green. I could hear the dry voice of Beaumont trying to indicate to Letitia where English camp was, and saying 'Dash it, I should have brought my field glasses.' To the North, where the slope pitched away from us steeply, we looked out over the long peninsula of Saanich, spread out as if on a map, mostly wooded but with a few clear patches of farmland, its coast curving away from us; then the archipelago of the Gulf Islands stretching Northward, intensely green in a dark blue sea.

The vivid colours, the huge distance on all sides, the sense of standing windswept and suspended in space with all the land falling down and away from us, the heat of the sun somehow pulsed by strong breeze, provoked in me a sense of excitement which the others must have been sharing: the girls' voices, though not Aemilia's, reached me in shrill tones, the men's sharp and pitched more high than usual.

We began to wend our way downward, on the Eastern side, over rocky hillocks tumbled with boulders, with dwarf oaks and arbutus growing out of the rock at odd angles, then becoming gnarled in turning to reach up as high as the wind would let them. There were hollows and small grassy plateaus between the rocky outcrops, which were sheltered from the wind. Aemilia picked her way down, using her folded parasol for occasional support, looking like a gauzy lilac and white butterfly, wisps of her chestnut brown hair blown loose from under her bonnet. I followed. The other couples were heading in different directions, as if the energy of the mountaintop had entered into them and was provoking them to be somewhat risqué about the normal conventions. Aemilia and I reached a grassy hollow where we were suddenly out of the breeze in a baking heat which made the grass smell like hay. Aemilia sat down, very carefully, as her dress required, on a smooth rock. There was nowhere similar for me to sit, yet I felt like resting, so I sprawled down as elegantly as I could on a grassy slope facing her, as if I were a young peasant, and she a lady shepherdess sitting demurely on her rock.

With the point of her parasol she began indicating wild flowers growing in cracks between the rocks – stonecrop, saxifrage; and in the grass – ragged starflower, blue camas, columbine, and pink and white fawn lilies. Her manner was light, but conventional. I knew that in this kind of relationship, of interested young man and modest young lady, it might take months before any serious conversation was possible. I was reconciled to this, and now even welcomed it as a way of raising myself above the level of my passions for Lukswaas, which seemed to lurk like hidden animals in the dark forest hundreds of feet below and behind me, invisible behind the slope, crowned with dwarf oaks, against which I was sprawled.

The other young ladies and the men were invisible too, although I could occasionally hear Frederick's voice. But now Aemilia began to quiz me, gently but firmly, about why I had joined the police.

I explained about my letter of reference to Mr Justice Begbie, and my role as an investigation officer for Augustus Pemberton, allowing myself to confide in Aemilia that eventually I might go back into the law but for now I found police work an invaluable experience, even though it did consume much of my life. 'I even live in the courthouse,' I said, 'where I have a room. And since it's also the jail, in effect I live in a jail.' I had meant to make this sound amusing, but it was merely dull and drab.

'Somebody has to look after the prisoners I suppose,' she said gently.

'Well there is a jailer, Mr Seeds, who also lives there. I've taken the prisoners out on chain-gang, I'm ashamed to say, to build the James Bay Bridge.'

'You did that?' She laughed, as if 'gaily', but with an artificial effect. 'So when you go home this evening, you go to jail.'

'Certainly this evening, when I give Mr Seeds a hand – literally, since we play cards together on Sunday evenings.'

'And discuss the criminal mentality?'

'Not with Seeds. The only discussions I've had on that subject have been with Mr Pemberton, a most intelligent man.'

'Can you think yourself into the criminal mind?'

'I try.' I thought of Lukswaas's advice to be like a hunter putting on bearskin. 'But it's not easy for someone of my rather naïve upbringing and education.'

'Do give me some examples. Do you encounter any really sordid people, plotting to murder their relations to profit from their legacies, or to swindle the banks on a large scale?'

'Not really. My detective work has concentrated on very ordinary burglaries, and a couple of small scale frauds – until this recent tragedy, of course, which has occupied most of my attention.'

'Still? I thought the murderer had been apprehended and all but hanged by now.'

I was surprised by Aemilia's bluntness. 'Admittedly it doesn't look good for him, since the circumstantial evidence against him is very strong. But I'm not satisfied with the way the case stands.'

'Really? I should think it would give you pleasure to assist in the punishment of such a dastardly crime.'

'It would make me sad, should there be a miscarriage of justice.'

'But that's not possible, surely.'

'Yes, it is. It's of course difficult to discuss with you the case under investigation. But for one thing, it's not absolutely certain than an Indian committed the crime, and for another it's in my opinion even less certain that *this* Indian committed it.'

'It probably doesn't matter *which* one committed it,' she said flatly, 'since I'm sure they're all as thick as thieves. I shouldn't be too surprised if they *all* did it, or if one did, they covered up for him. That makes them all guilty, doesn't it?'

'I suppose so.' My eye was distracted by two large birds high above us, their wings stuck out rigidly, wheeling in rising currents of air.

Aemilia glanced up. 'Eagles,' she said. 'We often see them from the farm. They are as common here as I suppose hawks are in England.'

'I've never seen them on my tramps in the winter with Frederick.'

'They like high places.'

We watched the eagles slowly turning, seeming to follow each other deliberately in dips and slides, doubling back on each other. One was larger. Perhaps it was their mating season, I thought – an unmentionable subject. But after a minute or two the light of the sky was too brilliant for the eyes. I came back to earth and looked across at Aemilia. As if my eyes had been changed by looking near the sun, I saw a sort of soft glow on and around her. She was beautiful, a shepherdess of the Versailles or Dresden china type. Inaccessible, of course, under the layers of silky, frilly clothing, and the layers of conventions we lived with. I smiled at our silence, and she smiled back prettily. Indeed she seemed to be letting herself be lighter today. There was no trace of her melancholy. But there had been that vehemence when she had spoken about the Indians. And now it came back, her eyes becoming colder, her voice sharp again:

'And do you see much of this Indian murderer?'

'I don't believe he is a murderer. But yes, I see him. He talks little. I'm afraid he's hopeful that I can find the real criminal so that he can be free. He knows I've been given the case. But I'm afraid I'll let him down.'

'You really believe he's innocent! I thought you had the air of a more sensible person.'

'Which I hope I am.' I bowed my head politely, although I felt rebuked.

'You believe in the *Noble Savage*, is that it? You think a man like that has a sensitivity like yours?'

'At times I feel that, or that in some respects he is *more* sensitive.' I was thinking of Wiladzap's 'song'.

'You're an out and out romantic, Mr Hobbes. Fie on you!' This old fashioned phrase – one of a number which could be heard from the Somerville girls' lips, as if at least some of their expressions came from the reading of novels – was perhaps meant to be playful, but was accompanied by a genuine curl of the lip in contempt.

'Of course I'm not a romantic,' I said. 'If I had ever been one, I should not be now, after six months in the police.'

'So what does he tell you, your Noble Savage?'

'Not much, I must confess. I know little or nothing about him. Nobody does, that's part of the problem. When these particular Indians do talk' (I was thinking of Lukswaas) 'they do so rather elliptically, and in images. And Chinook is not a help, It's a touching sort of language, in a baby-talk way, but inadequate for explanations…' I stopped because I realized that I did not believe this, and I felt that I was letting Lukswaas down since, although slowly, she had communicated to me some fairly intricate thoughts.

'I know Chinook,' Aemilia said loftily. 'Mesika nanitsh chack chack klatawa copa stick stick'. This meant 'I see eagle go tree tree'.

I glanced up, then looked back to her.

'Where did you learn it?'

'Comox.' She was referring to the place her family had once settled in, some 150 miles up the Straits, beyond the Gulf Islands we could see from where they were sitting. 'We had to use Chinook in trading with the Indians. We would have liked to employ them for farmwork but they think themselves too good for it. They are a shiftless lot.'

'I understand the settlement, er, failed.' This was dangerous ground, in view of what had happened to her father.

'Oh yes, it did indeed fail, Mr Hobbes. It failed. In a rotten, *bloody* way.'

'Bloody', even in the literal sense, was not a word supposed to come from a young woman's lips.

'Yes. I had heard that, vaguely,' I remarked.

'No need to be so polite. Not to mince words, three of the settlers in our little pioneering village were massacred, Father being one of them. If it had not been for the timely arrival of Her Majesty's Ship the *Trident*, whose guns razed the Indian village to the ground, we should all have been killed. My father had sent a message to Victoria. He knew trouble was brewing. They were smiling and childishly simple, the Comox; in that way Indians have which seems to have charmed you so, Mr Hobbes. But every now and then they would let a remark drop that we were only having the *use* of *their* land. It was not ours, no, not even though we cleared it with the sweat of our brow, and made fruit and vegetables and grass grow where formerly was miserable, gloomy forest and swamp. The women worked as hard as the men. Myself, between ten and fourteen years old, for four years, and who had known nothing more in the way of hardship than the savannah lands around the Columbia River, I worked like a boy. It was a dream for us all. Foully ended in a treacherous and vile attack by the Indians to whom we were introducing the benefits of civilization. One of them came up behind my father – I saw it myself, with *these eyes*, Mr Hobbes, and I screamed, but too late – and he pulled an axe from his blanket and struck my father down, just as you might fell a tree. From *behind*, Mr Hobbes. They like to attack from behind. So remember that when you turn your back on *your* Indian.'

Not surprisingly, Aemilia was trembling with agitation as she said this. But she shook her head abruptly, as if to cast drops of water from it, and said, 'Enough. I don't need to bore you with that old story.'

This was, of course, far outside the realm of my experience. 'I'm very grieved that you had to live through that, Miss Somerville.'

'Keep it in mind, Mr Hobbes. Keep it in mind when you deal with Indians. If you can't learn from your own experience, then you must learn from that of others.'

I winced. Goodness, she had a sharp tongue. I could not resist saying: 'But Miss Somerville, I'm sure your heart is not without charity towards these people. I mean, in your own household there is the little Indian boy of the Joneses – a nice looking little chap he is too, and I'm sure you don't think ill of him.'

'That's none of your business,' Aemilia said sharply. She rose to her feet, in a swift movement which had more strength than delicacy. 'He is indeed a nice little boy,' she added, '*adopted* by Mrs Jones as a mere infant, I believe, and therefore uncontaminated by the society of his own people. But if *I* were Mrs Jones, I should wonder about the *blood* coming through, and I should worry a great deal.' She turned to look for the others, and rose to her feet. I scrambled up, but maintained a respectable distance as we walked in the direction of Frederick's voice, which could be heard from within a group of dwarf oaks. But Aemilia stopped again and looked at me, her eyes steady and not at all emotional. 'All the same, you believe your Indian will hang.'

In short order, I'm afraid. He'll be tried within a few weeks, and on the present evidence found guilty. Then no doubt he will be hanged in the public square within a day or so afterwards. Then his band will disperse, and we shall have no more trouble with these particular Tshimshian.' I felt almost relieved to abandon all hope, and present the stark facts.

'Good,' Aemilia said. We went to join the others.

Aemilia and I were both silent on the way back to the farm, although Frederick and Cordelia chattered inanely. Beaumont and Letitia, who although they did not seem particularly excited by each other, seemed to get on well enough, occasionally added comments. I could not identify my feelings for Aemilia. I had begun the day in a state of romanticism about her, which I now realized had been forced, although I still felt there was an affinity between us. Only this affinity seemed to extend itself to a capacity to irritate each other, in an intimate way. Although our language had been formal, we had got to the point swiftly, and our conversation had not been empty like – I thought unkindly – that of Frederick and Cordelia.

But although I acknowledged to myself that the affinity between me and Aemilia still existed, I did not feel able to revive it this afternoon. We had said enough. Aemilia's bluntness had made me articulate, more clearly than ever, how dangerous Wiladzap's situation was. This might require desperate measures, and I was ready to abandon politeness and caution.

So when we arrived at the Farm, and climbed down from the buggy to the sound of the usual polite murmurs of assistance from the men, and the giggles of Cordelia, I announced that I would have to take my leave shortly, since I was on duty that evening 'in the courthouse' (meaning the jail). But if Mrs Somerville was not indisposed, I should like to have a word with her.

This caused a slight flurry as the younger girls looked questioningly at me and Aemilia as if perhaps a hasty proposal of marriage was in the works. I found myself blushing with embarrassment, but Aemilia walked off to the house in a demonstration of indifference, if not hostility. Then the others looked at me as if pityingly... 'Aemilia does have her moods,' Cordelia whispered to me. 'I shall go and fetch Mamma so that you can have your talk with her on the veranda.'

Since the sun had moved around to the other side of the house, the veranda was in the shade. It was really a simple wooden 'porch' with hanging baskets of flowers, and wickerwork chairs. Pleased not to be going inside for a stifling 'tea', I stood waiting until Mrs Somerville arrived, carrying a small bottle of smelling salts, as if she expected at any moment to be overcome.

'I'm very sorry to bother you,' I said. 'But I have to ask you a few questions, in my official capacity.'

'Oh, it's quite all right. I shall survive, it's only a small headache. And

Mr Quattrini will be well looked after by the girls. Did you enjoy your "promenade" on Mount Douglas?'

'Indeed yes. I had never climbed it before. The prospect is magnificent.'

Mrs Somerville sat down in a wicker chair. I took the chair beside her and shifted it so that I could partly face her. Her chest was heaving in short, sharp breaths: she was much more nervous than her words would admit. But I did not feel sorry for her. I realized that her nervousness and over-refinement were shields. She was in fact a robust-looking woman, with penetrating eyes, an unlined face, and a solid although rather plump body. She was not merely 'well preserved', but a woman not very far past being young.

'It's of course about Dr McCrory,' I said. 'I do understand that under the circumstances, anyone who knew him well must tend to deny it. His medical approach was so original that it must be hidden from prying eyes, so that anyone who became his patient must do so in strict confidence. And why should such confidence not be preserved after his death?'

'Are you implying I was a patient of his?' Mrs Somerville asked, with a sharpness similar to Aemilia's.

'I'm certain of it.'

'*Certain* of it? Well, I must say, young man, both your information and your judgment are wrong. I was never his patient.'

I felt stumped. I had indeed been certain that, like her friend Mrs Larose, Mrs Somerville had been the alienist's patient. She had then, I thought, become more intimate with him. But now she seemed too righteous to be lying.

'In that case,' I said, 'I am wrong for having misinterpreted the facts. Your relationship with him must have been of another kind.'

'Mrs Somerville's breast began to heave, and she clutched her smelling salts. 'What an *unspeakable* accusation. Are you saying I had an *improper* relationship with the Doctor?'

'I don't know what your relationship was.' I felt too clumsy to be able ever to get at the truth. 'But that it was a close and intimate one I have no doubt.'

'*Intimate*?' Mrs Somerville suddenly put aside her nervousness and became angry. She leaned forward and thumped me on the knee with her bottle of smelling salts. 'Listen to me, Mr Hobbes. You're using a variety of words – "relationship of *another* kind", "intimate" – in a quite disgusting "double-entendre". I will *not* allow you to talk to me like this.' Like Aemilia she tended to stress certain words heavily when agitated. 'About a *dear* friend of this family!' She reverted suddenly to her usual sentimental upset. Now she took a handkerchief from her sleeve and dabbed her eyes, although I could see no tears.

'I don't mean to be offensive,' I said. 'But Mrs Somerville, do make an attempt to understand me. Dr McCrory was foully murdered. It's thought by many to have been by the Indian who has been charged with the crime. But our investigations have revealed a world – a whole world – of bizarre and even vicious entanglements of the Doctor. It's more than possible that it was the hand of someone from this other world – or of a patient in an excess of nervous derangement – that struck the Doctor down. Anyone who knew the Doctor well may be in a position to enlighten us about this other world in which he lived. If you knew him well, you may know the names and circumstances of others who wished him ill. Do you not see that?'

'These are wild words, Mr Hobbes. "Bizarre. Vicious". You're too carried away by your zeal in this case. And you do not stop short of slandering the dead! I'm appalled at you. Of course the poor man will have had deranged patients. He was an *alienist*. He was not afraid of the deranged, the obscure, the hidden in people's lives. But it seems you know very little about them. Who *were* these patients? I'll wager, from your manifest confusion, that in almost all cases you don't know. All you can do, to feed your conjectures, is to come and ask a lady who received the doctor into her house, on quiet Sunday afternoons, what *she* knew about him. It's disgraceful, Mr Hobbes. I must ask you to leave.'

She sat looking at me haughtily, and I realized I was no match for her. For one thing, she was more intelligent than she normally allowed to appear. For another, if she had in fact been McCrory's patient she must be fortified by her knowledge that he did not keep records. But perhaps she had not been the patient. It must have been Aemilia! Why had I not asked Aemilia these questions? Because I had even less information to go on than in the case of Mrs Somerville. Perhaps Mrs Somerville could be so adamant because she was protecting her daughter's reputation. Yet as I looked at her, I still suspected her. When revealed in all her strength, she was a dominant woman. I found myself thinking, sordidly, that if any woman in the family was to have McCrory to herself, Mrs Somerville would make sure it was she.

'You must leave, Mr Hobbes,' she said. 'You are no longer welcome in this house.'

Beaten, and angry at myself, I rose to my feet, restrained the instinctive urge to apologize, and left.

On my long walk home I stopped at St Mark's to see if Firbanks was there. He was, fussing around the empty church in his vestments, preparing for Evensong.

'I thought I'd see you at the farm this afternoon,' I said.

'I thought I'd give it a miss. Not sure I like some of the company they receive.'

I resolved not to be drawn into the nastiness of our previous conversation. 'Just a small question,' I said. 'Or rather a confirmation you can help me with. I know I asked you about this before and you denied it, but,' I shrugged my shoulders, 'I thought I'd ask anyway. I have reason to believe McCrory supplied you with contraceptive sheaths. I assume this was to prevent transmission of disease to any young lady you might be with. Am I right?'

'You insolent…'

'Wait!' I interrupted, with a gesture to remind Firbanks that we were in church. 'Give the dead their due, at any rate. It was a very decent thing of him to do.'

''All right, all right. Yes, you're correct. He was most concerned about such matters of hygiene. Now does that satisfy you?'

'One more thing. Did he ever subject you to a "criticism"?'

Firbanks' waxen cheeks flared red. 'None of your business.'

'Thank you.'

On the long walk into Victoria, I reflected that it had indeed been decent of McCrory to want to protect prostitutes and 'squaws' against the curate. It had served no use to my investigation of the murder, to establish with Firbanks the truth about sheaths. But it had served some use for myself. It was part of getting into McCrory's skin – no pun on lambskin intended. What an odd man McCrory had been. I could not understand him. Who *had* understood him? Perhaps no one. His whole life seemed to have been devoted to the understanding of others, although not, as I saw it, from the best of motives. He knew so many people's secrets, yet they must not have known his. The end result must have been a sort of delusion in McCrory. He could not possibly have understood *himself*.

But did anybody I had interviewed? With the exception of the morbidly joking pharmacist, everybody else had been so sure of themselves, so certain of their positions. Even the snivelling schoolmaster Hadley, or Frederick when confronted with the locket, or Quattrini who had slept with his servant girl. Each fully justified themselves. Even Sylvie had her story, her excuse for what must be really a soiled and dirty life. She was the proverbial whore with the heart of gold – really! Her warmth was real. She was true to type. But weren't they all? Or rather, each was a type containing a sort of opposite other type. Hadley was the timid and fussy schoolmaster – but he drank. Frederick was the jovial young man about town – but he was an opportunist. Quattrini was the busy and pious merchant – who bought and sold people. Beaumont was the clock-work soldier, the man of power – who had a secretly humiliating life with women. Firbanks – the whited sepulchre. Mrs Somerville, the silly and pretentious widow – who was hard as nails when it came to a confrontation.

Who was it said 'character is destiny'? Heraclitus? A cliché. But it seems to be true. I feel these people are all acting out themselves. What they are is what they do. What they do is what they are. They all seem so unshakable. I can extract information out of them, or they can spill it out to me because I am a good listener, but all they are giving is themselves. It comes easily.

I am a good listener from listening to my mother. I too am what I do, do what I am. But I cannot see myself from outside. Am I as rigidly bound in the system of my character as these others? My character, like theirs, is my history – extending from the past through the present and perhaps even into the future. Do we have free will at all?

Shut up, Chad. This is an introspection, if anything is. But I am now leaving it in the story. After all I am part of the story.

Some characters I have not mentioned. Aemeilia. I don't understand her. She is quite fluid, less stamped out from a mould. Or rather, her mould is unique. Are some characters unique while others are not? Or is that uniqueness just coming from my interest in them? But one thing that is different about Aemilia is that she confides her own thoughts and feelings – as about her father at Comox. She is not pretending. No, that's not true. She is pretending, I know she is. But I am not sure when she is and when she is not.

And McCrory? I am beginning to understand him. But I am putting a picture together of him piece by piece. He is already in the past tense, he is part of history. He can be defined – eventually. But he must have been complex when alive. Perhaps, as with Aemilia, there were moments where genuine light shone through the veil of the character as presented to the world.

Wiladzap? At first he was to me the type of 'the Indian Chief', as if from a novel. And yes, I suppose the Noble Savage. I think he has spoken to me from the heart. Actually he speaks rather often from the heart – and seemingly listens from the heart too. But he too is hiding something, I know it.

And last of all: Lukswaas. I tremble with adoration for Lukswaas. She is to me, of all the people in my list, the most *true*. Yet she is betraying her husband! And I am too!

23

The following afternoon I walked out Cedar Hill Road to what I was determined – again – would be my final meeting with Lukswaas. I knew however, that we would make love one more time. Only afterwards could I have the resolution to break with her. I hated myself for calculating this, but called it necessity.

The previous night I had visited Wiladzap in his cell. Wiladzap had been eating some of the smoked salmon which had been brought to him, of a sort so hard and dry that it preserved well. He would not speak, but smiled slightly at me, as if he knew there was a special relationship between us – which there was, in the sense that I was working to try and exonerate him, but also in the sense that Wiladzap did not know about: that while he lay on his paliasse in his bare brick-walled cage, his wife had been giving herself to me, out in the wild forest.

When I arrived at the usual meeting place, I stopped and looked around. There was a rustle in the bushes near the path, and Lukswaas stood up. I went toward her, and her tawny cheeks blushed. She looked confused. She reached out and stroked my light grey frock-coat. I realized it was the first time she had seen me in civilian clothes. She would understand nothing of these clothes – that they were in English taste rather than American, or as I saw it, in good taste rather than bad. She was only curious. I felt the gulf between us: me, used to living in layers of civilized concealment, she living with that nakedness which came most naturally to her and which now I desired. But first I held her by the shoulders and looked at her handsome chilcat of light blue and black patterns, clasped over her breasts with a carved wooden pin; her arms with their silver bracelets; her hair with its central parting and neat braids hanging behind her ears with their abalone earrings; at her face, brown but flushed, wide-cheekboned but refined in its length and the firmly cut mouth; her teeth scrubbed whiter than those of most white girls I had seen; her nose fine and straight; her black almond eyes quick and sensitive. 'I love you', I could not help saying in English as I stooped and kissed her and held her to me, feeling her hand stroking my back.

We moved apart and she told me we could go down through the forest to a place she had found by the sea. Instead of following her, as I usually did in the dark, I held her hand and we made our way side by side down through the trees. The firs began to be interspersed with arbutus and oak as the land became rockier and better drained by gullies and ravines, then the forest ended at the edge of a bluff, almost a clifftop, though only fifty feet or so high, the sea azure below. Lukswaas pointed out a path descending a gully, and we followed it down over rocks and an almost dried-up stream and into a mass of brambles, with berries like flattened raspberries but yellow and unripe. Pushing carefully through these on the almost invisible path we emerged suddenly onto a beach of soft white sand, in a tiny cove hemmed in by rocky bluffs out of which arbutus trees stuck at crazy angles. The sea splashed gently in white lines along the beach, which was only a hundred feet or so across, half of it blinding white in the sun, the other half, where we stood, in the shade.

Without a word we abandoned ourselves to our usual feverish embrace, taking off clothes, throwing ourselves onto Lukswaas's chilcat on the sand, giving ourselves to each other, and ending with a convulsive sigh. Then we lay dreamily as usual, although this time there was the glow of multicoloured light through my eyelids. I opened them and looked up through a net of weird red arbutus branches and their dark green leaves to the sky. Lukswaas stirred. She smiled and ran her fingers through my hair. 'Boo woo', she said imitating our last shuddering breath. Then she pointed to the sea and explained in her halting Chinook that 'Boo woo' was the noise of the whale as it spouted, and it was the word the Tsimshian used for the moment at the end of loving, when the man and woman blew out the breath of life like whales…

I could have, I should have, allowed myself to enjoy this innocently pleasurable remark. But how many other times had she experienced this 'boo woo'? It hurt me to think of how naively I gave myself to her – to her sweetness, her 'cleanly wantonness' as I remembered from some old poem. She gave herself too, but for her it was an episode among many.

I sat up, and Lukswaas too. I got to my feet, and she too, as if wanting not to lose me. She even took my hand – shyly, it seemed. Perhaps the Indians did not usually hold hands. I walked forward into the sun, and could not help enjoying its heat on my skin as I stood looking at the sea. I stepped forward, Lukswaas still holding my hand trustingly, and into the leading wave as it crossed the sand. We both gasped. It was freezing. We stepped back. I looked at us both. A naked woman, tall, brown and lithe, and a naked man, taller and white. In fact, since both of us were slim and smooth skinned, our body hair curly and fine, we looked not much more than a gangling boy and a very pretty girl.

I asked in Chinook how old Lukswaas was, wondering if she knew. She said she was eighteen, and held up ten fingers, then eight. She asked me the same question. I said I was twenty three, and held up all ten fingers twice, then three. We smiled at each other. I could have cried. It was time for me to speak.

I said we could not see each other again. It was not possible. It was not right.

Lukswaas said, changing the subject in an illogical way, that Wiladzap was in the jail. When would he be free? Was I closer to finding the murderer?

I said that I was still working to find the murderer, and I hoped I would, although time was short. In truth, although I did not tell Lukswaas this, I was more hopeful, since I was planning to ask Pemberton for permission to interview Beaumont on San Juan Island: I found it hard to believe that Beaumont could have murdered McCrory, but there were more questions and more of a mystery surrounding Beaumont than anybody else, and this gave me a sort of twisted hope – like one of the arbutus growing crazily out of the rock.

Lukswaas bit her lip and looked at me, frowning. Then she begged me to do all I could to find out who had killed the doctor. Wiladzap must be set free of the jail. How was Wiladzap? Did he eat? Did he walk? What did he say to me?

Yes, he ate a little. And he walked once a day. But he had said nothing. I returned to my original subject. I reached out, took Lukswaas's hand, and looked into its palm. As I did so I could feel my desire returning, my body coming alive to her. 'Halo nanitsh nika mesika, mesika nika.' I said vehemently. ('Not see I you, you me'). I dropped her hand and turned away.

'Kahta?' I heard her say. ('Why?').

I turned back wearily to face her, my desire at least gone as I was out of reach of her, and I was trying not to see her as I spoke. 'Kehwa Wiladzap', I said. ('Because of Wiladzap').

Lukswaas said with what seemed to me unreasonable stubbornness, that while Wiladzap was still in jail we could see each other.

It was as if she did not understand complex feelings at all, I thought. I hated her for the brutal simplicity of her mind: yes, so long as Wiladzap was in jail we were free to see each other. So we would. Enough.

She was looking at me with an intense, worried expression. Then this softened and turned vulnerable. 'Mesika tikegh nika?' She asked. ('Do you love me?')

I felt deeply touched. 'Nika tikegh mesika' I said. Then, for good measure I added what I had said earlier in English. 'I love you.'

She recognized the words, and smiled. Then she said that when Wiladzap was free from jail, I could have a talk with him. She said that if she could not be with me she would cry and cry. This was as simple in Chinook as English: 'Nika cly, cly, cly.'

She turned away as if afraid of having said too much. She had. It was indeed too much for me. Was she proposing a sort of trade, where Wiladzap would sell Lukswaas to me? I felt excited, flattered, horrified, and sick.

'Mesika klootchman Wiladzap, halo klootchman nika', I said. ('You woman Wiladzap, not woman me').

'Ihtah?' ('What') She looked at me in surprise. 'Klootchman Wiladzap? Nika klootchman Wiladzap? Wake. Nika ats Wiladzap. *Ats*.' ('Woman Wiladzap? I woman Wiladzap? No. I sister Wiladzap. *Sister*.')

I felt as if I had walked into a wall: my body tingled with shock from head to toe. 'Mesika *ats* Wiladzap?' I said numbly. ('You *sister* Wiladzap?').

'Mesika *ats* Wiladzap', she repeated. Then for good measure she added that Wiladzap was her brother. She looked at me impatiently, as if this was obvious and I was being stupid.

'Nika tum tum mesika klootchman Wiladzap,' I said slowly. ('I mind you woman Wiladzap'). I remembered the question she had been asked by Pemberton at the courthouse: 'Mesika klootchman Tyee?' Literally, 'You woman chief?', meaning the chief's wife. I repeated it to Lukswaas now: 'Mesika klootchman Tyee!'

'Klootchman Tyee? Ah-ha. Klootchman Tyee! Nika Klootchman! Nika Tyee!' Lukswaas's voice had risen in a kind of panic.

At last I understood. She was saying 'Woman chief. Yes. Woman chief. I woman. I chief.' She was a chief in her own right – there was the mistake.

Lukswaas was backing away from me, her eyes open wide in horror.

Her mouth also opened wide and she raised one hand and covered it, still backing away. Horror … I had never seen anything like it, and I felt myself invaded by it, my own eyes and mouth opening wide, as I felt a deep internal chill which seemed to freeze even my heart. I had been making love to a mere girl, thinking she was another man's wife. My God. I struggled with Chinook: 'Kunish, kunish man kopa mesika elip nika?' I called out to her in agony – how many men had been with her before me?

'Halo man, halo man. Ikt. Ikt. Mesika!' ('No man, no man. One. One. You.') She was shaking her head, still in horror. 'Klootchman Wiladzap?' She repeated. ('Woman Wiladzap?').

'Nika wake kumtuks', I said desperately. ('I not know').

'Wake, wake'. ('No, no'). She clamped her hand over her mouth again, shaking her head slowly, eyes still horrified.

I felt like death. Our love had been killed on this beach. Of course Indian women were different, she had been more forward with me than a white girl would have been, but I had asked her to meet me in the forest, and she had accepted under the same innocent and overpowering compulsion as mine. But my compulsion must now be seen as a cynical adultery. What we had done was no longer the same, because while we had done it I had thought she was merely another man's wife in an act of betrayal. I could see all this clearly, but tried to redeem some of it with what was, after all, the truth, calling out in Chinook that while Lukswaas was in my arms I forgot the whole world. 'Lukswaas!' I called, but it was as if my words bounced back at me off a stone.

Lukswaas broke suddenly from her position of rigid horror, and dashed across the beach to our clothes. She seized her apron and slipped it on, stepped into her moccasins while pulling her chilcat around her shoulders, and ran away, scrambling through the bushes and into the gulley. I followed her, but half-heartedly, half-paralysed by a huge sense of guilt and stupidity. I stood naked on the beach, hearing the rocks scrape as she made her way up the gulley, then nothing.

I went over to the pile of clothes. She had abandoned my ring, on its leather thong, throwing it in the sand, I picked it up and put it around my neck with her stone, and dressed wearily. All my movements were slow. I looked listlessly around from time to time. My eyes kept being drawn to something which at last I went to examine, dragging my feet. It was a gouged out area behind some rocks just above the high water mark. I realized it was a place where a boat had been pulled in and beached. I thought of Beaumont's possible trips alone from San Juan, although Beaumont had mentioned landing at Telegraph Cove, a mile to the East. It would take a strong man to haul a boat this far up on the beach. I crouched down and examined the pebbles. Some were marked with brown varnish. But this was common to all boat bottoms.

Who would beach a boat in such an isolated place? But this was soon lost in a return of my agony about Lukswaas.

I trudged through the forest and back to the road, aware of nothing until I saw a figure on the road in front of me. My heart leaped. I thought it was Lukswaas. But no, it was a man who, to my surprise immediately jumped off the road and took to the woods. Suddenly alert, I tried to follow the man with my eyes, but lost him almost at once. A man in a straw hat darting into the bushes. I might have followed him, out of suspicion, but felt too crushed and weary. I trudged back through the forest, and along Cedar Hill Road.

The implications of what Lukswaas had told me were too painful to consider. Instead I tried to think of the implications for Wiladzap. These seemed so important that I decided to take the unprecedented step of calling on Augustus Pemberton, whose house at the top of Fort Street I would pass on my way into town.

It was late afternoon by the time I reached the house, too early for Pemberton to have dined. I rang, and was admitted by the maid, then shown into a small sitting room or 'parlour'. It was amusing really, to contrast this simple wooden house – which nevertheless by Victoria's standards was quite elegant – with the grand Georgian terrace in which no doubt a man of Pemberton's standing would be living in Dublin, where he had come from.

Pemberton did not keep me waiting, nor did he seem annoyed to see me. Victoria is informal compared to the Old World. 'Well, Sergeant,' he said. 'Not on duty, I see.'

'No. But I have just learned something of importance in the case of Wiladzap, which I feel I should communicate to you.'

'Of course. What is it? Sit down.' We sat facing each other in stiff wooden backed chairs.

'I have learned from the Tsimshian a fact about which we have been in error. The young woman Lukswaas is not Wiladzap's wife, she's his sister.'

'Really? Yes, that is a surprise. Did we not establish the relationship clearly in our interrogations?'

'I don't think so. Superintendent Parry and I merely assumed she was Wiladzap's wife, out at the camp. And then, with the vagaries of Chinook…'

'That's no excuse,' Pemberton interrupted. 'Chinook's all right if you know how to use it. There's a word 'ats' for a younger sister, and 'klootchman' means either 'woman' or 'wife' – understandably, since among these people we are not always talking about formal marriages. A wife becomes a woman, becomes a wife again, if you see what I mean. But did she not admit she was Wiladzap's woman?'

'I've gone through it in my mind, and what I recall is that you asked, "Mesika klootchman Tyee?" Meaning "You are the chief's wife?" But Tyee means any chief or highly placed person. She herself is highly placed. I think she understood your question as "Are you a chief woman?" Which, in her own way, she seems to be. So she said yes. Of course it would be far from her mind to guess we might consider her the wife of her brother. But from our point of view, she seemed to be treated as his wife: to have a status in relationship to him, to be dressed similarly, and wear bracelets of silver which somehow seems appropriate for a chief's wife. And at the same time, according to the man Smgyiik's accusation, she was the object of Wiladzap's murderous jealousy.' Here my vehemence might have betrayed some of my agony, if Pemberton, always hasty, had not interrupted again.

'Nothing more natural,' he said. 'The Northern tribes, the Tsimshian and the Haida, are not very well known to us, of course. But I remember Mr Begbie saying that among them the descent of property is matrilineal, that is from mother to daughter. It gives the women a certain status. And I think you're correct. It was stupid of me not to have been more precise in the interrogation. I too was making assumptions according to my prejudices. Of course she may have a sort of 'Tyee' status in her own right. At the same time, as a woman in a matrilineal tribe she would be in the custody, as it were, of her brother. In fact this woman Lukswaas is probably more precious to Wiladzap as a sister than she would be as a wife. These people tend to take on wives and put them away rather easily. But I suppose a sister is always a sister.'

'Oh God, I've been so stupid,' I said passionately.

'Come, come. You've done a good job, you can't be perfect. At least you've found out this detail now. But mind, Chad, it will if anything make Wiladzap's case more difficult.'

'What?' I snapped out of my own self-pity.

'You and I may well feel that the case is mitigated by the, let us say, "chivalric" aspect of Wiladzap's avenging his sister's honour. A jury may even feel the same. But they'll send him to the gallows as readily as in the other case. The jealousy of an Indian over his squaw may occasionally provoke murder, but more often he merely sends her away. If she repents and behaves well he may accept her back, although he may have a new wife by then. The old one, the sinner, may have to become the servant of the new. It's like that among the Salish tribes around here, at any rate. No one knows about the Tsimshian. But a man murdering another for an insult to his sister! It's punishable by the rope. In law it establishes the *mens rea*, the intention to commit the crime. Forgive me, you have a law degree, so you know this.'

'Yes, I see.' I sighed. Pemberton was hasty, but quick-minded. I could find no argument to contradict him.

'On the other hand your report was very provoking,' Pemberton went on. 'I must confess I was left disturbed by your revelations of this secret world of McCrory's. It's out of just such a secret world that the most heinous crimes often emerge. Yet the circumstantial case against Wiladzap is strong enough! And your insinuations about various citizens of this Colony, while disturbing, are not enough to cast doubt on Wiladzap's guilt. I'm afraid you've failed to make an alternative case. Therefore the trial must proceed, and I'm sure Mr Parry has other duties for you. The Sergeant's stripes will of course remain on your arm. You've done a fine and conscientious job.'

'Thank you, Sir. But I have one more request. An awkward one.'

'Oh dear. But go ahead.'

'I talked to George Beaumont, yesterday, the Marine Lieutenant.'

'Ah yes. From English Camp. I don't know the fellow. The one who haunted the Windsor Rooms with McCrory. Nothing surprising there. These military chaps have spent time in foreign parts, and they often don't have wives. At least his case is not so utterly *foul* as the pox-ridden "man of the cloth" your report so unkindly mentions.' Pemberton laughed. 'But I can tell you, having lived in Dublin, that nothing about men of the cloth comes as a surprise to me.'

'This chap Beaumont. I saw him socially yesterday. Last week he lied to me about his association with McCrory – saying he had only met him at Sunday afternoon teas.'

'Ah yes, the Somervilles. The mother was a "looker" in her time, but I'm sure there has been no hint, ever, of impropriety in her life.'

'I'm sure there has not. At any rate Beaumont admitted to me yesterday that he had in fact been pretty thick with McCrory, gone to the Windsor Rooms, and so on.'

'You wouldn't expect him to admit it the *first* time, Chad.'

'Perhaps not. But Sir, the most important thing is this: I asked him where he was on the afternoon McCrory was killed, and he couldn't really say. He made a remark about doing some rough-shooting on San Juan Island. I'm sure that if he had been on duty he would have said so. I know he has rowed or sailed across the Straits in the past, even on his own.'

'All right, Sergeant, sum it up for me,' Pemberton said rather wearily.

'Three things, Sir. First, his name is George, and he's a "King George Devil" if ever there was – something Byronic about him.'

'Really, Chad. *Evidence,* not mere impression.'

'I meant that the vivid impression of him as a "King George Devil" or a 'George Devil' might be communicated, in a few words, by a dying man.'

'All right.'

'Second, there's the association, the sexual imbroglio, if you like, between the two men – so productive, as you say, of violent feelings, and especially in this case where there is evidence he was being treated by the Doctor, either formally as a patient, or informally as a friend, for a nervous problem to do with women.'

'Yes. "Witherspoon"', said Pemberton dryly.

'Third, he does not provide an alibi for the day of the murder. My point is, Sir, that under ordinary circumstances – if he were, say, a merchant in this town – I know that I should have no compunction in *requiring* him to provide an alibi for that afternoon, and in submitting him to formal questioning.'

'You're right, of course. It's so damned inconvenient, his being a military man. If guilty of a crime he must be tried and sentenced by military court. Those are the rules here, even if the crime is against a civilian. A city policeman doesn't even, I think, have the right to question him in a case like this, except in the presence of a superior officer. A *most* embarrassing situation it would be if we – it would have to be you and I together, they would merely shoo a junior like you away from the Camp – if we quizzed a man on the details of his intimate life in front of his commanding officer, and our suspicions were proved to be groundless.'

'We might start with the alibi, not the more sordid details; and he has admitted to keeping company with McCrory.'

'Do you seriously think he was involved in this murder?'

'On the one hand I don't believe he could have been – as an officer and gentleman, of course, and a civilised chap, although somewhat strange. But his involvement with McCrory is unexplained. What I might call the logic of the situation seems to involve him,'

'Of course, my boy. But to get back to *mens rea*, where is it? Why would he murder McCrory at that moment? Where was the provocation? And so on. But I take your point. Although it's most distasteful to me. I shall think about it for a day or two, then if I still feel as I do now I shall compose a most tactful note to Captain Delacombe, Mr Beaumont's commanding officer on San Juan, and suggest that you and I pay a visit to ask a few "official questions, for the record" to Mr Beaumont, early next week. There's no hurry. Myself, I used to rush into things when I was your age – a tendency I've curbed with great difficulty. It will be three weeks, I think, before Wiladzap comes to trial, so there's time. I think you're leading us on a wild goose chase, but I'm ready to back you up on it. One thing, Chad. If an interview with Beaumont should prove to be *very* embarrassing, your head will fall.'

'I understand, Sir.'

I had meant to pursue with Pemberton the subject of getting Wiladzap a better lawyer than Mulligan, but now was not the time. With a rather stiff return to formality, Pemberton showed me to the door.

24

'Dear Mr Darwin:

Just before I left England for British Columbia, where I am now a Sergeant in the Victoria police (my university degree was in jurisprudence), an Oxford acquaintance, Mr Browne, of All Souls, mentioned to me that you were engaged in researches for a study of the 'Expression of Human and Animal Emotions'. He was not sure of the exact title or direction of your study, but said you had been circulating among your acquaintances, and in particular among missionaries and residents of far corners of the world, a list of questions along such lines as: do the natives in your area express anger with a frown and with clenching of the teeth? Do they express astonishment by a raising of the eyebrows? Do they jump up and down for joy? And so forth. Perhaps I misrepresent what Mr Browne told me, but I gather your interest is in the possible universality of emotional expression. This letter is to say that, should you wish to send me a copy of your questions, I should be most happy to see if I could answer them with reference to the Indian peoples of the Northwest Pacific coast, with some of whom I deal in my work – though not all as criminals, I hasten to say.

'My preliminary observations would seem to indicate that there is little if any difference between the emotional expression of these Indians and that of the Englishman, save in degree. The impassivity of the Indian face in moments where an Englishman might show agitation, anger or grief, is of course notorious. I imagine it is at the root of such clichés as that the native 'cannot be trusted', is treacherous, cunning, etc; for the impassive expression cannot be 'read' with regard to intentions. Similarly, I have heard it said by Americans in this Colony that the English, and in particular the official class, 'cannot be trusted'; and of course we have been trained to more self control than many of the more 'easy-going' (as they put it) Americans.

'It seems to me beyond doubt, however, that when the usual control of emotions, for social ends, is overwhelmed by events, a certain universality is revealed. I have seen a chief of the Tsimshian tribe, imprisoned in a cell, maintain his habitual impassivity for long periods, but at times I have caught an expression in his face which I should call 'sadness': a drooping at the corners of the mouth, a sagging of the cheeks, a downcast expression of the eyes. Yet, in moments of hope, his smile has been identical to that of an Englishman, with the eyes and mouth partaking in the familiar expression of narrowing with a light contraction of the surrounding musculature. I have also seen a Tsimshian woman in a state of extreme horror, her eyes and mouth opened to their widest extent, one hand raised to cover her mouth, all the while backing away slowly from the source of her horror.

'Please let me know if I can be of any assistance to you. Should you suggest particular avenues of observation, I should be most happy to pursue them and to attempt precise descriptions. I do not have to say how honoured I should feel at being able to assist in any way the author of *The Origin of Species* which has wrought fundamental changes in my view of life, as I know it has done in that of others.

Yours truly,
Chad Hobbes.'
TELEGRAPH

In this way I tried to hold my mind together. Every daily act – the routine of license fee collecting, responding to complaints, arresting vile drunks – had to be accomplished by an effort of the will. I felt my heart was breaking, and feared my mind might be too. I was eaten up by remorse – that literal (in Latin) 'biting back' on the self. I could not live with what had occurred between me and Lukswaas. Yet I could take no action to resolve it. At first, wild ideas had rushed through my brain: to go to Cormorant Point, do the honourable thing, marry her. How preposterous! Even if such a thing were possible, I would not be accepted by her now. I felt as if I had befouled her – not with my body, which was as 'cleanly wanton' as hers, but with my mind. Her face of horror had shown she knew this. Her own mind was pure. Mine was not. It was contaminated with something. And I had an idea of what it was: my mother again. My dear mother whom I love and to whom I can talk about anything – as I feel I can with Lukswaas. *Do I expect married women to be perfidious?* That is the question that haunts me. Why did I not simply ask Lukswaas what she felt about being with me when she was, as I thought, Wiladzap's wife? Because at some level I took it for granted that she *could* be perfidious. Her reaction showed she could *not!* Horror!

Then the day after I posted my letter to Darwin I received a letter, delivered by messenger to the courthouse, on a rather feminine speckled grey paper in a matching envelope.

'Dear Mr Hobbes:

I am afraid I was rather short with you on our mountain-top walk, because of the natural strain of recent events. Our conversation has been much on my mind, and I should like so much to redeem myself with you, and take up our relationship again at the civilized level of discourse about music and ideas where I feel sure it belongs. But unfortunately my mother no longer sees you as 'persona grata' in this house, because she says you asked her 'offensive' questions (although she will not name them). I have told her that in your line of duty it must be difficult to proceed with tact; indeed it must be necessary at times to proceed *without* tact, and for that you can surely be forgiven. As you discovered on our mountain-top, I myself am not always tactful.

'Since I am old enough, at twenty four, to take care of my own reputation without always paying heed to my family, I have a proposition to make to you: please meet me this Sunday, at 3 o'clock, at the small side road which you may have noticed about half a mile before the main Elk Lake Road. I often take the cart or a horse over the hill to there on my own, and I shall do so this Sunday. I shall bring a small picnic and we can talk at our leisure. Please do not think this forward of me. Else, how can I make amends for my rudeness last Sunday? But do, in tactful consideration of the circumstances, destroy this missive once read.

Yours truly,
Aemilia Somerville.'

This letter, written in a somewhat spiky hand for a lady, but with a dainty flourish in the signature, lifted me from my gloom. There was something appealing in its naiveté ('destroy this missive'), its forthrightness, and of course in its risqué proposition. I destroyed the letter, crumpling it and throwing it into a stove, and waited. Weary of the longing and sadness for Lukswaas, which made me literally drag my feet from task to task, I let myself feel flattered, excited, apprehensive and grateful that Aemilia had taken her reputation into her hands and made this overture. I also could not help wondering it I might question her further about McCrory. This prospect caused a lightening of the heaviness the case had assumed. My best hope would be the interview with Beaumont: Pemberton had written to Beaumont's commanding officer. Otherwise all would be lost. Aemilia's letter helped me survive the rest of the week. It also prevented me from following my daily impulses to get a horse and gallop – in sofar as this was possible on one of Victoria's hired nags – out to the Indian camp and throw myself at Lukswaas's feet. Which, after all, would have been ridiculous. Although I feel my mind has been emancipated by Darwin and by the scientific spirit of the age, my whole life has been framed by the social proprieties. There is no question of me throwing myself at the feet of an Indian girl who in society's eyes is a mere 'squaw'. There is every question, as my friend Frederick has known from the start, of me, of modest means but a gentleman, paying court to Aemilia Somerville, of somewhat more prosperous means and – well, certainly by Colonial standards – a lady. Only in flashes of despair as I toss and turn at night in my narrow bed in my courthouse prison do I allow myself to think that Lukswaas is an Indian princess.

The place I would meet Aemilia was a little over five miles North of town, along Douglas Street, which runs parallel to and West of Cedar Hill road. I hired a horse, since I wanted to be sure of getting back in time to my jail-guarding – or rather card-playing – duties with Seeds. This road was busier than Cedar Hill, with people in buggies, on horseback, or walking, taking the air. Some at least would be heading for Elk Lake where the water had warmed up enough for swimming, and where there were Ladies' and Gentlemen's bathing places. I am not experienced in Victoria weather, but I have been told that a hot spell like this is not uncommon in early summer, although it could turn cool and foggy any time. This day, like so many in the past three weeks, was like the best of English summer days – hot in the sun, cool in the shade.

I reached the place just before three o'clock, dismounted, and walked my horse into the side road so as to profit from the shade and to maintain discretion about this clandestine meeting. The road was really a track through towering firs, like the forest on the other side of Mount Douglas, and as silent. I could hear Aemilia's buggy before I saw it turning in from the main road. Less pretentious than the two horse buggy which the Somervilles used for formal excursions, this was a small one-horse cart. Aemilia's lilac dress was dappled by sunlight and shade. She was wearing a wide-brimmed straw hat with ribbons. Behind her on the cart was a picnic hamper. As she pulled up she seemed to smile and frown at the same time. 'You have a horse,' she called. 'I thought you always walked.'

'Just a hired nag.'

'Can you hitch her to the back or do you want to ride behind?'

'I'll hitch her.' I did so. The nag was tranquil enough. Then I climbed up and sat beside Aemilia on the cart seat. She moved over to give me room, but not too far. I could smell her lemon scent mingled with that of fir-resin from the forest, along with the inevitable smell of the horses. We smiled at each other intimately, as the presence in our minds at least, of the destroyed letter, allowed us to. I felt a stir of excitement and a pleasurable relief. 'Thank you for your invitation.' I said. 'It'll be so nice to let go of my work and be with you on an afternoon like this.'

'Good. I'm glad you don't feel I was indiscreet.' That being settled, Aemilia turned her attention to encouraging her horse along the narrow and bumpy road. 'This leads into what they call Beaver Lake,' she said, 'a Southern arm of Elk Lake, much less popular with the bathing set. But I've found yet another track to an even nicer part of the lake. I often come here when the strain of Mamma and my sisters becomes too much.'

She now directed the horse down a side track so narrow that the cart wheels brushed through bushes, and after only a hundred yards or so, she stopped. 'This is as far as we can go,' she said. 'Since no one comes here, I just leave the cart on the path, and tie the horse to a tree. There's a small stream and I have a bucket, so we should water them.'

Very practical. We both got down and worked together to unhitch the horses, tie them to trees on opposite sides of the path, and water them using a dented bucket hooked on the back of the cart. Aemilia maintained a mood of cheerfulness, but at moments when in the sombre patches of shade, I thought she looked pale and anxious. Then with an eager smile she directed me to take the hamper, while she took a light brown Hudson's Bay blanket and a table cloth.

The hamper was quite heavy, but I could carry it in front of me. I followed Aemilia into the woods. At once the path was only wide enough for walking single file, through the usual rocks and ferns among fir trunks. Then there was light ahead and we came out into a sunny glade of grass and bare smooth rocks which jutted out as a small peninsula into the blue waters of the lake which formed a narrow arm with the same dense forest on the other side. At the end of the little peninsula was a clump of bushes, so that there were two short stretches, one on either side, where the grass ran down to a fringe of bull rushes and lily pads at the edge of the lake.

Aemilia set down the blanket in the shade, still within the embrace of the forest, and showed me where to put the hamper, between the blanket and a rock. This done, we gazed around.

'It's Paradise,' I said.

'I think a settler must have cleared this little patch to build a house, but I dare say something went wrong and he gave up.' In spite of the touch of cynicism in this remark, Aemilia looked happy now, radiant in the sun in her lilac dress and broad straw hat with its lilac and white ribbons. She walked forward toward the lake and I followed her. Pairs of sapphire coloured dragon-flies were cavorting in the air over the water, some of them joining in flight, tail to tail, into a tumbling S-shape, then coming apart again. This might have embarrassed Aemilia but apparently did not. 'They're early this year,' she remarked lightly. 'Damsel flies. Do you have them in England?'

'Not like these. I believe all ours are brown and drab. I've never seen anything like these except as jewelled brooches or pins. We do have swallows though.' A couple of swallows were swooping here and there over the lake. I could not see if they were catching the damsel flies or something smaller. There were no midges as there would be in England.

As if attuned to my thoughts, Aemilia remarked that there were not enough insects to support a very large population of swallows. The birds which flourished best at the edges of forests were the crows. Sure enough, some crows, which I would have called ravens, were cawing hoarsely from the fir tops. We continued this naturalistic discussion, then when it became too hot standing in the sun we withdrew into the shade. Aemilia spread out the blanket and we sat down. I half sprawled on one elbow, which was the only comfortable posture, Aemilia demurely sitting, I supposed cross-legged, within the hoops of her dress, like a huge inverted flower.

It was indeed a rather intimate tête à tête, of a sort quite out of bounds for the unmarried or unrelated. It was totally compromising. As if both were thinking of this, the naturalistic conversation flagged, and we looked at each other.

'I'm glad you forgive me for last Sunday,' Aemilia said.

'Of course. There's nothing whatsoever to forgive. I appreciate your frankness in expressing your thoughts. Sometimes the truth is painful.' I stopped.

'But we don't need to discuss it now, do we? I don't want to talk about the Indians, Dr McCrory, or even your work. Do you mind?'

'Of course not.' For a moment I did mind: I would have to abandon all ideas of questioning Aemilia. But then, why bother? It was agreeable and exciting, to be here with her. I would have willingly discussed the moon …

'Let's talk about music. Tell me where you learned to sing.'

So we talked about Handel, church music, the songs I had learned from my mother, the execrable quality of the music at Oxford, only slightly improved by the wave of ardent liturgical revivalism. We even discussed the liturgy, then, rather abstractedly, the difference between social and religious morality. Aemilia had obviously done a lot of thinking about this. I was inhibited by her prohibition of discussing police work, and she too, perhaps out of sense of privacy, kept the discussion general.

'No matter how much we talk,' I said eventually, 'you're something of a mystery to me.'

'So I should be.' She smiled and fluttered her eyelids in a coquettish way which was uncharacteristic of her. 'A woman should always be a mystery to a man. He may try very hard, Mr Hobbes, but a man can never really know a woman – no, not even when he has "known" her in the biblical sense.' She bit her lip, obviously aware that this was too shocking a remark for a young lady to make. 'Let's begin our picnic.' She said. 'It's a small one, but quite special. Look.'

Without rising, she moved under the tent of her dress over to the hamper. She reached beside it for the folded tablecloth and passed it to me. As I spread it, she brought out plates and glasses, then a small packet wrapped in cloth which she opened to reveal neatly cut sandwiches. 'Inside these', she said, 'is the flesh of a trout I caught myself in the brook this morning. And here is a piece of cake.' She unwrapped another package. She reached into the hamper again and brought out a stone flagon. 'And this, still cool as it should be, although perhaps we could have put it in the lake for a while, is last year's raspberry and apple wine.'

Ah, that was the weight in the hamper.'

'Yes, although it's light to the taste.'

Aemilia served the sandwiches and poured the wine, which was straw-coloured. We raised our glasses in a silent toast, and drank. The wine was at least as dry and strong as any French white I had ever tasted, and just as good. The sandwiches were exquisite.

We ate delicately, as manners required, but in the heat it was easy to drink too much of the wine. Although I protested after the second glass, Aemilia insisted on filling a third, and after the third I did not care. She drank a glass for every one of mine. We ate a slice each of the cake, and washed it down with more wine. I was invaded by well being. I sprawled sensually on the blanket near this vision of womanly beauty in her dress like an inverted flower, talking on and off about old times in England, picnics in Oxford on the banks of the Isis – 'though nothing like as lovely as this.'

'No? I should like to go to Oxford and have you take me out on the river in a punt. I've read about that in a book for boys – *Tom Brown at Oxford*. It must be delicious.'

'It is. But do you know, I was lonely at Oxford. I was always longing for… I don't know what.'

'What young men usually long for, I suppose. It must be such a strain, all that study in those stone cloisters or whatever they are.' Aemilia was losing some of her coherence, but I did not mind, since I was losing some of mine.

We drank more of the wine. 'We must finish this,' Aemilia remarked. 'It doesn't keep, once it has been opened.' More obviously emotional, now she sounded sad. 'My goodness it's hot,' she added. 'We should get up and walk. I should like to put my feet in the water.'

We finished our glasses. I held out my hand and Aemilia took it to rise to her feet. She did not let go as we walked into the dazzling light and down to the water's edge. I was not really drunk, but the wine had gone enough to my head to make me giddy and carefree. I squeezed Aemilia's hand, and she squeezed back. I felt very happy, just like that, side by side, looking out at the sun playing on the water and the damsel flies dipping and swooping. I was vaguely aware that afternoon was getting on. 'I'll be sorry to leave this.' I said, 'which I'm afraid I'll have to shortly.'

'You can stay a while. Wait.' Aemilia disengaged her hand and stooped to unlace her shoes. She set them on one side – small, of white leather – then to my surprise pulled off her stockings which were short, and of white silk, setting them carefully on the shoes. Her bare feet disappeared back under the dress, but now she held this up and advanced into the water with a slight splash, and stood there. Then, holding the dress up with one hand, she reached with the other and undid the ribbon of her bonnet, which she passed back to me. Her chestnut brown hair was piled in a knot on the top of her head, her neck was slim and white. I stood holding the bonnet, excited. She spoke to me over her shoulder, not turning her head enough to meet my eye.

'Do you think we've drunk enough wine to forget conventions?'

'Not all of them, I'm sure.' My heart was pounding.

'Do you know what I should do if I were here alone? I should take my dress off – it's so infernally hot in these things, you cannot imagine it – and go for a swim in my shift. Perhaps if you could turn your back, I might do it now. Or, I tell you what – I dare you in fact, Mr Chad Hobbes – you go to the other side of that clump of bushes and take *your* overclothes off. You can swim from that side, and I can swim from this. A gentleman's and a lady's beach. Who can quarrel with that?'

'I certainly shan't,' I said, shocked at her invitation but ready to cast caution to the winds. I turned and placed Aemilia's bonnet on her shoes. Then I walked to the other side of the little peninsula, where I was hidden from her, and in the mindless state induced by the wine, I took off my coat, tie, boots, socks, then trousers. Should I leave on my shirt? No. I took it off, and dropped it on the ground, then set on it the pathetic intertwined burden of Lukswaas's stone and my own signet ring still on its thong. I was now only wearing my cotton summer drawers, which reached to just above the knee. I walked into the water, and felt my way through the lily pads. The lake was cold and very clear. To block my apprehension I breathed outward with a whoosh and threw myself forward with a tremendous splash, then came to the surface and swam out from the shore.

Aemilia had entered the water more quietly from her side. She came swimming slowly towards me, doing a breast-stroke, her head clear of the water, her shoulders with white straps on them, very pink. We smiled at each other rather guiltily. In the freshness of the water the haze of the wine was gone, and we looked clearly into each other's eyes for a moment of truth, fully aware of what we were doing and, at least on my part, happy to be doing it. Yes, I had learned something from Lukswaas, I thought complacently as Aemilia and I swam round each other in slow circles. I would never be so shy with a woman again. But in my heart I felt a pang: I would have given anything to have been swimming happily in this pristine lake with Lukswaas. Then I came back to the pleasure of being with Aemilia. She too had cast caution to the winds, and I was grateful to her. 'This is lovely!' I called, and rolled over on my back to kick along. I had only swum in fresh water in the Isis, never in a lake. It was glorious.

After a while Aemilia called, 'I'm going in now.'

'All right.' Dutifully, I swam over to my side of the little peninsula. I swam a few more circles, breathing easily, then came in to the shore and stepped up onto the grass. My feet were muddy, and water poured off me. I shook myself, and felt exhilarated. I was standing in the shade and began to feel cold. No towel, of course. I thought of drying myself with my shirt, but decided against it. Instead I stepped into the sun, toward the centre of the peninsula. Aemilia had done the same on her side, thirty feet or so away. She looked like a slim white ghost in her shift, which reached from her shoulders to just below her knees but clung wetly to her body. I moved at once back toward the shade but she called out 'Wait! It's all right. You'll catch cold back there. The sun will dry you in no time.'

I moved back into the sun which was now lower in the sky and shining directly on us from across the lake, its warm rays bathing my skin. Neither of us spoke. After a while, dry on my front, I turned to put my back to the sun, and noticed she had done the same. Still we did not speak, although as my body became warm and dry again I could feel a return of some of the headiness from the raspberry wine, and was becoming aware of an increasing tension between me and Aemilia across the yards of clearing. It was as if the afternoon had permitted my body to uncoil from my state of contraction I had put it into since the débâcle with Lukswaas, a state almost of self-punishment which might have endured for ever if Aemilia had not drawn me out of it. Now, coming back to my full self, I came back to an overwhelming sense of desire. This had, of course, been awakened by Lukswaas. I had struggled for years like any other celibate young man to suppress needs which must be kept for marriage or channelled into the adoration of ethereal young women in their crinolines – to convert, through constant effort, the animal into the spiritual, as I must do with Aemilia, to rise above what Lukswaas had awakened. But now, for reasons I could not understand and in my sensual state could not guess at, even Aemilia had made it clear that she was willing at least to play at the edge of the abyss of sensuality. She did not seem to want to be spiritualized. I did not really believe she wanted to embrace me at the other, animal level either. But there we were, not far away from each other, in a state of half undress, slowly turning and drying in the sun. As I filled again with heat it seemed to pour downward in my body and stirred me. Without looking at Aemilia I turned slightly so that my back was more toward her. Then I heard her:

'Chad!'

'I turned to face her. She was facing me. She raised her arms slowly, reaching for me. I walked towards her across the tufted grass and into her arms, holding her to me. She was trembling slightly, and warm through her shift now dry. We kissed, rather clumsily and wildly, our lips slipping across each other. I felt her pulling me back toward the picnic place and the forest. Still embracing, as if afraid that letting go would cause us to reflect on what we were doing and stop, we stumbled across the grass to the blanket and almost fell onto it, scrambling to push aside glasses and plates with a clatter onto the ground.

We lay in a tight embrace on the blanket, rolling, panting, kissing, clutching each other. Gradually she allowed me to become free with her body, pushing against me as I touched her, and she became free with mine, running her fingers down my back and in and around my thighs. Although we never pulled back to look at each other or caught each other's eye, for a long while we caressed each other, to an almost unbearable extent. I could not help thinking of Lukswaas, her skin which moved on her body like that of a cat. Aemilia was different, her skin more taut, but the lines of her body exquisite. Our clothes were peeled off and shoved aside but still we caressed each other. Although Aemilia had seemed eager for this embrace she did not now seem eager to consummate it. I faltered, aware suddenly of the seriousness of the situation – one move and we would be into the abyss, if that was what it was. But Aemilia whispered into my ear, her breath roaring and hot: 'I'm not so innocent as I seem, and nor are you. Do it.' She moved slightly, and I did. We were together, again for a long time. I was surprised that although bursting with need, something deep inside me was slow to give way. It was not the same as … My movements became almost mechanical. 'Be careful, darling,' she said, 'Don't make me pregnant.' I pulled back and out of her, and tried to jam myself forward between her and the blanket and finish it by friction. But I couldn't. I began to think of Lukswaas – but not in *that* way. Instead I felt like crying. Aemilia was clutching me tightly as if locked or frozen.

We lay still. I opened my eyes so that I could see her face. Out of one closed eyelid, next to me, a tear was trickling. I almost said 'What's wrong?' Instead I closed my eyes and lay in her arms, my heart sinking, trying to answer the question for myself. I realized, numbly, the obvious fact that she was no virgin. (Not like Lukswaas!) And that she had known all along what this afternoon might lead to. And that her heart was not in it. No: I knew, from Lukswaas, what a woman was like when her heart was in it. My heart had not been in this either. But of course I had wanted it. She must have wanted it too: she had drunk a glass of wine for each one she had poured me. Why should she give herself away like this? It was, in conventional terms, a horrendous, a fantastic step for a girl of good family to take. In theory it destroyed all chances of a marriage. She had even said to me – out of honesty, cynicism, or despair? – 'I'm not so innocent as I seem, and nor are you.' Yet neither of us had been able to go all the way through with this. There had been no 'Boo woo'…

I moved back from her. Now she was looking at me seriously, but she broke into a not quite real smile. 'Chad,' she said, 'keep holding me.' She pulled me back towards her. It was warm in the declining rays of the sun, and we could have stayed there a long while. She snuggled closely against me. 'Don't worry', she said, 'I'm afraid I disrupted you. It will be all right.'

'Of course it won't', I said. 'Now is not the time for us. And I must go. I'm on duty. I shall be late as it is.' I moved away from her but she pulled me close again and stroked my naked back.

'It doesn't matter. Let's wait until the sun is down. I don't need to be home yet. As you see, I'm a free agent. But don't let's even talk. It's so nice, just like this.' She began caressing me, and indeed it was lovely, in the warm sun, in this lovely woman's arms, and I could have started all over again except that it had gone wrong for a reason and in part of me – which seemed to be my mind, rather than my heart – a cold logical train of thought was asserting itself. It said to me that Aemilia had prostituted herself to me. She had not done it for money, and she had prostituted something more than the Windsor Rooms girls: her reputation. For what? For time. For nothing but time.

I pulled out of her arms and scrambled to my feet. 'I'm sorry, I must go,' I said. And although not with the horror in which Lukswaas had backed away from me, 'the source of horror,' I turned away from Aemilia, the source of temptation – and comfort, and an honest warmth which I realized was not love but friendship – and went across the clearing to put on my clothes.

To my amazement she leapt up and followed me, tugging at my arm. 'Chad! Chad! You mustn't go. My God! You can't just have a woman and then go away and leave her!'

'I pushed her hand away and began pulling on my trousers. I reached for the stone and ring and slipped them over my head.

'Did she give you that, your little Indian squaw? Aemilia spat.

'How do you know about that?'

'Just a guess. I know Indian girls wear these. The sluts!' She clutched at me again. 'Chad!' She began to cry, genuinely, her face a picture of despair.

'Aemilia, I know what you've been doing. You've been keeping me here. I don't know why. I'm on duty. I hope your keeping me here has nothing to do with that.' In fact, my guiding thought, though confused, was that she must be keeping me from my job in order to have me lose it, or to ruin my reputation in some way.

I can't believe this!' She said passionately, standing there naked but apparently careless of it. 'I give myself to you. I give my body. You *have* me. And you abandon me! You're an absolute bounder! If you go now I'll tell the world you have assaulted me and raped me! Her eyes were blazing.

But this excess of hers enabled me to stand my ground. 'You can tell the world what you want. I shall remain silent. And I didn't truly have you. Nor did you truly have me. Let's not pretend. Aemilia I'm most grateful to you, but …'

'Grateful! She shrieked. She reached out to restrain me as I made a lunge away.

'I *must* go. My duty is my honour. Please respect it, as I respect yours.'

'Oh God! What rubbish you Englishmen speak. You will stay here with me. You cannot abandon a defenseless woman in the forest like this.'

'Get dressed, and I'll see you out to the road. Then I must go. Believe me. I know you're upset, but I have to. I can come and see you tomorrow if you wish, and we can mend our fences. Aemila, my dear …' I felt real tenderness, 'please let us be friends.'

'In order to enjoy me properly next time! No. If you wish to avail yourself of my embraces, you shall stay with me now.'

'I'll have to go.' Almost blindly, I pushed her aside and walked across to the hamper. In the dying light I began stacking the picnic things in it – the plates, glasses, a piece of cake, the empty wine flagon.

Down by the water Aemilia stood stepping into her drawers, then her hooped petticoat, then pulling her dress on over her head. She stooped to put on her shoes. Then she picked up her stays, which she had not bothered to put on, folding them into a stiff bundle. She came over to me and turned her back. 'Button me up.'

I buttoned the fabric, now grey in the dull light, up her back from waist to neck over her white shift. I could have cried with anguish.

'Chad,' she said softly, and turned toward me, embracing me. 'We *can* be friends. One more time…' She snuggled in closely.

I pulled free of her with a jerk, almost ran to the hamper and picked it up. 'Come!' I said, setting off into the darkened forest. I heard her footsteps behind me as I hurried along the path. I reached the cart and went round to the back, pushing the hamper behind the seat. Aemilia was beside me, throwing on the folded cloth, the bundle of her stays, and the blanket.

'Will you please escort me home?' she said quietly. 'It's getting dark.'

'Aemilia!' I yelled, losing my temper. 'I *must* go. I'm already almost two hours late. I'll escort you to the road only.' But I hesitated. In truth it would not be chivalrous to let her go home in the dark – not that it was actually dark, but it soon would be. My resolve weakened. Suddenly I hardly knew why I *was* leaving her. To hell with Seeds, to hell with the jail.

'All right,' I said. 'I'll turn the cart for you, and I'll escort you home over the hill.' It would only be an extra mile. 'But you must promise to go as fast as you can. In fact I shall ride in front.'

'She said nothing. She helped me, rather listlessly, hitch her horse to the cart and turn it, not an easy thing to do in the growing dark. Then as I helped her politely up into the seat, she turned and embraced me gently. 'Forgive me, Chad. Oh, please forgive me.'

'Nothing to forgive. I have nothing but the most tender feelings for you Aemilia. Let me come and see you soon and I hope we can be friends again.'

'All right.' She climbed into the seat.

I unhitched my horse, mounted and set off down the path and out of the forest. We emerged onto the main road at a point where it crossed a rise, and as we turned South we could see down to Victoria and the Straits. The jagged line of Hurricane Ridge, in Washington Territory, was incredibly clear, like a long serrated blue blade against the pink light reflected from the sunset on the West, which flared above the lower mountains of our own Vancouver Island, tinted a green-blue such as would never be seen in England. I trotted my horse along in front of the cart, down the road a little way, then up the cross road which led over a low hill between fields and woods to the Orchard Farm valley. I did not look back. It was nothing like completely dark when we reached the road a hundred yards from Orchard Farm. Some light might even hold until I reached town. I turned as the cart came up behind me and called 'Goodnight!'

'Goodnight,' I heard distantly.

I kicked my horse in the sides and set off down the road to the nearest thing to a gallop it could manage, a sort of sporadic canter, so bumpy that I had to hold on frantically to avoid being thrown, wild thoughts racing through my head. My corrupt, savage mistress had turned out to be utterly clean and pure; my civilized ideal had turned out to be mysteriously corrupt. Aemilia had been detaining me, keeping me away from something I would find at the jail.

25

I arrived in Victoria after dark and returned my horse to the stable, putting down an extra dollar since she had been ridden hard and would need walking. I hurried down the street to the courthouse, but approached it cautiously along the side of the square. Two things Aemilia had said had stuck in my mind: 'I'm not so innocent as I seem, and nor are you.' And her remark about my getting the stone ornament from a squaw. So far as I knew the stone was unique, at least to the Tsimshian. Aemilia must know the Tsalak in some way, and I wondered if she was conspiring with them in an attempt to get Wiladzap out of jail when only the feckless Seeds would be on guard. It seemed an insane suspicion, but I was assuming the worst.

As I approached the courthouse I could see no one about. Sunday nights were quiet in Victoria, and there was no street lighting, since there was no gas. The courthouse, like other large buildings, had its own lamp above the door. On the far side of the square it was totally dark. Anyone could be there. The door would be locked. Normally I would have sauntered up to it and stood digging in my pocket for the key. Now I took the key firmly in one hand still in my pocket, walked very briskly up to the door, unlocked it with a single movement, tugged it open, leapt in and slammed it behind me. As I did so there was a scurry and a movement in the shadows outside, lost immediately to me as I rammed the inside bolt into its socket. My ears were assaulted by the sound of singing from the jail wing. I walked cautiously across the dimly lit vestibule, bringing out my second key in case the jail gate was locked. I peeped round the corner.

From my angle of vision I could see down the cell corridor through the barred gate, which was hanging slightly open, and at the same time across the corridor into Seeds's quarters, a comfortable room where Seeds and I could play cards near the open door and at the same time keep an eye on the cell corridor. Now, in the larger part of the room, not visible from the cells, there was a scene like a theatrical tableau or a coarse painting by some ribald artist, such as Rowlandson, of the previous century. Seeds was sitting in his usual armchair beside his table on which was a whisky bottle and some empty glasses. On his knee was an Indian woman, naked except for her woven bark apron, under which Seeds was feeling with one hand while he nuzzled his big head into her breasts. She was playing with his member which she had brought out of his trousers.

There was a sudden roar of noise interrupting the singing from the cells – an outburst of whistles and cheers.

I dashed forward past Seeds's door, pushed the gate open, and rushed down the corridor not sparing a glance for the cells although I was inundated by a racket of shouts and a smell of liquor. I reached Wiladzap's cell. Lukswaas, crouching in front of the lock, was working through Seeds's key ring. I struck it from her hand and it hit the floor with a clash. She jumped back in fright. I faced Wiladzap who was standing up against the cell door, holding two of the bars with his hands. Wiladzap's teeth were bared in rage like those of an animal. I stood panting, looking into Wiladzap's eyes which were blazing with the same rage and determination as his whole face, but suddenly they shifted to one side in a brief glance past me.

I felt a sudden strange tingling sensation of alarm, and instantly froze. Wiladzap glanced to the side again and shouted a word I did not understand.

I turned slowly, painfully, all my courage gone. Lukswaas was standing just behind me. In her right hand was a very long knife which she had drawn back, ready to plunge it forward into my back, at about the level of my kidneys.

The uproar from the cells subsided. There was silence. The prisoners could see what was going on. But I could only look at Lukswaas. My life, or my death, was in her hand. In my mind's eye I flung myself forward, grabbed her arm as the knife came to me, and pulled her down … But I did not move and nor did she. We looked at each other. Her eyes were dark with an intense expression of pain and grief.

'Lukswaas.' I could say no more, but I could feel my own anguish pass from my eyes to hers.

She turned her hand so the knife handle was facing me, and held it out to me. I took it carefully, then pulled out my large linen handkerchief, wrapped it round the blade, and put it in my pocket.

There was a grunt from Wiladzap just behind me, and an exhalation of breath, a sort of communal sigh, from the prisoners. Then I heard Wiladzap say: 'She no kill you.'

The cells broke into uproar again, with drunken cheers, and the smash of a breaking bottle. At the same time, Seeds came stumbling down the corridor with a revolver in his hand, his shirt open and his trousers almost falling down. Behind him was the half naked figure of the other Indian woman – Wan. There was a roar and a chorus of whistles and moans from the cells.

'Shut up!' I yelled sharply. 'Seeds, put that damned thing away!'

The hubbub subsided, and Seeds stopped in his tracks. 'If you fellows don't shut up I'll put you on a chain gang for a month solid!' I yelled. 'Finish your booze if you want, but calm down! Seeds, for God's sake go back to your office and get dressed. Nobody's got loose. I'll take care of this.'

Seeds turned and reeled back along the corridor. Wan flattened herself against the wall as he went past. There was another mass sigh from the cells, and someone said wistfully, '*There's* a girl.'

'All right, boys,' I said, finding it hard to blame them for their exuberance. 'I know she's pretty, but she'll have to go. 'Wan!' I told her in Chinook to go where the men could not see her, and wait. She looked at me questioningly. I heard Lukswaas's voice just behind me talking quietly in Tsimshian. Wan nodded and walked away.

I turned my back to Lukswaas on the one hand, Wiladzap on the other. I glanced at Lukswaas then fixed my eyes on Wiladzap and said: 'You speak English.'

Wiladzap looked at me but said nothing. His face had returned to its usual impassivity. I thought of a way to break the silence, although it was based on the logic of association rather than any clear reasoning. I said very distinctly: 'Aemilia.'

Wiladzap gave a start. 'Aemilia,' he said, almost as distinctly as I had.

'You know Aemilia.'

'I speak little English,' Wiladzap said slowly, but pronouncing the words clearly. He looked past me at Lukswaas, then back to me. 'Why she no kill you?' Then he began speaking to Lukswaas in his own language, urgently, but I raised my hand to cut this off:

'Wake. Spose mesika wawa Lukswaas mesika wawa Chinook'. ('No. If you speak Lukswaas, you speak Chinook').

I stepped closer to the bars so that I was only a few inches from Wiladzap and no one could hear us except of course Lukswaas.

'You want me dead?' I said to Wiladzap.

'You my friend. I love – I like you. But you not make me out this place. I die. You not find man who kill McCrory.'

I could hardly quarrel with this logic, although it did not please me. 'You not help me. You speak English. Why you not tell me you speak English?' I found I was speaking English to Wiladzap as if it were Chinook.

Wiladzap looked at me for a while silently, then said: 'I not want you know Aemilia know me.'

'Why not?'

'I not say. You talk Aemilia.'

'When did you last see Aemilia?'

'You talk Aemilia.'

'All right. I'll talk to Aemilia. But now you tell me one thing. McCrory. Dying. What did McCrory say to you when he was dying?'

Wiladzap frowned. 'King George Diaub. King George Diaub.' He muttered. Then his face lit up slowly, his lips moved silently as if he was trying to remember or rehearse something, and he said: 'That Devil George! That Devil George!'

He seemed quite excited, and had raised his voice.

'Good,' I said. 'You remember my Tyee? Pemberton?

'Yes.'

'Pemberton come tomorrow morning. You tell Pemberton: 'That Devil George'. All right?'

'All right.'

'You know George?'

'George? King George? You are King George.'

'Yes. But a man named George. You know him?'

'No.' Wiladzap shook his head, as if even George as a personal name was unfamiliar to him.

'All right.'

Lukswaas was still standing quietly behind me. I turned and looked at her more calmly. She was wearing one of the atrocious grey HBC blankets. I asked her to tell Wan to ask the Indians waiting outside the jail to go home peacefully. How many men? I asked.

'Waaks. Tsamti.' Then she said at some length that the other Tsalak had left their camp and were waiting at another bay, nearer Victoria.

Then Waaks and Tsamti and Wan must tell them to go back to Cormorant Point, the old camp, and wait, I said. After two or three days Wiladzap would come. I turned to Wiladzap and said in Chinook that I thought I knew who the killer of McCrory was. His name was George. I would go and find this George but it would take a day or two. I would go with Pemberton. But first it was important that Wiladzap tell Pemberton McCrory's words. Wiladzap nodded. 'All right,' he said in his slow but uncannily precise English. 'Lukswaas,' he added. 'Where she go?'

'She go with me.' Seeing suspicion instantly cloud Wiladap's face, I continued, hoping I could in fact do what I was saying: 'I'll take her to Pemberton's house. Pemberton's wife good woman. Take care of Lukswaas.' I repeated this in Chinook for Lukswaas.

'Good,' said Wiladzap. Then, 'Why she not kill you?'

'You ask her,' I said, playing Wiladzap's game of earlier. 'In Chinook please.'

'Kahta mesika halo mamook wind Hops?', Wiladzap asked abruptly. (Why you not make dead Hops?')

'Nika tikegh hyas kloshe.' Literally, 'I love great good.'

I had not dared expect her to say this, but I should have known better: she is as naive as I am.

Wiladzap was looking puzzled. He chewed his lips for a moment. Then he nodded and said, 'All right. You take her Pembaton house.'

I closed the door again and Lukswaas and I were alone in the huge vestibule lit by its single dim lamp. I reached for her and held her close to me for a while, feeling an intense relief at having found her again, and a desire to wipe out my experience with Aemilia by making love with Lukswaas at once. But I felt I could not do this: my mind was not yet clear, and I doubted hers was either. So I let go of her. I stood for a moment thinking of my impulsive and gentlemanly promise to take Lukswaas to Pemberton's. Then I took her by the hand and led her to Seeds's room. I could feel her shrinking slightly as we entered, and felt a pang of pain at what she must have planned with Wan. Seeds sat up and looked at us blankly.

'Go and splash some cold water over your face.' I said, giving orders again, 'and then go and knock up Harding: you know his lodgings on Herald Street. Bring him back here and he can take over duty with you. I have to go out for a while with this young lady. I'll see the Commissioner, and I'll say something of this matter to him, but I'll try and make sure it doesn't reach the Superintendent. I imagine our friends in the cells will sleep off their party and be no worse for wear. But you'd better treat Wiladzap well: I'll wager my last sovereign that he'll be due for release shortly.'

'All right.' Seeds got up wearily. 'I don't know why I done it. Well, yes I do. You may say this one's a lady, but that other one! And I ain't had female company since Florence ran off with that Yankee bastard.'

It suddenly struck me that it might be easier for Mrs Pemberton to agree to look after Lukswaas if she was dressed like a white woman rather than in a filthy HBC blanket. 'Sam! Your Florence: did she leave any clothes behind?'

'Course she did. She took off in such a hurry.'

Was she a big woman?'

She was tallish, but skinny. You'd never think sh …'

'Where are the clothes?'

'In the store room. Blue cabin trunk in the corner.'

'Can I have them? I'll pay for them.'

'You crazy? Awright, awright. I'll get Harding.'

Seeds shuffled out to put on his coat, and I made sure the cage door to the cells was locked. I asked Seeds for the store-room key. Then I led Lukswaas, who had been waiting patiently, across the vestibule and down a kitchen passage. I unhooked the lamp from the wall beside the store-room, struck a match and lit it, then opened the door. The room was large, cold, dirty, and cluttered. I set the lamp on a box and opened the trunk. It was packed with neatly folded woman's clothing. We stood looking at it.

I began to explain to Lukswaas that it would be best if she wore white woman's clothes, so that I could take her to Pemberton's. But she interrupted me, saying that she had already understood. Then she said stubbornly that she would not go to Pemberton's house that night. She would stay with me.

'But… I reminded her of what I had said to Wiladzap.

She interrupted again. She said she was not a belonging of Wiladzap's. She would go to Pemberton's in the morning and stay there until I found the murderer and Wiladzap was released from jail. She agreed it was a good idea since she would not be happy going back to the Tsalak camp. There would be much anger among the Tsalak. But now she wanted to be with me. It was too long since we had talked and held each other.

I was excited by her fierce affection, as well as struck by her stubbornness. I told her I had only a small room and a small bed. I was not a rich man with a big house.

Lukswaas tapped her forehead and then her heart, and said I was rich inside myself. Then she turned back to looking at the clothes, picking up carefully a black shawl which lay on top. I dusted the lid of the box, so that we could lay clothes on it. Then together we began to take out the clothes and sort them into piles. The dresses were the least problem. The prettiest, yet most discreet (some of the others were too frilly and vulgar) was one of yellow cotton – the sort of dress a young girl might wear about the house. I held it against Lukswaas and it looked the right size. There was a hooped petticoat, not so wide as a full scale crinoline, collapsed down like a round concertina. There were several shifts, like Aemilia's, any of which would be suitable. Bloomers, which were out of fashion and not necessary. Cotton drawers – like mine, only finer and with a slit between the legs. Knee stockings with garters. Some miscellaneous ribbons which Lukswaas took all of. The main problem would be the stays. No young lady could *not* wear these 'iron maidens.' But perhaps Mrs Seeds had been some what loose in dress, as in behaviour. Her stays were of the minimal kind – from bosom to waist rather than to upper thigh. They were still formidable. I held one of them up with distaste and made a gesture of despair. Lukswaas merely shrugged and added it to the pile. I rummaged in the bottom of the trunk and found a pair of black, rather severe shoes. Lukswaas kicked off one moccasin and tried a shoe against her foot. It would be a little wide but its length was right. We gathered up the clothes Lukswaas would need, I blew out the lamp, and we left the lumber room. The jail was quiet. Before going to bed, I would usually visit the filthy water closet off the vestibule. I asked Lukswaas if she needed to make water. She nodded. With some words of apology I showed her to the closet. Her nose wrinkled in disgust. I realized it would be better to use the chamber pot in my room, and tried to explain to her. At any rate she followed me, up the half flight of stairs to my door. I took my own lamp, hanging outside, and lit it. Then I opened my door with my key, and showed her in.

Although small the room at least had a window onto Bastion Street, which I opened, letting in the cool air. I set the lamp on my table where Lukswaas spread the clothes carefully on a chair. I showed her the chamber pot, then left the room again for a minute. When I came back she had put it on one side. I picked it up and brought it downstairs and emptied it, and my own bladder, in the water closet.

When I came back to the room Lukswaas was sitting at the table, her chin on one hand like a student, looking carefully at one of my books she had taken from the wall shelf. It was *The Voyage of the Beagle*. I supposed she had been attracted to it because it was the most worn of my books, and was especially well bound – in red leather with gold engraving. She stroked the spine and smiled. She said she would like to learn to read. I said I would teach her. Then for some reason our eyes instinctively turned to my looking glass, on the wall to one side. There we were, a strange sight: Lukswaas sitting seriously at the table with the open book in her hands, me leaning around her. There was on the one hand a striking contrast between us: her face coppery, mine pink and of course bearded; her eyes almond shaped and black, mine round and green-grey; me wearing a dove grey frock coat and navy blue cravat, she wearing a grimy Hudson's Bay blanket; me a white, she an Indian. Yet on the other hand there was a similarity: both were young, tall and upright, naively serious, with long faces and intense eyes. We looked well together.

Without speaking or even smiling, we studied ourselves for a while. Then I took Lukswaas's hand, and she turned to face me. With a sense of doing the right thing, but a certain dread of the consequences, I asked her if she would be my woman for always. She nodded her head and said yes. I fumbled to undo my collar stud and the buttons of my shirt, and drew out the things with her stone and my signet ring. I unthreaded the ring and gave her a brief kiss on the lips. We drew apart. It was odd how we understood each other. I had an innate aversion to fussing, and Lukswaas apparently the same. We needed to say no more. But she took the stone from where I had set it on the table. Then she spat on it and rubbed it briskly with a corner of her blanket. She held it up at an angle, to catch the light from the lamp, and beckoned to me to look. I leaned forward and saw a dim but precisely detailed image of our two faces, close together and in miniature, on the shiny black surface. She stood up and put it over my head.

Then she stood back and began to undo the braids of her hair, shaking it loose and letting it fall thick and lustrous over her shoulders. We embraced, held each other, wriggled out of our clothes, and fell together onto my narrow camp bed. The afternoon with Aemilia came back to me for a moment with a pang of sadness, then a brief panic: would I be able to do it again, with Lukswaas? But nothing could stop me wanting her. She and I, although of different races, different continents, and unable to understand each other's different languages, came together in our usual effortless way.

I pulled the sheet over us and we lay close. The lamplight was steady and golden on the wall. It was true, what the Oneida people said, that giving in completely in love led to a close bond. I was happy to let go of the outside world and retreat to this room where in a magic circle of giving and receiving Lukswaas and I lay as one. Depleted energies? Spending? This was the peace the religious sought.

Yet thinking of our separation from the outside world brought it to mind. The day had been too eventful for me to be able to sleep. I even had questions for Lukswaas although, as often happened, she anticipated them. She asked what I had done with Aemilia.

I explained that we had had a picnic, describing what this was. I said it had been very nice but I had a feeling Aemilia had wanted to keep me there. However, I had had to come back to the courthouse. I knew I could not lie to Lukswaas, and grew tense in the expectation of more intimate questions. But she did not ask them.

I asked if Lukswaas knew Aemilia, although I knew the answer.

Yes. She did.

They had planned together to free Wiladzap from the jail?

Lukswaas explained that she had wanted to free Wiladzap but could not think how. Then Aemilia had come and together they had decided: Aemilia should keep me away, so that I would not be at the jail. Lukswaas would free Wiladzap.

Lukswaas clutched me urgently in the narrow bed and asked me if I now knew who had murdered McCrory.

I said I thought so, that the murderer had almost certainly been a King George soldier called George, who was now on another island where Pemberton and I would have to go and find him. But, I asked Lukswaas, how did she know Aemilia?

Lukswaas's answer was the same as Wiladzap's: I must talk to Aemilia.

I acquiesced in this, saying I would go and see Aemilia in the morning.

Then I changed my theme to one which had often tormented me. Why did Smgyiik say Wiladzap had killed McCrory? Why did he say Wiladzap had been angry at Lukswaas going into the woods with McCrory?

Lukswaas said nothing for a few moments. Then she said it was because Smgyiik had wanted to marry her. But she had never wanted to marry him. Nor had Wiladzap liked him. Smgyiik was an unlucky man, she said. He had probably gone to his cousins – other Tsimshians. He could never return to Tsalak.

Why had he not taken the money?

He was not so small in heart that he would take money for his words. He had spoken them out of anger.

Anger that Lukswaas had gone into the forest with McCrory?

McCrory had had no 'skookum' – no power. But Lukswaas had been interested in what he had said about plants. Perhaps Smgyiik had thought this meant she had liked the doctor. Anyway, once Smgyiik had burst out and said that Wiladzap had killed McCrory, he had to run away. If he had stayed, Wiladzap, or Waaks, or Tsamti would have killed him. Why had he spoken? Because when my chief (Parry) had started to count out the gold pieces, it showed that the death of McCrory was important – it was as important as all that gold. This meant that Wiladzap would be killed by the King Georges if they thought he had done the murder, and Lukswaas might be killed by them too. Smgyiik had been very angry.

Lukswaas killed too?

Among the Tsimshian, revenge was not limited to one person, Lukswaas said, it included the whole family. That was very cruel, I said, returning tit-for-tat Lukswaas's comments back at the camp about the cruelty of the whites in the case of poor drowned Cathy.

Lukswaas said philosophically that Indians and King Georges were cruel in different ways.

Some King Georges, and especially Bostons, might be cruel to me and Lukswaas, I said. They would not like a white man marrying an Indian woman.

Many Tsimshian would not like it either, Lukswaas said. But she liked it.

She began stroking me again. Our desire should have been 'spent' only a few minutes before. But it was still there, like a circle including us with no end but itself. After a while we fell asleep, clasped together so closely that our lips were still touching.

We awoke not long after dawn, Lukswaas snuggled into my arms with her back to me. After a kiss of greeting we both sprang out of bed and stretched ourselves. We took turns with the chamber pot, all shyness gone, and scrubbed ourselves with soap and cold water from the ewer and basin, sharing my towel. Then I got dressed in my uniform. But Lukswaas stood tall and naked in front of the looking glass and began to work on her hair with my brush. She took one of the black ribbons she had picked up from Seeds's cabin trunk, and tied her hair behind her head in a ponytail such as some white women wore. She was transformed – still an Indian but possessed of a haughty beauty like that of a tall Spaniard or Italian. Then she turned her attention to the pile of clothes. She reached for the stays, and slipped them on gracefully, turning to me to lace them, which I did, though not tightly. Then she put the drawers on the wrong way round, then corrected this. She did the same with the shift. When it was on she looked questioningly at me. I nodded approval. Then she put on the hooped petticoat. Then I helped her into the dress, buttoning it up the back as I had done for Aemilia. She then put on a plain white bonnet, although I had to tie a bow for her. Then she sat on a chair, awkwardly adjusting her dress, and put on the white silk stockings. Then the shoes. Of all the clothes, Lukswaas liked these least. She tapped her feet on the floor and winced. Then she put on the black shawl – these were fashionable in Victoria, although in England they would be strictly for servant girls. She got up and looked at herself in the glass. I said she looked lovely.

I asked her if she was hungry and when she said yes, I asked her to wait in the room. I went downstairs. There was no one around. I went out and walked over the Ringo's. I could not have faced bringing Lukswaas there. There would be no question of Ringo, an ex-slave black as soot, admitting an 'Injun' to his restaurant. But he would, for a fee, send out breakfast. In a short while I was on my way back to the courthouse followed by a boy carrying a breakfast tray.

It was still early. I got the boy to set the breakfast on the long table in the room which Pemberton had used for the interrogations of Wiladzap and Lukswaas. The boy would come back for the tray later. I went upstairs.

Again Lukswaas had been leafing through my books. She had found a small album in which I kept a few drawings and photographs of my parents and the vicarage in Wiltshire, and was studying it with great interest. I said she could bring it downstairs. We ended up having a leisurely breakfast at the big table – ham, toast and muffins, all of which Lukswaas liked, and tea for her (the Tsimshian obtained tea from traders so she was used to it), coffee for me. Then we sat sipping our tea and coffee, looking through the album.

There was something unreal in the fact that Lukswaas was dressed as a white woman, but at the same time I realized that, to an unprejudiced eye, she would do well in the part. For one thing she was unusually beautiful but in a quiet way. For another she was good at copying my movements with knives and forks and cups and saucers. I made no comment on this but could see she was, in a sense, working hard. This touched me. I would do the same, in reverse, if I were among Tsimshians.

When we had finished we went out of the vestibule. Seeds spotted us from his office where he had been talking with Harding, and came out, looking forlorn but inquisitive. 'I put this young lady up on the spare camp bed in the store-room,' I lied. 'I'm now going to take her to the Commissioner's house. I imagine he'll come here shortly to talk to Wiladzap.'

I asked Lukswaas to wait for a moment, and stepped into the armoury. I dropped a Colt 45 revolver and ammunition into my pocket, for later. Then I rejoined Lukswaas and we walked out into the square where, with luck, Wiladzap would not be hanged …

Lukswaas took my arm. At first she had a little trouble with her shoes, and if I was not mistaken she cursed under her breath. But she soon found her natural grace again. There were few people on the sidewalks, but those few stared at us curiously.

We walked as we had done that first night, up Fort Street and out of town until we reached Pemberton's house. It was now half past eight, and I assumed Pemberton would have finished his breakfast. I felt extremely nervous. I was taking a gamble on my sense of the Pembertons' kindness and that as Anglo-Irish they had a more flexible attitude to human nature than English people. I paused at the garden gate. Lukswaas waited docilely, her hand on my arm. I opened the gate, then closed it behind us. We walked along a short path and up the steps to the front porch. I pulled the bell cord.

The door was opened by Pemberton himself. Perhaps it was the maid's day off. Pemberton was wearing a smoking jacket and an old fashioned smoking cap with a tassel. 'Good morning, my boy.' He said looking surprised.

'Good morning, Sir. I'm afraid I must talk to you urgently.'

Come in, come in.'

We stepped over the threshold, and Pemberton bowed slightly. 'Good morning, Ma'am. Augustus Pemberton.'

Then his face became transformed from its usual solemnity to comic puzzlement, almost an expression of pain, then a smile with a mischievous twist. 'Why this is …'

'Lukswaas. Wiladzap's sister.'

'Of course. Good morning, child. Come this way.' He showed us into the 'parlour' in which there was a small fire burning, unnecessary on such a mild morning, on one side of which Mrs Pemberton, elegantly but simply dressed, and wearing a white mob cap, was sitting stitching at a sampler. Between them was a trolley with the remains of breakfast, and a pot of coffee I could smell along with the smoke from Pemberton's pipe, which he picked up from the side table where he had left it. 'Forgive the informality. Maid's morning off. My Dear, it's Mr Hobbes. He must talk to me urgently. Perhaps I can take him to the dining room and we can sit there …'

'Please don't bother,' I said, seizing my opportunity. 'I have a favour to ask of Mrs Pemberton, and if you don't mind her hearing our discussion…'

'Not at all. I have no secrets from her – not even official ones – though of course they go no further. Young lady, do sit down.' Pemberton was apparently incapable of speaking Chinook to someone dressed as Lukswaas was. She had grasped that Pemberton meant her to sit in the chair his eyes had involuntarily glanced at as he spoke, and she sat down gracefully, although once she had done so she remained preternaturally still.

'Pemberton indicated another chair for me, and we formed a fireside circle. Mrs Pemberton was staring intently but not unkindly at Lukswaas. 'Do you speak English? She asked quietly.

'None at all,' I said. 'She is Lukswaas, the sister of the Tsimshian chief who is in jail. Sir,' I said to Pemberton, 'I don't want to make a long story of this, since it's very embarrassing to both Seeds and myself. I don't think it's fair to report Seeds to Superintendent Parry, since all came out right in the end. As for myself, I was foolish enough to let myself be detained elsewhere and I arrived late for duty last night. A group of Tsimshian from Cormorant Point had come to the jail with some idea of persuading Seeds to let Wiladzap free. He was careless enough to let a couple of the women in, but he was unpersuaded. Nevertheless the incident caused a bit of a ruckus and Wiladzap, when I returned, lost his usual poise. In fact he became quite upset, and in the process he uttered several words in English.'

'My goodness,' Pemberton interrupted in his brisk way. 'That's a new one.'

'I couldn't ascertain where he had learned it or why he had concealed it. But he knows – either from the past or recently – Aemilia Somerville. There is some secret they are concealing, which I can guess at but which I want to discuss with Miss Somerville this morning. It may only be incidental. The most important thing is that now Wiladzap admits he knows some English, he has come clean about what McCrory actually said to him: 'That Devil George.''

'Beaumont! But why? Does Wiladzap know Beaumont?'

'He says not – convincingly. I don't think he even knew George was a name, apart from 'King George'. Hence part of his error, I suppose. But if I may suggest so, Sir, you might go to the jail and interview Wiladzap – in English. I told him you might do so.'

'Good idea.' Pemberton, with one of his bursts of energy, leapt to his feet. 'And you'll want us to go to San Juan, no doubt.'

'If possible.'

'Why not? There is now justification for doing so at once. I wrote to Delacombe last week saying we'd come this week, and received a note from him saying he would expect us. I shall order up a boat to be ready at Telegraph Cove at noon, and I shall meet you there. I see from the bulge in your pocket that you already have a revolver. I shall bring one too. The man may be dangerous.'

Certainly the common description of Pemberton as 'resolute' was a true one. Although capable of dithering, this must have been, as he himself had said, part of a control of his own rashness. He was now quite excited.

'I hope you'll take care, Dear,' Mrs Pemberton said. She knew her man. 'Don't risk coming back across the Strait after dark.'

'Of course, of course, my Dear. At any rate, Captain Delacombe's very steady. There will be no great surprises.'

'And have you saved this young lady from her own people, Mr Hobbes?', Mrs Pemberton asked cannily.

'In a way.' I found I was blushing like a boy. 'Not that there's much wrong with them, but they're upset about the situation.'

'And you'd like us to take care of her until her brother is – we hope – released?'

'Mrs Pemberton, you're a brick!', I burst out in relief. 'As you have guessed, that's exactly what I was going to ask you, although I fear it's an imposition.'

'She'll be no trouble at all. We have an extra servant's room, if you and Augustus are delayed until tomorrow. No! She held up her hand as if to stop me from saying something which might have been silly. 'I shan't *treat* her like a servant. I shall enjoy teaching her a few things around the house. I have the impression she has never been in a house like this before.'

'Plank houses, my dear,' Pemberton interrupted. 'Much more grand than the Songhees. Great big plank houses, like school dormitories I suppose.'

'Well, she's clearly a cut above the Indian girls I've seen around here. I'm afraid I don't have a word of Chinook, but we'll manage.'

'Thank you,' I said, getting up. 'I know she'll be very well with you.'

'All right then', Pemberton said. 'Noon at Telegraph Cove. I'll go and see the man Wiladzap at once. His statement should be ample justification for a very vigorous questioning of Mr Beaumont.'

I said goodbye to Mrs Pemberton and turned to Lukswaas who – perhaps copying Mrs Pemberton – had remained sitting. I had meant to say goodbye coolly, so as not to give anything away to the Pembertons, but when I saw her eyes looking at me with a clear trusting expression, I did not hesitate to do what came naturally: I bent and gave her a kiss on her cheek, then held her hand for a moment while I said to her in Chinook that I hoped to see her the following evening at the very latest, but in any case she should stay here until she heard from me.

'Kloshe nanitsh', she said. Literally 'good see', meaning I should take care – an unknowing echo of Mrs Pemberton. I straightened up and, aware that it would not be fair to Mrs Pemberton – quite irrelevantly to Lukswaas being an Indian – to leave with her a young lady with whom

I was obviously on intimate terms, without explaining the relationship, I said: 'She is my fiancée.'

Mrs Pemberton rose to the occasion, although her eyes widened: 'you may be sure I shall treat her as such.'

26

I arrived on horseback at Orchard Farm soon after ten o'clock. The sun was already high in the sky, the dew had burned off, and it was hot. In the Orchard, along the roadway behind a zigzag snake fence, a young man in a straw hat was apparently inspecting the trees, although as soon as he saw me he came to the fence. It was Aemilia.

I was less shocked than I might have been. I had never seen a woman in trousers before, but my visit to the Indian camp, where some of the women wore leggings and the others were bare-legged, had disabused me of the idea that women were somehow born in dresses … The greater shock was my recognition that this 'young man' was the one who had bounded into the forest to escape meeting me when I had plodded wearily along the road after my break with Lukswaas. But I was prepared for something like it. There had been a conspiracy.

'Good morning,' I said, dismounting and tying my horse to the fence.

'Good morning. I thought you might come.' Aemilia looked very pretty in man's clothes. They consisted of blue dungarees and a striped shirt, but her body was pleasantly curved, her bright eyes and fresh face more clearly displayed as her hair was pinned up under her hat. She looked ready to brazen out the interview.

I swung myself over the fence and landed just in front of her. 'Aemilia. I want you to tell me everything. The whole story,'

'Why should I?'

'For one thing because Wiladzap – *your friend* Wiladzap – is still in jail.'

Suddenly she looked as if she might cry. She bit her lip. What happened?' She said tightly.

'I arrived in time, that's all. Waaks and Tsamti were lurking outside but I got in past them. Lukswaas and Wan had almost suborned the jailer, but the procedure was not complete. I had a good talk with Wiladzap who in the excitement of it all blurted out a few words of English. I sent the Indians back to camp, except for Lukswaas who is now with friends of mine in town. The name "Aemilia" created a strong effect, I noticed in Wiladzap. But he would answer no questions about you. Very gentlemanly of him. I said I'd ask you. So here I am.'

'I have nothing to say.'

'Yes you do. You must, in fact. There's a murderer on the loose and the only way to get your friend Wiladzap out by *legitimate* means, is to find him. And you can help.'

'But who *is* the murderer?' Aemilia said angrily.

'You don't know?'

'God knows! I don't. There are several people I might suspect. Everybody who knew McCrory ended up hating him.'

'You too?'

'No one more than I.'

'Perhaps *you* killed him.'

'Don't be silly. Chad, if you know no more than this, stop playing cat and mouse with me. Stop this torment. Just go away.'

'I could arrest you, as a matter of fact, for conspiring to break a prisoner out of jail.'

'Do you like this power, Chad? You're becoming a brute.'

'I'm reluctant to be completely honest with you, because even then I'm not sure you'll be honest with me.'

She thought for a moment. 'Let's be honest, then. But please don't use what I say as evidence against me.'

'As a matter of fact the law requires that I must – if for example you were tried for an offence. I cannot undertake not to. But so far, I have kept the jailbreak incident quiet, and I doubt it will come to the fore. My own aim, in fact, is to get Wiladzap out. I think I know who the murderer is too. I'll tell you shortly. But please, I want your story: about you and the Indians.'

'All right.' She turned and went over to the shade of one of the apple trees, and sat down on the dry grass. I followed and sat near her. I realized, unhappily, that my feelings toward her were still strong. I was very much aware that I had embraced her the day before, and I felt a kind of desire – for caressing her but not for the moment of consummation itself. That belonged to Lukswaas. I was not experienced enough to be able to label such an ambivalent feeling in any but naïve terms. I told myself that I 'liked' Aemilia, even sensually, but did not 'love' her.

'Lukswaas will have told you,' Aemilia said, as if wanting to put off her story.

'I didn't press her to.'

Aemilia looked puzzled. 'Are you in *love* with that girl?'

'I am.'

'That explains a lot. You might have been just cynically using her, as so many white men use 'squaws.' But I couldn't quite believe it of you. And she was terribly gone on you. She said she had given herself to you, like a crazy woman, and then later she learned you had thought she was Wiladzap's *wife*!' Aemilia laughed harshly. 'You're given a cherry to pluck, and you assume it's an over-ripe plum! *I'm* the plum, not she.'

'What do you mean?'

'*I'm* his wife.'

This went so much further than my suspicions that I was speechless. I waved a hand to tell her to continue.

'Starting from the beginning: I was fourteen years old. Daddy was killed, as I described, by a filthy Comox. I was with him. We were both some way from the village. The Comox, several of them, grabbed me and took me away. Needless to say they decapitated Daddy. I've told this before, so I don't cry about it now. It's history. The Comox tinkered around with me a bit but did not violate me, as they would have an Indian girl. They were in fact very frightened. Most Indian violence is committed out of sheer terror, I think. Perhaps white violence too? Anyway, this particular band set off fast, with me, to the territory of the neighbouring Kwagiutl. They had, I think – I didn't speak Comox, which is a kind of Salishan – decided to sell me as a high quality virgin slave. I was too dangerous for them to keep, but the Kwagiutl are the most bloodthirsty tribe along the upper Straits so perhaps they would have the power to take me on. At any rate, as I later heard, the HMS Trident had arrived and shelled the Comox village, which was a pity since women and children were killed, and the culprits had got away.

'We went toward the Kwagiutl territory by canoe. But we didn't meet the Kwagiutl. Instead we encountered a really grisly sight: a huge canoe full of Tsimshian who had come hundreds of miles down the coast for a raid on the Kwagiutl. Their canoe had eleven, as I recall, Kwagiutl heads stuck on poles down the middle. There were thirty or so Tsimshian men, and three Kwagiutl girls they had taken as slaves. All this, by the way, is rare now. That was in 1860, only nine years ago, but much has changed. Anyway, my Comox literally befouled themselves with fright. As the other canoe swept up, they made me stand up and they called out in Chinook that they had a beautiful white girl to sell. The canoes wallowed side by side. And Wiladzap, who was only twenty one but who had done particularly well in their raid – he had killed four Kwagiutl – bought me. For the entire stock of his personal booty from the Kwagiutl – skins, argillite, blankets… You should understand, this was a very high price. He could have simply cut the throats of the Comox. I wish he had! There were only five of them. But it was a question of pride, and largesse. The canoes grappled together. The goods were handed over to the Comox, and I to the Tsimshian.

'Then they brought me to Tsalak. The journey took two weeks, camping on shore at night. They treated me very well, all of them. Wiladzap did not even molest me. He was waiting to show me to his mother, as it happened. But after several days I became suddenly ill. A reaction, I suppose, to my father's death. I had been stoical, but I collapsed into tears and trembling which wouldn't stop. Wiladzap had the journey delayed for two days so that we could stay encamped. First he disappeared for a whole day into the forest to collect herbs, but also to ask the spirits for guidance. He came back with herbs for an infusion, which I drank. But he also came back with a 'vision'. He said my father (the Comox had told him my father had been killed) had appeared to him: he described him very accurately. My father had told him that my mother and my sister were safe – the vision seemed to condense my two sisters into one. Wiladzap said he would take care of me, and nobody would harm me: he had promised that to my father. All this was soothing, although I was as if paralysed, trembling like a caught rabbit, and weeping. Then he held my head very gently and put his mouth against it, on top, and for a long while seemed to breathe into my skull. Then he took each foot in turn and breathed for a while into the sole. I was too weak to resist him, and I'm glad I didn't because I suddenly went into convulsions and found myself screaming. Then I slept and woke up feeling clear and almost happy. It was night, and Wiladzap was sitting beside me in the firelight. I saw him and I fell in love with him – just like that. He could see it. He told me later that he had known it would happen: there were only two alternatives – I would die of grief, or I would love him. He treated this as a responsibility above all, but he truly loved me, I knew. He still did nothing improper. He wrapped me in a blanket and I slept again.

'Tsalaks is quite an impressive place, up from the mouth of a river on a very large island – Princess Royal – well placed for coastal and interior trade up in the mainland rivers, and very prosperous. Big plank houses along the river bank, with totem poles in front. About four hundred people, in four clans – eagles, ravens, backfish, and wolf. Wiladzap is an eagle. This comes through his mother who is now, I'm sorry to hear, dead. The women in tribes down here are, as you know, treated like dirt, although I dare say they have the kind of secret influence that women always do. The Tsimshian are what I believe the new science of ethnology calls 'matrilineal'. That means property descends from mother to daughter, or from uncle to nephew – meaning to a man from his mother's brother. It doesn't mean the women rule. It's not what I believe the more romantic ethnologists call a 'matriarchy'. As always the men rule, though the women know everything. But women can accumulate reputation. They can even inherit certain names. Do you know, it makes me think of *Ivanhoe* or other novels of Walter Scott. The Tsalak are by our standards medieval. Their concerns are reputation, courage, and chivalry. And the amassing of material wealth, of course.

'At any rate, Wiladzap was already a "chief" – although this is a flexible term since a chief has to live up to his title. Even women can be of the chiefly class, and they must be industrious and well behaved – as with us! Wiladzap was also what they call a "halayeet", what we might vulgarly call a medicine man. But that was not by choice, it was more a sort of inspiration. He had been possessed several times by a "spirit illness" which they value very highly, and almost died, and in the weakness of this, had brought out songs which could be used as formulas for curing illness. So he was already a very special sort of man. He was, of course, also brutal when it suited him. You must *not* romanticize these people. They completely lack conscience about the taking of human life. The only thing that might stop them from killing someone would be the material consequences – a bloody feud, revenge, and so on. They can be prudent. But not what we would call moral. They are however fairly moral about sexual relations between members of the same social class – which I suppose comes under prudence. Wiladzap freely enjoyed the embraces of one of the new slaves, in the first few days of our journey – before his cure of me, after which he remained chaste. But even he would not feel free to have relations with a girl of his own class. If he did, demands for marriage, exchange of property and so on, from her brothers, would follow. This is hard on the girls, of course. Unlike their brothers they can't enjoy fornicating with slaves and social inferiors. It's the same as among us! But worse for them, since they are not kept sheltered but are constantly stimulated by nakedness, sexual talk, and romantic stories which do not stop short, as ours do, before the crucial moment. But I'm digressing – thinking of Lukswaas.

'Wiladzap consulted his mother about me. The nearest thing you can imagine to her would be the sort of 'dowager duchess' type you find in English novels, although she was not very old, perhaps the same age as Mamma is now. She had an eight year old daughter, Lukswaas, who was even then very pretty and thoughtful. At any rate, the old lady – which is what I thought of her as – interviewed me as best she could, established by a discreet examination that I was a virgin, and said Wiladzap could take me as his first wife. I was, of course, not consulted on this, although Wiladzap was so enamoured of me that he swore there would never be a second wife, I would be the only one. They were all very kind. Becoming Wiladzap's wife entailed no particular ceremony beyond dressing me as one of them, Wiladzap giving me fine clothes and ornaments, and my going to live with him in his area of the clan house. To tell the truth, the nearest comparison I can come to is that Wiladzap's area was like a stall in a very large stable. Or perhaps the great hall of medieval castle was like that?

'Although the worst of my misery had gone, I had seen my father murdered. I had lost my mother and sisters. My heart ached. I felt violated by Wiladzap. He was not harsh with me, but I could not enjoy his demands on me. I found them disgusting in fact, much as I loved him – but it was a love full of ambivalence and conflict. I learned Tsimshian, and weaving, and all sorts of lore. Then after about six months I became pregnant. This changed things. I was filled with strange sensations. Morning sickness, of course. But then, of all things, intense desire. I became passionate for Wiladzap, and could not have enough of him. We would retreat to bed early, or lie out under the stars – it was summer – and make love and talk. I began to teach him English, which he regarded as a gift, learning it very quickly and talking it quite beautifully. This stage lasted about three months. I had become quite big. And I now had a sort of power over Wiladzap. Yet I could see that once I had the baby I would be one of the Tsalak for ever. I didn't want to be. I had to do something, then or never, to get away.

'Since I knew by then many of the things they believed in, I thought of the one way in which I could appeal to Wiladzap. Children have a more complicated status with them than with us. For him, for example, his greatest material responsibility would be to his nephews – the children of his sisters, Guyda (she's still at Tsalaks, apparently), and the younger sister, Lukswaas. But there is often great love and affection between fathers and sons or daughters. So I told Wiladzap, and his mother, that if he did not take me back to my people at once I would poison the child in my womb and it would be either aborted too early to live, be stillborn, or horribly deformed. They understood this at once. They think, perhaps rightly, that the pregnant woman can kill her unborn child by evil thoughts, or by stilling what they call the breath of life in her body.

'Wiladzap pleaded with me – insofar as he can plead – to stay. But I was determined. His pride and largesse were touched. You see, I was not a slave. It would be unthinkable for a man of Wiladzap's renown to keep a wife against her will. If I needed to go back to my own people, well then Wiladzap would take me back. For a while only, to have the baby with my mother. That became the official reason.

'It was autumn, and the weather was steady, though cold. Wiladzap and some of his men – and their women, to keep me company – brought me by canoe all the way back to Comox. They ran the gauntlet of the Kwagiutl who might have attacked them at any time. The Comox settlement had been abandoned. They brought me further South, to the first British settlement, North of Nanaimo. They left me there. My mother was sent for, from Victoria, and I came here.

'I had said to Wiladzap that one day I would come back. But as we approached the white settlements he became very gloomy and said he had lost me for ever. If I did come back, I said, I could come in one of the Bay's trading ships, when my baby was old enough to travel. But he must not try to come and get me. He said he would not. I cried when I said goodbye to him. I almost asked him to take me back! I wish I had! None of the present troubles would have happened. But then I was naïve. I was not old enough to understand what would happen to me.

'My mother was of course happy I was still alive. She called it a miracle. But pregnant! She was her usual helpful self at the birth, as kind as could be. But it was all hushed up. And she found the Joneses to take little William.

Wiladzap: William. Sometimes I call him my little Eagle. He's such a fine little boy. But he thinks I'm his 'auntie'! It's so painful. And this has suited everybody. I believe my mother has 'forgotten' even who William is. And my sisters practice the same deception. The little hypocrites. Can you understand all this?'

'Of course.' It was, in fact, predictable. Reputation was more important for 'eligibles' than life itself.

'It has put me in the most horrible position. I've returned to the life of a blushing maiden. For nine years! But it's a lie. I've not known how, in all conscience, I could even marry – the Indian marriage being a nothing in Christian terms. Not a *respectable* man, anyway. I have – as you know – the appetites of a married woman. At the same time I have the attributes of an old maid in the making. I like that too, in a way. I'm more interested in books and music and grafting apple trees than in most things. I can't play the game my sisters can.'

'Did you ever think of going back?'

'Incessantly. But it would have broken Mamma's heart. She too was living in agony. She too has the appetites of a woman – as I *now* know – and had lost her man. She couldn't have Daddy back. Why should I have Wiladzap? Who was a painted savage anyway…

'At the same time there is much about the life of the Indians – even the Tsimshian – that repulses me. It's not merely that they do not always wear clothes, that they do not play Handel, or eat seedcake at 'tea'. Nor are they much dirtier than we are. They have no baths but they wash more often… But up at Tsalak it rains constantly and the clouds become stuck gloomily for weeks on end against the mountains. And it's like living in a combined butcher's and fish market. They are always bringing in animals they have killed, and chopping them up, and skinning otters, and gutting and cleaning fish. One is always washing off blood or fish scales. And it all stinks. It's not the work. They work, especially the women, all day long, but some of it's pleasant. I picked berries and crushed them into cakes, I cooked meat in skunk-cabbage leaves, I wove blankets. But it's a constant harvest of living things. I prefer to work on my apple trees. This orchard was my idea, by the way, and I love grafting and pruning. Civilization seems to depend on agriculture, which the Indians just don't have. Indeed they consider it ridiculous to cultivate plants. That's why Indians are so unreliable as farm workers. Another thing is that they live in terror! Now the whites are more established up the coast I've heard there's much less head hunting and raiding. Many of the Tsimshian – the so-called Kitkats, even, from near Tsalak – have even moved up to the missionary settlements. But I'm sure there are still the permanent revenge feuds that go on between tribes. They remember atrocities from decades back, and brood on them, then take action when they can. I shouldn't want to go back there with my son – although, my God, I'd love to *own* the little dear – only to be butchered in some raid by the Haida.

'Then, on the other hand, if raids are less common, if the Tsimshian are becoming less wild, I sometimes worry that they'll become corrupted, like the Songhees, and degenerate. Although at other times I think they may not. They have more energy, and they are terrific traders. If we, the whites, will let them be! Lukswaas tells me the trading routes are being taken over by the HBC, and have been prohibited to Tsimshian. She says Wiladzap is afraid of becoming mangy and diseased like a bear in a cage. That's why he's worked up about this old fashioned quest of earning the Legex name. How could I go back to all that? Yet you know, when I saw them at Cormorant Point last week I cried with emotion and gratitude to be among them. Even talking about them now with you makes me want to be with them...' Aemilia stopped talking, her face flushed and excited but her eyes abstracted.

'Did Wiladzap come to Victoria to fetch you?'

Aemilia laughed, rather wildly. 'I don't *know* for sure. He didn't tell them. It was a trading expedition, that's all, to find new markets. Lukswaas says he wants me back. He has had slave girls, of course, and sired children on them whom he could acknowledge and raise to his level if he felt like it. But he has not done this. He 'dreams', as Lukswaas put it, of me. She says that when they arrived at Cormorant Point he told the women who go from farm to farm seeking housework, to keep an eye out for me. They always remember a face, by the way. Lukswaas recognized me at once, even though I was dressed as a man and she had not seen me since she was nine. She thinks he meant to search for me once they got really settled in at the camp. I would have known last night! – if he had got free. I told Lukswaas to tell Wiladzap he could send a messenger for me if he wanted. I waited up all night! I was ready to take the buggy to wherever they were, and to take

William too. But it's my fault, all this mess!'

'How?'

'When I heard a band of Tsimshian had camped on the peninsula I was terrified. I thought at once it must be him. I suppose I had half-wished, half-feared such a thing might happen one day. So I sent McCrory to spy on them.'

'*That's* why he went...'

'He would have anyway. He loved Indians because he could buy valuable herbs from them for almost nothing, and because they told him things which by their standards are commonplace but which he could use in his practice. I told him to find out, without asking of course, if Wiladzap was there, and to report to me on what he looked like, what his mood was. Wiladzap is extremely intelligent but he's as temperamental as a child...'

'Wait. McCrory knew about Wiladzap? You had already told him your story?'

'Yes.'

'I must ask you to tell me everything about your relationship with McCrory.'

'It's an ugly story – much uglier than the Tsimshian, even with their canoe-full of heads. Uglier, in its own way, than my father's death which was at least sudden!' Aemilia was transported by her own vehemence, and stopped short.

'Go on, please.'

'I'll try. I can talk to you, Chad. But please, if this must become public, censor it, won't you? Like Bowdler's *Family Shakespeare*. Bowdlerize it, won't you? Because to you I'd rather tell exactly. We've been close – though My God it fizzled out, didn't it – as it had too. We've been with *them*. Anyway I want you to tell me what you think of my tale of McCrory.'

'I shall.'

'All right. He turned up in Victoria last year as you know, and he made a great impression on Mamma. She went to see him. Not, ostensibly, about *her* "nerves". About mine. My melancholia. I had refused to go. I had told her only a charlatan could pretend to cure melancholia, since it was the result of life. Emotional conditions are not diseases.

'But eventually I went to see McCrory. To keep Mamma happy. I was not sure why she was so urgent that I go. I don't understand human motives,

302

and certainly not hers. Could it be that she was drawn to him, and did not want to be, so threw me in his way instead? I wondered that even at the time. I went. He was a charming man, of course – a bit of a ruffian under the gloss, one sensed, but then that can be charming too. He was extraordinarily sure of himself. When I told him my objections to coming – not that he was a charlatan, but that emotional states were the results of life, not diseases – he said 'Aha! You must think I'm a charlatan to attempt to cure such things!' Then he explained that even physical diseases were the results of blockage in the flow of life – or universal fluid, animal magnetism and so on and so forth – through the body. Emotional states could cause these blockages too, he said. In short, he disarmed every criticism, often before it was made, but at the same time accepted completely that I *was* critical, that I *had* doubts.

'I had never met a doctor like him. You can see that part of his appeal was that his pseudo-scientific jargon described things I had learned from Wiladzap! Of course there is a 'breath of life', and a flow of it through our body. Any Tsimshian 'halayeet' works to dissolve the blocks to this flow, although he may see them as places where evil spirits are encamped. So I was impressed by McCrory. I went into treatment. The lying on the couch. The breathing deeply. The magnetic passes. You know it all, I suppose.'

'How about what one lady described to me as "the electric testicles"?'

Aemilia laughed rather nervously and for a moment I regretted having been so forward. But she went on. 'I wonder who that was? No, don't tell me. Thank-you, you make it easier for me. Yes, the electric testicules. To which I did not react at all – I mean electrically. I withdrew my hand, sat up, and asked him what in God's name he meant by this. With characteristic aplomb he buttoned his trousers and explained. There was a special concentration of magnetism in that area, and so forth. Then he said it was clear from my reaction that although I was annoyed, I was not an innocent woman. He said he had already deduced that my melancholia and what he called my "hysterical" symptoms – such as aches and pains and dizziness and oppression around the heart – were the result of an early awakened sexual impulse that had not been satisfied… At the time I did not know something I know now: that he had seen my mother privately on every trip she had made into town, and that they were in the way of becoming pretty intimate – I'll explain later. So of course she had told him something of my story. He was able to tell me little things about myself which he presented as the result of clinical deduction, but which of course were not. This was over many appointments. I had fallen under his spell enough to come back regularly. I, who am always so critical! But usually my criticism has frightened people: they feel it as sharp, and they shrink from it. It was wonderful to have a man receive barbed remarks from me with perfect calm.

'Meanwhile the magnetic treatments continued and they were very stirring – in my intimate female parts, although he was only making passes in the air and never actually touched me. So after a while I, who had abjured men, was in a perfect state of emotional and sexual crisis about this man whom I did not find handsome or cultivated and whom in fact I found vulgar. Not that I should ever have embarked on an "affaire" with him...' Aemilia seemed lost for words.

'But,' I said, to make it easier for her, 'what about "magnetation", "male continence", and so forth?'

'Did he do that with everyone?' Aemilia looked horrified.

'I don't know. They are practices which originate in the Oneida Community in New York, where McCrory spent some time. A Christian Communist sect – so called "perfectionists."'

'How vile. Yes. He told me of an aspect of possible treatment which would surely assuage my tensions and "hysterical symptoms". I would undress and lie under a sheet with my eyes closed and he would, without lifting the sheet in such a way as to expose me, insert his – 'self' was how he put it. Shielded by a lambskin membrane (I had never heard of such things) which would prevent any accidental conception. Not that the aim of this treatment was his own pleasure! He swore it would not entail much movement on his part and certainly not a "spending", if you know what I mean. Also the membrane would prevent contact of our skins directly and thus preserve the propriety and the medical nature of the treatment. It was *not,* he assured me, an act of lust or even love that he had in mind – although of course he liked and respected me. It was a way for the universal fluid, through this conduit as it were, to establish its balance. The coupling of two organisms, he said, served its purpose in lust and in love, in marriage and in procreation; but it had another function, which was to establish a magnetic equilibrium, through the opposition of the male and female poles: this function I might benefit from without the perils of an illicit relation with a man... And so on! I think I tell you all his suave glozings and explanations in a way to excuse myself.'

'It's not necessary.'

'Because of course I gave in! As Byron put it in the poem: "and saying she would ne'er consent, consented." And the experience was something as he said, in that he held to his end of the bargain, as it were, and went no further – never, *so far as I could tell,* did he experience pleasure or ecstasy for himself. Unless he did so stealthily, like a snake within that cursed sheath which was – you know – strangely cool, as if all warmth to it came from me. Uggh! But my melancholia did abate, and the aches and pains. I wonder if it was merely that I had something to fill my life, and a sense of doing something unconventional, and of occult power, on my visits to him.

'Then something happened on his part. He began to want to see me more often. For the treatment, you understand. And then when in a treatment he suddenly leaned forward and took me in his arms! I shrieked and pushed him away, and of course he apologized. He said he was falling in love with me! Well, the scales fell from my eyes and I saw him for what he was: a man like all the others. This of course was what his superhuman, as it seemed, control of himself in the treatments had made him *not* seem.

'So I stopped the treatments, and felt no worse for it, although a little wiser in the ways of the world, and self-disgusted at having let myself be used. Yet he had begun coming to the farm on Sundays as a family friend, and this continued. I teased him and ribbed him in front of others and he took it in good part, so I ended up not exactly disliking him. We used to take little walks together around the house. He liked getting *out,* even under an umbrella in the winter rain, and so do I. He would confide in me even about his patients, although not usually mentioning their names, as if wanting me to see him as an ordinary struggling human, not as the magician he had wanted me to see at first. In a moment of candour I once told him he was no better than a prostitute. I said 'you are nothing more than the masculine equivalent of a fricatrice.' Nasty word that, fricatrice, with its implications of rubbing, and I wanted to hurt him. 'But', I said, 'when a woman is a fricatrice she knows it: only a man would deceive himself that he was a healer or a daring pioneer of science, while being a fricatrice...' And he said – lyrically – that perhaps he was prostituting himself, but healing required sacrifices: the doctor had no hope of a cure unless he gave something of himself…'

'And your mother?'

'Mamma! I have only this week found out *exactly* what was going on – by dint of the most appalling screaming matches between us. She is in a state of *terror* that you or someone else will find out about her and McCrory and that this will come to the ears of Mr Quattrini who is worth hundreds of thousands and a Catholic and views her as a saint! Orchard Farm has been an inferno this past week!

'Of course I shouldn't tell you about Mamma but I shall, because it bears on my case. In a word: she was McCrory's mistress, almost from the beginning. No nonsense about 'treatments' and lambskin sheaths. She is past child-bearing, and although ten to fifteen years older than he, it would seem she was an avid and greedy partner in… You see? My mother whose reverence for my father, for 'what he would have thought of the betrayal' if I had gone back to my Indian because my animal lusts had been awakened! Mamma calls a spade a spade 'en famille' I assure you, in spite of the smelling salts and flutters…' Aemilia's voice trailed off, and she looked so upset that I decided to change the subject.

'You must tell me everything you know about George Beaumont.'

Aemilia's eyes widened. 'Is it he? Is it really he?

'I think so. What do you know?'

'Very little. He met McCrory here. They became thick, would see each other often. Poor George had some kind of affliction… Oh Lord! Chad, must I be honest? I'm sounding like a woman of the street. McCrory told me of course, mentioning George by name. George could not become excited, in the physical sense. When he lay with a woman he became angry. McCrory was even afraid that one day George would *kill* a woman! So he wanted to cure George, and last time we talked he said he had a *plan* for George. He said one other odd thing. I had asked him about his visit to Cormorant Point and I had, I'm afraid, teased him about being 'my spy'. He laughed and said he didn't mind being a spy, since he too had a spy – 'our friend George', he said. But he would say no more. He liked to be mysterious, of course.'

'You know nothing else?'

'Nothing. Conversations about George were usually tempered by the fact that he was nearby paying court to Letitia.'

'And Firbanks? You know about his…? I stopped, out of discretion or fed upness.

'Yes. His… what I believe the French call 'chaude-pisse' – I read that in a book. McCrory told me to make sure the little rat did not get *really* close to Cordelia – of which of course there was no chance.'

'Aemilia. Why did you… I mean why did we do what we did yesterday?'

'It was not *really* part of the plan. But once I saw you had a horse and could get back to town quickly, I knew there was no other way I could keep you. And I wanted to do it. I still sort of want to, though as before it might not work, and I hardly dare…'

'Why – hardly dare?' I felt choked with an emotion I could not understand, as if I could love Aemilia after all.

'I knew you had been with Lukswaas. By the way it was me whom you met…'

'I know. Young man in straw hat.'

'I was going to Cormorant Point because of our talk the day before. I had realized that you had lost confidence in finding the murderer, and poor Wiladzap would be dead before long. At first a certain part of me was glad he had been arrested. 'See how the mighty are brought low', sort of thing. And honestly I had a sort of hope for you. I liked you and I thought if any man could understand my story and forgive, you might. You're such a prig, but honest and good-hearted. Though I don't love you. You don't love me?'

'Something very like it, but not it.'

'We should marry, you know. We'd be very well suited. We don't love each other. But perhaps that doesn't matter in marriage. And we've had a similar experience with – with them. I think yesterday for a moment I had the idea: Chad and I can make love and escape from *them* – escape all that violence and danger. But we couldn't. You can't escape from Lukswaas, now, anymore than I can escape from Wiladzap. And maybe that's as it should be. They are both *good* people!'

'Lukswaas. You were telling me that you went to see her.'

'Yes, because I knew that if nothing was done to get Wil out of jail he'd be hanged as soon as nothing. I had provoked you into admitting it. At one point I had thought I would be glad to be rid of him. But when you really admitted it would be the end for him, I knew I had to do what I could to get him out. So I thought of the obvious scheme. Nothing is unknown in Victoria. The story of Seeds the Jailer's wife running off with a miner is an old one. And I guessed he would be tempted. And whisky would keep the prisoners quiet. So it was my scheme. I arrived at the camp, having seen you, and was told Lukswaas was ill. She had just got back from being with you and was desperate. I tried to explain to her that if you had known she was a virgin you would *never* have put a finger on her, and on the other hand you must have felt terrible being involved with another man's wife. She agreed you felt terrible about something. But she said she would never want to see you again. All right. We made our plan. That's all. I'm sorry you got back in time – unless you *do* get the murderer. But if it's poor George!'

'Why *poor* George?'

'Well, he *is* poor George. If he killed McCrory he must have been driven beyond endurance.'

'Why did you say earlier that many people might have killed McCrory? From your account, everybody liked him. He could get away with anything. Even you, although you said earlier that it was an ugly story, seem to have ended up on the best of terms with him. You asked me earlier to tell you what I think. I think it's amazing that you could allow that relation with McCrory to happen…'

'Don't judge me, Chad. And don't be jealous: I know you don't love me but I can see from your face that you're angry, in that way men feel when a woman they are attached to doesn't see through another man. But how could I have seen through McCrory? He had an answer to every objection, he was so suave… but I'm excusing myself. Yes, it was my fault. What happened between us was *evil* – more so by far than if we'd had a real sexual affaire! That shocks you… But it was evil to have a sexual congress which was so stealthy, so unconsummated. I think I put up with him afterward because he had exposed to me an evil part of myself: we were like conspirators. After all, if he had deceived himself that his lust for me was really a medical treatment, I had deceived myself in the same way. But it was even worse: we each must have *known* we were deceiving ourselves. At moments I knew clear as day that, treatment or no treatment, I just wanted a man in my… I was using him too! But God how I loathed him as I did so. Then I used him as a spy on the Tsalak. Which was equally vile…'

'Don't torment yourself about it. After what you went through…'

'No, I must accept that I was vile. As he was vile. You, for example, are a prig. I mean it kindly: you are, for a man, over-concerned with virtue. But a man like McCrory exudes a sort of false virtue no matter what he does. You could not cheat people, or lie to them, or promise falsely and betray them, and at the same time be convinced of your own virtue. McCrory could. Perhaps it's the Yankee in him: I don't even believe he was from Virginia – more likely New England or New York. You know the Yankee attitude: whatever a man does is not judged in itself, or by how it makes him feel in his heart, but by its success. McCrory's treatments were a success in his estimation, so they were beyond question. I once asked him, as I thought nastily, whether he really *believed* in the animal magnetism. 'Of course I do', he said. 'Because I know it *works.*' I think there is something evil in that. Because I have a point of comparison: Wiladzap. Wiladzap did not 'believe' in the breath of life, he *lived* it. And he would never touch someone he was asked to heal unless he had gone into a kind of retreat, for hours at least and I believe at times for days, and purified himself by washing scrupulously, and fasting; and if he did not receive the answer to the problem in the form of a song – what we might call a poem containing a magical formula – he would not try to cure it. He did not, like McCrory, have an answer to everything.'

'Do you still love him?'

'You're a goose, Chad. Of course I "love" him. Whether I could possibly go with him is another question. I might be ready after all this. A while ago I still would not have been. I distrusted my memories – after all, I was only fifteen when I last saw him! – although they are as clear as day. And although I say he is 'good' he is in some ways an *awful* man. Ruthless...'

'I know. He yelled at Lukswaas to kill me – I'm sure of it. She was standing behind me with a knife ready to plunge it in. He was quite puzzled when she didn't.'

'As well he might have been. You have caught that girl. But then she has caught you too. We are both caught, you and I. By them. We are doomed. But so are they.'

'I hope none of us is doomed.'

'It's no easier for them. We've all caught each other. If Wiladzap is free I may go with him, and bring my son too, and be cast into that elemental world again. Perhaps to live through its dissolution: I worry about the

Tsalak. And if Lukswaas stays with you – which she would without question, she is all loyalty, that girl – you are both blighted in the eyes of respectable society. You can marry her, and she can change her name to Lucy and learn to lace herself in stays. But you will still be seen as having sacrificed your good name for the lust of a squaw. You'll lose your employment. Nobody will talk to you. You'll be ostracized. They'll never believe it's more than lust, no more than with me and Wiladzap. It used to terrify Mamma. If I went back to Wiladzap it would show that the itch of lust could not be satisfied otherwise. Too true, from her point of view, as I see it now! But not mine. It's more than lust. I tried to experiment with that yesterday, with you. And you know, I said 'Don't make me pregnant', to get you to withdraw, as you did. It was a last minute effort to preserve *something* I have only had with Wiladzap. You understand?

'Of course. It preserved something for me too.'

'Aren't we goody-goody?' Aemilia smiled ruefully, although the words had shown her usual sharpness. 'Now please, go and sort things out with George, but be careful. He's like a toy soldier, that man. It must be very frightening to be inside his body. One lesson I learned ten years ago is that murder is the offspring of terror.'

'Thank you.'

We got up, and embraced each other briefly. Then I swung myself back over the fence, mounted my horse, and rode away. Aemilia was left as before, studying the apple blossom against the sky.

27

Pemberton had hired a pinnace rowed by four boatmen with another as helmsman. Once they had pulled out beyond Ten Mile Point in a brisk breeze the men set a small triangular sail to help us along, then rowed on and off. Although the water was choppy there is not the same deep swell on Haro Strait as in the Straits of Juan de Fuca, which are directly open to the Pacific. It was not hard to imagine Beaumont rowing and sailing a small boat across on such a day as this.

Pemberton and I were squeezed in the bow, side by side on a narrow seat facing backward. I summarized what Aemilia had said about George. The 'spy' remark puzzled both of us. McCrory had perhaps been spying, or had liked to think he was, against the English. But there would be no point in this since it was impossible to keep a secret in the Colony, and while the San Juan dispute awaited arbitration there were no military manoeuvres in prospect.

Pemberton had interviewed Wiladzap and was satisfied that there was enough chance that he was telling the truth for a thorough questioning of Beaumont to be warranted. If this revealed that Beaumont was the murderer, then he would be left in the hands of his commanding officer. Pemberton had seen no need to bring extra constables with us. But, although dressed in civilian clothes, he had a small pistol in a shoulder holster, 'in case there is unexpected trouble.'

I did not ask about Lukswaas, nor did Pemberton mention her. For most of the voyage we sat squeezed together but looking in different directions across the waves at the receding forested shoreline of Vancouver Island, with the low rocky cone of Mount Douglas behind.

After about an hour and a half we began to approach San Juan, and by turning my head to look behind Pemberton I could see the shoreline in more detail than ever. From the other side of the Strait it had seemed always low, peaceful and green. I could now see that the Southern end was a sort of heath, golden, and dotted with small bushes. Towards the end of this heath, four or five miles away, was a tiny cluster of white buildings which I knew must be the American Camp. The English Camp was about half way along the island's Western shore which at close range was revealed to be high and rugged, with rock outcroppings and stretches of thick woods. Above the island was a line of sparkling clear sky and above this a huge tower of cumulus clouds whose underside shone like mother of pearl.

By sitting half sideways while Pemberton did the same, I could see that we were approaching a small gulf or bay which we would enter through a channel between two wooded promontories. On the shore facing the channel was a white blockhouse, jutting out onto a beach, and behind it a clearing with houses, and figures moving here and there.

The water became suddenly choppier as we approached the channel, and the bow dipped and splashed. Pemberton and I were drenched with spray. We cursed – 'Damn it' from Pemberton, 'Blast!' from me – but could do nothing. Then the pinnace hit a sudden calm in the landlocked bay, the sail flapped loosely, and two of the men stopped rowing as the helmsman guided the other two in across the water which was glassy as a pond. Pemberton and I sat stiffly, backs to the shore, half soaked. It would have been undignified to be seen craning our necks. There was a naval sloop at anchor, with eight guns on the deck, and a variety of pinnaces, barges and rowing boats attached to buoys.

The boat ran onto the beach with a rasping noise and I felt myself being lifted up. Two of the boatmen jumped overboard to tug the boat further in. When it stopped moving Pemberton stood up and stepped over the gunwale. I followed. We were on a rocky beach just below the blockhouse, which looked brand new, sparkling with fresh paint. It was four floors high, hexagonal, and built of square logs on a foundation of rock extending onto the beach. Cannons peered from rows of embrasures. The roof was conical with a flagpole from which the Union Jack was flying. Behind the blockhouse the clearing looked like an English park – a big level field of short grass like a lawn, with a parade ground on one side, oak trees scattered here and there, and long low buildings of brick and white-painted wood. In the shade of the trees, Marines in their blue uniforms but without their usual white helmets, were sitting reading or talking – being early afternoon it must be a rest time. Down the grass a small group of men came stepping smartly, in white helmets. The first was an officer, with behind him a Sergeant and a Corporal.

As they approached, I noticed that the officer's trim was spoiled by the fact that he was extremely unshaven. But his bearing was erect. He was probably in his late thirties, his unshaven cheeks golden brown, his eyes blue.

'Commissioner! He said, using Pemberton's obsolete title, as most people did. 'I wasn't expecting you so early in the week. But you're very welcome.'

'How do you do, Captain.' Pemberton shook hands, then introduced me. 'This is Sergeant Hobbes. Sergeant, this is Captain Delacombe.' I shook hands with Delacombe who was slightly taller than me. 'Good God, Delacombe.' Pemberton said, abandoning formality, 'you look like a real ruffian with that fuzz.'

'Sorry.' Delacombe stroked his face ruefully. 'Didn't you know? Queen's Regulations changed. Navy can now grow beards, like the rest of the civilised world. We no longer have to look like a bunch of schoolboys. But it takes time.' He turned to his Sergeant and Corporal. 'Dismiss, Sergeant.' He said quietly.

They saluted smartly. 'At ease,' the Sergeant said to the Corporal, and they walked back toward the buildings.

'Looks like Hyde Park, doesn't it?' Delacombe remarked. 'Awfully hard to stay formal. We stand at ease after lunch. Come with me and I'll give you a tour. Mr Beaumont, whom I know you want to talk to, is with a detachment over at Roche Harbour for provisions. He'll be back within the hour, I should think.'

Delacombe showed us the blockhouse, whose walls were four feet thick. It contained a store of ammunition and food, and the whole garrison could retreat into it if necessary. The four Marines on guard duty snapped to attention and stood like statues. Everything was spic and span. The armoury was a stone reinforced cellar within the foundation, packed with carbines, mortars and ammunition. Above it was a command room with tables and chairs, and maps on the walls. Above this were sleeping quarters with bunks. The hexagonal, white-washed rooms with the light striking across them from the embrasures, were curiously attractive. The building had been completed only the previous year, and Delacombe was proud of it. Outside again, he led us across the grass to show us a boat house, stables with a dozen or so horses and various carts and wagons, store-rooms, a dormitory block for the men, and a small elegant house which Delacombe, Beaumont and another Lieutenant shared, along with their servants. Apart from the house, which was of brick and clapboard, the buildings were all of square logs, but the scene was very English, with something of the atmosphere of a public school. Delacombe even mentioned that his men went to 'Chapel' at Roche Harbour.

We sat down on the veranda of Delacombe's house in the sun, our splashed clothes drying, with glasses of cold light ale. When Delacombe's servant had withdrawn, Pemberton said, 'We shall have to talk with your man Beaumont. I hope it will not be unpleasant, but I should warn you that there's a strong implication that he may know more about this atrocious murder than is good for his reputation.'

'You mean you have learnt more since your letter? I can't say I didn't take it seriously – dashed disturbing, in fact. But I couldn't believe that old George would have any really disagreeable associations. He's an odd fig, old George, but very upright – perfect wooden soldier, you might say.'

'Does he go off often on his own?'

'You put your finger on it, Commissioner. When he has a moment off duty he's never around. Does a lot of rough shooting – the place is swarming with rabbits and grouse, and they come so close you can even pot them with a revolver. But he usually takes a shotgun. When he has a day's leave, he's off to Victoria. I rag him about having a lady friend there, but he denies it – I won't say hotly, because there's nothing hot about him – coldly rather. He's a very private man. But why not? We can't live in each others' pockets. It would get on the nerves, rather, wouldn't it?'

'You mean he'll even go to Victoria during the week at times?'

'Oh yes. I assume so. Another thing he likes is boating. Very active man. Strong as an ox. He'll take off in one of our keeled skiffs and row or sail half way round the island, or across to Telegraph or Cadborough.'

'And on the Wednesday of the murder? Do you know where he was then?'

'Yes, I thought of that after your letter. The truth is, he had a day's leave. I believe he went out boating. At any rate, he disappeared.

'Well, we can question him about that. In your presence of course.'

'If it turns out he has done something criminal I shall place him under arrest, much as I should hate having to do so. I shouldn't exactly call him a friend, but one becomes fond of one's officers.' Delacombe seemed to be rather light hearted by nature, but his brow clouded, and I guessed that he was very worried. 'Queer cove, George. In a way I shouldn't be surprised if there were some murky secrets about him. He's too good to be true. Not, I'm sure, that his secrets involve the commission of an actual crime of violence.' Delacombe's face brightened, either naturally or by an effort of will. 'Thinking of crimes, and Indians, isn't this infernal news about the *John Bright*? Do you think those fellows ended up being eaten by cannibals?'

This was not a change to a brighter subject, but at least a change. Delacombe and Pemberton sat talking, waiting perhaps as tensely as I for Beaumont's return. Then there was the crunch of marching feet, and as we turned to look along the verandah to our left, a squad of six Marines appeared with Beaumont, wearing a white pith helmet like those of the others, marching beside them. Behind came two wagons with their drivers erect as puppets in their seats. The distance between the squad and the nose of the first horse, and the back of the first wagon and the nose of the second horse must have been precisely the same. This procession disappeared behind a clump of trees and the barrack house. Then came muffled shouts and the crunch of the squad falling out.

Beaumont appeared around the barrack house, marching briskly. He stamped up the steps to the veranda and saluted Delacombe. 'Provisions detail duly accomplished, Sir.'

'At ease Mr Beaumont.'

Beaumont relaxed. 'Good day, Gentlemen,' he said in his dry voice to Pemberton and me as we rose to our feet. I introduced him to Pemberton. They shook hands. Beaumont seemed imperturbed by seeing us.

'The Commissioner and Sergeant Hobbes want to ask you a few questions,' said Delacombe. 'Perhaps around the table in the library would be a good place.'

'Certainly, Sir. Allow me one minute. I shall be with you directly.'

'Of course. We shall be waiting for you.'

Beaumont stepped briskly into the house, and they heard him stamping up some stairs inside.

'Let us go in.' Delacombe said, and allowed Pemberton and me to precede him.

Inside, the house was like any Colonial farmhouse – four or five not very large rooms downstairs, with a staircase in the hall facing the door. Delacombe showed us to the right into a sort of conference room which had a long table and hard-backed chairs, a wall of bookshelves, another of maps, and windows to the side of the house and onto the veranda. Delacombe pulled out a chair for Pemberton at one side of the table, and went to the head. I moved around to the other side, facing Pemberton. He took out his notebook and pencil. We waited.

Beaumont's footsteps were heard on the stairs, mechanically regular as the man himself, and he came into the room. He sat down at the foot of the table.

'Mr Pemberton? Delacombe began.

'Sergeant Hobbes will ask you some questions.' Pemberton said. He and I had agreed that it would be best to start with a gentle presentation of the facts, and related queries. If a severe interrogation became necessary, Pemberton would take over.

'Mr Beaumont,' I began. 'As you know, Dr. McCrory, an acquaintance of yours, was murdered near Cormorant Point on the Wednesday of three weeks ago, when you had a day's leave. Could you tell us what you did that day?'

'I believe I went boating. There was a good South-westerly breeze. I sailed over to Darcy Island. There's a sand bar there. Walked along it with a shotgun, but did no shooting. No ducks in that heat.'

Darcy Island was a few miles North of Cormorant Point off the Vancouver Island Coast.

'Do you remember,' I said, 'when we were walking from St Marks the Sunday before last and I asked you where you had gone that day?'

'I think so.'

'What did you say?'

'Believe I said I went shooting, didn't I?'

'Yes. Here on San Juan.'

'I believe I said "on the Island". But I meant Darcy Island.'

'But you didn't actually shoot?'

'No.'

'You mentioned to me the grouse, as I recall – not ducks.'

'I must have been thinking of the grouse here.'

'On a previous occasion, you may remember, the Sunday before, I asked you if you had known Dr. McCrory apart from at the Somervilles. Do you remember what you said?'

'I said no. Which was a lie. But I was being asked rather casually, not in formal interrogation. I felt my relationship with McCrory was a private matter.'

'Were you a patient of his?'

'No.'

'He told someone that you were.'

'Really? He must have been joking. It was not the case.'

'So you were merely a friend of Dr. McCrory's?'

'As you put it, "an acquaintance".'

'Did you ever visit his house?'

'Once or twice. I would ride into town, having hired a horse at Cadborough, and I would stable it at McCrory's. We would then walk into town together for dinner.'

'Where?'

'Ringo's. Or the chop-house.'

'Where did you go after dinner?'

'The Windsor Rooms. A dancing establishment. Which many gentlemen, in so far as there are any gentlemen in Victoria, patronize. I say, Sir!' Beaumont addressed Delacombe. 'I don't believe it's fair to have to answer questions of this nature.'

'I'm afraid they must be *asked*,' Delacombe said, 'if the Sergeant believes they shed light on your relationship with this McCrory. Of course you may choose not to *answer* them. But frankly, since we are all men here, and since it is no crime in the eyes of either the Navy or the police to visit certain "establishments", even if they are disreputable, I suggest you be as informative as you can.'

'Where did you stay the night when in town?' I asked.

'At the Hotel Argyle.'

'We can check that in the hotel register. Perhaps you can tell me the dates of the times you have stopped there since last September.'

'Really! I resent this questioning. If I go to the Windsor Rooms, it is with the likely prospect of spending the night with a lady, is it not? I might not, in fact go to the Argyle. But naturally I don't wish to discuss such occasions.'

'As a matter of fact, the ladies of the Windsor Rooms don't usually receive guests overnight.'

'Well, *part* of the night. I would then walk back to Cadborough or Telegraph. As you know I'm a very restless man. I walk miles.'

'Then what about the horse?'

'What horse?'

'The one which you left at McCrory's.'

Beaumont was silent, although he showed no signs of emotion. 'What are you implying?' he said at last.

'Please answer the question.'

'There wasn't always a horse. I might have walked. If there was, then I would have picked it up on my way out of town.'

'At night?'

'You never stayed at McCrory's?'

'I won't say never. I suppose I might have.'

I remained silent for a while, so as to emphasize Beaumont's sudden awkwardness. Then I remarked: 'The trouble is, Mr Beaumont, that your responses to my questions about your relationship with Dr McCrory are so reluctant. I believe there is much to hide in your acquaintanceship. The evidence I have received indicates the following. First, you were a frequent companion of Dr McCrory's at the Windsor Rooms. Second, that you were his patient. Third, that your visits with him to the Windsor Rooms were connected with attempts to treat a nervous disorder for which you were in treatment with the Doctor. These points have been attested to by various informants. A fourth point is that you may have stayed overnight at Dr McCrory's guest room. Now, since you have been evasive about these points, to an extent which goes beyond your natural desire to protect your privacy, how can we assume you are telling the truth about where you were on the afternoon McCrory was killed? Even about this you have been evasive. Rough shooting on San Juan, instead of on Darcy Island. Grouse, instead of ducks. Yet as an officer and a gentleman I know it's your instinct to tell the truth.'

'Really, Hobbes, I don't know what you're driving at. Naturally I'm not proud of my association with the ladies of the night of a miserable Colonial town, in the company of a Yankee doctor who was probably a charlatan. I regret it. But it was my way of amusing myself. There's nothing wrong with that. And here you are seeming to accuse me of a murder when you've given no evidence whatsoever to link me with it.'

'There is another matter. I have a report from the United States that McCrory was cashiered from the Confederate army on suspicion of spying for the Yankees. And a report from a naval man at Esquimalt that McCrory seemed to be spying there, asking about naval dispositions and so on.'

'The rotter,' Beaumont said, although his voice was still unmoved. 'He was indeed one of the most nosy characters I've met.'

'He once remarked à propos of you: "George is my spy".'

'Good God!' Beaumont stiffened, to become more wooden. 'That's a slander. A rotten slander. To whom did he say this? Sir!', he said to Delacombe. 'I request that I be allowed to clear my name in this regard.'

'Of course, Mr Beaumont. I'm sure the Sergeant will tell you who reported this allegation.'

I was put on the spot. 'Miss Somerville,' I said.

'Aemilia! I know that none of those dear girls would slander me. I must assume that McCrory was doing so, out of malice or a twisted sense of humour.'

'Did he ask you about our dispositions here?' This was Delacombe.

'Yes. I must admit he did. But, dash it, I hardly took it seriously. We have no secrets. I assumed he was merely being nosy, in that Yankee way. Perhaps it pleased him to claim acquaintance with an officer here and tell his friends that I was "his spy". If, Sir, it came to the ears of anyone in Victoria, then I must answer for my indiscretion in choosing such a friend. It was stupid of me.'

I continued: 'Do you always come to Cadborough Bay or Telegraph Cove when you take a boat over to Vancouver Island?'

'Yes. Telegraph, since it's slightly nearer here, if I'm going to walk. Cadborough if I'm going to hire a horse from the farmer there.'

'I thought you sometimes came to another cove – it doesn't have a name, but it's backed with rocks and arbutus – about a mile West of Telegraph Cove. Toward Cormorant Point.'

'Really?' I don't believe I know it.' Beaumont's face was a mask as usual, but he had become very still as if his breathing had almost stopped.

Mr Beaumont, do you have a habit of whittling at sticks with a knife?'

'I dare say I do occasionally.'

Out of the corner of my eye I saw Delacombe make a sharp movement forward. 'Mr Beaumont.' He said. 'You know very well that your habit of whittling is so prominent as to be a source of friendly jokes in this camp.'

'I dare say, Sir.' Then to me: 'And what is the relevance of my whittling to the death of McCrory?'

'The path near where he was murdered was sprinkled with wood chips. I should remind you that McCrory was knifed to death.'

'I know that, Hobbes.' Beaumont looked at me as steadily as he could look at anyone with those strange eyes of his, which had always a fine vibration or wobble.

'Or at least,' I said 'he was knifed and left for dead.' I looked at Beaumont narrowly, but apart from the wavering in his eyes he did not flinch. 'He did not die for some time,' I added. 'Then an Indian found him. He said something to the Indian before he died. He said: 'That Devil George'.'

Beaumont's eyes froze and for a few moments he looked directly and unwavering at me. His pupils were very large, like black holes. Then he pushed back his chair and stood up.

'Sit down, Mr Beaumont,' Delacombe said.

Beaumont reached into his tunic pocket, as capacious as mine, and pulled out a revolver, at the same time raising his left arm horizontally. He set the barrel on his arm, pointing it at Delacombe and releasing the safety catch with a soft click. 'I shall be going now', he said in his usual level voice.

'You know it's a capital offense to draw your weapon on your commanding officer,' Delacombe said coolly.

'I reached for my own pocket, but Beaumont swung round and pointed the revolver at me. 'Put your hands on the table, Sergeant.' He said. I obeyed.

Beaumont sprang like a tiger in the direction of the door and was gone with a clatter of boots on the hall floor and the veranda.

I scrambled to my feet and kicked my chair back, hearing it fall on the floor as I ran round the end of the table – glimpsing Pemberton pulling his own pistol out from under his coat – and out of the room onto the veranda. The sun was dazzling. I too clattered down the steps, but had to pause to see where Beaumont had gone. There he was, running and bounding like a goat across the grass to the South edge of the camp. From behind my ear came a loud bang: Pemberton firing his pistol – useless at such a range. With a leap over some bushes, Beaumont vanished into a wall of forest.

I sprinted across the grass, pushed through the bushes Beaumont had leapt over, and plunged into the sudden cool darkness of the forest. There were firs and cedar, as around Mount Douglas, but interspersed with hardwood trees – alders and maples – and with a disconcerting amount of nettles in the undergrowth which I charged through like a bull with a tremendous crashing noise. I stopped abruptly and listened. There was a faint crashing in the woods over to my right, toward the sea. I headed in that direction, then stumbled onto a path which I ran along. It humped up and down around rocks and fallen trees, thick and decayed. I tried to listen as I ran, but it was no good. I stopped. I heard the faint sound of rocks grinding on rocks far ahead. I started running again, leapt over roots which crossed the path every few feet. The path descended into a gully and petered out as I charged down it, kicking rocks with a scraping sound, bounding across a broad stony steam bed, and splashing through a stretch of shallow water. I climbed the other side, finding the path again at the top and renewing my original pace, although by now my chest was hurting and my heart pounding. On and on the path went, through endless avenues of tree trunks, then it became a narrow channel between knee high bushes. Ahead, the forest looked more open. The path began to descend, crossing an area of swampy ground. Here and there planks had been thrown end to end and fixed in place by pegs. I leapt from plank to plank. The path rose again for another stretch through the forest. But now ahead there was more light through the trees, and after a hundred yards I came to the edge of the forest and a rail fence which I scrambled up and over.

I ran out into a big sloping field of tufted grass, dotted with oaks and outcroppings of rock from which arbutus were growing, with the sea only a hundred yards or so to my right over a bluff. To my left was a farmhouse with paddocks. A barking dog was standing on a knoll. On the other side of the field was another rail fence, and behind it a rocky slope on which the blue-uniformed figure of Beaumont was climbing at a run. He was about three hundred yards ahead – not more than a minute running flat out, I found myself calculating as he dashed across the field. But I would not be capable for long of running at this pace, although I was getting my second wind and the sheer pounding agony of the first few minutes had abated. I reached the other side of the field, thought of trying to vault the fence but scrambled over instead, then began to pick my way at a half run up the slope around boulders and tree trunks. I was nothing like as fast as Beaumont.

I was soaked with sweat by the time I reached the top of the hill, a crest of dry grass and rocks. There was Beaumont climbing like a fly up another steep slope on the other side of a valley which opened down to the sea. I staggered, catching my breath, and glanced behind me: two figures in blue were running across the field, just out of the forest. I waved frantically at them for a moment, then flung myself forward again.

Now I was running down hill, having to rear back now and then so as not to fall, stumbling over tussocks and tree roots. Rabbits bolted away in all directions. At the bottom of the hill a gulley contained a stream about a foot deep. I splashed through it and scrambled wearily up the facing hill, grasping at bushes and small tree trunks. At the top was a plateau, covered with long rough grass, rocks and patches of flowers. A pheasant with a long crimson tail watched me from a boulder. More rabbits dashed this way and that. There was no particular path, and Beaumont was lost to view, so I ran Southwards, parallel to the sea a hundred yards or so on my right below steep bluffs.

There was another dip, full of thickets of bushes and brambles, which I plunged into, cutting my hands as I flailed through. I came out onto a rising slope again and plodded warily up it, gasping for breath. At the top I doubled up for a moment, so exhausted I could almost have vomited on the grass. I straightened up and looked ahead. There was the open heath I had seen from the boat, golden-green, with dark bushes, stretching as a long ridge beside the sea on the right, with forest on the left. A long way ahead now, perhaps half a mile, the blue figure of Beaumont was moving fast, though not running, across the heath.

I glanced behind me but could see no one. I began running again, in a crouch, at a steady rhythm. There were a few rocks, and I ran over grass between and around bushes. Rabbits scattered in all directions and now and again I flushed a grouse which whirred up and away. The sun, straight ahead and high in the sky, beat down on my bare head. My mouth was parched and my eyes kept filming over with sweat pouring from my hair. I mopped my brow as I ran. Although Beaumont was stronger, my long legs helped me on this open terrain. This gave me hope of catching up. Beaumont slowed down at the top of a rise against the metallic blue sky. He crouched down in the grass. I kept running flat out. Then I saw a flash and a puff of smoke beside Beaumont and heard a gunshot. I kept running.

A crack to one side of me and another gunshot. Beaumont was shooting at me, I realized rather stupidly – now from about a hundred yards away, too far to have much chance of hitting me. But I slowed down and began dodging from bush to bush crouching as low as I could. As I tacked across my original direction I noticed two figures coming up from behind – Delacombe and another marine. I darted forward again.

Beaumont was about fifty yards in front of me, leaning forward with his back to me over a boulder in a clump of bushes, resting the barrel of his revolver on his left arm to fire ahead. He fired. Then I heard a crack in the air to one side, and another shot from behind me. At the same time I could see what Beaumont was firing at – a white building not more than a hundred yards in front, where some blue uniformed soldiers were scuttling around. I drew my own revolver from one pocket, and its ammunition clip from the other, stumbling as I slammed the clip in, and yelled 'Beaumont!' Beaumont fired again, but my shout had caused him to jerk. He steadied the barrel carefully for another shot. A shot cracked past me again from behind, and Beaumont swung round as I leapt on him and tried to grapple him to the ground. Panting harshly, we wrestled in a crouching position. I felt a bang on my head as Beaumont hit me with his revolver, and fell. But I managed to hook Beaumont with an arm and he came tumbling over on top of me. His gun went off with a terrific crash just beside my ear, then I saw his leg near my right hand, pressed the muzzle of my revolver against the calf, and fired. He screamed angrily and pushed me away with superhuman force. I rolled across the ground feeling a moment of terror that I would be shot. But suddenly there was an ear-splitting noise of bangs and thuds from up in front. I stopped rolling, lay on my stomach and lifted my head, but I could see only a bush, and to one side Beaumont lying clutching his leg with an expression of agony on his face.

The din was terrific. The Americans in front of us must be firing at random, but since the ground sloped down behind me and Beaumont, the bullets were all cracking overhead. Then I saw a long blue figure scuttling along the ground up to Beaumont, grappling briefly with him, then pulling away holding Beaumont's revolver. It was Delacombe. Leaving Beaumont, he wriggled across to me, and shouted 'Have you got a white handkerchief?'

'Yes.'

I dug for my handkerchief as Delacombe shouted, 'Damned Yankees!

Typical! Civil War tactics. Massive waste of ammunition. It's quite safe really! Unaimed!'

Delacombe took my handkerchief, shook it out, then to my surprise leapt to his feet, with the bullets still cracking all around, and waved the handkerchief. It took what seemed a long time, ten seconds at least, for the fire to slacken, and still a few bullets snapped by.

The firing stopped. My ears were ringing. There was a smell of gunpowder. Smoke drifted by in wisps. I decided to stand up, and did, although my legs were like jelly. I walked over to Beaumont who was sitting up holding his leg, biting his lip. His face looked yellow. Delacombe's companion, a Marine Sergeant, appeared at my elbow. 'I'll have it fixed up in no time, Sir', he said to Beaumont, and took a field dressing from his pouch. Beaumont rolled up his trouser leg, soaked with blood, a sick expression on his face. I turned to look around. Delacombe had stopped waving the handkerchief and was standing waiting for a group of Americans who were ambling across the grass, revolvers and carbines dangling in their hands. They were dressed in a similar blue to the Marines, but with brown leather belts and cloth caps. Their uniforms were crumpled and untidy. The front man, evidently an officer from his gold braided epaulettes, had a thick black beard, a hooked nose, and big brown eyes.

'Ep!' Delacombe called out.

'Del!' Said the officer. 'What the hell's this?'

'No one hurt I hope?'

'Naw. But what *is* this?'

The two men shook hands. 'Just old Beaumont here, out potting rabbits.' Delacombe said. 'Got too enthusiastic. Potted himself in the leg.'

'Oh yeah? And who's *this*? Doesn't look like one of yours.'

'Friend of mine. Sergeant Hobbes, Victoria police. Over for lunch. Hobbes, this is Lieutenant Epstein.'

'Good day,' Epstein said. We shook hands. 'You potting rabbits too?'

'Oh yes. Never saw so many in my life.'

'We thought you were 'potting' *us*. In fact I'd swear a bullet or two came our way.'

'I'm terribly sorry,' Delacombe said. 'If the truth be told, Ep, I'm afraid our friend Beaumont got a little "corked" at lunch. We all got somewhat carried away, I'm afraid. But goodness, your chaps know how to raise a storm. I thought we'd run into the Battle of Gettysburg.'

'American firepower,' Epstein said, and winked. He turned to look at Beaumont, and stepped over to him, crouching down to examine the leg. 'Point blank range,' he said. 'You fall on your revolver, George?'

Beaumont did not reply. He sat looking glumly down at the leg where the blood was already seeping through the field dressing.

'Bone broken?' Delacombe was asking the Sergeant.

'We can lend you a stretcher', Epstein said, 'and a wagon to get him back to your camp.'

'Very handsome of you,' said Delacombe. 'The stretcher would be very handy. No need for the wagon. I have a detachment coming along the main road. They can carry him.'

'They're not potting rabbits too?' said Epstein, raising his eyebrows exaggeratedly.

'Heavens no. On patrol. Sergeant!'

'Sah!' The sergeant saluted.

'Go and find the detachment and get two men to come and take the stretcher.'

The Sergeant stepped off briskly.

Epstein turned and issued his orders: 'Schwartz, Watson, go get a stretcher for this officer.'

The men saluted with their palms facing down, and ambled off across the field.

'An army of free born Americans,' said Epstein.

'Fine-looking chaps,' Delacombe said soothingly.

'You look as if you've run all the way down the island,' Epstein said, looking at my filthy torn trousers.

'I was chasing a rabbit through some bushes. Not worth it really.'

'This war started up over a pig,' said Epstein. 'I'm sure glad it didn't start up again over a rabbit. Tell me the whole story some time, Del.'

'When I know it all, I shall, Ep. I appreciate your forbearance.'

'Not at all. Let's get together soon. I believe Mr Eliot in Friday Harbour is going to invite us both to a luncheon party Sunday week.'

'Oh good. Then we'll be able to have a chat.'

The two men saluted each other. 'So long, then,' Epstein said with a wry smile at us all. Then he headed back across the grass, his soldiers ambling behind, to the white house where the stars and stripes flew listlessly from the rooftop under the beating sun.

28

The road back to English Camp, farther inland than the way I had come, went dead straight through the forest and past occasional patches of cleared land with farmhouses exactly like those around Victoria. It was mainly in the shade, so the walk was less tiring than I had feared. I felt physically buoyant, although mentally oppressed at the prospect of interrogating Beaumont again, and at having shot him and probably broken his leg.

Pemberton had come along the road with the Marine detachment, and he and Delacombe and I walked back side by side. Once Pemberton had been told what had happened there was little to say. 'Decent chap, Epstein.' Delacombe remarked. But he looked cross and grim. Beaumont followed in a stretcher carried by shifts of Marines. He and Delacombe did not look at each other.

At the camp Beaumont was brought to the blockhouse. His leg would be bandaged and splinted by a 'surgeon' – a Corporal who specialised in First Aid. After a drink of ale on Delacombe's verandah, during which little more was said, the three of us walked across the grass to the blockhouse. It was late afternoon, and it had been decided that Pemberton and I would stay overnight.

Beaumont was in a bed in the third floor dormitory of the blockhouse. A small table had been brought in, and a marine secretary, a Corporal, would take notes. The four of us sat around the table on plain wooden chairs, leaving one side open facing Beaumont's bed. He was half sitting up, propped by a bolster and pillows. His face looked grey in the diffuse but bright light which entered from the embrasures and was reflected from the whitewashed walls.

Delacombe opened the proceedings by warning Beaumont that he should take heed of the fact whatever he said might be used as evidence in any of three possible charges against him: that he was guilty of a civil murder; that he had drawn a weapon on his commanding officer; and that he had fired against an opposing army during a state of truce.

'I admit to all three,' Beaumont said in his strange mechanical voice. 'I killed McCrory. I drew my revolver on you, Sir. I shot at the Americans.'

'Then we shall have to hear your account of these events,' Delacombe said coolly.

'Sir, with respect, I decline to explain why I killed McCrory. It's a sordid little story which I find utterly undignified. If you pass me a piece of paper, I shall write on it that I killed him, using the Bowie knife which you can find in my quarters, in revenge for a personal insult. But that's all I shall ever say for the record. I believe it's all that is necessary for the civil authorities to clear up their case. Not for the record, but for personal reasons, I should appreciate it if I could have a private interview with Mr Hobbes, to whom I shall tell my motives for the crime – to satisfy his curiosity, and to relieve myself of a certain burden. But, to repeat, all I am prepared to do for the record is write a simple confession of the fact. To do more would be humiliating. And I can't stand humiliation.'

'Would that be acceptable to you, Commissioner? Delacombe asked Pemberton.

'It's in your hands, Captain. You're the authority in this case. Certainly a signed confession will be enough for me to clear up the civil case at once.'

'With regard to the murder, Mr Beaumont, I find your proposal acceptable,' said Delacombe. 'It would also make procedures simple if you acknowledge in writing that you drew your revolver on me. But I must have your explanation of why you fired on the Americans.'

'I did so in order to provoke a renewal of hostilities. I hate the Yankees,' Beaumont said drily, 'and I should like to see the rotters removed at once from this island by force of British arms. That's all.'

'You can write that down too. You know that all three of these crimes are capital offenses.'

'I am aware of that, Sir.'

Delacombe asked the secretary to give Beaumont pen and paper. We all sat very still as Beaumont scratched out three statements on separate sheets.

When he had finished, the secretary took the sheets to Delacombe, who read them. Then he and Pemberton witnessed them, signing them as in the presence of the secretary and me, and we also signed.

Delacombe stood up, and the others did the same. For a moment, I thought Delacombe might say something to Beaumont, or even shake his hand. Instead he turned away, his face grave. 'I suggest you stay and have your talk now,' he said to me, 'then join us at the house for dinner.'

Everyone left the room except me. I put my notebook and pencil in my pocket, and pulled my chair over to the bed. Beaumont and I looked at each other.

'I hold no grudge against you, Hobbes,' said Beaumont calmly. 'You were merely performing your duty, as I should have in your place. I can see you deduced I was the culprit by a process of elimination. There could have been no evidence that I was on Vancouver Island that day. I'm sure nobody saw me – apart from McCrory. "That Devil George" he said, did he?' Beaumont paused for reflection. '*I* should say *he* was the devil. "Shouldst thou see the devil, cast him out!" A favourite quotation of my mother's. She's a very religious woman. I'm afraid her heart will be broken by all this. But no. I don't believe it will. Nothing will break her heart. She will stay alive for ever.'

Beaumont paused for thought, his wavering eyes gone still. Then they began wavering again as he looked at me. 'Now I shall tell you my story. Please repeat it to no one. Not even Aemilia whom I suppose you will marry some day.'

'I don't think so.'

'No? Too bad. But I shall tell you because I know you put a lot of thought into the crime – I mean solving it. And of course a short statement on paper is not a satisfactory confession. I believe in confession, don't you? Such a shame our church has abolished it. I'm not really a bad man, Hobbes. I do my duty. Always have. But I have not been happy. I joined the Marines because my father was a naval man. I should have joined the cavalry. The Marines were a compromise. Never compromise, Hobbes. It's bad for the soul. Of course the Marines did a superb job at Sebastopol, and their reputation was high when I joined. But since that they have not seen much action. Cavalry have, of course – in India. Most of my career has been spent at sea, actually. I become sea sick easily – unless I am in control of the boat. That's why I like sailing and rowing. The last two years I've been here, and it has been very agreeable. But I couldn't have asked for a worse commander than Delacombe. He gives a man too much leeway. It may be good for some chaps. But not for me. I have to be kept busy all day long. Otherwise I brood. I become melancholy. And since I don't like drink much – it can make me ill – I can't soothe myself that way. Delacombe is of course an excellent soldier. No criticisms there. Brave man. Proved himself in the Crimea. But he's what the Yankees call "easy going". Like this whole island. It's a sort of little terrestrial Paradise, for one thing. Where a bloodless war was started over a pig! There's nothing much to do except visit among the English settlers and the better sort of Americans. And of course supply and provision the camps, do manoeuvres, and so on. It is, mind you, a jolly well run camp.

'At any rate, I developed the habit of going across to Victoria. A Herculean trip from here, but it would spend my energy. I've always been possessed with a restless energy for women. I don't know if you understand that, Hobbes. You seem somewhat of a Laodicean to me – lukewarm, like Aemilia. I like to be with women who have a bit of spice to them – and are vicious, even. I become very excited with prostitutes. Of course many men who have spent time at sea become used to them. But I have always had a difficulty with them, Hobbes. And this is the sort of thing I should find humiliating to make a public statement about. In a word, my virile member lets me down. Or, from their point of view, lets them down. I cannot penetrate a woman.

'I've given much thought to why. At first I assumed it was an organic lack of some kind. But some of the women themselves averted me that it was not. They would ask me if I was upset, or frightened of them. They would make jokes like: "It's not going to bite you". I would become very angry. Not that I would show it. The bitches.

'I'd never been in love. But when I met the Somerville girls, as St Mark's church, I believe I fell in love with all of them! At least I thought they were wonderful. They all have an ethereal quality, don't you think?'

'I know what you mean.'

'You see when you're deeply excited by a fricatrice – a woman of spice, so to say – but the final pleasure, the consummation, is denied to you, you become very angry with women. Not that I ever hurt one. But I sometimes thought I might. A very distressing feeling. Not that they are ladies, the fricatrices. On the other hand I have never been drawn to them if they were not lady*like*. I never wanted to, as they say in Victoria, "hump squaws". Forgive my language, Hobbes, I can see it disturbs you. But we're both men, after all.

'At any rate, I fancied myself in love with each Somerville girl in turn.

And it was very diverting. Last summer I was as near to being happy as ever in my life. The mother is common, of course, and some of her little mannerisms have rubbed off on the daughters. But the father must certainly have been a gentleman. They all have a streak of refinement. God, I loved those Sunday afternoons!'

For the first time, I saw signs of emotion in Beaumont: his face was briefly animated by an expression of grief and longing, then it became wooden again.

'Then that beast McCrory appeared on the scene. Every Sunday. Showing off to the girls. Always trying to make them giggle. *Not* a gentleman, I assure you. But he seemed to take an intense interest in me. He told me, very seriously, man to man, as we walked down the road one evening, that he wanted to be my friend. Well, dash it, Hobbes. It's not the sort of thing one chap says to another. Sort of thing girls say. But I have such restless energy that when he proposed we meet in town the following Saturday night, I accepted.

'When we did meet we went to a few taverns for drinks – although I don't drink more than a glass of ale, and he drank very little. And he became very intimate in his way of speaking to me, asking me about my home, my mother, my childhood, my aspirations. I must admit it was new to me to have a man ask me such things. It's the sort of thing a woman might do to pass the time in bed when the other thing had not worked. But I felt flattered, I suppose. We ended up going to the Windsor Rooms – which of course I knew already – but where he was doing what he insisted on calling "field work". This consisted, I believe, in his asking the girls all sorts of indecent questions. He didn't do this at the same table as me, of course. But we enjoyed ourselves, dancing with the girls, and so forth. Then he asked me if I was going to have a girl for the night. I opened up to him and said I didn't want to, because it would lead to the same old failure. At this, he whisked me out of the Windsor Rooms, and back to his house for what he called 'a good talk'. He had a way of worming information out of a man. As I say, I realize I have needed confession in my life. I have always been too shy to confess my thoughts to friends. Besides, among Englishmen, it just isn't done, is it? My father was very remote, and usually away at sea, so we hardly ever talked. With my mother the talk was mainly about scripture. So I'm afraid the dam burst, so to say, with McCrory, and all of my thoughts came out in a flood. The man was a swine, at bottom, but awfully good at listening.

'So when I would come into Victoria every week or so, I would go out with McCrory on his "field work", and stay the night in his spare bedroom. Then the next morning he would do private treatments with me. Animal magnetism, universal fluid, and so forth. This had what he called "paradoxical results" in me. I would become filled with the most unpleasant sensations – creepy crawly feelings, tingling, and pains in my muscles. At the same time I would get into a funk and break out into a stinking sweat. This interested McCrory very much. He said it smelt of sulphur and brimstone. I say! Can you imagine: sulphur and brimstone. As if I were Old Nick himself! I suppose that's why he called me a "devil".'

Beaumont paused as if in awe at this, his mouth hanging slightly open. Then it resumed its usual rictus, and he began talking again in his thin, flat tone.

'He saw I didn't like his saying this, so he explained that I was suffering from "stagnant humours". The universal fluid had become too still, as if in a swamp, so to say, and although it would be the devil's own job to get it flowing again, he and I should "work on it together", and eventually I should get better.

'But I was not exactly his patient. He said, in his rather over-candid way, that he preferred to have me as a friend. He did, however, accept some financial contributions from me, to buy medical supplies and equipment. A new phrenological head, for instance, which he sent for from San Francisco.

'I shall list to you some of the treatments. They were mostly suggestions of things I could do on my own or with a fricatrice. They are too embarrassing to explore in detail. One was onanism into a lambskin sheath. The idea was that this imitated the woman's sheath, and that I should become habituated to the sensations of confinement of the member, and so forth.

'Another was that I extend the breathing down into my abdomen. He said my diaphragm did not move adequately. But this "breathing down" as he put it, made me dizzy.

'Another was that I should always lie with a fricatrice from behind. The girls themselves call this 'spooning'. The idea was that this would make me less shy than I might be face to face, and more "comfortable at being an animal". I objected to being thought an animal, of course, but he soothed me by pointing out that "animal" meant "animated" by spirit. I should let my spirit move my body. Here the breathing usually came in too, since he pointed out that "spirit" meant "breath". He would come out with such etymologies as if they were magic, forgetting, I suppose, that every Englishman of breeding has had years of Latin and Greek at school.

'I am avoiding the question of spooning in this digression. It was actually a promising suggestion, though I'm not sure if this was for the reasons he suggested. I achieved a sort of onanism, once or twice, with a girl. An improvement – in retrospect. I could not see it at the time. I was becoming ruled by my difficulty, and obsessed with it. All the attention McCrory brought to it, so much a relief at first, made it more important – fanned the flames.

'Then McCrory made a new suggestion. Playfully. He had adopted a manner with me which I would normally permit no one, a sort of bantering. He suggested that perhaps what I really wanted was to sleep with a boy. To behave like a Greek. On other words, that I was a pathic. In favour of this idea he instanced the comparative success of the "spooning". Ridiculous! I said at first. After all, there are some rather notable differences between a woman, even a girl, and a boy. The girls from the Windsor Rooms, at any rate, are rather voluptuous. Anything less like a boy I cannot imagine, even when embracing them from behind. Besides, as I assured McCrory, and I'm afraid most Englishmen of breeding might, I had occasionally shared a bed with another boy at school and indulged in the sort of practices which are not at all uncommon. Even then, at school, I had never *desired* a boy, in the sense – all too painfully – I now desire a woman.

'He jumped on this! He was most interested. Said it was fascinating that I had no *fear* of boys, as I had of women. I said, why would I ever fear boys? I had been one myself, after all. But I thought I feared women – by then he had convinced me I feared women – precisely because I desired them so much yet at the same time felt, as I supposed, somewhat awkward about defiling them. I am merely guessing: for me these things are unbearably complicated. But McCrory then said that there are things about ourselves that we do not wish to know, and that we put them into recesses of our mind and forget them, but they are still there as part of us. It is just like putting an object we don't like in a disused room of a house or in the cellar, and pretending to forget it. We know it's still in our house, but we pretend it is not.

'I said I found that a rather fanciful idea, and at any rate logically impossible to prove.

'He said, "It's a great idea and it came from an Englishman, Francis Galton. It means that in each person there are things put aside and buried, whose existence is denied. You, George, have put away your desire for boys but it's there all the same."'

'"Rubbish!", I said, and reiterated that I most decidedly preferred women to boys, even though they made me nervous. But he wasn't listening. Then in his usual way of jumping from one simple idea to another, he said suddenly: "A berdache! What you need is a berdache!" And he explained to me something unutterably vile: he said that in certain Indian tribes, boys who were pathics were allowed to dress and behave as women, even to the extent of becoming the concubine of a man!

'Now, at that time, which was not more than five or six weeks ago, McCrory had Indians on the brain. The Tsimshian had arrived and set up camp at Cormorant Point. McCrory was full of the idea of going to see them and buy medicines from them and learn "ancient methods of healing" as he put it. Oh yes, I forgot to mention, he had given me several very expensive medicines – which of course I paid for – for my "condition" as it was coming to be known. Powdered rhinocerous horn, reindeer horns, bull's testicles, concentrated oysters – all obtained through his Celestial servant, Lee. None of it did the least good. He said he felt sure the Indians would know the kind of herbs and medicines which would be found in the woods here, and given *fresh* – which would make all the difference.

'At the same time he was egged on to visit the Indians by Aemilia, who seemed very curious about them. So he went and saw them. He reported that they were going to find him the appropriate herbs. He said they were very open about such matters, not hypocritical the way we whites are. He was very taken with them. He had not asked about the "berdache" yet, because the camp was mainly full of women and what looked like warriors. But he would.

'There was another matter.' Beaumont paused. 'A different matter. Once McCrory had got to know me fairly well, he began to ask questions about our camp here, our dispositions, our arms, and so on. Of course I told him.

There are no secrets in such matters. Then he would ask about our plans if an arbitrator ruled against the British claim. Would we stay on San Juan? Would we fight? Now, I ask you! Ridiculous! These Yankees of course have no principles, so they assume *we* don't. I assured him that if an arbitrator ruled against us, which was highly likely in view of the envy other powers have of Great Britain, then of course we would pack our bags and leave.

'He could not believe this. "Albion perfide!" and all that – not that he was educated enough to know the phrase, but he had the idea. We almost quarrelled about it. Then after that, from time to time, he would say, "What would you think if it turned out I'm an American agent, sent to this Colony to spy on the English?"'

'I said so far as I could see there were already at least 3,000 American spies in Victoria, and the English had long since given up trying to hide anything from them. Besides which, there was nothing to hide. Even on the island here, Delacombe and Epstein know each other's every intention. It's a way of avoiding accidents. But McCrory would still tease me about it, and it began to rankle somewhat.

'My account is almost at an end, Hobbes. On that dreadful day, McCrory arranged to meet me near Cormorant Point, after he would have visited the Indian Camp, at one o'clock. There is a small bay just West of Telegraph Cove where I sometimes tie up if I come over alone, and from there a path leads to the main road and then to Margaret Bay or Cormorant Point. We arranged to meet just below where the path met the road. The idea was that McCrory would be able to give me a batch of fresh herbs for my "condition", which I would take for the next few days. Then on the Saturday evening I should try their effects on Grace at the Windsor Rooms, with whom McCrory had already, as he put it "discussed the case." All very humiliating. Then he would ask the Tsimshian about this famous "berdache" idea of his, which I must say did not appeal to me.

'I arrived at the place quite early. Not wanting to be seen talking to McCrory up on the main road, I waited a hundred yards or so down the path, near the stream, knowing he would look for me there. I remember I paced up and down, whistling through my teeth, and whittling on a stick. It's a habit I have, being so restless, I know people laugh at it, but I can't help it. I've wondered since what I was thinking about. The real answer is: nothing. I just waited. He was late. I waited. Then he arrived, coming rather cheerfully down the path, carrying a basket like a woman going to market.

'"Well, how's my spy today?" he said. Then seeing that didn't go down well he said "I mean, I've been doing some spying on the Indians, just as you spy for me on San Juan." I said "I say, old chap", or some such meaningless thing. Then he sat down on a rock, and tapped on his basket. "Just the stuff for you in here," he said. "Mind you I'm afraid I have to disappoint you about the *berdache*. Poor old George. These particular Indians don't have 'em."

'Meanwhile I was going on whittling my stick, you might say mechanically.

'"What you want", he said, "is to get it up as straight as that stick. But whittling at yourself all day long won't help you with a woman. You know what? Just now I was collecting these herbs in the forest with the prettiest squaw you ever might see. I said, does this herb make a man grow big? – talking fluent Chinook, of course. She blushed like a white girl but she said yes, it made a man big. What about this, I said. Is an Indian's thing as big as this? You know what I did, George? I pulled out my organ and showed it to her! And her eyes went wide as little saucers, then she turned away. So I repeated my question: is an Indian's thing as big as this? You know what the little trollop did? She turned and looked very carefully and said in Chinook, "siwash elip hyas, elip toketie". Which means "The Indian is more big and more pretty!" Then she ran off, back to her camp. But I could see from her eyes that what she had said was a lie. "The point is, George, *old boy*" – he used to mock my way of speaking, at times – "if you take these herbs your organ will end up even more big and more pretty than *this*!" Whereupon he jumped up from where he had been sitting, unbuttoned, and pulled out his organ – in a state of erection, although in fact I suspect the squaw had been telling the truth because it was not very impressive, being rather thin and curved. "Touch it, George," he said, "It's excited at the mere thought of a pretty girl like that squaw. *This* is animal magnetism!"

'So I threw my stick far off into the bushes, took one step forward, raised my knife, and drove it straight into his rotten, grinning face. He dodged his head out of the way and I hit him just below the neck, and pushed down hard. Then I tried to pull it out but it seemed to have got stuck against the collarbone. For a moment he struggled – spitted, so to say, on the knife. Then it came up and out. Be he didn't fall. He stood there, staggering, looking at me with a sort of dopey expression. So I changed the position of the handle in my hand and plunged it straight for his rotten heart from under the ribs. But I must have missed it, for now he started squealing like a pig but still would not fall down. I pulled out the knife and pushed him with the other hand. He stumbled and fell over a boulder in the stream. I went over and looked down at him.

'I was calculating how best to finish the job. My only thought was "good riddance". Then I realized it would be an easy thing to cut him up so it would look as if an Indian had done it – perhaps the medicine man he had been visiting. I knew medicine men sometimes tried to eat people alive by tearing at them with their teeth. What fun it would be, I thought, to leave this reptile cut up and bitten so that whoever found him should be sick! He was writhing and moaning but seemed incapable of moving off the boulder. So I put my knife handle between my teeth, like a savage. Then I reached down and tore his coat off and his waistcoat and shirt and flung them away. I pulled his trousers down to his boots. I took the knife in my hand again and slashed him across the belly a few times. Then I knelt down in the stream and seized him by the shoulders and bit him in the arm. That made him scream in a gurgling kind of way. I picked up my knife which I'd let fall in the water, and I looked at him in the eyes which were sort of dreamy. Then I surveyed my handiwork, as it were, the gashes on his body. His member, damn the thing, was stiff as if he were still thinking of that foul squaw. I looked back to his eyes, still dreamy as if he were going away. "Look at this!" I yelled. Surprised myself, really. I reached down and grabbed his organ in one hand and chopped it off with the knife. I held it up in front of his eyes. Then I stuffed it in his mouth. Like a gargoyle. But by this time I assumed he was dead. What a shame, I thought. He probably didn't feel that last bit at all.

'To complete the Indian impression and, I must say partly out of curiosity, I then attempted to scalp him. I held that horrid red hair of his in one hand and hacked around the edges against the skull. I could feel the scalp come loose a little but it would have taken an almighty tug or a lot more work with the knife to get it off. Besides, he already looked like the devil himself and I didn't want to disturb the picture. So I gave up. Then I went away.

'I don't know how he could have stayed alive though. Do you mean, the

Indian came and found him and he *spoke*?'

'Apparently,' I said. 'Pulled the – thing – out of his mouth, and spoke. Then died.'

'I'm sorry I didn't do a better job. Usually when you see an animal's eyes go like that – a rabbit's for example – it's finished.'

Beaumont was apparently unmoved by any of this. 'All over for me anyway.' He went on. 'You see I knew – perhaps that was what was on my mind as I stood waiting for him, whittling the stick, although it was not in the form of words – I knew that all this rubbish would never work for me. McCrory either thought, or pretended to think, that he could change people. It's not possible of course. That's why we have to fight wars. He was "helping me" for a bit of money and to convince himself that he was a very important man – a "great healer", or an intriguer or spy. But he was really a very miserable wretch. It was like a fairy tale he was making up as he went along. Like my loving the Somerville girls. First Aemilia; then when she wouldn't have me, Cordelia; then when she wouldn't have me, Letitia. It would have been the same with Letitia. I didn't *want* them to have me. What would I have done with Letitia? She didn't even attract me in that way. I should have continued, even after marriage, to visit the Windsor Rwatooms or similar haunts. But I was tired of that. I think it has been all over for me for a long time.'

Beaumont's voice had grown so dry it was like that of a ghost. I got up and stood looking down at him. 'Thank you.' I held out my hand and Beaumont shook it firmly. 'Good luck.' I turned to go.

Beaumont called after me: 'Just one thing, Hobbes. Give my love to the Somerville girls, all three of them, will you?'

'Of course.'

The room door was locked from the outside, but I knocked on it and a guard standing there with a pistol in his belt let me out.

Dinner at Captain Delacombe's was excellent, at a long table with silver candlesticks, cut glass decanter, and plates with the Marines' crest and blue and gold rims. There were several bottles of first class claret. The main dish was a rack of lamb with tiny new potatoes, and currant jelly. Pemberton and I both had good appetites, but Delacombe picked at his meat in a state of gloom which gradually infected us so that by the time the Port was circulating with the inevitable Stilton, we sipped and nibbled in morose silence.

Delacombe seemed to be waiting for something. He had asked the servant to fling the window open and let some air in. It was pitch dark outside except for a dim glow from the barracks. There was a distant echoing thud. Delacombe raised his head mournfully. 'Poor George,' he said.

Pemberton said tentatively, 'You mean you…'

'They were all capital offences. The inevitable result would have been a firing squad, here at English Camp. Awful for morale. I sent him his clothes, with a pistol and one round in the coat jacket. Not strictly speaking wrong on my part, since I was waiting for his leg to get a little better before officially charging him.'

Delacombe waited silently. There was the sound of footsteps outside, then a knock at the door. One of the servants came in. 'Sorry to bother you, Sir. Lieutenant Liddell must speak with you.'

'Show him in then.'

This was the other Lieutenant, whom Delacombe had preferred not to have at dinner, and had detailed to the blockhouse. A small man, he marched in and saluted. 'I'm afraid Mr Beaumont has shot himself through the head, Sir. He's dead.'

'Good old George,' Delacombe said. 'I knew he'd come through all right in the end.'

29

I parted from Pemberton at Cadborough Bay late the following morning, and rode over to Orchard Farm. I wanted Aemilia to know Wiladzap would be released that afternoon. She came out onto the porch as I was hitching my horse to the rail. She was wearing a simple grey dress. She waited with perfect poise as I climbed the steps, her face showing no emotion.

'George Beaumont sent his love to you all,' I said. 'He's dead. Shot himself. But he wrote a confession to the murder. The Commissioner will be able to release Wiladzap this afternoon. I thought I should let you know.'

'How horrible about George! But...' She smiled. 'Thank you Chad. The rest is good news. I don't know what Wiladzap will want to do, but I shall find out. Do you know?' – She looked grandly around her – 'I am mistress of this farm for a while. The Joneses are still here of course, and little William. But Mamma and the girls are gone.'

'Where to?'

'They're in town for now, but this evening they all leave for San Francisco on a long holiday – with Mr Quattrini. Mamma and he were married yesterday afternoon, in the Catholic church, very quietly.'

I was not greatly surprised: sudden marriages were common in Victoria, and the law required no advance publication of banns. Nevertheless I said 'My goodness!'

'Yes. A surprise! But not really. My mother, you see, was almost exploding with panic that something awful would come to light about her and McCrory, especially if Wiladzap were released and George was charged with the murder: I told her you and Mr Pemberton had gone to San Juan to question him. I had to. I hope that was all right.'

'As it turns out, yes.' I realised that Aemilia must have used all the knowledge she had in some kind of decisive emotional battle with her overpowering mother, and I did not begrudge it to her.

'It was perhaps a *little* immoral of her,' Aemilia said. 'I think she thought, 'it's now or never'. Mr Quattrini is such a very moralistic man. I think she told herself that if he found out any bad things about her after the marriage had been consummated, there would be some way of persuading him everything was all right. So now I assume it has been consummated, and no one will find out anything now, so all is well. I guessed it would be – from the look in your eye yesterday morning. And now you look unscathed.'

'Physically yes. Though I feel as if I've aged.'

'That has been a continuous process since I first saw you: a year a week, I should say.' Aemilia was clearly in a happy mood from which nothing could dissuade her. 'Anyway, I persuaded Mamma I should *not* go to San Francisco, since I must take care of the farm. In fact the Joneses can do that, if necessary. It's all a polite fiction between Mamma and me, to avoid having to discus the *possibility* that I and little William might leave with Wiladzap. It is of course *only* a possibility. So I'm a free woman. I shall make up my own mind for the first time in my life.'

'Good. But I don't envy you the task. I dare say I can make up my own mind about Lukswaas, hoping that her mind accords with mine, but all I see ahead is difficulty and struggle.'

'That's life, Chad, and it's shorter than you think.' Aemilia's brow clouded.

'I suggest you come to the jail for three o'clock. We should have released Wiladzap by then.'

'Good. Only don't tell him. We shall do our own talking. I'm very frightened, but underneath I know it will be all right.'

We gave each other a peck on the cheek, like brother and sister.

As I rode down from Spring Ridge to the Pemberton's house on Fort Street my nerve began to fail me. I was even, after all that had happened between me and Lukswaas, as frightened of her as Aemilia was of Wiladzap. And as Lukswaas was of me, no doubt. Did Wiladzap fear Aemilia too? How strange, that combination of love and fear. I could almost understand how poor Beaumont's body, stiff with fright instead of soft with pleasure, had failed him where his desires and affections were most aroused, in a woman's arms.

The servant who answered the door directed me around the house: 'The Commissioner and Mrs Pemberton are out the back.' I walked along a narrow gravel path to an extensive garden, with roses on trellises, in full bloom, and beds of carnations and pansies around a croquet lawn. A striped awning had been slung on poles from the back of the house over a paved terrace. Here in wicker chairs in front of small tables were sitting Pemberton and Mrs Pemberton and Lukswaas. As soon as she saw me,

Lukswaas made a movement as if to get up, but Mrs Pemberton made a gesture that she should remain seated and said very distinctly, 'No need to rise, my dear, you wait for him.'

Lukswaas sank back into her chair but her whole body was taut, her cheeks flushed and eyes bright. She was wearing a white muslin hooped dress with red ribbons, and a broad brimmed straw hat.

Very much aware of the Pembertons, but stubborn with pride in my relation to Lukswaas, I took her hand and at the same time bent down and kissed her on the cheek. She smelled not of herself but of a light flowery scent.

I reassured her in Chinook that Wiladzap would be released that afternoon. Aemilia would come to the jail and meet them.

Lukswaas said she had been told Wiladzap would be free. Her heart was happy for Aemilia.

I turned to Mrs Pemberton. 'Thank you very much for looking after Lukswaas.'

'No trouble at all, Mr Hobbes. I declare she is the most intelligent girl I've ever met. And not just in an imitative way either: she works things out for herself. I was very pleased to have her as my guest. I've given her some clothes which of course she can keep. But what will you do with her now?' Mrs Pemberton looked at me with an expression of sharp inquiry. 'Must she go back to her own people?'

'She and I will have to discuss that. We have not had enough time. There's a sort of understanding between us which... Let me speak frankly, Mrs Pemberton: I am absolutely devoted to her, I want to marry her, yet I'm appalled by the implications for her of such a step.'

'And for you, my boy'. Pemberton interrupted.

'People can be so very cruel,' Mrs Pemberton cut in. 'I fear for you both.'

'Yes!', said Pemberton. 'I remember the filthy slanders Governor Douglas had to endure about his wife being half Indian and possibly – so it was whispered – "illegitimate". As if these pioneer marriages needed benefit of law! No more than do the common law marriages of Scotland even to this day. Douglas and his wife have endured it all, and their daughters have married well. But the tendency in this Colony is toward increasing harshness. Even Governor Douglas did not have to deal with such as Amor de Cosmos and our American residents. The Americans cannot, as we

British do, consider themselves and the Indians as common subjects to the Queen, God bless her!' Pemberton paused, perhaps in a rush of sentiment, then resumed vigorously. 'I hope the Canadians, who are also subjects of the Queen, will do better than the Americans – but not if Amor de Cosmos is an example! Consider Mr Begbie: some years ago he could count on some good feeling toward the Indians, but more and more, every effort he makes on their behalf – to have them recognized as landholders and eventually as citizens – is spurned. You'd be better off even in India where an Englishman can marry a Hindu girl and though it might not be a perfect match, at least their children are accepted. Here your children would be damned. You could keep a squaw in a shack by the Upper Harbour and no-one would blink an eye. But marry one! I would try and ensure that you could stay with the police, but I would fail! Better for both of you to go back to England, even, if you marry.'

'As you must, my dear,' Mrs Pemberton said. 'I feel it in my heart.'

'You were always a romantic,' Pemberton said to his wife with a tight-lipped smile. Then to me: 'I know you're a man of principle. If you wish me to marry you both, I'll do it at the drop of a hat. You can always have a church marriage at a later date.'

'Thank you.'

'I hear Mrs Somverville has gone and married Mr Quattrini,' said Mrs Pemberton, as if trying to lighten the sense of doom which hung in the air since Pemberton's tirade, and which Lukswaas, ignored, had obviously caught: she sat like a rock, looking at the rug.

'Oh dear,' said Pemberton with a rueful expression, no doubt thinking of poor Kathy Donnelly. Then briskly, 'Have you eaten, Chad?'

Sandwiches and iced tea – an American habit – were called for. I ate, and talked with the Pembertons. The subject of marriage was put aside and a certain calm could re-establish itself. Lukswaas sat quietly listening and I agonized for her. She must feel like a wild bird caught in a cage. I didn't want that fate for her.

Eventually it was time to go to the courthouse. Pemberton, out of magnanimity or resignation, invited me and Lukswaas to walk down with him.

Lukswaas shook hands with Mrs Pemberton and said in clear English, 'Thank you.'

'Bless you, child,' said Mrs Pemberton.

I walked with Lukswaas on my arm, and Pemberton on her other side. People on the path beside Fort Street and then on the board-walks moved aside to let us pass, but with unfriendly expressions.

At the courthouse, Pemberton signed the papers for Wiladzap's release, in Superintendent Parry's office off the vestibule where Lukswaas and I waited side by side, not touching. Pemberton had given me a week's leave. I explained quietly to Lukswaas in Chinook that I would not have to come to the courthouse for seven days. She nodded. She seemed to accept everything as it came and took it for granted that we would be together. But she caught me looking worried. Without a word, she tapped the signet ring I had put on her left hand, and made as if to take it off. I stopped her and took her hand.

Then the outer door opened and Aemilia came in. She was wearing a gingham dress, checked blue and white, and a straw hat under which her hair was bunched up. In her ears she had silver earrings, obviously Tsimshian, and on both arms just below the frilly cuffs of her sleeves she wore wide silver bracelets engraved with dense and complex designs.

Lukswaas exclaimed with pleasure in her own language and she and Aemilia hugged each other. They spoke in Tsimshian, which Aemilia pronounced slowly but with clicks and glottal stops.

Pemberton came out into the vestibule with Parry and greeted Aemilia, whom he knew. I introduced Lukswaas to Parry, who had not recognized her. Parry inclined his head, but looked embarrassed, and focussed his attention on me. 'You've done a good job. But my God what a mess it has all been! For myself I'll be thankful when the Indians have left Cormorant Point and made their way North again, though I do regret that the Tyee had to cool his heels in jail for over three weeks. But then it turns out that he speaks English! He could surely have saved his bacon before now.'

'Very complicated matters,' I said.

'Hobbes, I believe you should release the prisoner,' Pemberton interrupted. 'Miss Somerville tells me she has invited him, and you and his sister, to her house for a period of rest, which I'm sure he'll need.'

'Thank you, Sir,' I said dutifully. Parry accompanied me to the jailer's office were Seeds, looking a reformed character in a well ironed uniform, gave me the keys obsequiously.

I walked down the corridor, ignoring the other prisoners, to Wiladzap's cell. Wiladzap was waiting, standing squarely in the middle of the floor, his arms folded across his chest. He let them down when he saw me. 'Hops', he said simply, and smiled.

I turned the key in the lock and opened the door. I reached out my hand, and Wiladzap shook it with a firm grip, holding onto it for a moment as if to feel the pulse of my blood, and looking me steadily in the eye. Wiladzaps' eyes I realized now, were like Lukswaas's in shape, although he had a dominating way of using them, even now as he said 'Thank you. You find man who killed McCrory. Good. He died?'

'Yes. He's dead. He killed himself.'

'Killed self? Too bad.' Wiladzap looked genuinely sorrowful. Presumably he had expected the killer to go down fighting.

'I'll tell you more later,' I said. 'You come with me.'

I walked beside and slightly ahead of Wiladzap along the corridor. 'Bye Chief!', someone shouted. Wiladzap ignored this. Then someone else said, 'Lucky dog!' Wiladzap stopped and looked into the cell the voice had come from. One of my chain-gang, an armed robber.

'Lucky', Wiladzap repeated. 'Wiladzap name lucky'. Then he walked on.

In the hall Pemberton stepped forward and shook Wiladzap's hand, apologizing in Chinook for his detention, wishing him well in the future. Wiladzap listened, his eyes entirely focused on Pemberton's face. But I had noticed one flickering glance to where Lukswaas and Aemilia were standing behind and to one side. After this it must have taken extreme control for Wiladzap to pay attention to Pemberton who became quite carried away on his own words, as could happen easily in Chinook, but he listened patiently. Then when Pemberton stopped, Wiladzap kept looking at him and launched into an equally long speech about how his heart had been sick in the jail, very sick, but he knew that Pemberton and 'Hops' had been trying day and night to find the real killer of the doctor. He knew the good hearts of the King George men and of their great white Queen Victoria. He knew that in the city named after the great white Queen he would be safe from evil.

Pemberton looked pleased at this. They shook hands again, and Wiladzap was free. He walked straight across to Aemilia and stopped just in front of her. 'Aemilia,' he said. He stood straight as a spear but tears burst out of his eyes and began to flow down his cheeks.

There was a spell in the air. No one in the vestibule moved. Aemilia stood looking at Wiladzap, her grey eyes peaceful. Then Wiladzap reached out one hand to her. She reached out to him. They linked just their little fingers, like children, and stood looking at each other.

Everyone else began to move again. Parry clattered off to his office. Pemberton smiled at me and Lukswaas and walked to the door. Lukswaas and I moved toward each other and did what we had wanted to do for a long time, embracing each other tightly and rocking on our feet, oblivious of the others. I felt a great calm invade my body and hers.

When we broke apart, standing hand in hand, Wiladzap and Aemilia were still standing looking at each other, but now both their hands were joined. Aemilia looked across at us. 'Are you ready to go, Chad? Jones is waiting outside.'

'Yes.'

The spell was broken, and we all moved toward the door, Aemilia and Wiladzap now talking to each other in Tsimshian.

Outside in the sunbaked square we climbed into the farm buggy on which Mr Jones was sitting as upright as the most elegant of coachmen. Lukswaas and I faced backward, snuggling close into each other and not talking; Wiladzap and Aemilia opposite us faced forward, and looking each other in the eye talked all the way to Orchard Farm.

The next few days were not exactly easy. They were too intense for that. But when I look back from some time later I think that for all of us – me, Lukswaas, Wiladzap, Aemilia – this was our Happy Land.

Orchard Farm became transformed into a sort of camp, with open fires outside in hearths built by the Tsalak who visited constantly in small groups, bringing and cooking salmon and other fish. I was unable to understand what was said between Aemilia and the Tsalak, but they seemed respectful of her in varying degrees. I was more directly concerned with their relation to Lukswaas. Sometimes she would wear English clothes and her hair in a tail, sometimes Indian and her hair in braids, as if feeling her way between the two styles. She told me she *felt* better in Indian clothes, but *looked* better in English ones. I thought she looked lovely in either. But the clothes were only a symbol of something deeper. Just as Lukswaas was attracted to something in me, she was attracted to something in English life. Conversely I was attracted to her and to something in Tsimshian life. It could become confusing. The only steady times were when we broke away from the farm and walked in the woods or over the fields hand in hand, or when we grappled passionately at night.

Even our sleeping arrangements were a compromise. (Perhaps George Beaumont could not, as he had told me, live with compromise – but I knew that Lukswaas and I could not live long without it.) Lukswaas enjoyed the neatness and order of an English house, and immediately began teaching herself to use kitchen utensils – Mrs Jones was given leave to stay in her own house for this period – and she experimented with samplers and sewing. But she preferred to sleep outside, since it was summer. Wiladzap could hardly bear to be in a house at all, although he was highly interested in all mechanical things, from kitchen taps and the pump, to the draft regulator of the fireplace. All four of us ended up sleeping every night on paliasses and blankets on the porches, Aemilia and Wiladzap in the front, Lukswaas and I in the back of the house.

Several times a day Wiladzap and I sat talking or went on a walk together over the fields. Not that Wiladzap was capable of walking for its own sake. For him everything had a goal. I was astonished at how the so-called 'savage mind', at least in Wiladzap, was ruled by ideas of purpose. If we walked over the fields it was to be away from the others and for mutual instruction. I taught Wiladzap how to shoot a pistol – he was only experienced with rifles. Wiladzap taught me how to shoot a bow and arrow. I taught Wiladzap what I knew of the economics of trade from the English point of view – a subject which Wiladzap grasped very quickly even when it was presented in a mixture of simplified English and Chinook. Wiladzap taught me various uses of a Bowie knife.

We also had laborious but always intense conversations among all four of us, about the future. There was no doubt that Lukswaas would stay with me although 'one day' I would visit Tsalaks. As Wiladzap said with his usual simple arrogance: 'You save my life, I give you Lukswaas.' The case for Wiladzap and Aemilia was more complicated. An Indian woman could be taken as a concubine by a white man and become adapted to white life, although the couple were despised and shunned as exemplars of sheer lust, the coupling of a civilised man and an animal. But it was unheard of for a white woman to live with an Indian man, despite the fact that at least a few such as Wiladzap were in material terms richer than many whites. Then since the Northern tribes, Tsimshian and Haida, were known as skilled traders, and therefore the HBC in cooperation with the Colonial government was keen to restrict their activities, Wiladzap's future was precarious. In spite of his extreme, naively boastful confidence, he feared on the one hand being cheated and hemmed in by the white traders, and on the other being deserted by his own people.

Chieftainship among the Tsimshian had to be maintained by glorious deeds, trading successes, and potlatches. The competition for the eagle name 'Legex' which Wiladzap had mentioned after his arrest, absorbed much of his ambition. Aemilia made some attempts to persuade him to settle down and farm with her. We even discussed the possibility of all four of us working Orchard Farm: in an alliance of strength, perhaps we could set our own social rules. We could perhaps buy the farm from the former Mrs Somerville who would not want it now that life as Mrs Quattrini would provide her and her younger girls a finer house in town and one in San Francisco as well. But Wiladzap could not understand agriculture. For him, only slaves carried things and chopped wood, and the idea of trimming trees so that they produced fruit was alien to him. Were not the woods full of berries anyway? Unfortunately the only attraction farming might have had for him, that of money, was in short supply in the depressed economy of the Colony. Aemilia knew, as she told me, that she would have to go with Wiladzap. She even looked forward to meeting old friends at Tsalak. But in time, she said fatalistically, things would get worse for the Tsimshian.

There had been a reunion between Aemilia and the little boy William. His character had, to my eyes, the same mixture of the happy-go-lucky and the stoical which was evident in Wiladzap. The Joneses had treated him well but he had always sensed there was something special between him and his 'auntie' Aemilia. And since he had grown up, in spite of being well protected, with some idea of shame at his own Indianness, he was pleased to find he had a big chief like Wiladzap for a father. All this made Aemilia look happy and light as a girl.

Aemilia when at Tsalaks had been adopted by a woman of the Raven clan, as a necessary formality since Wiladzap could not marry an Eagle like himself. This adoption would have to be confirmed among the band before they left Victoria. Luckily there was a Raven woman among them who remembered Aemilia's adoption and could attest to it. Then there was the difficulty that William, although Wiladzap's son, derived no status from this: all inherited status came from the mother. (New status could be won later). But Aemilia had no particular 'names'.

This question of names I did not understand well, since I found most Tsimshian words difficult to pronounce. But it was explained to me that familiar names were not the important ones. Wiladzap, for example, meant 'lucky in hunting' – as the telegraph from Fort Simpson had said. Hence Wiladzap's remark to the prisoner that he was 'lucky'. Lukswaas, I was touched to hear, meant 'a sudden shower of rain on a sunny day'. But Lukswaas, as her mother's daughter, had several hereditary names of great renown. She decided, with a shrewd generosity which resolved Aemilia's status completely, that she would gift Aemilia her names. Wiladzap, therefore, would gain status by association, and William's status was assured. In return for this, all Lukswaas would receive, I thought ruefully, was the humble name of Hobbes…

The conversations among all four of us, perhaps partly because they were so difficult using two and three languages and therefore words were chosen and explained carefully, were like windows into our minds – so different, but we liked what we saw through those windows. We once had a long discussion starting from Darwin's remark, which I quoted, that the difference between the savage and the civilised person is 'the difference between a wild and a tame animal.' We agreed that within both the Tsimshian and the English societies there was a range between wild and tame people. And that each could turn upside-down, as it were, and become the other. The most tame people could go wild, and vice versa. Furthermore, the idea of the civilised and the savage could be used in such a reversal of behaviour. Wiladzap was fascinated by how Beaumont, although he only knew him from my and Amelia's description, who was the incarnation of the 'King George', when he carried out the killing of McCrory did it in imitation (and a bad imitation at that) of a savage. And I proposed, as a counter-example, that when the famous Chief Freezy decapitated his wife on the beach opposite Victoria, he was actually imitating the ways of the white man: instead of killing his wife in a fury, he carried out a staged execution, just as the English did in public hangings. He thought he was being civilised.

So far as we could see, each civilisation had its refinement and its barbarity. Wiladzap admitted that among the Tsimshian murders were frequent and treacherous. But at least they were always, in the long run, paid for. He was disgusted at the Christian doctrine of hellfire, which he knew of from the missionaries, the 'Metakatla men', and which I could explain in more detail. But eventually the conversation turned to the idea of whether in fact animals and humans were different at all. The Tsimshian identified with the virtues of the eagle and the salmon, they incorporated these animal virtues into themselves. Wiladzap said that in a trance he could hear animals speak to him. But Lukswaas pointed out that what the animals said was about the life of animals, not the life of people. The eagle would point out something in distant sight or vision. The salmon would speak from its experience of travelling the seas. But she did not think the feelings she had for me were those of an animal. Animals could not deliberately change what they did, as she was doing in learning to dress like an Englishwoman and to cook on a stove. Then Aemilia broke in passionately: 'Darwin thinks that because we have evolved like animals we *are* animals. But show me the animal that has experienced repentance and remorse!'

After these words had been translated and clarified, we all fell silent. I thought of my own remorse at having made love to Lukswaas thinking she was Wiladzap's wife. Perhaps Aemilia was repenting having left Wiladzap for so long. Or Wiladzap repenting not having come to seek her earlier. I do not know what Lukswaas, the most innocent of us all, had to repent or feel remorseful about. But I found myself wondering if she felt remorseful at abandoning her own people, at not going further with them on their voyage.

Could it be that my dear old father had been right? Did all humans have a conscience after all? Then I thought of Beaumont, 'that Devil George', and I could see no signs of conscience. I doubted if McCrory had had a conscience either. There was a paradox: Beaumont was in a way the most 'tame' of the lot of us. And I suddenly realised that McCrory was tame too: his life was spent and his money earned in taming the wild, forbidden impulses of others. Suddenly I loved all four of us, sitting on the porch at Orchard Farm, for our innocent wildness – the wildness that had led

Wiladzap to pursue Aemilia to the ends of his known earth, that was leading Aemilia to throw over the civilisation her family so fussily cultivated, that had led Luskwaas and me impulsively into each others' arms.

Does conscience go with wildness, not tameness?

Wiladzap was eager to leave, partly because of an innate restlessness, partly, Aemilia confided in me, because the band were fretting at having stayed so long in a place where they could no longer trade. Wiladzap's release had been accompanied by much less public attention than his arrest. The fact that McCrory had been slain by a Marine officer in a fit of 'melancholia', a code-word for anything from dementia to alcoholic frenzy, was rather shameful. It was as if popular indignation was an end in itself: if it could not be provoked, as it so easily could against Indians because of an underlying terror, then the murder was less interesting.

The Tsimshian knew nothing about this, but they did feel they were still unwelcome. Wiladzap decided that rather than return home at once they would go South into Puget Sound, in Washington Territory, where years ago bands of Tsimshian had traded. Now the prosperous towns of Port Townsend and Tacoma might provide a chance for them to recoup their losses, sell their otter skins at a good price, and go home with a profit in hand. The band would come to Cormorant Point for a few days on their way back North. The parting now would not be so complete or so painful.

On the morning of the day the Tsimshian left, there were two simple ceremonies. First Pemberton, with Mrs Pemberton, came to the Farm and conducted a brief marriage of Wiladzap and Aemilia, to legitimize their union with their son William in English eyes. Then he married me and Lukswaas. This was clearly to the relief of Mrs Pemberton, who wept.

Then at Cormorant Point, now a bare clearing with a small fire burning in the centre, there was a brief ceremony in which the adoption of Aemilia as a Raven was confirmed, and in which Lukswaas, in a speech which seemed to me quite fiery, like that of an orator, gifted her names to Aemilia. Lukswaas was dressed like an Englishwoman, although she had followed Aemilia's example of wearing Tsimshian earrings and bracelets. She seemed almost delicate, she was so fine in feature and movement, but she had an authority as she spoke which I had never seen in a woman.

Aemilia had dressed as a Tsimshian, in a magnificent chilcat blanket

Wiladzap had given her, its blue, black and silver designs so fresh that they shone, with bare legs and moccasins, and her hair in braids. With her pale skin she looked like a visiting Goddess.

Little William was dressed in a chilcat and leggings, made at the last minute by one of the women. He was clearly nervous, but made up for this by holding himself very erect, like his father. He had said goodbye to the Joneses at the farm, and shed a tear or two – but he would see them again, and his fear was obviously mixed with excitement and pride.

Wiladzap and I had exchanged gifts: an otter-fur coat and a first-class Bowie knife for me; a pistol and ammunition and a pair of riding boots for Wiladzap. Aemilia was taking various personal items, and Lukswaas was retaining some of hers.

The Pembertons had also come to the Cormorant Point ceremony. There were general farewells, accompanied by hand clasps and embraces. Aemilia had tears in her eyes, although perhaps of joy more than sadness. Wan cried deeply at leaving Lukswaas. I shook hands with Waaks and the gloomy Tsamti, and embraced Wiladzap like a brother. We looked long into each other's eyes and I saw such an unexpected sadness in Wiladzap's that I almost cried. Lukswaas showed no signs of grief, but she had become, after her speech, lustreless and stony-faced.

Lukswaas and I and the Pembertons stood on the bluff overlooking the beach, as the men, some totally naked, others wearing leggings, held the canoe, already heavily loaded with chests, baskets and other gear, parallel to the shore in the shallow water. The women and children and finally Aemilia and Wiladzap climbed in. Once in the canoe, Wiladzap stripped off his chilcat, and some of the women, who would also paddle, stripped to the waist. Many of them had used sticks from the last fire to smear black patches on their faces. The canoe itself had a weather-beaten mask painted on planks on both sides of its high prow. It was a barbarous sight – such as Captain Cook had seen over a hundred years before when the first white men had come to the Northwest.

The last three men pushed the bow outwards, entering the water up to their thighs, then climbed in over the gunwale and took their paddles. There were now ten paddles on each side. A man's voice rang out in a chant and the paddles swept down in unison. The canoe shot forward with amazing speed, and leaving a wake as straight as an arrow headed

East to the other side of the long curve of Margaret Bay, eventually to turn South around Ten Mile Point and across the Straits of Juan de Fuca into Puget Sound.

It was not the way among the Tsimshian to wave or call goodbye. Lukswaas and I and the Pembertons stood silently until the canoe disappeared around a rocky point.

Aemilia had said Lukswaas and I could spend the next weeks at Orchard Farm, at the very least until she and Wiladzap returned on their way North. She had even suggested that if the Quattrinis did not wish to return to the farm, as seemed likely, I might wish to lease it, and work it with Lukswaas and the help of the Joneses if they wanted to stay on in their little house.

I felt happy to be alone with Lukswaas. We had come to the Tsimshian camp in the Pemberton's buggy, and now since the sun had become unpleasantly hot we were content to take our time walking back through the cool forest. I was teaching Lukswaas English, so our conversation consisted of such remarks as: 'That is a cedar, a good tree for making planks for houses', or 'This path is stony'. And Lukswaas repeating them clearly. But we liked this. Lukswaas became more cheerful. We came out of the forest into the little fertile valley where I was beginning to feel at home, and walked down the road to the farmhouse. For now it was all ours. We made a simple meal, then watched the sunset from the back porch. It was unusually clear and pink, so that the distant blue hills turned an unreal green before darkness fell. The air was so clear that it became rapidly cold.

We decided to sleep inside. We had already re-arranged the rooms upstairs: we would use Aemilia's as our bedroom, but with the younger girls' double bed moved in. The room was under the eaves and had slanting ceilings. A double window faced out front over the roof of the porch. The wallpaper was old fashioned and striped. Lukswaas had liked this room best from the beginning. She was pleased to be going to sleep in it, and in a bed with fresh sheets and counterpane. We had already made sure that the straw mattress was suitably hard, for Lukswaas would have been unable to sleep if it had been soft.

We went to bed and lay side by side on our backs, with a candle burning on the bedside table, watching the flickering light on the ceiling. We had never so far lain down together and not made love. But Lukswaas seemed abstracted as never before and although she snuggled into me closely it was not an embrace. I was exhausted, emotionally as much as physically. Eventually the candle guttered and went out. Lukswaas was breathing quietly. I fell asleep.

I woke because Lukswaas had moved abruptly. She was sitting up in the bed beside me, completely still, as if listening for something. The room was very dark, and there was only a faint dark blue light through the white curtains, which were hanging motionless although the window was open. The air was cold. None of this was unusual except for something in the way Lukswaas was sitting. I had never seen her rigid like this.

'Lukswaas,' I said quietly.

She said nothing, so I sat up beside her and put my arm around her naked body.

'Cold,' I said.

Then she spoke to me in Chinook, saying she was afraid, she was certain that something terrible was happening. What was happening outside? She asked wildly.

I got out of bed, went over to the window and pulled the curtains aside to look out. There was no moon, but the night was extremely clear with thousands of stars, glittering and hard. There was not a breath of wind. I described this to Lukswaas and went back to bed.

She clung to me and we pulled down together under the bedclothes to get warm again. I held Lukswaas from behind – spooning as the girls at the Windsor Rooms had called it – and since I often embraced Lukswaas this way I would have been ready to do so now, but she remained still, although her skin became warmer, and unusually tense. She said again that something terrible was happening, and she began to cry. I held her gently and stroked her hair, but after a while could no longer do so, she was sobbing so violently, with loud cries as if her heart was breaking. Then she calmed down, I held her again, and although she still felt warm to the touch, she began to shiver, moaning that we would never see the others again. When I tried to reassure her she would not listen. I drifted off to sleep, then woke again. Lukswaas had stopped trembling and was lying still in my arms but I knew she was awake. Although I slept on and off, I knew she had not, and as the room began to lighten, the walls and furniture revealed in a dull grey light, she said to me once more that we would never see the others again.

In the morning Lukswaas slept, waking at noon in a sort of daze. She then became so distraught that I sent Mr Jones into town with an apologetic request that Pemberton telegraph to Port Townsend to ask if there was any news of the Tsalaks' arrival in Puget Sound. Lukswaas and I waited for the rest of the day and went to bed with a feeling, which I now shared through infection, of oppression and terror.

Pemberton's reply did not come until the following afternoon, when it was brought by messenger.

'Dear Chad: I cannot express in words how sad I am to have to enclose this copy of the reply by electric telegraph to my enquiries to Washington Territory. Warmest regards to you both – Augustus P.'

The telegraph read:

```
IN RESPONSE TO YOUR QUERY PARTY OF TSIMSHIAN TEN
MEN TWENTY FIVE WOMEN AND CHILDREN MASSACRED AT
DUNGENESS SPIT NIGHT BEFORE LAST STOP NO SURVIVORS
STOP TWENTY FOUR CLALLAM INDIANS NOW AT SNOHOMISH
RESERVATION UNDER ARREST STOP SIGNED WILLIAM KING US
AGENT PORT ANGELES
```

EPILOGUE

'Dear Mr Hobbes:

I thank you for your most interesting letter. I am indeed preparing a work on Expression, a subject which has preoccupied me, on and off, for thirty years but will have to wait a little longer before I can treat of it in a book, since I am much occupied with my *Descent of Man* which I hope will see the light within a year or two. I did indeed, in 1867, prepare a set of printed Queries, of which I enclose a copy with some manuscript emendations. I have so far received some twenty five replies from missionaries and other observers, and I should be pleased to receive one from you with regard to the Indians of the British Columbia coast. I must urge you, however, under no circumstances to rely on *memory*, in compiling your notes, for it is notoriously fallible. Trust only *observations*. Indeed, the observations in your letter, of the Expression of sadness and horror by the Tsimshian, had all the vividness of having been penned, as I suppose, very shortly after you had made them.

My aim is, in comparing the Expression of Emotion in man and in animals, to provide a rational explanation of how various Expressions, now rendered innate, might have originally been acquired as habits. Expressions may be in fact subject to the laws of Evolution. But before I can formulate the principles which suggest themselves to me after thirty years of observations of Expressions in man, in animals at the zoo, and even in my own children (whose emotional Expressions I have endeavoured to record through photographs), I wish to collect as many trustworthy observations from other sources as possible. In this I should be glad of your help.

Thank you for your kind remarks. I am sorry to have missed British Columbia on the Voyage of the Beagle, which did not proceed farther North than the Galapagos. In those days your coast was nothing more than a wilderness inhabited by the cannibals whom Cook had described.

I envy you the opportunity to make the most interesting observations of all, namely of the differences between civilised and savage man which are, as I put it in the *Voyage,* no less than those between the tame and the wild animal. Yet, as your observations so clearly show, in states of deep emotion, the differences are less than we might suppose.

Yours truly, Charles Darwin.'

Mr Justice Begbie and I picked our way carefully along the rocky shore of the Goldstream, every now and then stopping for a long while, observing, and saying nothing. The rain had stopped earlier in the day, but drops still fell in showers from the drooping branches of the tall fir trees every time a gust of the raw November wind shook them, and big yellow leaves would float down through the air from the cottonwoods interspersed with the firs along the riverbank, to become strewn on the surface of the water, some of them sticking to the backs of the salmon as they broke the surface. The river was about fifty feet wide and only two or three feet deep, gravel bottomed, and scattered with rocks and boulders on which some of the dying salmon became stranded, flapping weakly as the shrieking seagulls tore with their beaks into the flesh, starting always by pecking out the eyes. The corpses of salmon were littered along the rocks and along the banks, skin gashed and ripped to expose half eaten flesh, the eye hollows mere rings of bone. Cawing crows feasted alongside the gulls. Every so often along the river were rapids where the water ran shallowly and where the salmon cut their bellies wriggling upstream, so that the water behind them carried dissipating streaks of blood. In the deeper pools the females circled over their 'redds' – scooped out hollows in the gravel on which they laid spawn clusters of eggs, while the males circled around them, quivering and ejaculating clouds of white milt.

From further down the stream, behind us, came the heavy splashing sound of some Songhees, in dungarees and floppy hats, standing in the water at the edge and gaffing the largest salmon, the Chum, some of them up to four feet long. Most of the salmon were smaller Chinook, two to three feet long. All were emaciated from their long struggle back from the sea, into the Saanich Inlet and up the Goldstream to spawn and die. Here and there in a deep pool under a cottonwood or fir, a pair of Coho, smaller and darker than the others, circled around each other. Chum, Chinook, and Coho had different life spans, but all ended here.

The dark green gigantic firs dripped, the yellow cottonwood leaves drifted down and strewed themselves on the living and the dead, and the thousands of salmon struggled first and later circled in their slow dance, shuddering first in ecstasy and later in death. All silently. Only the gulls and crows cried raucously as they plunged their beaks into dying or dead eyes and flesh. The river flowing over the stones and boulders made a low, constant, gurgling.

Rather than pick our way back along the shore, Begbie and I pushed through bushes to a path which led parallel to the river. As we walked down it we could have been in any part of the forest, and the gurgling of the river faded, although we could still hear the gulls and the crows. 'I've seen a hundred people out here from town on a Sunday afternoon,' Begbie remarked, 'and none of them ever makes a sound when they are by the river. All keep silence, as if visiting a holy place – which in a way it is.'

I could think of nothing to reply. We both fell silent again. Begbie was still a dandy, even in his wet-weather riding gear. His boots were elegant, and he wore a sort of highwayman's cloak with toggles of silver braid, and a top hat.

After a while he said: 'I find the whole story sad. Then that final blow for you in the hour of your triumph. I'm sorry I was in the Interior. But I dare say I could have done nothing Pemberton didn't do. And if I'd tried to help I should have been accused of being an interfering Indian-lover. But, as you've found out for yourself, there are Indians and Indians, just as there are English and English. In fact English were all Indians once – so I often think. The Britons whom Caesar discovered even covered themselves with war paint! And the Druids who were their medicine-men would burn human sacrifices alive in wicker cages hanging from oak trees – which is worse than many things the Indians have done. Civilisation is, as they say, skin deep.'

'Yes. I had a letter from Charles Darwin the other day in which he reminded me of that.'

'Really? You're in correspondence with him?'

'I wrote to him six months ago with some observations about the expression of various emotions among the Tsimshian. He replied very generously. I can show you his letter, if you have time to pass by my house for tea. Or might I ask you to supper?'

'Why not? That's very kind of you. I want very much to meet your wife. But since it gets dark so early and the roads are muddy, you may have to put me up for the night. Excuse my pioneer ways, inviting myself.'

'Of course. I had thought of it but was shy of asking. We don't live in grand style, though I can provide a couple of bottles of claret with supper.'

'My boy, I've spent many a night with no roof over my head at all, and at times the accommodation they provide for me in the Interior is a shack such as a man would be ashamed to erect even on the Upper Harbour in Victoria. I'd like you to show me that letter, the terrible one, from King, the Indian agent.'

'I liked the man – Mr King – behind that dreadful letter,' I said. 'I also liked Epstein, the American Lieutenant, and I preferred his band of free-born soldiers, ambling behind him, to our mechanical Beaumont. I had feared all Americans, except the obvious rogues, were Perfectionists – like McCrory – trying to create the best of all possible worlds and not seeing how they are doomed to fail. Epstein, and Mr King, are realists.'

'I'm not afraid of the Americans,' Begbie said. 'Whether Europeans or Jews or even Negroes, they *are* our cousins. But I think only a *British* Columbia could include us and our friends the Indians in the same society. Not a Utopia! But there's land enough for all of us here: we don't need to despise God's children for the colour of their skins. I wish for your sake and your wife's that the impossible could come to pass. But I'm getting too old to leave here, and if we must be Americans or Canadians I know myself well enough to predict that I shall make the best of it.'

We reached the clearing where we had left our horses in the care of a Songhees to whom Begbie gave a dollar. Before mounting his horse, Begbie stood as if looking back towards the river, but he was obviously thinking of something else.

'One thing, Hobbes, I'd like to ask you. But I'd like you to forget about it once you have answered it. This whole sordid affair of the alienist McCrory is very disturbing. I've heard rumours that so-and-so or so-and-so were patients of his. Do you know who was, in fact?

'He kept no records. I'm sure of that. But yes, I know who most of his patients were.'

'Could you tell me, was Mrs Blum among them?'

Begbie was looking at me almost haughtily, but the question rendered him totally vulnerable. He was said to have recently fallen in love with this Mrs Blum, a married woman. The nature of their relationship was shadowy, although as I saw Begbie now, I could guess what it was.

'I can tell you truthfully that her name was never mentioned to me in connection with the alienist.'

'Thank you.'

We mounted and rode off along a muddy track, parallel to the river and hemmed in by mountainous walls of moss-covered rock, on which the sun's rays never fell, presenting a scene which might fashionably have been called a 'romantic prospect', but which in reality was one of utter gloom.

I had resigned from the police after the seven day leave Pemberton had given me. I was too heart-sick to continue, and Lukswaas and I needed each other. I had been able to rent Orchard Farm, at a pittance, from Mrs Quattrini. The Joneses had left to settle on Saltspring Island. Lukswaas was pregnant – probably from one of our first encounters in the forest. But I had managed to bring in and sell the fruit harvest which I regarded as Aemilia's. We would be all right for the winter. I had bought a few pigs. This was far from romantic, but practical. Mrs Pemberton had told me that in Ireland a pig was known as 'the gentleman that pays the rent.' And this horse I was riding, as well as another, had come with the farm.

By the time we had arrived, the wind had become more blustery, and behind us in the West the sky was blackening. It was good to enter the house in which Lukswaas and I, in spite of all that had happened, had been so happy that light seemed to leap out of the walls. There was a roaring fire in the sitting room grate, and Begbie and I sat ourselves in front of it, Begbie wearing a pair of my slippers, while Lukswaas prepared hot toddies of spiced cider and brandy. Begbie had learned enough Tsimshian from the Interior branches of the tribe to pay her some gallant compliment which had made her smile.

She brought the hot toddies and sat down close to me, but I got up for a moment to fetch the two letters for Begbie to read: Darwin's, and the other.

Lukswaas and I sat looking into the fire, holding hands. We were at peace with each other. This did not change even when I went on to think about the salmon dying on the rocks of the stream. Lukswaas and I had circled each other many times like the salmon in their dance, but it had been granted to us to live a while longer before the beaks of the gulls pecked out our eyes… Like the eyes of Wiladzap, Aemilia, and their little boy, of sturdy Waaks, gloomy Tsamti, and gentle Wan.

Begbie had read Darwin's letter, and was now reading the other one which I knew by heart:

'Dear Mr Hobbes:

It has taken time for me to get back to you with this, but the life of a U.S. Indian agent is very busy, and I wanted to make this a long enough letter to explain to you fully these barbarous events which, as you write, deprived you at one blow of your dearest friends.

'First, the Clallam. The name means "the strong people", and they are indeed big and warlike. They are a Salishan tribe, unfriendly cousins to your Sooke and Saanich and Cowichan. I say unfriendly because even now a Clallam canoe will occasionally head North and return with a cargo of their cousins' heads. These expeditions are carried out with the utmost stealth, and I dare say they creep up on their victims unawares. To my knowledge, the Salish in general avoid pitched battles (although they used to fight them at sea, from canoes) preferring sudden assassinations and ambushes. Their villages, set back from the long sandy beaches we have here, were often fronted with rows of sun-bleached skulls set on stakes, and these can occasionally still be seen. The Clallam are now in a precarious state of half-civilisation. Some of the older ones when young, prior to 1849, became great favourites of your British sailors, who gave them names which they still keep, such as: Queen Victoria, Prince Albert, the Earl of Clarence, and the Duke of York. They are amiable old rogues for the most part. The younger ones find themselves caught between the old ways and the new, unable to prove themselves in feats of hunting and blood feuds, since the Territory is filling up very fast with settlers and, unlike in British Columbia, they are heavily outnumbered.

'As to what happened at Dungeness Spit. This is, as the name suggests, a long curving peninsula of sand and shingle, covered with only a few low bushes, which juts out Northward into the Sound. It is the obvious stopping place for any Indians arriving from the North, wishing to camp for the night and then move on without contact with local Indians. However in this case the Tsimshian party, which arrived an hour or two before sunset, was spotted by some Clallam who recognized them as Tsimshian by the size and shape of their canoe, and the designs on its prow. And here is the nub of the story: some fifteen years ago, as precisely as I can ascertain, a party of Tsimshian passing through these parts abducted two Clallam women and brought them North from where they have never, needless to say, returned. Now for the Clallam, all Tsimshian are the same, though I understand they occupy some two hundred miles of coast and consist of many different tribes. So at the sight of these travellers, the Clallam began instantly plotting revenge. Messengers were sent out to the villages where relations of the abducted women lived. By midnight a war party of twenty five young men was gathered at Tsiskat, the Clallam village at the base of the spit. This presented, in fact, a long awaited opportunity for them to prove their valor, although not everyone would call a night attack on a party of sleeping people an act of valor.

'The day had been very clear and at this time of year, on the Straits and in the entrance to the sound, such a day is usually followed by heavy fog. Sure enough this had come rolling in and covered the spit, so that a man could not see much farther than the end of his arm, but the Clallam knew the spit well, having dug clams there all their lives. They were armed with the guns they use for hunting – long barrelled rifles for the most part – and knives. They set out in canoes and paddled up the West or outer side of the spit, landing quietly at a point somewhat below where the Tsimshian had camped on the Eastern or inner side. At this point they seem to have lost their nerve. Some urged turning back, for fear of punishment by the U.S. government (through its agent, myself, whom they hold in some fear). Then someone suggested they build a small fire and blacken their faces with the charred wood. In the excitement of this, they got their resolution back again. They re-embarked in their canoes and paddled silently up to a point just opposite the Tsimshian camp. They waited on the shore while two scouts made their way across the narrow spit to survey the camp. It was a makeshift affair of mats spread from stakes and logs, under which the entire party was lying. There was a large fire which gave some light through the fog. The scouts could see that there were many more women than men, which was encouraging. One woman got up to replenish the fire, searching around for driftwood, and almost stumbled into one of the scouts as he lay on the ground. This unnerved him, and when she had lain down again, he was so impatient for his comrades to come up from behind and attack that he fired his gun at the sleeping Tsimshian.

'The Tsimshian of course jumped up and seized their own weapons, but in the light of their own fire and looking out into the night and the fog they must have been at a great disadvantage. Almost at once the entire Clallam party was up at the level of the scouts and they poured bullets into the Tsimshian until all were dead. In the old days, the Clallam would have taken women and children as slaves, but since slavery is now illegal, they had already decided to spare no one. Such are the workings of the savage mind! To replace one crime by another even worse!

'They then rushed in and decapitated the men. Since there were only ten heads to go round among twenty five Clallam, they began to yell at each other and quarrel over them, some indulging in an indecent tug of war for their possession. In this rage they went around the other bodies, mutilating them, and cutting off ears and fingers where there were rings. Then someone discovered that a body he found and was about to decapitate was that of one of his companions. This Clallam had been killed apparently by a pistol shot, which makes a different wound from a rifle. There was a terrific quarrel. These men who had massacred thirty five men, women and children were heartbroken and furious at the death of one of their own. They came to blows, the scout who had fired the first shots being blamed for his recklessness. Then in another of those sudden losses of nerve which afflict them, they decided to embark for home, leaving their trophies, by which I mean the heads, on the beach although carrying off a fair amount of trinkets and silver jewellery, along with the body of their fallen companion.

'The next day the matter came to my attention and since the elders of the Clallam, those named after your English Dukes and Earls, live in great fear of the U.S. Government, all twenty four of the remaining offenders were swiftly handed over to me. I have put them to work on the Snohomish Reservation, secured with ball and chain, cutting trees and pulling out stumps from dawn to dusk, which I assure you is back-breaking work. But I regret to tell you that I will have to release them after some months. U.S. law is not fussy about one Indian killing another. These are viewed as domestic altercations, and left alone. The life of an Indian is not viewed in the same way as that of an American. I do not know if the same view is held in British Columbia.

'So there the matter rests, and an ugly story it is. I hope you find this account satisfactory.

Yours truly, William King, U.S. Indian Agent, Port Angeles, W.T.

'P.S. the bodies of the Tsimshian were terribly cut up, and I had the Clallam bury them at once. It was remarked to me that one woman looked pale for an Indian. But then the Northern Indians are lighter skinned anyway, so I did not give the matter any attention. No doubt this was the woman you mention, who had married the Tyee, God help her. But rest assured, in the state of things, you would not have wanted to retrieve the body.'

Begbie put down the letter with a sigh. The three of us remained looking into the flames, listening to the gusts of the November storm outside ripping the last leaves from the trees around the house and bringing in squalls of rain from the West. After a while, Lukswaas took my hand and placed it against her belly where I could feel the kicking of our child, impatient, so I imagined, to be born.

AFTERWORD

Many of the characters of this story, apart from the obvious ones like Charles Darwin and John Humphrey Noyes, are in the historical record: Judge Begbie, Augustus Pemberton, Captain Delacombe, Lieutenant Epstein, William King the Indian agent, and even Chief Freezy. Begbie and Pemberton have streets named after them in Victoria.

Aemilia's remark about animals not experiencing repentance or remorse comes from a critique of Darwin by his friend Frances Power Cobbe.

The various sexual therapies practised by McCrory – even the 'electric testicules' – are well documented in 19th century North America and Europe.

British Columbia joined Canada in 1872, on the promise of a railway from the East to the Pacific coast, which was eventually built, and a causeway to Victoria, which was not. Amor de Cosmos became Premier of the new province, was so corrupt that he fell into disgrace, and died insane and almost forgotten. Judge Begbie soldiered on, adapting to Canada, and died peacefully in his beloved Victoria, but his dream of justice for the Indians was not realized. By the end of the century the Tsimshian and other coastal tribes, their populations halved by epidemics, were reduced to poverty and working in salmon canneries.

An account of the massacre of the Tsimshian on Dungeness Spit in 1869 can be found in Edward Curtis, *The North American Indian,* Volume ix, 1913. Curtis's informant was Naehum, the scout who fired the first shot, 'now an old man and a devotee of the Shaker religion. After this confession he fell into a violent fit of "shaking", prayed volubly, and asked God for pardon, all the while ringing a bell and weeping copiously.'